I... are broken, and an entire country has been laid waste. Now an uneasy peace settles on the land.

Into Sharn come four battle-hardened soldiers. Tired of blood, weary of killing, they only want a place to call home.

But the shadowed City of Towers has other plans. . . .

THE
DREAMING DARK

Book One
CITY OF TOWERS

Book Two
THE SHATTERED LAND
December 2005

Book Three
THE GATES OF NIGHT
December 2006

THE CITY OF TOWERS

THE DREAMING DARK
BOOK 1

KEITH BAKER

CITY OF TOWERS

The Dreaming Dark · Book One

©2005 Wizards of the Coast, Inc.

Distributed in the United States by Holtzbrinck Publishing. Distributed in Canada by Fenn Ltd.

Distributed to the hobby, toy, and comic trade in the United States and Canada by regional distributors.

Distributed worldwide by Wizards of the Coast, Inc. and regional distributors.

Cover art by Mark Zug
Map by Dennis Kauth and Rob Lazzaretti
First Printing: February 2005
Library of Congress Catalog Card Number: 2004113599

9 8 7 6 5 4 3 2 1

US ISBN: 0-7869-3584-7
ISBN-13: 978-0-7869-3584-0
620-17643-001-EN

U.S., CANADA,	EUROPEAN HEADQUARTERS
ASIA, PACIFIC, & LATIN AMERICA	Wizards of the Coast, Belgium
Wizards of the Coast, Inc.	T Hofveld 6d
P.O. Box 7071702	Groot-Bijgaarden
Renton, WA 98057-0707	Belgium
+1-800-324-6496	+322 467 3360

Visit our web site at **www.wizards.com**

DEDICATION

To all my friends and family, to those who have played in my games and listened to my stories; and most of all to Ellen, who has always been my greatest inspiration.

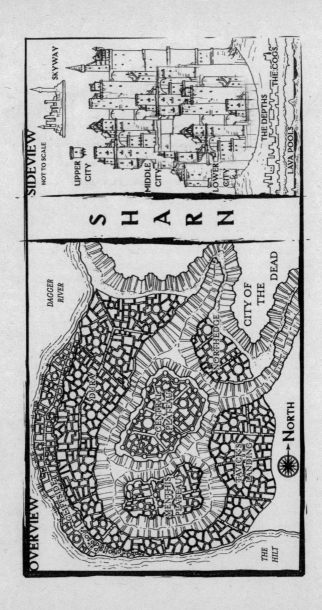

OVERVIEW

DAGGER RIVER

CLIFFSIDE

DURA

CENTRAL PLATEAU

MENTHIS PLATEAU

NORTHEDGE

CITY OF THE DEAD

TAVICK'S LANDING

THE HILT

→ NORTH

SIDEVIEW
NOT TO SCALE

SKYWAY

UPPER CITY

MIDDLE CITY

LOWER CITY

THE DEPTHS

THE COGS

LAVA POOLS

S H A R N

PROLOGUE

CYRE
KELDAN RIDGE
Olarune 19, 994 YK

There was a moment when they might have won the battle. The Cyran troops were seasoned veterans, though they had little choice in the matter. In these troubled times a man became a soldier the moment he was old enough to wield a scythe or a flail. The troop had been taken by surprise, but within moments of the initial assault the Cyrans had formed ranks and were holding their own.

A roll of thunder heralded the arrival of the stormship, then terror dropped from the night sky. Painted black, the sleek longboat herself was almost invisible from the ground, but the lightning flashing around the ring of elemental air holding the ship aloft flickered off the bottoms of the clouds, painting the battlefield in bright light and black shadows. Within moments a wave of arrows rained down upon the Cyran army.

Fiery explosions rocked the battlefield. Hundreds died, and the tide of battle altered.

۞ ۞ ۞ ۞ ۞ ۞ ۞

Daine swore as he strode into the ruined camp, cursing Flame and Sovereign alike. Behind him, the warforged Pierce surveyed the carnage, two arrows held to his massive longbow. Jode examined the bodies of the fallen, but the halfling's healing touch could not raise the dead.

"Saerath!" Daine shouted. "Saerath, if you're already dead I swear I'll find a path to Dolurrh so I can torture you for eternity!"

A pale face peered around the open flap of a singed tent. "But captain!" the balding half-elf whimpered, his face pale. "It's an ambush! There are enemies all around! You know I'm not supposed to place myself at risk!"

Daine reached inside the tent, grabbed the collar of Saerath's robe in one mailed fist, and hauled the wizard forward and almost off his feet. Though slightly built, Daine was surprisingly strong.

"Damn the Queen's rules, Saerath! Ten more minutes and there won't be an army left—and that includes you!"

He released his grip, and the portly half-elf staggered back a few steps. As if in answer to his words, a massive ball of flame came whirling out of the sky. Striking forty feet to their left, the explosion filled the night with the smell of burning flesh and the screams of men and horses.

Daine pointed at the stormship as it swept overhead. "We'll serve as your shields, but I need that ship down *now!* Rules of war or no, if you don't help, I'll kill you myself!"

As if to put Daine's vow to the test, an enemy soldier emerged from the smoke and into the flickering light of the burning tents. It was a creature out of an artificer's nightmare—metal, darkwood, and leather merged into a human shape. Its mouth was filled with daggers, and its metal torso was studded with shards of sharpened steel; with every motion the spikes scraped again its joints, generating a painful whine. The warforged soldier held a gory morningstar in each hand, and seeing Daine's badge of office it raised its bloody weapons and charged.

It never reached him. From his right a silver blur flew forward—Pierce, his own warforged companion. Pierce crashed into the larger warrior and knocked it flat on its back. Daine stayed with the wizard while Jode and Lynna raced to help Pierce. But even from the ground, the warforged was a deadly opponent. With one swift motion it hurled a morningstar into Lynna's chest, tearing flesh and crushing bone. Before Pierce and Jode could respond, the armored beast rose to its feet and

2

battle was joined in earnest. Sparks flew as the two warforged rained blows on one another. As Lynna's life ebbed into the dirt, Daine looked back at the cowering wizard. *"Now,* Saerath! The ship's making another pass, and this may be the last chance we have!"

Trembling, the wizard looked up at the approaching stormship. He wove mystical patterns with shaking fingers, whispering words of unbinding and dismissal. As he finished the incantation a ball of flame fell from the sky, struck, and the world disappeared in fire.

❀ ❀ ❀ ❀ ❀ ❀ ❀

Lei saw the fireball strike the center of the camp, and she wondered if Saerath had been caught in the blast. Alive or dead, he'd accomplished his task. As powerful as the stormship was, it relied on a web of delicate enchantments, and the abjurer had managed to disrupt this tapestry of spells. The ring of stormclouds wrapped around the waist of the ship buckled. Bereft of its elemental propulsion the ship plummeted toward the ground. The disruption was temporary, but it lasted long enough. The stricken stormship came crashing down, timber and bodies scattering across the Cyran camp. There was a gust of hurricane wind as the elemental was released from its bonds, and Lei staggered against the gale. But even as a ragged cheer went up from the Cyran survivors, a second wave of warforged emerged from the night.

Two of the enemy soldiers—a massive warrior with a long cleaver fused to one arm and a smaller scout with a dagger in each hand—reached Lei's position. Like Saerath, Lei was a non-combatant. As a member of House Cannith, she maintained the warforged and other magical weapons that the Cyran army had purchased from her house. According to the rules of war, she was a forbidden target—and likewise, she was not allowed to participate in any violence. But the enemy wasn't playing by the rules. Paralyzed with fear and surprise, Lei just watched as the soldier raised its razored arm. Having worked with warforged all her life, it seemed impossible that she would die this way. She saw her reflection in the blade as it fell toward

3

her face, but at the last moment she was shoved aside by a small figure—Jholeg, the goblin scout. Behind him Cadrian, Donal, and Mal moved in to engage the warforged with their halberds. Jholeg grinned at her, even as he darted back in to stab at the construct's leathery guts with his curved blade. He dodged a cleaver blow that would have removed his head, then made a quick thrust at the knee of the armored giant.

Lei had never seen warforged like these before. Despite their heavy armor, these 'forged moved with an unnatural speed, and they had strangely diverse set of weapons and designs.

"Get out of here, Lady Lei!" Cadrian shouted. "We'll—"

His order was cut short as the 'forged's cleaver sheared through his helmet and split his skull. Mal was next to fall, and as Lei saw his blood dripping from the blades of the warforged something inside Lei snapped. Almost without thinking, she walked up to the massive construct. Ducking under a blow intended for Jholeg, she reached out and placed her hand on the warforged's chest. She concentrated, and time seemed to recede as her senses expanded. She could feel the layers of magic binding the myriad components of the warforged together, the mystical energies that gave the creature thought and motion. Since she was a child she had been taught to weave these webs, to create magical artifacts and bring life to the lifeless. Now, with Cadrian's ruined face fixed in her mind, she hardened her thoughts into a blade and struck at the glowing core of the mystic web. There was a moment of timeless discontinuity, and then she was back in the battle. As she removed her hand the warforged soldier simply fell apart, collapsing into a heap of metal and stone.

Although the giant was down, the smaller warforged scout was still on its feet. Still covered with the blood of her friends, it danced straight for her like a ghastly silver puppet. There was a flash and a warm sensation across her belly, and she found herself falling to the ground. As the fires and the sounds of war grew faint, she was vaguely aware of a new group of people arriving on the scene, of the tiny construct being overwhelmed and shattered. But it was all so far away . . .

A cooling sensation filled her, icy water running through

4

her veins. The world snapped back into clear focus. Jode was kneeling over her, the dragonmark on his head glowing with a pale blue light.

"I've got you, Lei," the halfling healer murmured. "Just relax."

She closed her eyes and let the soothing light flow through her.

Daine looked over from the shattered ruin that had been a warforged soldier. "I need her on her feet," he said. "Now. Pierce is almost in pieces." He scowled and looked out over the battlefield. Burnt corpses were mingled with the twisted remnants of warforged warriors. "We don't even know which side those 'forged were fighting for. We need to regroup as quickly as possible. Warforged, a bloody *stormship* . . . who knows what else is out there?"

As if in answer to his words, the third wave appeared.

CHAPTER I

Flickering flames cast long shadows. But this was no battlefield. The fire blazed in a beautiful hearth of blue marble, filling the chamber with the rich smell of cedar. This was the home of Lord Hadran d'Cannith, and the trappings spoke of his wealth and power. The floors were covered with soft Sarlonan carpets, each one embroidered with a labyrinthine pattern of twisting, thorny angles. Portraits and glamerweave tapestries adorned the walls, depicting the glorious deeds of his Cannith ancestors. Dominating the room was a vast darkwood desk, its surface covered in golden sigils that glittered in the firelight.

Lord Hadran d'Cannith sat behind the desk, pulling at his chin as he listened to the messenger's report. It had been over a year since the battle of Keldan Ridge and the devastation that had wiped Cyre from the pages of history. Over a year since he had heard anything of his betrothed. Hadran was a wealthy and influential man, and he had spent a fortune on inquisitives, messengers, and diviners. Although he feared the worst, he had always clung to an ember of hope. And now, it seemed, his prayers had been answered.

"Lei was injured at Keldan Ridge, Lord Hadran," the inquisitive said. She wore a long cloak of dark green leather, a hood pulled low over her face. "It has been difficult to gather any sort of information about the battle, but it seems her troop was faced with an overwhelming force of unknown nationality.

6

They were driven west into contested lands between Thrane and Breland, and that's the only reason Lei is still alive. On the Day of Mourning, she was just outside Cyre—just beyond the effects of the disaster. I imagine she's one of the few people who actually saw the Mourning with her own eyes."

"But she's alive? You're sure of it?" Hadran chewed on his gray mustache, a habit his first wife had always despised. "Why didn't she arrive months ago? Why hasn't she sent a message through the stones?"

"I'm not a diviner, m'lord," the messenger replied, pulling her emerald cloak tight around her body. "I believe her companions took her back into the ruins of Cyre to search for other survivors. As for the stones, I wouldn't be surprised if she has no coin. But I know for a fact that Lei d'Cannith is alive and on her way here. I expect she and her companions will arrive in Sharn within the week."

"This is glorious news!" Hadran cried, jumping to his feet. He found that he was shaking. "I . . . I know you can't rely on such things, but months ago I spoke to an augur about Lei. She said we would never be married, that death would come between us. I prayed and I prayed that it was a false vision, and oh, Olladra be praised, it was!"

He moved to embrace the messenger, but the cloaked inquisitive took a step back.

"Be careful, Lord Hadran," the messenger said, her voice seeming deeper and darker. "It is all too easy to misread prophecy. I said that your betrothed was coming to Sharn. I never said you would see her again."

"What?" said Hadran, his joy turning to anger.

"Your oracle said that death would come between you and Lei." The shadows in the room seemed to grow deeper, and beneath the hood the messenger's face was lost in darkness. "You assumed the death was hers."

She threw off her cloak and Hadran cried out in horror.

❧ ❧ ❧ ⬤ ❧ ❧ ❧

Moments later, the messenger wiped her bloody hands on Hadran's shirt. She picked up her cloak and wrapped it around her shoulders, pulling the hood down over her head. She took one last look at the ruin that had once been a dragonmarked lord.

"I'll give your love to Lei, Lord Hadran," she purred. "I have great things planned for her. Great things."

No one saw her leave.

CHAPTER 2

BRELAND
THE OLD ROAD
Dravago 25, 996 YK

Daine woke in the mud. Cold rain fell from the gray sky, and his woolen blanket was soaked and filthy. At least it's just water, he thought. Compared to what they'd been in over the last six months, rain was a welcome change of pace.

The memories came unbidden to his mind, images far worse than any nightmare. For centuries Cyre had been a jewel in the crown of Galifar, a fertile land renowned for its crafts and culture. Now Cyre was a barren wasteland filled with corpses. As he traveled south, Daine heard the peasants whispering about the horrors to be found in this so-called Mournland. According to the tales, blood fell from the sky instead of rain, and the spirits of the dead howled with the wind.

The truth was far worse.

The battle at Keldan Ridge happened the night before the Mourning. The final hours of the battle were a blur. None of the survivors could remember how they escaped from the warforged marauders, and no one could actually recall when the disaster took place. How did it happen? What force could have devastated an entire country yet leave a few soldiers completely unharmed, a mere twenty feet from the border? Perhaps this amnesia was a side effect of the force that destroyed the realm, or perhaps the event was simply more than the human mind could bear.

On that terrible morning, Daine had led the remnants of his

troop back into Cyre, passing through the dead-gray mists to see what lay beyond. How could they have known how vast the devastation would be? Who would believe that an entire country could be destroyed in so brief a time? For months they had pressed deeper and deeper into the wastes. All that they found was horror and death. As the weeks went by Daine's soldiers fell one by one to the terrors of the twisted land, and only five survived the long trek back to the border—Daine, Pierce, Jani Onyll, the healer Jode, and Lei d'Cannith. But that was far from the end of their troubles. Every day brought a new clash with the soldiers of Thrane, and Jani fell victim to a last gift of Cyre—a lingering infection Jode's touch could not cure.

Finally they moved south into Breland. After a few skirmishes, the active aggression of the Brelish soldiers faded into muted disgust. The destruction of Cyre had thrown the entire world into a state of shock, and the common folk were weary of war. The chroniclers said that King Boranel of Breland had offered sanctuary to the refugees of Cyre. Others claimed that princes and ambassadors were hammering out the terms of peace far to the north, laying the foundation of a new world that would take the place of the ancient kingdom of Galifar. The frontier garrisons held the borders against any signs of treachery, and Daine's troop had received a bloody welcome in Thrane. But further south the people had begun to lay down their swords and return to their plows. After years of battle, it seemed that the conscripts were returning home for good.

It had been many years since Daine had a place to call home. Any past he might have returned to was buried in the ashes of Cyre. Pierce had been built to fight in a war that was all but over. Jode had never spoken of his family. Lei was the only one of the survivors whose future was clear, and so the others traveled with her on the road to Sharn—not because the city had any particular promise for them, but they had no place else to go.

Daine rose and shook the water out his blanket. Pierce was struggling to keep the fire alive, and Lei was starting to break camp, gathering the tarps and blankets. Daine joined her.

"Another fine day, hmm?" he said, handing over his blanket.

Lei smiled and shook her head. Her hair was covered with

mud, but it still seemed to gleam in the firelight, as if there was true copper mixed in with the red. Folding his blanket and placing it with the others, she produced the wooden rod she used as a focus for simple magic. With a few deft gestures, she wove a domestic cantrip into the wood. A wave of this makeshift wand drove mud and water from blankets and clothes, and scoured the dirt from her skin and hair. A dry blanket was hardly the most important thing in life, but without Lei's magic their clothes would have rotted away months ago—and her ability to conjure food was all that stood between the soldiers and starvation.

"We're almost there," Lei said, handing him a mug of water and a plate of cold gruel. It was about as pleasant as eating mud, but it had them alive. "If it wasn't raining, you could see the towers from here."

"You're really going to go through with this?"

"Of course. You don't understand our ways, Daine. I am an heir of the Mark of Making, and I have a responsibility to my house."

Dragonmarks. Daine swallowed a spoonful of gruel with a grimace. No one was born with a dragonmark, but members of a select few bloodlines carried the potential to manifest a mark and the magical power that came with it. It was Jode's dragonmark that allowed him to heal injuries with a touch. Lei's mark had a similar effect, but where Jode could knit flesh and bone, Lei repaired metal and wood. The powers of her dragonmark were the least of Lei's talents, but the mark defined her place in the world. In an age ravaged by war, a weaponsmith could hold more power than a king, and the dragonmarked artificers of House Cannith were the greatest weaponsmiths of modern times. House Cannith blazed the trail that led to the invention of the stormship, the wand of eternal fire, and of course, the warforged. Dragonmarks were rare even within the families that carried them, and Cannith often formed matches between the dragonmarked in the hopes that children would inherit the powers of the parents. So it was with Lei and her betrothed. Hadran d'Cannith was a widower and almost twice Lei's age, but his gold was good and his mark was strong.

"Blood above love," said Daine. "I've heard it before. All I'm interested in is the gold you promised us. It's just . . . I've seen you covered in mud and blood. I have a harder time seeing you as lady of the manor."

"You think I like sleeping in ditches and watching my friends die?" said Lei as she handed a plate of gruel to the groggy Jode.

"None of us *like* it. But it's those who can do it without letting it kill them that make soldiers. You lived through things that killed hardened veterans. You're one of us."

Lei shook her head. "My service in the guard was duty to my family. Just as my marriage is. Of the two, I'll enjoy marriage far more."

"Ever been married before?"

Lei opened her mouth to retort.

"Please, Captain Daine, my lady Lei!" Jode interjected with a brilliant smile. "If we have only a day's travel ahead of us, let us enjoy one another's company while we still can, yes?"

Lei and Daine mumbled apologies and returned to the gruel.

❀ ❀ ❀ ❀ ❀ ❀ ❀

Though the sun was still buried behind the clouds, it was just past dawn when they broke camp and headed back toward the Old Road, the path that connected the great cities of Breland. They'd chosen to sleep in a clearing well away from the road so Pierce could watch for enemies. But a tangle of the King's Woods lay between the travelers and the road, and it was there that trouble struck.

From behind a tree stepped a man out—a rangy, pock-faced Brelander wearing the patched leather tunic of a Brelish soldier. Perhaps he was a deserter or a retiree with nowhere to go, but Daine thought it just as likely the man had torn his ill-fitting armor from the corpse of its true owner. A gray woolen cloak shielded him from the rain, and he waved a wooden cudgel in their general direction.

"Ho there, travelers!" the man called, his voice a gravelly rasp.

Daine stepped to the front of the group, signaling the others to halt.

"Morgalan's the name. By your dress, I take you to be strangers in our lovely land. Mourners, are you?"

"Mourners?" asked Daine.

"Refuse from what's left of Cyre. They're calling it the Mournland now, on account of there being nothing for you lot to do but mourn for what you lost."

"If you've got a point, make it quick." Daine's hand went to his sword, but he held his temper in check. This was far from the first time they'd been harassed, and Daine smelled a trap.

"I have a bit of a nose for the energies of the arcane, and I can see that there's more to the young lady's backpack than meets the eye. I'll be taking that, along with any coin you might have on you."

"Four to one, by my count. Not odds in your favor." Daine scratched the back of his neck, using the opportunity to make a few swift gestures to his companions with the tips of his fingers.

"Things are rarely what they seem." A crossbow bolt flew from the trees and struck the ground near Daine's feet.

"True," Daine said, but he was already in motion, charging at the highwayman, drawing his sword and dagger as he ran.

From the corner of his eye, Daine saw Pierce raise his enormous longbow and send two blue-feathered arrows back along the path of the crossbow bolt. There was a cry from the woods and the sound of a man falling from the trees.

Two men and a woman, all three dressed in tattered leathers and armed with hatchets, burst out of the woods to Daine's left. He slowed his charge long enough to be sure the others had them.

Lei was waiting for them. She hurled a small stone in their direction. It burst with a blinding flare of golden radiance. As the bandits threw up their hands to shield their eyes, Pierce was already loosing more arrows. Within seconds, all three lay stretched out on the ground.

Morgalan met Daine's charge head-on. With a furious cry and a blow of his cudgel, he knocked Daine's blade from his hand. But the sword was the lesser threat. Daine's dagger was Cannith-forged from adamantine and could slice through steel with ease. Daine ducked beneath the bandit's next blow, and with one swift stroke he cut the cudgel in two, leaving Morgalan with a bare stump of wood.

Dropping the ruined remnant of his club and stepping back, the bandit made an intricate gesture with his left hand while muttering words in a language Daine had never heard. Daine felt the touch of enchantment, and for a moment it was difficult to focus.

Morgalan . . . Morgalan . . . why were they fighting, after all? Surely this was a misunderstanding. His friend Morgalan needed his help, needed his assistance against these three brutes . . .

Daine had dealt with sorcerers before, and Saerath had occasionally tried a charm when he'd been ordered to dig latrines. Gritting his teeth, Daine shook his way free of the intrusive thoughts and drove his dagger into the shoulder of the bandit.

Morgalan gasped and the mystical pressure faded. Daine grabbed the man by his neck with his free hand, yanked the dagger free, and threw Morgalan into the mud. He leaned down, his foot on the bandit's neck and his blade at his throat.

"Listen to me, Brelander," he growled. "I've been fighting your kind for six years. Every instinct I've got says I should slit your throat and leave you bleeding in the dirt." He struck the pale man across the face with the pommel of his dagger, slamming his face into the mud. "But the war's over, and I am a stranger in your land. Don't give me a reason to start fighting again."

Daine stood up, deliberately cutting Morgalan's purse from his belt. He tossed the leather pouch to Lei and picked up his fallen sword. Across the way, Jode was tending to the wounds of the bandits Pierce had feathered, while the warforged kept the injured ruffians covered with his massive bow.

"Leave them be, Jode," Daine called. "We've got other business in this 'lovely land.' "

❋ ❋ ❋ ❋ ❋ ❋ ❋

There was little conversation following the attack, and they eventually joined the stream of travelers on the Old Road to Sharn. Jode rode on Pierce's shoulders, singing an occasional song in the liquid tongue of his distant homeland. Daine brought up the rear, watching Jode and wondering. After all the years they'd spent together, the many battles they'd been through, Jode was still an enigma to him. The halfling had come from the distant Talenta Plains, a barren land said to be home to huge lizards. The glittering dragonmark of Healing was spread across his bald head as plain as day, but Jode had never acknowledged any ties to House Jorasco, and he did not wear the signet ring of a dragonmark heir. He was always ready with a cheerful story or a song, but his own past was a mystery. Daine had never pushed him. He had pain enough in his own past, and if Jode had secrets, it wasn't Daine's place to steal them.

Midday the clouds cleared, and there it lay before them—Sharn, the City of Towers. Even at this distance, the towers stretched up to the sky—dozens of shining spires, each bristling with minarets and turrets. The Old Road passed through flat farmlands, and over the course of the day it seemed less as if they were moving and more as if the towers themselves were growing, rising up higher and higher with every passing hour. Slowly details emerged. Daine noticed that a few of the smaller towers seemed to be floating in the air, unconnected to the main columns. Tiny dots moved to and fro—boats and other vessels darting through the air. As the sun sank beneath the horizon, the lights of the city became visible, twinkling like stars.

"House Cannith lit the city, you know," Lei said. "Casalon d'Cannith perfected cold fire almost seven hundred years ago. The impact on Galifar was truly remarkable. In many ways it set the stage for—"

"I thought the elves developed cold fire thousands of years ago," Daine said.

Lei scowled. "Yes, well . . . Cannith brought it to Khorvaire."

15

Daine smiled, though Lei did not see it. The elves of Aerenal had been working with magic for more than three times the length of recorded human history, and Daine had once met an Aerenal ambassador who was over seven hundred years old. It was only natural that elven skills would exceed those of the younger race, but it was one of the only ways to derail Lei's effusive monologues about the virtues of her house.

"How do they keep the towers from falling?" asked Pierce.

It was as much as he had said in the last week. The warforged warrior, never talkative in the best of times, had become positively taciturn in recent months. Daine was hardly surprised; Pierce had been built to defend Cyre, and now the country was destroyed, the war over. What purpose did Pierce serve in this broken world? So far he'd continued to follow Daine's orders. But how long would this loyalty last?

"There are places in the world where arcane energies behave in an unusual manner," Lei said. "Many sages believe that this is the result of other worlds touching this one. So a place touched by Dolurrh is filled with despair, while Lamannia causes vegetation to bloom. Along these cliffs, spells of air and flight are empowered. The enchantments that support these towers could not be performed in most places. The city itself is drawn to the sky. You'll see flying boats and similar things—all the result of the magic of this place."

"So if they're all supported by magic . . . what happens should the spells unravel?" Daine's mind flashed back to the stormship tumbling from the sky after Saerath disrupted its bindings.

"Well . . . actually, I believe that towers have fallen in the past. During the war. Presumed sabotage, though it was never proven."

"And I imagine your beloved lives in one of the highest towers?"

"Yes." Daine didn't turn to look, but he could hear the frown in her voice.

"Wonderful."

❀ ❀ ❀ ❀ ❀ ❀ ❀

As the sun slipped below the cliffs, the Old Road came to the tower called Tavick's Landing, then ran beneath a vast bronze statue of Queen Wroann ir'Wyrnarn, her sword raised in defiance of the laws of Galifar. Black-cloaked guards manned a dozen separate gates, listening to the tales of merchants, travelers, and peasants. The traditions of a century of war were still in effect, and no one entered Sharn without passing the Guardians of the Gate.

The gate to which Daine and his companions came was manned by a burly dwarf whose beard resembled a patch of black thorns. "You don't look like you're from these parts," he growled. He studied Pierce and then fixed on Daine's rank insignia. "Mourners, are you? Serves you right, you ask me." He nodded up toward the statue of Wroann, the queen whose rebellion had started the Last War. "Stand against Breland, and see what it gets you."

Jode stepped forward before Daine could speak. "I see that little escapes your keen eyes, sergeant. I take it you've encountered Mourners before, hmm?"

The dwarf studied him carefully. Jode's dragonmark was spread across the top of his head—and a dragonmark usually meant power and wealth.

"That's right. High Walls is lousy with 'em. Used to be where they kept traitors. Some would say it still is."

Again, Jode interjected before Daine could speak. "Well, it's a simple mistake to make, but ours is no simple tale, sir. Yes, Lord Daine wears the dress of a Cyran soldier, but there is far more here than meets the eye. Allow me to introduce the Lady Lei, heir to the Mark of Making."

Lei curtsied and extended her hand, revealing her Cannith signet ring. The dwarf examined the ring closely.

"Lady Lei is betrothed to Lord Hadran d'Cannith, whose name I certainly hope you recognize. As any child could tell you, House Cannith had its seat of power in the confines of Cyre, and after the disaster, Lord Hadran wished to ensure the safety of his beloved. Thus he hired the three of us—Lord Daine, a master swordsman trained by the Blademark of House Deneith; Pierce, a stalwart warforged warrior handcrafted by my lady's parents to ensure the safety of their only daughter; and myself, Jode d'Jorasco, a healer without equal."

Minutes passed as Jode wove his tale, describing the great dangers the trio had faced in their hunt for the lost Cannith heir. The dwarf stood spellbound as Jode recounted the battle with the warped warforged and the living darkness. A blackcloaked woman wearing the badge of a captain came over and rapped him on the side of the head, snapping him out of the daze. "Horas! Process this lot and move on! You're holding up the line!"

The dwarf blinked and shook his head to clear the cobwebs. "Uh, yes . . . yes. Sorry. Just . . . make a mark here on the ledger and you can be on your way. I trust you're not bringing dangerous materials into the city? Pyrotechnics, dragon's blood, dreamlily?"

"I do have three warforged in my pack," Lei said. "Is that a problem?"

Jode sighed.

"In your . . . May I see them, please, Lady d'Cannith?"

Lei took off her pack and unfolded the funnel-shaped cloth cone at the top. "Pierce, do you mind?"

A murmur ran through the waiting crowd as the massive warforged warrior crawled into the tiny backpack. A moment later he emerged, dragging the battered body of a small warforged scout.

"All three are inert," Lei explained. "I haven't had time to see if they can be restored, but we found them during our travels, and I wanted to return them to the house."

"I . . . see." Clearly Cannith heirs transporting damaged warforged were not a part of this guard's daily routine. "You . . . you can go about your business, my lady. Enjoy your visit to Sharn."

Lei smiled as Pierce pushed the wounded warforged back into her extraordinary pack. "Thank you, sergeant," she said. "I'm sure I will."

❂ ❂ ❂ ❂ ❂ ❂ ❂

Once they were safely out of earshot of the guards, Jode turned to Lei, shaking his head. Pierce and Daine were straggling behind, their eyes turned skyward to the towers, awnings, bridges, and buildings that stretched upward and out of sight.

"My Lady Lei," said Jode, "there really was no need to mention the warforged at all. I had the situation well in hand."

"I've always wondered if you had formal ties to House Jorasco, Jode. Why don't you ever talk about it?"

"I made that up, my lady. I had the sense that our sergeant would be more impressed by the emissaries of a powerful house as opposed to a few 'Mourners' in search of refuge."

"That would explain that bit about the fight with the cannibal children." Lei frowned. "My parents were involved in the early work with the warforged, though . . . it's entirely possible they did build Pierce."

Jode shrugged. "I was simply speaking extemporaneously, my lady. I had no idea my words held even one grain of truth."

"Huh. And Daine?" Lei glanced back at Daine and Pierce, neither of whom were paying she and Jode the least bit of attention. "He didn't actually train with House Deneith?"

"I'm no oracle, Lady Lei. I was just spinning a tale for our prickly sergeant. Besides, can you really see our captain in a house of mercenaries?"

Lei smiled, then broke into laughter. After a moment, Jode began to laugh with here. Daine scowled as he and Pierce caught up to them. "All right, you've had your fun. Now let's get on with it. I want to sleep in a bed tonight, and we still have to find your loving suitor, Lei."

"Follow me . . . Lord Daine."

Still smiling, Lei led them through the crowd.

CHAPTER 3

BRELAND
SHARN
Dravago 25, 996 YK

Daine had heard stories of Sharn, but mere words could not convey the overwhelming presence of the city. The wide street was filled with a churning mob. Half a dozen different languages filled the air. A Talentan merchant was haggling with a young gnome over the price of halodan meal-worms. A pale elf wearing a golden gown and a thin mask of beaten silver was walking down the street, accompanied by a massive ogre laborer, who was carrying a trunk formed from bronzed bones. A patrol of blackcloaked guardians watched the streets with suspicious eyes and the promise of swift retribution.

The most disorienting part was the sky—or the lack thereof. This district was entirely enclosed in one of the massive towers of Tavick's Landing, and above their heads the hollow core of the tower stretched up out of sight. Gargoyles and hippogriffs whirled in the air above them, darting between the different levels of the tower. The walls of the central tower were easily fifty feet thick, and buildings and businesses were carved directly into the walls. The interior of the tower must have been six or seven hundred feet across, filled with smaller spires and buildings.

"Nice place," Jode said, taking it all in stride. "At least you don't have to worry about the rain. I'd watch out for falling hippogriff dung, though. That's insult and injury for you."

"There's still rain," Lei said absently, studying the street ahead. "I'm not a specialist in weather, but apparently enough condensation builds up in the heights of the tower to rain on the people at the bottom."

"Isn't that always the way? So where are we going, my lady?"

"A place called Dalan's Refuge. It's on the upper levels of this quarter. That robber had a few sovereigns in his purse. Unless you feel like climbing a lot of stairs, I was hoping to find a coach."

"After all you've been through, my lady, I would say that you deserve a little luxury at the end."

Daine scowled.

"You disagree, Captain?" Jode inquired.

"You never know what's going to happen," Daine said. "We only have a few coins to our name. I hate to waste even one."

"You worry too much, my captain. Once we arrive at Lord Hadran's estate, Lady Lei has promised to see us well-compensated from his lordship's treasury."

"I know Hadran will look after you," Lei said. "He's a good man, and— Oh, there's one!"

She waved, and a vessel dropped from the air to meet them. At a glance, the skycoach was a long, narrow rowboat built from firepine and darkwood. A figurehead of a swan was embedded at the prow of the ship; the image of its outstretched wings was engraved along the length of the boat, glittering in the cold light of the mystical torches. The driver was a young woman dressed in a simple white gown bearing the emblem of a swan on the left breast. Her short, silvery hair and wide eyes hinted at a touch of elven blood.

"How may I help you?" the driver inquired.

"There's four of us," Lei replied, stepping into the floating boat. "To Round Wind in Dalan's Refuge."

Money exchanged hands, the rest of them climbed in, Daine taking the seat next to Lei. Jode and Pierce sat across from them.

The boat rose into the air. The skycoach rose along the central core then entered a tunnel. Within moments they emerged into open air, skimming past the bridges and smaller spires of

Tavick's Landing as they ascended toward the heavens. It gave Daine an eagle's eye view of the city. There were towers upon towers, buildings that dwarfed the tallest tree he'd ever seen, and bridges ran between many of them, spanning chasms that would mean certain death to anyone foolish enough to climb the guardrails.

"Round Wind?" Daine asked, turning to Lei.

"People give their mansions names. You know, like 'Friendly Arms' or 'Welcoming Light.' "

"I'm familiar with the tradition. But Round Wind? What does it mean?"

"Oh, don't argue over trivialities. This is *it*, Daine! It's over! All those years of war, all the blood, the death . . . it all ends here. I'm going home."

Daine's mouth tightened. "This isn't your home."

Lei dropped her eyes and looked away for a moment. "Look, I'm angry too. My parents, my closest friends . . . I lost them, too. I know this isn't Cyre. But our old life is gone, Daine, and it isn't coming back. You've seen what's left of our homeland. It's time to move on. To start again."

Daine said nothing. Pierce and Jode stared out at the spectacle of the city stretched before them, staying well out of the conversation.

"Have you thought about my offer? I'm sure there's a place for you in the household."

"As what?" Daine snapped. "A guard? Patrolling Round Wind and making sure no hippogriffs crap on his lordship's roof?" Daine slammed his fist on the railing.

"Would it be so different—"

"Don't, Lei," Daine warned. "I fought for Cyre. You may think you know me, but you have no idea what I've sacrificed or why I served the Queen. I'm no sword for hire, and the last thing I'm going to do is work for a dragonmarked house."

Lei looked away. When her temper was hot, she was more than a match for Daine, but clearly her heart wasn't in this battle. "Why? What do you know of the houses? Is Lord Daine too good to work for a craftsman's daughter?"

"How can you of all people ask me that? Have you forgotten

what happened at Whitehearth? Do you expect me to forget?"

She looked back at him, and he saw the glitter of a tear in her eye before she turned away again. "Have you?"

Her words were cold water on Daine's fiery temper. "Lei . . . look, Lei, I'm sorry. I didn't mean it like that." He paused, trying to find the right words. "There's a lot about me you don't know. You and Jode are the only 'marks I've ever had as friends. And I . . . I'm no sellsword, all right? I've got to find another path. I just don't know what it is yet."

He held out his hand, and after a long moment, she took it. "I'm sorry," she said. "Can you at least stay the night at Round Wind? A hot meal, a nice bed . . . and in the morning, I'm sure Hadran will be willing to give you a good breakfast and enough gold to get you started on whatever path you choose."

He took a deep breath, then nodded and looked away. "Yes. Thanks. Though I think I might prefer a last bowl of your gruel. I think I'm going to miss it."

"Not me!" Jode broke in. "No offense, my lady, but I'd just as soon never see that goo again."

Lei smiled faintly. "I'm looking forward to real food myself. How about you? Will you be finding a place in one of the houses of healing?"

Daine had wondered this himself. If the war was truly over, it was the obvious role for a man with Jode's talents, but healing was the domain of House Jorasco. Jode's dragonmark hinted at a tie to the house, yet he'd never spoken of it . . .

"Oh, I'm not ready to settle down yet. Pierce and I thought we'd stay with the captain and see where fortune took us. Right, Pierce?"

"You won't be coming with me, Pierce?" Lei said, surprised.

The warforged soldier glanced over at them. "I'm sorry, Lei." His voice was deep and resonant, slow water running across stone. "I would not have survived the war without your aid. But I wish to remain with Captain Daine. The war may be over, but he is still my commander. House Cannith sold me to Cyre. The house does not own me now."

This time, tears finally began to flow. "I knew we'd be going our separate ways, but Pierce—" Lei looked up at the armored

23

warrior. "I thought . . . I just thought that you'd . . . " While she was casting about for words the boat dropped sharply, stealing her breath.

"Round Wind!" shouted the driver.

Lei dried her eyes and nodded. "We'll discuss this later tonight," she said, her voice tight. "I'm going to have a lot to explain to Hadran."

❀ ❀ ❀ ❀ ❀ ❀ ❀

As impressive as the lower streets of Sharn had been, Dalan's Refuge was on an entirely different level—literally and figuratively. The district was built on a massive ring encircling one of the largest towers of Tavick's Landing, and they were thousands of feet above the waters of the Dagger. Despite the altitude, the breezes were warm and light, and Daine had no trouble with the air.

They were surrounded by the ostentatious display of wealth. Statues surrounded the streets, prominent citizens of Sharn captured for eternity in bronze and marble. At the edge of the ring, a fountain of illusions threw shimmering columns of rainbow light into the air, dropping off the edge to fall towards the lower districts. Night had fallen, and there were far fewer people on the streets than there had been below. Dalan's Refuge was a residential district, and most of its inhabitants had either retired for the evening or were off seeking entertainment in more exotic regions.

Round Wind proved to be true to its name—at least partially. The manor was formed from large spheres of different stones, merged together to create an unusual aesthetic effect.

"Hadran's grandfather was an architect," Lei explained.

"And insane?" Daine muttered.

Two men in Cannith livery stood at the front gate, but they allowed the group to pass once Lei displayed her Cannith signet. They walked down a long corridor with rounded walls. Statues of Hadran's ancestors watched from either side—proud artificers and wizards bearing the symbols of the house.

Eventually the hall opened into a large atrium, but a bulky warforged that dwarfed even Pierce blocked the path. Where

Pierce was designed for battle, this guardian seemed to have been built to impress. He was armored with plates of silver, and gemstones adorned his torso and faceplate. Lei seemed to recognize the 'forged and stepped out in front of Daine.

"Domo, I have returned, and I have three guests. I apologize for arriving unexpectedly. It's a very long story. Please inform your master at once."

The warforged did not budge. "You are not unexpected. Nor are you welcome in Round Wind. Leave now." Its voice was a deep, rolling rumble, and the hostility was unmistakable.

Lei frowned. "What are you talking about, Domo? I am Lei d'Cannith of Metrol!" She held her signet before her like a sword, and her anger caused the Cannith seal to blaze with light. "You will announce me to Lord Hadran at once, or I'll see you melted into scrap!"

The air seemed to ripple around her hands, and Daine had a flashback of a warforged soldier exploding in the battle of Keldan Ridge.

"I do not take orders from excoriates," said Domo. "You have no place here. Return to the streets or I shall summon guards and have you removed."

The words hit Lei like a blow. The fire went out of her, and she took a step back. Daine half-expected Jode to jump in, but even he looked pale. Lei looked back at the warforged, seemingly dazed. "Ex . . . but . . . why?"

Domo raised a hand, and Daine heard guards approaching. He stepped forward and took Lei's arm. "Back off, gemstone. We're leaving."

Lei followed blindly, still in a state of shock. As they walked down the long path, Lei paused to look at the statue closest to the door. It was a work in progress—a masculine figure in the robes of a Cannith artificer, but the features were still unformed. Lei stared at the blank face in silence, and then allowed Daine to pull her toward the street.

❖ ❖ ❖ ◉ ❖ ❖ ❖

"We spent all of our silver on the coach," Jode said, "so I'm afraid we're going to have to take the long way down. I think we should go to that High Walls district the gate guard mentioned. If there are other Cyrans there, it's probably our best chance for finding shelter. Still, we're going to need coin, and quickly."

Lei still seemed to be in a daze. She had taken off her Cannith signet ring and was idly turning it around in her hand. Daine couldn't remember seeing her cry before today, but for the second time today her eyes were glittering in the light of the cold flames.

Pierce was bringing up the rear of the group, and he approached Lei. "My lady, what is wrong? I am afraid I did not understand the conversation at the manor gate."

Lei stopped walking. Anger and sorrow warred on her face. "I'm *not* your lady, Pierce! Not anymore. I'm ex . . . ex . . . "

"Excoriate," Jode said quietly.

Lei wheeled to face him with fury in her eyes then clenched her fists and turned away. She grabbed Pierce in a fierce embrace, sobbing against the mithral plating of his chest.

Pierce had been forged for war, and none of his companions could match his skills in battle. But he knew little about soothing distress. He put his hands on Lei's shoulders as if he was worried he might break her.

"My lady, I do not know this word. What is this . . . excoriate?"

Lei continued sobbing. "Why?" she murmured.

"Excoriation is a tradition among the dragonmarked houses," Jode said, his tone more subdued than usual. "It is a punishment reserved for those who have severely violated the precepts of the house, not unlike excommunication in the Church of the Silver Flame. It was first put into practice around the time of the War of the Mark . . . though back then they would actually flay the skin from the victim, stripping away his mark both literally and figuratively."

"You can't actually cut away a dragonmark, can you?" Daine asked.

"No, you can't actually take the mark away. The flaying was a symbolic gesture—though many excoriates must have died during the process. The social implications are what matters. An excoriate is no longer part of the house. Other members of the house are not to speak with him or aid him in any way. He is barred from all enclaves and estates. He cannot marry within the house. If he claims to be an heir of the house, he can be prosecuted under the laws of Galifar. It's a serious charge, and it takes the authority of a baron or a house council to order it."

Daine approached Lei and gently put his hand on her back. "Lei," he said softly. "Why would they do this to you? What have you done?"

•Lei pushed away from Pierce and Daine. *"I don't know!"* she howled. "All I've ever done I've done for the house! *How could they do this to me?"*

Blind with rage, she made a savage gesture with her left hand. There was a glitter of silver, and Daine realized that she'd hurled her signet off the great ring of Dalan's Refuge to fall thousands of feet to the peaks below.

Jode sighed. "That would have bought us at least a night's lodging." He shrugged. "Look, Captain, we need to get moving if we're going to get a roof over our heads." He made a sidelong gesture with his head. "And I think the natives are getting restless."

Indeed, a few Brelish guardsmen were watching them from a hundred feet away, and one was idly toying with his crossbow.

"You're right." He sighed. "Lei . . . Lei, we'll sort this out. Just . . . give it time. Pierce, could you . . . " He gestured at Lei, and the warforged soldier carefully picked her up.

"Take heart, my lady," he rumbled, as they began the long journey down. "This battle has just begun."

INTERLUDE

Rasial hated the deep tunnels of Khyber's Gate. The smell of sewage and smoke filled the air, and the cold torches were few and far between, leaving long pools of shadow in the subterranean passages. But business was business. He stood beneath the flickering torch, cleaning his fingernails with his dagger and trying to look calm.

"Rasial?" The voice from the shadows was soft and oily. A moment later, three people emerged from the darkness. As promised, they were unarmed. The man in the lead wore a tattered brown cloak and his face was hidden by a deep cowl. A man and a woman stood behind him, dressed in roughspun cloth patched with burlap. They were covered with dirt and scabs, and their faces were almost devoid of expression. How did I ever come to this? Rasial thought.

"Yeah."

"Rasial . . . *Tarkanan?*"

"That's me."

"I thank you for meeting us so promptly. I trust you have the merchandise that we discussed?" The voice of the hooded man seemed to shift slightly every time he spoke . . . it was barely noticeable, but the pitch and inflection changed from moment to moment.

"Yeah, I got it." Rasial tossed the small pouch in the air and caught it with his left hand, revealing the glistening black

28

dragonmark and the sores upon his palm.

The hooded man seemed hissed. "Yesss, good."

"The question is if you can uphold your end of our bargain," said Rasial. "Gold is a start, but until you prove that you can deliver on your promises, this—" he tossed the bag and caught it in his right hand— "stays with me. And if you're thinking of trying anything stupid—" he extended his left hand, and for a moment the shadows seemed to be drawn toward his palm— "I'd stop now."

The hooded man laughed, a horrible, gurgling sound. For a moment his face was revealed by the torchlight, and Rasial gasped. It was a horrible ruin, with exposed muscle that seemed to pulse and twitch with his laughter.

"Oh, have no fear, Rasial," the stranger said. "All your problems will be over soon enough."

His two companions leaped forward without a sound, moving with unnatural speed and in perfect unison. It was clear Rasial couldn't outrun them, so he hurled the pouch at the wall of the tunnel, hoping to smash its contents and steal their victory, but to his shock a fleshy tentacle lashed out from the spokesman's arm and snatched the purse from the air. The next thing he knew, the man with the vacant stare was right in front of him, slashing at him with claws that had grown from his hands.

What were these people?

Rasial spun to the side, but even as he did he felt a burning pain along his ribs. The stranger's claws tore into his side.

But now it was Rasial's turn. He slammed his left hand into the man's face, letting his power flow through his palm and into his attacker. As always, the pain was excruciating, but as bad as it was for him, it was far worse for his victim. The stranger cried out—the first sound he'd made—and fell to his knees, clutching at his face. Rasial smiled. But he had forgotten about the woman. The next thing he knew there was a sharp pain in the pack of his neck, and he found himself falling.

Darkness stole his senses before he hit the ground.

CHAPTER 4 BRELAND
SHARN
Dravago 25, 996 YK

They must have walked half a mile before they found the lift. Now they were slowly dropping toward the bottom of Sharn on a large disk of floating metal. Daine tried to ignore the fact that the only thing standing between him and a drop of two thousand feet was a thin, invisible field of arcane energy. Pierce was carrying Lei cradled in his arms. She had finally fallen asleep. Daine stood at the center of the disk, talking quietly to Jode.

"How do we even know this is real? What if that whetstone of a warforged was playing some sort of a joke?"

Jode shook his tiny head. "It's just not something you joke about, captain. *Especially* a warforged, doubly so a servant in the house of the lord she's to be married to. That 'forged belongs to the household, and if the lord wanted to melt him down, he could."

"What about Hadran, then? Could he have put the 'forged up to it? Or condemned Lei to get out of the marriage? They haven't seen each other for years, right?"

"No, it still doesn't make sense. Lei's family died with Cyre. If Hadran wants out, who's going to challenge him? Besides, there are established grounds for excoriation. You know that as well as I do. It's not something you do on a whim, lord or no lord."

Daine sighed. "Meanwhile, we're high and dry. So much for

30

Lord Hadran's fabled generosity. And if Sharn is anything like Metrol, I imagine the guards won't like us setting up camp on the street corner."

Jode smiled. "Leave it to me, Captain. Have I ever let you down?"

"I'm going to pretend you didn't just ask me that."

⊙ ⊙ ⊙ ⊙ ⊙ ⊙ ⊙

Once a residential district, High Walls had been converted to serve as a prison—a fortified ghetto for those deemed a security risk to Breland and Sharn. Now that the war was coming to a close, the gates were open and the portcullises were raised, but the guards remained, and black-cloaked archers walked the walls that gave the region its name. Beyond the gates, the district was a dismal sight. Walls were cracked, windows broken, cobblestones had even been lifted from the streets. The few people who were still about were filthy folk in torn and soiled clothes, watching from alleys or peering out of shattered windows.

"Well, it looks like there aren't any guards to keep us from sleeping in the street, but I wouldn't recommend it," Jode said. "Seems to me like our friend Morgalan would be right at home here."

"What exactly are we looking for here?" asked Daine.

"I'll know it when I see it." A few moments later Jode held up a hand, motioning them to stop. "This'll do."

A rather melancholy manticore was painted on the sign above the door, and not with any particular skill. In one corner was the horn of the hostel along with a small Star of Cyre. "Well, it looks like Cyrans are welcome," said Daine, "but we still have one problem—the complete absence of coin."

"Trust me." Jode threw open the door and strode inside as if he owned the place. Daine followed, while Pierce set Lei's feet on the ground and gently shook her awake.

The interior of the Manticore Inn was as uninspiring as the façade. The sullen people sitting around the common room studied the travelers suspiciously. Here and there Daine did see the tell-tale look of Cyre in some of the faces—a narrow chin, hazel eyes ringed with brown—but if Jode was banking on an outpouring of love, he was sorely mistaken.

To Daine's surprise, Jode called out loudly in the tongue of the Talenta Plains, and a moment later the innkeeper appeared. She was a stout halfling with streaks of gray in her brown hair, and she returned Jode's query in the same tongue. An animated discussion followed, as Jode indicated each traveler in turn and went through a bizarre series of pantomimed actions. Even the other patrons took an interest, leaning forward to watch the antics of this seemingly mad halfling. The innkeeper seemed dubious, but eventually she nodded, and Jode embraced her. Pushing him away, she went back to the kitchen.

"I've got us a few days of credit," Jode whispered. "Now whatever she says, just nod."

A moment later, the innkeeper returned with a set of keys and led them upstairs. The keys seemed almost unnecessary, as most of the doors were on the verge of falling off of their hinges. She opened the door and the end of the hall.

"I know it's not what you're used to, General," she said. "But hopefully it will suffice until your letters of credit are cleared by the bank."

Daine glanced over at Jode. *General?* "We've been in the field for many days, lady. Your generosity is appreciated." He knelt to kiss her hand, and she looked away and blushed.

"Oh, not at all, General. To think, one of the Queen's trusted advisors in my humble inn. And after you risked so much to save those Talentan orphans. Truly, a few days is the least I can do." She smiled again. "Breakfast is served at the eighth bell. I look forward to hearing more tales of your valor in battle."

"Of course, of course," Jode said. "But at the moment, the general needs his rest."

❀ ❀ ❀ ❀ ❀ ❀ ❀

Once upon a time, the room might have had a cold fire lamp. It might have included a bed. But furniture had been stripped away, leaving only a pair of mildewed pallets set against the floor. There was a single oil lamp, and spiders scattered into the shadows when Jode managed to get it lit. Daine had seen prison cells with more ambiance. He sighed. "All right, Jode. *General?*"

Jode shrugged. "Dassi likes war stories. I trust you can spin a few. She seemed especially interested in your efforts to help halfling children escape Cyre in the last days of the war, despite great personal risk and constant attack by the undead warriors of Karrnath."

Daine shook his head, smiling. "And what did this buy us?"

"Well, she likes stories, but she still drives a hard bargain. She's extending credit for five days, at which point she expects to be paid in full and then some. Luckily for us, her prices are quite reasonable."

"Hardly surprising, considering the luxurious accommodations."

"This from a man who woke up in a muddy ditch?"

"Fair enough. Any thoughts on how we're going to pay her?"

"A few. I'll get the lay of the land in the morning, Captain. For now, I think that rest is called for."

Daine nodded. "Yes, you're right. You and Lei take the . . . beds. Compared to my nice ditch, the floor will be fine."

Pierce helped Lei to the pallet, then got their blankets out of her pack. Within moments, Lei and Jode were fast asleep. Pierce drew his long flail and turned to face the door, preparing for the night's watch. Daine turned down the lamp. He lay in the darkness for what seemed like an eternity. Occasionally there was a shout or a cry from the street or movement outside the door. At such times, Daine found his hand was resting on the hilt of his sword before he'd even thought about it.

But eventually, he found his way to sleep.

Interlude

The first thing Rasial noticed was the smell. His nostrils were filled with it—a cloying blend of cinnamon, sulfur, and burned flesh.

The second sensation was sound—bubbling, dripping, a vast assortment of liquid noise.

Sight returned before touch. He was lying on a curved table, staring up at an arched ceiling hewn into solid stone. The table was slightly tilted, his feet higher than his head, and his head throbbed with the rush of blood. After a moment he realized that he was spread-eagled on the surface, his numbed limbs attached to the table with steel manacles. He could only move his head a little, but he could see that he was surrounded by large glass tanks, each filled with a different shade of luminous fluid; the only light in the chamber came from this rippling liquid. Vague shapes were moving in some of these tanks, casting shadows across the ceiling. Writhing tentacles, pulsating amoebae . . .

Was that a hand?

His own limbs were completely numb. Tentatively, he tried channeling the shadows through his dragonmark.

Nothing. No flow of power, no pain. Was it just a side effect of the venom or spell that held him paralyzed? Or was there something else at work?

"I thank you, Rasial Tarkanan. You have proved doubly useful to our cause."

Rasial stiffened at the sound of the oily voice. With an immense effort, he lifted his head to look for the source of the sound.

The hooded man stood at the foot of the table, but he wasn't hooded any longer. His visage was even more horrific than the momentary glimpse had implied. Hands, neck, face . . . all a horror. In place of skin the man had pulsing, bloody muscle. The cords and sinews seemed unnaturally thick, and they moved of their own accord, twitching in ways that normal muscular contraction couldn't account for. He was larger than Rasial had realized—layers of wet muscle bulging beneath simple brown robes. His eyes were sunk deep within his sockets, and they glittered with madness. His mouth was a bloody ruin, and bony talons tipped his spidery fingers.

"What are you?" Rasial whispered. Simply moving his jaw was almost impossible, and forcing the words through his throat took every ounce of willpower he possessed.

"What I am is irrelevant. The question is what I will become. Thanks to you, I am one step closer to the answer." His mouth . . . there was something wrong with his mouth, but Rasial couldn't quite make sense of it.

"What . . . become . . . ?"

"Don't struggle, Rasial. You have served us well. My master comes, and he shall grant you the rest you deserve."

Rest? Was this monster going to kill him? After everything he'd done, all he'd been through, was this how he was going to die?

You will not die. Embrace eternity in me.

It took a moment for Rasial to realize that the thought was not his own.

CHAPTER 5

BRELAND
SHARN
Dravago 26, 996 YK

The ninth bell was ringing when Daine opened his eyes. He was alone. His hand dropped to his sword—and found nothing. The door to the room began to open. He rolled to the side and rose up behind the door. A large armored figure crept into the room, moving with eerie silence. Daine clenched his fists together and prepared to deliver a mighty blow to the back of the intruder's skull . . . and then checked himself.

It was Pierce.

"Pierce! Where are the others? Where's my *sword?*"

Pierce turned to face him, seemingly unsurprised. "Jode went out earlier this morning. I believe that he took your sword with him. Lady Lei is in the common room, finishing breakfast. Mistress Dassi is about to close her kitchen, and Lei thought you might want food. I'm supposed to tell you that she 'won't be conjuring food for anyone too lazy to get out of bed at a reasonable hour.' "

Daine scowled and reached for his chainmail shirt.

"I don't believe you need arms, Captain. I was studying the other patrons. There were a few knives, but I don't believe there is any imminent danger."

Daine shrugged. "Well then, let's go."

❂ ❂ ❂ ❂ ❂ ❂ ❂

Lei was sitting at a round table, talking with the innkeeper. Her eyes were slightly puffy, and she seemed more pale then usual. Her voice was cool and level. "You're in luck, Daine. Dassi saved the last bowl of gruel for you. By now I imagine it's cold. Just the way you like it."

The halfling scuttled off to fetch Daine's meal. Lei's conjured food had no taste whatsoever. After trying the innkeeper's cold, pasty porridge, Daine found that he missed it.

"How are you?" he asked.

Lei glared at him. "Fine. Wonderful. Oh, I couldn't be better. *General.*"

Her voice was sharp, but Daine let it go. At this point, anger might be the only way to hold back tears. "No sign of Jode?"

"No. The wretched weasel took my pack. If he does anything with my warforged, I'll skin him alive."

"Lei . . . " He tried to touch her hand, but she jerked away. "We'll get through this."

She glared at him. "Don't you dare tell me how I should feel, Daine. You have no idea. This is my family. This is my *life.* To be treated like this, to think that Hadran would *allow* this . . . "

"Is there anyone you can talk to? This isn't your first time in Sharn. Is there anyone who might give us information?"

Lei started to snap, then took a deep breath and began again. "Yes . . . it's possible. They'd never see me at the enclave, but there are a few people I might look to. But you have to understand, my family was from Metrol. I don't know many of the Brelish Cannith, and if Hadran won't see me . . . I don't know." She shook her head. "I don't understand."

"Try to be patient. We'll get to the bottom of this."

The door flew open, and Jode came in from the street. He was smiling and flushed, and half-dragging Lei's pack. "Drinks all around!" he called, tossing Dassi a gold galifar. "First round's on me."

"At tenth bell?" Daine remarked. But none of the other patrons were turning down a free round, and it had been some time since Daine had had anything other than water.

Unfortunately, the Manticore's ale was of the same fine quality as its porridge.

Jode climbed up on the table and slid the pack across to Lei. She watched him with narrowed eyes. He smiled disarmingly and took a long pull of ale, followed by a terrible face.

"How is it we're suddenly buying for the house?" Daine asked. Lei was already looking through the pack.

"Well, I thought it would be good if I got the lay of the land, got to know my way around town, and while I was at it I found a pawner who seemed like a decent woman, and I thought it would be good if we had a few coins to rub together."

"Where's my crossbow?" Lei said.

"Oh, come now. We're in the greatest city in the world! Do you really think you need a *crossbow* on the streets of Sharn?"

Daine put a gentle hand on the halfling's shoulder. "Pierce said that you took my grandfather's sword with you when you left this morning. May I have it back now?"

"I'm sure it will be safe, Daine." He tightened his grip. "You know I've got a good sense for people! Besides which, you've still got your dagger, right?"

"Jode . . ."

"I know, this may seem unwise, but I assure you, I've already put the coin to good use!"

"By buying watered-down ale for a group of strangers?"

"I tracked down an old friend of yours. Someone I'm sure can help us find our feet."

"I'm listening." He hadn't released his grip.

"Alina Lyrris."

Daine swore and knocked his tankard to the floor. He pulled Jode across the table. "Is this a joke?"

"No! She's been in Sharn for over a year. I thought that with your history . . . you know, perhaps she could offer us work."

Lei was lost in her thoughts again, but Pierce took an interest. "What history is this? Who is this Alina?"

Daine took a deep breath and let go of Jode. He forced a smile and sat down. "Alina Lorridan Lyrris is an old friend I . . . had dealings with before I joined the Queen's Guard."

"How might she help us?"

Jode answered. "Alina is a wealthy woman, and I'm sure she has a lot of connections in Sharn. I'm certain that she'd be happy to help an old friend like Daine. I've already talked to one of her associates and set up a meeting in one hour."

Daine bit his lip, but stayed silent.

"Then let us ready ourselves," said Lei.

Daine shook his head. "I don't know . . ."

". . . If we should concentrate all of our resources in one place?" said Jode. "Brilliant as always, General. Pierce, why don't you and Lei see what you can find out about House Cannith? There must be someone in Sharn who's willing to talk to you, Lei. Daine and I can speak with Alina."

Pierce glanced over at Lei, and after a moment she nodded.

"Very well!" Jode say brightly. "We'll meet back here at, shall we say, two bells?"

"I'm going to get my armor," Daine said, scowling.

❈ ❈ ❈ ❈ ❈ ❈ ❈

"Alina Lyrris? What have you gotten us into?"

High Walls was just as dismal by the light of day as it was in the dark. The ghetto was an exterior district, built along the outer wall of the great tower of Tavick's Landing. The alleys and streets were filled with refugees of all nations, but the majority of the beggars and miserable laborers were Cyrans. With the destruction of their homeland these unfortunate souls had nowhere else to go. They passed a one-armed veteran of the Queen's Guard, who stretched out his good hand in an imploring gesture. In a nearby alley, a pair of feral children were chasing a dog, stones in their hands.

"You know she's our best hope," said Jode. "You know she'll have money."

"And what will we have to do to get it?"

"Give her a chance. We don't have to agree to anything."

"I'm going to see Alina Lyrris. And you know what the best part of it is? You *pawned* my thrice-forsaken sword!"

"All the more reason to see Alina, yes? The sooner we get some money, the sooner you can get it back."

"You—"

A new voice intruded. "Pardon me . . . General?"

The voice belonged to an old man, who had come up behind the pair. Like all of the inhabitants of High Walls, it was clear he had seen better days. A horrible scar could be seen at the base of his neck, puckered flesh disappearing beneath his robe. But despite the dirt on his skin and his torn clothing, the stranger carried himself with a sense of dignity and pride, and his voice had an air of quiet authority. He studied Daine with an appraising eye.

"I thought I knew most of our generals, yet . . ."

"Ah, a simple mistake," Jode said brightly. "I know that there have been a lot of wild stories about the region, but my companion is *Captain* Daine of the Queen's Guard. He served with valor and distinction until the very end, and I'm sure you've simply heard how he saved the life of General ir'Dalas in the Battle of the Three Moons."

The old man brought an end to the tale with a raised hand. "Captain, then. I am—"

"Teral ir'Soras," Daine said.

The man nodded.

"I remember seeing you at court in Metrol when I was younger."

"You have a good memory, Captain. It has been many years since I advised the queen. And now it is too late to save her. Sovereigns guard her soul and save us all."

Daine inclined his head respectfully, then returned to his careful study of the old noble. "Lucky you were away from Metrol on the big day. How'd you end up here?"

"A long story, and not one for the street. Perhaps you'll join me for dinner this evening? There are many of us in Sharn, and I'm trying to bring the refugees together."

"Of course," Daine said. "I'm sure it can't be worse than what they'll be serving at the Manticore."

"Wonderful," Teral said with a slight bow. "It's the black tent in the central square. I'll see you at sunset."

Daine inclined his head respectfully, while Jode made a dramatic bow. The elderly man smiled slightly before turning away and disappearing into the crowd. Daine watched him go.

"What do you make of that?"

Jode shrugged and continued walking. "He's a generous man trying to create a bastion of Cyran values. Or he's an opportunist hoping to capitalize on the anger of the refugees to form a power block. I know which seems more likely to me, but does it matter?"

"I suppose not." They walked a ways in silence, eventually passing through the gates of High Walls and into the tower of Tavick's Landing. "So where are we meeting Alina?"

"It's called Den'iyas. It's in one of the other towers. It's going to be a long walk, I'm afraid. Unless you'd like to take one of the skycoaches . . ."

"After that worked out so well yesterday? I don't think so. I'm not about to let you throw away any more of the money you made from my family sword."

"Speaking of family," said Jode, "have you told Lei?"

"No. I'm not going to. And neither are you. Is that understood?"

"Whatever you say. But if there was ever a time—"

"No. And that's final." Daine stopped and knelt down, grabbing Jode and spinning him around. "Do you understand? No hints, no jokes. Leave it alone."

"All right. But I still think—"

"*Jode!*"

"All right! My lips are sealed."

"Don't give me ideas."

They walked on in silence for a few moments, until Jode tugged on Daine's leg. "Over there."

A line of people were shuffling onto a raised circular platform. It seemed to be some sort of stage—about twenty-five feet across and enclosed by a low metal rail. The wide ramp seemed to have been designed for wagons. "What about it?" said Daine.

"That's where we're going," Jode said, leading Daine onto the stage.

"We're meeting Alina *here?*"

Jode rolled his eyes. "No. This is how we get up to Den'iyas, Captain Can't-afford-a-skycoach."

At that moment, the platform began to rise.

* * * ● * * ●

The district of Den'iyas was located amidst the upper spires of the Menthis Towers, high in the sky. Daine was beginning to adapt to the noise and bustle of the lower streets, but Den'iyas was something else again. The lower levels fit Daine's vision of a large city—grime and poverty everywhere, with merchants hawking their wares and beggars assailing any who would listen. By contrast, Den'iyas was an image from a storybook tale. The streets were clean, the buildings bright and cheerful, the air filled with song and laughter. On a street corner, a troubadour was teaching a group of children to weave light from air, tracing hypnotic patterns of shimmering color with his fingers; as Daine watched, one of the onlookers produced a shaky but similar trail.

They were gnomes. Den'iyas was the heart of Sharn's gnome population, and Daine towered over the vast majority of the people on the street. Just over three feet in height, taller and stockier than halflings, the gnomes reminded Daine less of human children and more of miniature adults. They wore fine clothes in a rainbow of colors, and everyone was impeccably groomed. Most of the men had well-trimmed beards and long mustaches, while the women wore an astonishing range of elaborate hairstyles and headdresses. While there was as much variety in skin and hair tone as in the human crowds below, most of the gnomes had fair hair and pale skin touched with a golden sheen. It seemed almost like a circus or a dream, with wind chimes drifting through the air and entertainers juggling globes of light.

"Watch your step," Jode warned. "I know it looks pleasant enough, but trust me . . . watch what you say."

The buildings were as beautiful as the tiny denizens of the district, and most had two sets of doors—one sized for halflings and gnomes, and one for larger patrons. Jode led Daine past gemcutters and candyspinners, and the smell of warm cinnamon pulled at their nostrils. Eventually they arrived at a small park, where an elderly gnome dressed in burgundy and gold was tending a bend of fireblossoms. Jode approached the gardener. "I don't mean to tell you your job, but you really should watch out for thorns."

The gnome studied Jode carefully, scowling beneath an enormous blond mustache. Just as Daine was about to step between the two, the gardener grunted "She's expecting you." Despite his small size, his voice was a resonant baritone. The flowers shivered and dissolved, revealing a staircase dropping down into darkness.

Jode smiled. "After you," he said to Daine.

CHAPTER 6

BRELAND
SHARN
Dravago 26, 996 YK

The stone steps led down into a dark hall. It might have been a towering hallway for a gnome, but Daine had to duck to keep from striking his head against the ceiling. Once Jode had joined him, the illusionary garden shimmered back into place, leaving them isolated in full darkness.

"You found out about all of this in one morning?" Daine said, using one hand to feel his way along the stone wall.

"I've dealt with gnomes before," Jode said. "Once I heard Alina was in Sharn, it was just a matter of dropping the right names, passing a few coins to the right people. Spend a few months in Zilargo, you'll learn how it works. If you survive."

"I didn't know you'd been to Zilargo." Daine had never seen the homeland of the gnomes.

"Scary place, my friend. Like a poisonous flower."

The hallway was quite short, and within a few moments Daine came up against a stone wall. There was a loud *click* and the stone shifted forward, revealing the well lit chamber that lay beyond. Daine stepped through the doorway and stood up. The ceilings were just high enough for him to stand without crouching.

The room was an unusual sight. It was a square chamber, and each wall was about twenty feet long. A large, circular firepit dominated the center of the room, but instead of coals it was filled with amethyst crystals. Violet flames danced above the pit, and a pleasant, flowery smell filled the air. An assortment of chairs and couches ringed the pit, and while most were sized for gnomes there were a few built to human scale. One divan seemed to have been designed for an ogre, though Daine couldn't see how an ogre would fit through the entry hall. But the most disorienting aspect of the room was the mirrors. Three of the walls were entirely covered with mirrors, creating a dizzying sense of space. The fourth wall was a single window looking out off of the edge of the tower—a bird's eye view of the Dagger River and the land surrounding Sharn, with only a window and a few wisps of cloud between them and the cliffs thousands of feet below.

There were no obvious doors, no shelves or chests. Aside from the chairs spread around the firepit, the only objects in the room were a set of intricate birdcages set against the wall across from the window. There were six cages, each made from half a dozen different precious metals woven together and studded with gems. As beautiful as the cages were, they were overshadowed by the exotic birds contained within. Daine had never seen their like. He was no druid, but he guessed that they were from lands beyond Khorvaire—the jungles of Aerenal, perhaps, or the distant plains of Sarlona. Curiously, the birds were completely silent; they watched the intruders carefully but didn't make a sound or rustle a feather.

Then he realized. He could see the birds in the mirror, but . . .

"The mirrors . . . where are *our* reflections?"

"I don't think they're mirrors, Daine. If I recall correctly, we're on the wrong side of the tower for a view of the Dagger."

"Illusions?"

"That's my guess. I'll bet these images can be adjusted on demand." Jode studied the window. "The real question is—is this actually what's going on above the Dagger right now? Or is it all imagination?"

"That's what keeps it interesting, isn't it?"

It was a woman's voice, low and rough, but with a lilting, lyrical cadence. It had been a long time since Daine had heard that voice, but it wasn't something you forgot. Alina Lorridan

Lyrris was one of the most beautiful women Daine had ever seen—for all that she was only three feet tall. She was dressed in a diaphanous gown of white cloudsilk embroidered with intricate patterns of pure gold, which broke the light into thousands of shimmering shards as she moved. Her large violet eyes were a perfect match for the amethyst necklace. Her pale hair nearly matched the gold of her gown. It was split into dozens of braids, each bound with rings of silver and threaded into eyelets on the arms and back of her gown, creating a billowing golden cloak that shifted as she moved.

Daine hadn't see her a moment before. Either she'd been invisible, or she'd walked out of one of the mirrors. He and Jode appeared to be alone with her, but he knew from experience that there must be bodyguards nearby. If Alina could arrive unseen, the guards might already be in the room. Were the walls even real?

Alina showed her perfect teeth in what most people would see as a smile. "Daine, how lovely to see you again. When I received Jode's message . . . well, I never thought that our paths would cross again so soon."

"Eight years is a long time, Alina."

"I suppose it is . . . for you. Such a pity to fade so fast. Still, I was pleased to hear that you survived your service in the war, and the disaster that stole Cyre from us." She walked over to the menagerie and looked down at the birds. "Can I get you anything? Water? Wine? Dreamlily? I have a fine Cyran vintage. It might be the last chance you have to taste it."

"I swore I'd never drink with you again."

"Suit yourself." When Alina turned around there was a goblet of golden liquid in her hand. "You always drank too much anyway."

She walked across the room and sprawled languidly on a velvet couch. The amethyst flames flickered, casting violet shadows across the room.

"After I heard about Jode, I did a little investigation of my own, and I must say, I was pleasantly surprised to find that you were accompanied by a young lady." She gestured idly, and an image of Lei's face shimmered into existence in the air before her. "A dragonmark heir, no less. Coming full circle, Daine?"

"Leave her out of this, Alina!" said Daine, striding over to her seat.

"Are you certain about that, Daine?" Alina's face was expressionless, but her eyes glittered in the firelight. "I understand that the young lady is in a difficult position at the moment. Perhaps—"

"I said, leave her out of this! You're dealing with me."

"So I am." Alina closed her hand, and Lei's face vanished. "And what is it you want, Daine? What do you have to offer?"

Jode stepped forward. "I'm sorry if I misled you, Lady Lyrris. We are seeking honest work, not some sort of gift or exchange. With the loss of Cyre, we must all find our way in this new world. A simple job, a chance to make a few sovereigns . . . you employ dozens of people, don't you? Surely there's something you could use us for."

Alina laughed musically, sending a shiver down Daine's spine. "Honest work? You'd make a fine fool, Jode." She stared into the fire for a moment. "You must be truly desperate, to come to me for *honest* work. Yet . . ." She studied Daine carefully. "Perhaps there is something you can do for me. A servant of mine—a courier engaged in good, *honest* work—has gone missing. I believe that he has betrayed me and stolen my property. He wouldn't be the first. Until I . . . sort things out, yes, I imagine that I could use a little outside assistance. If you reclaim what has been stolen from me, I should think a reward would be in order."

Daine glanced at Jode. It sounded harmless enough. "What can you tell us, my lady?" Jode said.

Alina gestured at the wall. The image of a man appeared in the reflection of the room. Whether through coincidence or artifice, his location and posture mirrored than of Daine, and when Daine moved, the image duplicated his actions. Daine walked up to the wall to take a closer look at the stranger in the mirror.

"This is Rasial," Alina said.

He was human, early twenties, with lank black hair that fell to his shoulders and spread across his chin. Under the right circumstances, he might have been handsome, but his eyes were haunted and he had a hungry, desperate look. He wore dark cavalry leather and a short black cloak, and he held a dagger in his right hand.

"Rasial used to be a windchaser—an aerial racer—with a gifted touch for hippogriffs and daggerhawks. He stopped racing after a terrible accident, but he still had talent and ambition. I helped him get back on his feet, and in return he perform certain services for me—notably, bringing certain exotic goods to Sharn through the air. Recently, I paid him a great deal of money to bring a special package into the city. I know that he returned to Sharn yesterday, but I have not received my merchandise, and he has gone into hiding. There are many possibilities, but I suspect that Rasial's greed finally outweighed his loyalty. As I said, it's not the first time someone has taken advantage of my generous nature."

"So you want us to hunt him down for you?" asked Daine.

"You wound me, Daine. I am not a vengeful woman. You're still alive, aren't you? I don't care what becomes of Rasial, but I want what I paid for—the goods he was carrying, or at the very least the knowledge of who has them now. Deliver the shards, and I will pay you . . . say, three hundred dragons? That should be more than enough to get you established in Sharn or wherever you intend to settle."

"Four hundred," Jode said. "There are four of us."

"You actually think of your warforged as an ally? I've always seen them as pets."

"He's right," Daine said. "Four hundred."

"Three and a half," she said languidly. "Half the coin for half a man."

"He's worth more than I am, Alina."

"What made you think I was talking about your warforged?"

"Four or not at all."

"Oh, Daine," Alina heaved a dramatic sigh. "Do you suppose I can simply conjure platinum coins from thin air?"

"Do you really want an answer?"

The gnome studied him solemnly and finally allowed a smile to cross her perfect features. "Very well. For old time's sake. Four hundred it is."

"So what are we looking for?"

"Khyber dragonshards," Alina said. "A very rare form of Khyber shard, at that." She waved a finger at the mirror, and the dagger in Rasial's hand shifted into a shard of black crystal laced with purple veins. The veins were faintly luminescent. Every now and then, they would flare up with a brighter burst of light. "I could give you a tedious lecture about their origin and value, but I imagine that your lady friend can do that just as well as I can. I know Rasial hasn't left the city yet. He may still have the shards, or he may have already sold them. In either case, finding Rasial is probably the best place to start."

Daine studied his counterpart carefully. "Is he dangerous?"

"Who isn't?" Alina lazily swirled her wine about in the goblet.

"How do you know he hasn't left the city?"

"I have my ways."

"Helpful as always. Is there anything in particular about him that we ought to know?"

"Now that you mention it . . . if you should cross blades, I suggest that you don't let him touch you."

"That's it?"

"That's all you need to know."

"I'll bear that in mind." Daine turned away from the mirror. "Look, Alina, I'll be the first to admit that we can use this money. But why are you doing this? You could hire a Tharashk inquisitive for a fraction of what you're offering us. Are you telling me you can't find him yourself?"

"Daine," she said reproachfully, "you won't take my gifts. Can't I help out an old friend by giving him a simple job?"

"Your gifts are never free, and we were never friends. What's your angle here?"

She laughed. "It seems ten years isn't such a long time after all. You know me too well. You're right. I have a reason for wanting to use you for this."

"Fresh faces?" said Jode.

"Indeed. There is a delicate balance of power in this city. Rasial has friends. If he has betrayed me, there are people who can trace my usual sources. You're outsiders. You can't be immediately connected to me." She smiled. "And if anything bad happens to you, what have I really lost?"

"Funny," said Daine.

"Lady Lyrris," Jode interjected. "I assume that time is of the essence. What can you tell us about Rasial or his associates? How many shards does he have? How large are they?"

Alina reached under the sofa and produced a small packet wrapped in black leather. "All of the details are here." She tossed the packet to Daine and then produced a smaller purse. "Here's a few sovereigns. It should be enough to get you started. Let me know if you need more. And now, if you don't mind, I do have other business to attend to."

She gestured toward the door, and it opened again.

"By the way, Daine?" she said as they were leaving.

"Yes?"

"If I were you, I'd buy a sword."

CHAPTER 7

I f the dragonmarked houses held power to rival nations, then the district of Dragon Towers was where they maintained their embassies and consulates. Dozens of shops promised the mystical services of the true heirs of each house, and beyond these little businesses lay the enclaves of the houses themselves—massive towers where the heirs lived and learned their arts. The Great Healing Hall of House Jorasco was the largest to be found in Breland, and Sivis Tower was a nexus for communication across Khorvaire. The services of the dragonmarked were expensive, and the people who thronged the streets were not the peasants and beggars found on the lower level. Here aristocrats rubbed shoulders with knights and merchant princes. The street was a tapestry of colorful silk, and the air filled with the scents of rare perfumes and the exotic spices of the Ghallanda vendors.

Pierce and Lei made their way through this glorious chaos. Although the streets were crowded, most people made way for the warforged soldier. But even as Pierce scanned the streets for any possible threats, his thoughts were on the Lady Lei. Pierce had an intuitive understanding of combat. A shifting shadow, the glint of a blade, the smell of fire—he would know how to respond to such things. But he had no guidelines for the sorrow of a friend. It was not the first time he had seen pain or anger. He himself still felt the loss of each comrade who had fallen in the war—a hollow emptiness when he envisioned the faces of Jholeg or Jani. But no one had ever taught him what to do with these feelings or how to address the sorrow of another. So he cleared the way for the Lady Lei and waited for her emptiness to pass on its own.

Ahead he saw the sign of a smithy; the hammer-and-anvil seal of House Cannith was emblazoned below the name of the smith. "My lady, should we begin our inquiries with this armorer?"

Lei glanced up at the sign and shook her head. "No. Black anvil."

Lei was speaking less frequently than usual. It seemed reasonable to assume that talking would help repair her damaged spirit. "I do not understand the significance of the color. Is it not your—uh, the seal of House Cannith?"

Lei sighed. "The powers of the house extend far beyond the actual heirs of the mark, Pierce." While her voice remained dull, she began to fall into her usual lecturing cadence. "Each house has found ways to apply the powers of its mark to provide services to the people of Khorvaire. But the houses have extended their influence farther into these fields. The black anvil indicates that the smith has been trained and licensed by a Cannith guild and that his work will meet the standards set by the house. But he is not an heir of the blood and could be of no use to us."

"I understand, my lady."

"Cannith Tower is the central enclave of the house." She pointed at the silver spire rising up ahead. "That's where we'll get our answers . . . if they'll speak to me."

"You have doubts?"

"If . . . if what that Domo said is true," she said, "then yes, I have doubts." She reached out, resting her hand on his mithral shoulder. "I just don't know what to expect. I thought the war was finally over."

"Perhaps the war is never won," Pierce said. "We must simply find satisfaction in survival."

Lei tightened her grip on his shoulder, and they continued on their way.

❋ ❋ ❋ ❋ ❋ ❋ ❋

Cannith Tower was a masterpiece, a testimony to the architectural talents of the House of Making. Silver threads had been embedded into the surface of the stone walls, creating the impression of a glittering web of light rising into the sky.

"I remember when I first saw the tower," Lei said. "I came here to study firebinding." She pointed to a window high on the tower. "My cousin Dasei and I stayed in that room while we were learning. She couldn't bind to save her life, but she always managed to charm her way through the challenges." She shook her head.

While Pierce listened, his attention was on the defenses of the tower. For all that they appeared to be leaded glass, he had no doubt that the windows were mystically hardened to resist physical damage. There was one central gate, and five guards spread before it. All five were identical warforged—massive warriors built from gray adamantine alloy. They stood as still as statues, but Pierce had no doubt that they had already spotted him and were evaluating the threat he might pose. Each of the 'forged carried a long hammer and a shield bearing the Cannith seal. Pierce couldn't spot the slightest scratch on the polished skin of any of the soldiers. This could reflect a lack of combat experience, or it could be a fringe benefit of working for the House of Making. While combat seemed unwise, Pierce loosened the chain of his flail. Should Lady Lei be threatened, he needed to be ready.

"Are you certain this is a wise course of action, my lady?"

"Don't worry, Pierce. There is no question of violence here." Nonetheless, he could hear fear in her voice. "Follow my lead."

Lei took a deep breath and walked up to the gate. One of the warforged moved to block her path.

Lei made a sharp gesture with her hand. "Stand aside, guardsman. I have dealings with the baron of this house and have no time for underlings."

Pierce was watching the guard's face, and he saw a slight motion as the warforged looked down to examine Lei's fingers.

While Lei had the imperious manner of a noble, she no longer had her ring, and the guardsman held his ground.

"What is your name and the nature of your business?"

"I am Lei d'Cannith," she snapped, "an heir of the mark, and my business is not for you to know."

The speaker glanced at one of the other warforged soldiers. Pierce tightened his grip of the haft of his flail.

"Please inform the warden, Twelve," the sentinel said. One of the other warforged nodded and entered the building.

"You dare to keep me waiting on the doorstep?" Lei said.

The guard met her gaze. His face was a steel mask of indifference, but Pierce could sense a touch of uncertainty beneath. He wasn't prepared for this situation. "If you will wait one moment, I am certain that the warden will be able to assist you."

Pierce could see Lei's anger building, but she maintained her composure. She had expected a cold welcome.

Minutes passed, then a new figure appeared at the gate. A large man in his late forties, he had red hair that almost matched Lei's, but there were a few streaks of gray in his flaring mustache. He wore studded leather armor died a deep blue, and a harness bearing five rods of polished darkwood—each holding a potentially deadly enchantment, Pierce was sure. It had been two years since Pierce had seen this man, but he remembered him clearly enough—Dravot d'Cannith, whom they'd last seen as the warden of the Whitehearth armory.

Lei glowed at the sight of a familiar face. *"Dravot!"* she cried. "You're alive!"

She moved to embrace the warden, but a warforged guardsman stepped into her path. Her face tightened in anger, and for a moment Pierce thought she might actually attack the warforged; he had heard of her exploits at the battle of Keldan Ridge. But then Lei saw Dravot's face. She stopped, the energy draining out of her.

"You have no place here," Dravot said. His voice was as cold as his expression. "You have been declared excoriate, and have no rights to the name of this house. You are to have no dealings with this house or its heirs, and you are not to present yourself at enclaves of the house. Failure to comply with the dictates of the house will be . . . dealt with." His hand dropped to one of his wands.

"But Dravot . . ." Lei grasped for words. Clearly she hadn't expected such treatment from a familiar face. "Tell me why! What have I ever done?"

Dravot's face was as impassive as any of the warforged. "You have no rights to any answer, and you will receive nothing from any member of this house. You will leave this place now, and you will not trouble the rightful heirs of this house ever again. Do you understand?"

"Dravot—?"

"You will receive no answer from any member of the house. *Do you understand?*" Dravot drew one of his wands, glittering darkwood bearing a single band of gold.

Pierce studied the wand, determining whether he could shatter it with his flail before Dravot could unleash its powers. But as he let the chain slide free, Lei nodded.

"Let's go, Pierce," she said. Turning, she looked back at Dravot. "I'm glad that you're alive."

He said nothing, and the wand stayed level in his hand.

Slowly, Lei and Pierce walked away from the tower. Lei seemed dazed. Pierce put his hand on her back, holding her up and keeping her moving. They'd walked about fifty yards when there was a loud whisper.

"Jura still lives in Darkhart Woods." It was Dravot's voice.

Looking back, Pierce saw Dravot still standing at the gate of the enclave. Apparently he had used some magic to send the whispered words along the length of the street. Pierce looked down at Lei. The words had roused her from her shock, and now she was deep in thought.

"My lady?"

She raised a hand. "Let's go back to the Manticore. I need to consider this."

CHAPTER 8

BRELAND
SHARN
Dravago 26, 996 YK

I don't know why I let you talk me into this," Daine said as he and Jode walked back to the central lift. Nearby a merchant was haggling with a customer over the price of an iridescent doublet, while a tiny gnome girl with a bright red cap was playing with a shimmering ball of light woven from strands of illusion. The girl's pointed cap was nearly as tall as she was. "We're soldiers, not inquisitives. And I never planned to see Alina again, let alone work for her."

"You know, we've never talked about what you did for her."

"That's right."

"Daine, I know it's not what you had in mind, but the war is all but over. And Cyre is gone. Nothing's going to change that. We need a new start, and if you've got a better way to get four hundred dragons, I'd like to hear it."

They walked a ways in silence.

"Extraordinary collection of birds, wasn't it? Such beautiful coloring."

"True," said Daine. "I wonder who they were before."

Jode chuckled and let the matter drop.

Once they were on the lift along with a few other residents, Daine unwrapped the leather packet. There was a sheaf of parchment inside, covered with sketches and Alina's neat hand-writing. Daine and Jode split up the pages and began to sort through them. One page described the Khyber dragonshards.

It was mostly arcane gibberish, and Daine resolved to have Lei look it over. There was a map of Sharn, with brief notes on a few highlighted districts. The last few pages in Daine's stack concerned Rasial. One included sketches of his face from a few different angles, while the other was a brief biography.

"Rasial Tann . . ." Daine mused, studying the parchment. "Here's something Alina didn't mention—he used to be part of the Sharn Watch, a unit called the Gold Wings."

"Yes, that fits," said Jode, tapping the top sheet on his pile, a description of various sporting events. "Look over there. Those hippogriff riders? They're Gold Wings. The unit's trained for scouting and responding to aerial crimes, but apparently many of the riders also participate in the games."

"And as a former guardsman, Rasial would know how to avoid the patrols searching for smugglers . . . assuming he doesn't still have friends on the inside."

"So a guardsman down on his luck turns to crime. A tragedy of our times."

"Apparently he claimed the trophy in the Race of Eight Winds two years ago. Mean anything to you?"

"Yes, it's all here. Annual event in . . . Dura Tower. Biggest race in Sharn. Brings spectators from across Khorvaire."

"You'll never see anything like it!" The new voice managed to be high-pitched and gravelly at the same time. Turning around, Daine discovered a small goblin girl just behind his legs. "All manner of beasts chasing and fighting, darting between the parapets." Her red eyes gleamed. "Last year, the griffon turned on the eagle right after the bell was rung. You can still see the blood on Kelsa Spire."

Jode spoke before Daine could chase the goblin off. "What's your favorite beast?"

"The Gargoyle, of course," the girl said, as if speaking to an even smaller child. "Malleon's Gate used to be that Bat, but now it's the Gargoyle. He hasn't won yet, but he's fast and quick and clever, and I'm sure this year is when things will change."

"Who's won the last few years?"

"The stupid pegasus. The hippogriff was *going* to win, then it died."

"One of the others killed it?"

"No, that would have been more fun." The little green girl gestured with her hand, showing a path of flight followed by a sudden drop. "It just died. Left a big stain on Rattlestone Square. My friend Galt has two feathers."

The lift paused to take on two new passengers, both wearing the green and black uniforms of the Sharn Watch. The stocky dwarf glared at Daine suspiciously. His companion was a tall human woman whose face was a maze of scars. Daine absently ran a finger along the scar that ran down his left cheek, remembering past battles with Brelish soldiers. The lift began to move again, slowly falling the remaining thousand feet toward the ground.

"The Pegasus is really, really fast," the goblin girl said. "But Carralag is clever, and I know he'll get the best of it this year."

"Did you ever—?" Jode began.

The dwarf guard grabbed the goblin by her hair and pulled her back, causing her to yelp with pain. "You again!" he spat. "What did I tell you about riding the lifts, girl?"

The girl tried to turn, but the grip on her hair was too strong. "Dunno! Just wanted to see the sky!"

"You know what I said," the dwarf said. He put one callused hand around her throat and lifted her up into the air. Behind him, his companion smirked. "I said I'd throw you off the lift myself if I ever say you again. You should have stayed where you belong, girl."

The dwarf moved to the railing, the goblin kicking and gasping in his grip. Daine planted his foot behind the dwarf's knee and sent him tumbling to the ground. The girl darted behind Daine, huddling against the railing.

The dwarf rose to his feet. "Dorn's teeth!" he swore, drawing a short sword with a well-worn edge. "You've just made a grave error, Mourner."

The scarred woman was carrying a halberd, and she moved to flank Daine.

"I should watch you throw a girl to her death?"

"That's no girl. It's a goblin. The only reason she's on this lift is to pick the pockets of fools like you. But I suppose you can identify with that. I can't imagine a Mourner trash having any proper business in the upper wards." He studied Daine carefully. "You just struck an officer of the watch. I think you deserve another scar for that."

"I think I'll pass." Daine studied his opponents, shifting so his back was against the railing. He reached for his sword—and remembered it was gone. Damn Jode!

"Go ahead," the dwarf said. "Draw your knife, boy. Give me a reason to run you through."

The lift came to a stop and the other passengers scurried off, leaving only Daine, Jode, the two guards, and the whimpering goblin girl.

The dwarf walked toward Daine as the lift moved again. "Not so bold now, are you?" He stared up into Daine's eyes, putting the point of his blade against Daine's throat. Daine looked down. The halberdier watched as a tiny spot of blood blossomed on Daine's throat, and for a moment she lowered her guard.

Daine was waiting for an opening, but help came from an unexpected quarter. The goblin girl cried out and threw herself at the dwarf, clawing and biting at his leg. As the guardsman glanced down, Daine smashed his hand and sent his sword flying. The halberdier brought her point in line, then suddenly gasped and fell to the ground; unnoticed in the chaos, Jode had stepped up behind her and pierced her knee with his stiletto. While he spent most of his time treating injuries, Jode had a keen understanding of pain. He knew where it hurt and how to hit it. The woman dropped her weapon and clutched at her leg, oblivious to her surroundings.

"Let it go," Daine said to the dwarf. "This can end now. No more harm done."

The dwarf responded with an incoherent howl. He charged, but Daine ducked out of the way. Spitting with rage, the guardsman snatched the fallen halberd and charged again, blade leveled at Daine's chest. At the last second, Daine spun out of the way. He grabbed the upper haft of the weapon and threw all his weight into it. He meant to disarm the dwarf, but he overestimated his opponent's weight and momentum.

With a long cry, the dwarf went sailing over the railing and disappeared.

Daine ran to the edge of the lift, but there was nothing to be done. He turned around. "Jode!" he snapped. "Make sure that woman doesn't bleed to death. Quickly! We're getting off at the next stop."

Jode seemed unperturbed as he bent to his task. "And here I thought I'd get to keep a feather."

The goblin was crying. "You're fine now," Daine said, kneeling over her. "But you need to get up and get moving. You have a home?"

She nodded, brushing at her tears.

"Go straight home. Now. And don't come back to this lift. *Ever.* Do you understand me?"

She nodded again.

A moment later, the lift came to the next stop. The goblin girl disappeared into the shadows of the street. Daine and Jode sauntered off as nonchalantly as possible, passing through the crowd waiting to board. Back on the disk, the semiconscious guard clutched her knee and moaned.

⊛ ⊛ ⊛ ⊛ ⊛ ⊛ ⊛

"What do you mean, *you saw her take it?*"

"You didn't?" said Jode. "It was such an obvious lift, I assumed it was a gift. You're a soft touch, and I'm sure she needed the money just as much as we did."

"Oh, this day just keeps getting better. You pawn my grandfather's sword, convince me to take a job from *Alina,* watch as a pickpocket steals the money we received for expenses, and the best part? I just killed a member of the city guard."

"You don't know that. This is Sharn. The city guard very likely carries charms against such happenings." He smiled mischievously. "Or maybe someone caught him?"

"Against falling hundreds of feet?"

Jode shrugged. "This is Sharn."

Daine closed his eyes and groaned. They were sitting at a table in the Manticore, and now that they only had Jode's original stake money from the morning, they were drinking water.

It wasn't long before Pierce and Lei returned. "Was your mission successful, Captain?" Pierce inquired. Lei seemed lost in thought.

Jode answered for him. "Aside from Daine being a murderer and getting robbed by a little girl? I'd say so. We need to track down a smuggler, return some stolen goods, and if we succeed we're looking at more money than you'd have made in another thirty years in the army."

"I wasn't paid for my service."

"Proving my point. How about you? Any news?"

Pierce looked to Lei. When she said nothing, he continued. "The accusation was true. Lei has been outcast. No member of House Cannith will speak to her. However . . ."

"There is someone," Lei said quietly. "An uncle. Jura. I haven't spoken to him since I was a child. But now . . . he may be able to tell me what's going on or get a message to Hadran for me. I haven't seen Jura for a long time. He's . . ." She paused, but couldn't seem to find the right words. Finally, she looked up at Daine. "I'd appreciate it if you'd come with me."

Daine stood up. "All right, but if you don't mind, let's avoid the area around the Den'iyas lift."

CHAPTER 9

BRELAND
SHARN
Dravago 26, 996 YK

Your Cannith lords may be brilliant artificers, but I can't say much for their taste in architecture," said Daine, examining the mansion. Built from black granite with walls carved to resemble a dense thicket of trees, Jura's manor was named Darkhart Woods.

Lei said nothing.

At the gate to the mansion a warforged servant met them and led them inside without a word. Where Hadran's servant was an imposing, bejeweled figure, this construct was a spindly assembly of wood and leather that seemed on the verge of falling apart. It smelled of mildew, and clicked and clattered with every motion.

Entering the manor was like walking into a swamp. The air was unnaturally warm and moist, and the smell of rotting vegetation filled their nostrils. Glistening ivy covered the walls, and woven rushes were spread in place of carpets. Globes of mystical energy lit the halls, but these were shuttered and the ambience was dark and wet.

"The man likes his plants," Daine muttered. Why a man would spend good gold to grow weeds *inside* his house was beyond his understanding.

"Oh, Uncle Jura loves . . . plants," Lei said absently. Her thoughts seemed far away.

After leading them through a green maze of hallways, the

warforged guide paused at a large pair of double doors and rapped sharply. The doors slowly swung open, propelled by invisible hands. A wall of mist hid the chamber beyond. Daine glanced at Lei, but she just shrugged. More Cannith tricks, he thought.

The warforged turned to them and bowed. "Lord Jura awaits you," it said, its voice a raspy rustle.

❀ ❀ ❀ ❀ ❀ ❀ ❀

The fog concealed a forest. When Daine stepped through the mist, his boot sank into muddy earth. A dense grove of trees spread out before him. Tendrils of mist drifted across the ground, and he could hear the sounds of insects and the rustle of birds and rodents all around.

"What is this?" he whispered, his dagger already in his hand.

"Don't worry," Lei said as she came through the mist behind him. "Uncle Jura?" she called, peering into the woods.

"Over here, girl." The deep voice came from somewhere in the center of the grove. "Just follow the path. I'll give you more light."

With that, the sun came up—at least, the sky brightened to the color of full daylight. Studying the sky, Daine spotted a stone seam. They were standing in a vast chamber. The high domed ceiling was painted with a perfect illusion of a cloudy sky. Still, the mud seemed real enough.

Jode whistled. "Now, I've seen some fine shadow-work in my time, but this . . . do you know how much he must have spent just on the moisture? Do you think he can make it rain in here?"

Lei dismissed him with a wave of her hand. "Hush. And don't mention the trees. I'll explain later." She led the way down a wide, muddy path, and they passed beneath the canopy of the trees. After a few twists they came to a large clearing.

Jura Darkhart was waiting for them. He shared Lei's coloring—pale skin and red hair—but otherwise the two couldn't have been more different. Daine had seen corpses that looked healthier than Jura. The excoriate lord was little more than a skeleton, with leathery skin stretched across protruding bones. His fine velvet clothing hung from his emaciated frame, and what little hair he had was concentrated in a scraggly beard. Jura sat crosslegged on an enormous wooden throne carved from the stump of a fallen darkwood tree. He had a small knife in one hand and a long darkwood staff laid across his legs, and he was whittling figures on the surface of the staff. He did not look up to acknowledge his guests.

"Greetings, Lord Jura!" Jode called out before Lei could speak. "Thank you for allowing us into your home. What a fantastic throne you have. Truly, I've never seen its equal."

Lei gritted her teeth, but held her tongue.

Jura looked up from his work and studied the halfling carefully, his gaze lingering on Jode's dragonmark. "It cost me dearly, Jorasco. It meant a great deal to my wife, rest her soul." His voice was deep, but cold and emotionless.

"Did something happen to your wife, my lord? Allow me to extend my most sincere condolences. If we can—"

"Enough," Jura said, and his cold gaze was enough to silence even Jode. He looked at Lei and ran one hand along his dark staff. "I trust you had good reason to disturb me, girl."

"I . . . wanted to see how you were, Uncle." The air was warm and full of moisture, and Daine could see sweat on her brow.

"Don't insult me. I know why you're here. You want to know about Hadran and why you're not welcome at the family door anymore. And who better to talk to than old Jura, the last dog chased from the house?"

As he talked, Lei seemed to regain a little of her usual fire. "Spare me your self-pity, uncle, I've got troubles enough of my own. At least you have your own private palace to sulk in."

Jura chuckled, a horrible, rasping sound. "At least you still have spirit, girl. Very well. Ask your questions."

"Why won't Hadran see me?"

"Because he died a week ago."

Lei gaped at him, shocked to silence.

"I understand he was torn to pieces. The work of a wild beast, perhaps—or a shifter of exceptional strength. Or a well-crafted homunculus, of course."

Daine stepped up. "What are you saying? They can't blame Lei for this?"

"Don't be ridiculous," Jura said. "Even if she had been in Sharn, no one thinks she has the talent to build a homunculus with such power."

"Then why?" Lei trembled with rage. "Why am I outcast?"

"Lower your voice, girl," Jura said. "We may both be outcasts in the eyes of our house, but I am lord of this manor and I expect you to show proper respect."

For a moment Daine thought that Lei was going to attack the old man, then she stepped back and looked down at the ground. "Why have I been cast out of our house, Lord Jura?"

"The last year has brought many changes to House Cannith, girl," Jura replied. "The high council of the house was destroyed along with Cyre, and over the last month the barons have been fighting to establish a new order. Baron Merrix of Sharn is now the ultimate power in the south, and he personally ordered your excoriation."

"I've never even *met* Merrix! I've only been in Sharn once before. What have I done?"

"The council may be dissolved, but Merrix would still need to justify his action to the surviving elders. You know the possibilities as well as I do. Treason, conduct bringing shame upon the house, and of course, miscegenation." He cast a speculative glance at Jode. "You really don't know?"

"No!" said Lei. "I've done nothing to warrant this!"

"Then perhaps it's all a mistake."

"Will you speak for me, uncle? Plead my case to the baron?"

"Talk sense, girl! I am as much an outcast as you are. I may have made contacts in the house over the years, but the baron would never speak to me, let alone listen to my words. And even if I could get an audience, I wouldn't waste what good will I have built up on you. I have my own interests to look after. Now that my wife is gone, I hope to return to the house myself. Merrix needs powerful supporters, and gold I have to spare."

Jode jumped in again. "I see! So while you cannot speak

on behalf of the Lady Lei, you summoned us here to provide material assistance, yes?"

"You amuse me, halfling. No, I have no intention of wasting my coin on such a useless investment."

"Then if I may ask, my lord, why did you grant us this audience at all?"

Jura smiled. "I have been an exile for many years, Jorasco. Perhaps it amused me to see someone in a worse position than my own."

Daine's hand tightened on the hilt of his dagger, and even Jode seemed close to anger. Lei put her hands on their shoulders, holding them back. "Then I believe our business here is concluded, uncle."

"Not entirely," Jura said, rising to his feet. "In truth, I agreed to see you at the request of an old . . . associate, who wanted me to set up a meeting on her behalf. If you want to speak with her, go to the broken church in Malleon's Gate. Tell the keeper that you're looking for the wind. And when she arrives, you'll need to give her this." He tossed the dark staff to Lei, who winced as if it burned her hands.

"Who—?" Daine began.

"I have said all I intend to say," Jura snapped. "Now leave my house. Darkhart Woods is no place for unwelcome guests."

Daine turned to ask Lei's opinion, but she was already halfway down the path to the gate.

❉ ❉ ❉ ❉ ❉ ❉ ❉

Night was falling as they made their way back to Dassi's inn. Pierce led the way through the streets, his eyes ever watching for trouble. Jode tagged behind, lost in his own thoughts. Lei, walking next to Daine, held the dark staff as if it was covered with poison spines, and her expression was grim.

"Time to explain, Lei." said Daine, scowling. "You didn't tell us that Uncle Jura was another outcast. What did he do to get thrown out of Cannith? What are you afraid of?"

"Jura . . . always loved plants. He traveled to the jungles of Aerenal, the Eldeen Reaches, the forests of Karrnath. He met his wife in Aerenal."

"So? Don't tell me that expelled him for marrying an elf?"

"Actually, she was a dryad. He had her relocated to Sharn. As if the miscegenation wasn't trouble enough, after the wedding his behavior became . . . questionable. His parties were infamous. The stories say that he made most of his current fortune selling poisons and prohibited substances—dreamlily and the like."

"Because of a dryad? But in all the stories I've heard—"

"A *darkwood* dryad."

"Ah."

"Yes. Apparently, in his bid to be restored to the house, he's claiming that his wife ensorcelled him, that he wasn't responsible for his behavior. Whether or not that's true . . . he's not the man I knew as a child."

"Darkwood, hmm?" Daine reflected for a moment. "How did she die?"

"How do dryads ever die?"

Daine reflected on the wooden throne in the indoor grove, carved from the stump of a darkwood tree. He glanced over at the black staff. The top was carved to resemble the head of a beautiful woman, with long tresses running down the shaft. "So . . . that's . . . ?"

"Dark heart? Your guess is as good as mine."

"Charming."

The walked the rest of the way in silence.

CHAPTER 10

BRELAND
SHARN
Dravago 27, 996 YK

Little sunlight reached the streets of High Walls, and the filthy windows of the Manticore might just as well have been made of stone for all of the light they let through. Alina's parchments were scattered across the floor of the small room. Lei had woven an illuminating enchantment into a small crystal she'd been carrying, and she was using this light to read the documents. Daine paced back and forth and Jode sat on the floor, while Pierce remained as silent and impassive as a statue.

"Time is of the essence," Daine said. "For all we know, Rasial has already sold the shards. It's possible they will be smuggled out of the city before we can find them. If this is the case, Alina will at least expect us to find out who is in possession of the goods. Whatever happens, we need to find Rasial fast."

The fourth bell rang, pure tones echoing throughout the vast well of Tavick's Landing.

"We have a dinner invitation, if we want it," Daine continued. "Jode and I met Teral ir'Soras, an old councilor from the Cyran court. It may be a waste of time. He's a politician, so he may just be currying favor. But if he knows the residents of this district he could be a useful contact, especially if we're going to be here for a while. What else do we have to work with?"

Jode spoke up. "Rasial Tann served in the Sharn Watch for five years, serving with the Gold Wing guards for the last three years of his career. During that time he lived in the Dagger-watch district of Upper Dura. Most of the guardsmen are based there. Hopefully, our friend from the lift isn't going to pursue the matter, but I don't think it's a good idea for you to be asking questions in a garrison right about now, Daine."

"And you think she's forgotten about you? You only stuck a knife through her knee."

Jode shrugged. "Subtlety is my strength. I won't be recognized."

Daine scowled, but nodded. Jode was far better at digging up information than Lei or Pierce, and this might take a delicate touch. "As you wish. What else?"

"It seems that Rasial has a particular gift for handling hippogriffs. That's why he was recruited by the Gold Wings. But in his free time, he spent a great deal of time racing. Hareth's Folly in Middle Dura seems to be a center for windchasing and other aerial sports. Alina's notes provide the locations of a few arenas and gambling halls."

"But he's not racing anymore?"

"No. The largest race in Sharn is called the Race of Eight Winds. It happens once a year. Two years ago, Rasial won the race on behalf of Daggerwatch and the Hippogriff. Last year he rode for the Hippogriff again, but there was some sort of accident and he was almost killed. After that, he dropped off the horizon. Quit the guard. Stopped racing. And that's what we have to work with."

"What about the shards?" said Daine, looking to Lei. If she'd heard him, she gave no sign. "Lei? Lei!"

Lei looked up from the parchment she was studying. She had been distant since they'd returned from Darkhart Woods, and her voice was cool and emotionless. "Dragonshards are magically active minerals. Common Eberron dragonshards store and focus magical energy. These form the basis of many of the conveniences we take for granted, such as the everbright lantern. Sky shards fall from the Ring of Siberys. These amplify the natural powers of a dragonmark. Sivis message stones, Jorasco altars of healing . . . these all rely on sky shards."

"So what are we dealing with?"

"Khyber shards. These are found in veins deep below the earth and are said to be the dried blood of the dark progenitor wyrm. Just as the first fiends are said to be bound by the blood of Khyber, deep dragonshards are used to bind spirits and elemental energies. The lightning rail, airships, bonded sails . . . these are all made possible by Khyber dragonshards." Lei stood up and begin to pace, unconsciously echoing Daine's earlier movements. "But these are only the broadest categories. Purity, color, size . . . all of these things can play a factor in the value and use of a particular shard." She pointed at the page. "Your friend is trying to acquire a very unusual form of Khyber shard. It appears to resonate with dragonmark energy, much like a Siberys shard."

"So . . . ?"

"Siberys shards amplify energy, but Khyber shards bind it."

"I'm still not following. What can it do?"

Lei shrugged. "If this material truly can bind dragonmarked energies, you might be able to use it to create some sort of shield against dragonmarked effects. Or a manacle that could prevent a prisoner from using his dragonmark. But it's impossible to say. These notes are purely theoretical."

"How did Alina learn of the shards," asked Daine, "and who she was dealing with to obtain them?"

"I was hoping you'd tell me. My . . . family are the finest artificers of this or any age." For a moment her eyes went distant. "Yet I've never heard of these shards before. I can't begin to imagine what your friend would have to pay to find them, let alone to buy them. Who is this Alina? And why would she be interested in these shards?"

Jode spoke before Daine could come up with an answer. "I met Alina Lyrris in Metrol eight years ago, shortly after I'd begun fighting for Cyre. She was dealing in contraband goods, and I heard that she was selling secrets to the Cyran court. I am sure of three things. Alina is deadly, cunning, and has more wealth than you can imagine. She claims her fortune comes from gem mines in the Seawall Mountains, but don't believe it. From what I've heard, there are few things she hasn't tried—businesses and otherwise."

"So what does she want?"

"Control: knowledge, secrets, personal power. I don't think that she cares about money. It's all a game she plays with other people's lives."

"And now she's the new boss," Daine said with a scowl.

Lei looked at Daine for a moment, perhaps wondering how he had come into contact with Alina, what fueled his bitterness. But her own sorrow weighed heavily on her shoulders, and she said nothing. Daine took a deep breath and turned back to the matter at hand.

"So the shards are unusual. Can we use that? Could you track them, Lei?"

She considered. "I can craft a temporary divining rod easily enough, but it will only have a range of around a thousand feet. And the enchantment will only last for a few minutes after it's activated. So you won't want to use it unless you're pretty sure of yourself."

"It's better than nothing. Do it. Then we've got the matter of your Uncle Jura, and 'visiting the wind.' What was that?"

Lei shrugged. "I don't know." She glanced over at the dark-wood staff, which was leaning against a corner of the room. "That staff is magical, but so far I haven't been able to discern its function. Unless it's cursed."

"Not something we should rule out," Jode said.

Lei continued. "It seems unlikely Jura would give away a powerful item as part of a fool's errand. Even if it was cursed, what would be his motive for giving it to us?"

"I don't know," Jode said, studying a fingernail. "Perhaps he thinks getting rid of you will buy him favor in the house? Maybe he's trapped a banshee in the staff, and at the stroke of midnight it will kill us all with its horrible wail."

Lei just stared at him.

"Yeah, that seems likely," Daine said.

"Look," Lei said, "I don't know if I trust Jura. He's not the man I knew. But I . . . I don't think he'd try to harm me. Whatever's happened, we're still family. I think this could help us."

Daine scowled. "We should check it out quickly, then. What do you know about Malleon's Gate?"

"One of the most dangerous districts in Sharn—at least for humans. Most of the goblins and their kin live there, and I've heard that stranger creatures have been drifting east from Droaam."

"It's not likely that Uncle Jura is sending us into a bad neighborhood to be slaughtered and killed?"

"Daine . . ." Lei sighed. "I trust him." She considered a moment, then added, "Well, more or less."

"You fought an army of Darguul raiders at Sennan Rath, Captain," Pierce said calmly. "This can hardly be as dangerous of a situation."

"Spoken like a man who still has all of his weapons." Daine shot a glance at Jode, who at least had the grace to look embarrassed. "But you're right. Still, it sounds like we should stay together for this. Afterwards we'll split up to investigate Daggerwatch and Hareth's Folly, and meet back here for dinner with Lord Teral."

The others nodded.

"Very well," Daine said, as Jode gathered the papers and Lei picked up the staff. "Let's go talk to the wind."

CHAPTER II

BRELAND
SHARN

Dravago 27, 996 YK

High Walls, the newfound home of the Cyran refugees in Sharn, was a depressing ghetto. For decades, the government of Sharn had worried only about maintaining the gates and the guards and not about the comfort of those trapped behind the walls. Poverty, fear, and uncertainty were a part of everyday life.

Compared to Malleon's Gate, it was paradise.

When human settlers first came to Khorvaire, they found the remains of a great goblin empire—a civilization shattered long ago and left to ruin. Hobgoblins and bugbears lurked in the mountains and harsh lands, while goblins remained in the ruins of their ancient cities. But the humans of Sarlona were determined to claim this new land as their own. When Malleon the Reaver landed on the shores of the Dagger River, he enslaved the local goblins and forced them to work on his fortress city—a city that would be destroyed in the War of the Mark. Six hundred years later, King Galifar began work on the new city of Sharn, and he promised freedom to all goblins who would serve him as soldiers and laborers. But few human inhabitants of the city ever accepted the goblins as true equals, and racial violence was an everyday occurrence. Eventually, most of Sharn's goblins settled in a single district, trusting in numbers to provide safety and shelter. But safety and prosperity were two different things.

While Malleon's Gate had always been a place of poverty and misery, it was only over the last century that it had become truly dangerous. Two new nations had arisen in the wake of the Last War, taking advantage of the chaos and the fragmentation of the proud army of Galifar. Cyre and Breland had both used goblinoid mercenaries in the war, drawing the cunning hobgoblins and powerful bugbears down from the mountains to augment their armies. Eventually these creatures outnumbered the human soldiers in the eastern front. The hobgoblins ruled Khorvaire long before humanity had arrived, and a charismatic warlord was determined to use the fall of Galifar as a stepping stone for the future of his people. He managed to win the loyalty of many of the other mercenary chieftains, and at a critical point in the war the soldiers turned on both sides and laid claim to the territory they were supposed to be protecting, proclaiming the new nation of Darguun. With the Last War at its height, neither Breland nor Cyre could afford to retaliate. Both still needed goblin troops, though the commanders were considerably more cautious about the concentration of such forces. Even now, with the war winding to a close, the remnants of the five nations lacked the resources or resolve to move against Darguun. Representatives of the hobgoblin king were seated at the Council of Thronehold, debating the future of Khorvaire. A number of former and current mercenaries had settled in Sharn, and they naturally gravitated towards the greatest concentration of their own kind. But where the city goblins of Sharn tried to avoid conflict with the human citizens, the Darguuls viewed humanity with disdain. The Sharn Watch had long ago abandoned the Gate, and any human or elf who entered the district was on his own.

But the hobgoblins were not the only creatures to emerge from the shadows of the war. All manner of monsters—harpies, ogres, trolls, and even more terrible things— filled the lands around the Byeshk Mountains. Even the knights of Galifar had avoided the haunted woods and wastes of this land. While it had always been a place of dark legend, the horrors of Droaam never reached into the lands beyond—until the Last War. Over the last century, three terrible sisters—each hag a legend in her own right—seized control of the region and began to reshape and transform it, creating a nation from raw chaos. Over the last two decades the creatures of Droaam began to appear in the eastern lands, selling their services. Gargoyle scouts and couriers could be invaluable, and many businesses could use the raw strength of an ogre laborer. The monstrous population of Sharn had grown over the last few years, and while most of these creatures preferred to live in the tunnels beneath the city, a fair number had settled in Malleon's Gate, adding to both the color and danger of the district.

Over the course of the war, Daine had fought many Darguul warriors, and he could smell the aggression in the smoky air of Malleon's Gate. On his command, the group drew weapons as soon as they entered the district. With an arrow nocked in his massive longbow, Pierce took up the rear. Lei was resplendent in green leather vest studded with gold; this was an heirloom of her house, and the golden rivets were especially receptive to the temporary enchantments she could produce. She held the darkwood staff at the ready. Jode was a healer by trade, but he had served as a scout and could fight when he had to. Though his sword would be little more than a knife in the hands of a man, it was finely-crafted and razor sharp. Daine had his dagger drawn, the adamantine blade catching the guttering torchlight, and for the hundredth time he cursed sword-pawning halflings.

Malleon's Gate, one of the oldest districts in Sharn, had served as a ghetto since the earliest days of Sharn, and its age was obvious even to the casual observer. The stonework was rough and angular in comparison to the smooth curves of Tavick's Landing and Menthis Plateau. Mold and mildew covered the walls, inside and out. If there had ever been cold fire lanterns in the district, they had been shattered or stolen long ago. Most of the denizens of the Malleon's Gate could see in the dark, and outsiders had to find there way by the light of a few smoky torches.

The narrow streets were full of noise and chaos. Goblins were everywhere—haggling, arguing, or simply shouting in the harsh Goblin tongue. A massive bugbear forced its way through a pack of goblins, flinging the smaller creatures left and right. By contrast, when a trio of heavily armed hobgoblins emerged from a dingy tavern, the crowd instantly parted. Clearly the warriors of Darguun were not to be trifled with. The commander of the trio met Daine's eyes, and for a moment the former adversaries studied one another; then the moment passed, and the soldiers sauntered down the street. Daine breathed a sigh of relief. There could be any number of Darguuls within shouting distance, and if blood was spilled there was no telling how quickly the situation would escalate.

"So where do we find this broken church?" he said, glancing back at Lei.

"I'm afraid my family never visited Malleon's Gate on my trips to Sharn," said Lei. "Perhaps you should ask for directions."

Daine studied the few bystanders. "Somehow I think we'd be more likely to get a knife in the gut than useful advice. Let's keep on."

They explored the streets. Gleaming red eyes watched suspiciously from the shadows, but Daine kept his dagger in view and no one approached. On one street, a sharp shriek pierced the gloom as a harpy passed overhead. The half-human creature spun around and a ball of spit and phlegm struck Daine in the face.

Daine grabbed Pierce's arm before the warforged could release an arrow. "Let it go," he said. "We're the outsiders here." He wiped his face and rubbed his hand on his cloak.

Turning a corner they came upon a granite statue of a club-wielding goblin, its face frozen in rage. "I'm not sure about the taste," Jode said, "but it's nice to see an attempt to bring a little artistic flair to the region."

"It's not a statue," said Lei. She studied the perfect lines of the statue. "This unfortunate fellow was once very much alive. Something changed him to stone. Medusa, unless I miss my guess. Though I suppose it could be a basilisk."

Jode stumbled, and looking down found that he had tripped over the arm of a shattered second statue. "Lovely! Can we get this over with? Dinner with Councilor Teral is sounding more attractive every minute."

The next living residents they encountered were a pair of

goblins—a male and a female—engaged in a heated debate. Sheathing his dagger, Jode walked over and hailed them in the Goblin tongue—somehow managing to make even that harsh language seem cheerful. The goblins were momentarily dumbfounded by the interruption, but their demeanor changed once Jode produced a few copper crowns. The male goblin reached for the coins with a snarl, but as he did his companion struck him in the head with a mighty double-fisted blow and he sank senseless to the ground. The woman took the coins and engaged in a brief, animated conversation.

Jode returned to the group, and the goblin dragged her fallen comrade out of the street.

"What did she say?" Lei asked.

"She said that she sympathized, as her fool of a husband wouldn't ask for directions either." Jode grinned. "But I've got directions, and I'd say there's at least half-odds that she was telling the truth."

"Lead on, then."

❀ ❀ ❀ ❀ ❀ ❀ ❀

The broken church had been abandoned long ago, its holy trappings stripped away and only bare fragments remaining of the once-beautiful windows of colored crystal. Fire and acid had scarred the walls. On the steps, two monsters were engaged in a brutal battle.

One was a minotaur—at least eight feet tall. Powerful muscles rippled beneath a sleek coat of black fur. He wore a black loincloth embroidered with golden sigils, and his long horns were bound with bands of brass. His opponent was a bugbear—a seven-foot blend of ursine and goblin features. His light brown fur was unkempt and patchy, his clothes torn, and one of his fangs was missing. The two were fighting barehanded, and it was clear that the bugbear was getting the worst of it. Studying the steps, Daine noticed the bugbear's missing fang lying a few feet away.

Daine could see that the bugbear was barely standing. The minotaur ended the battle with a single mighty head butt. The bugbear fell down the steps, blood streaming from nose and mouth. It did came to a stop, its head resting on the second step, and did not move again.

The minotaur studied its fallen foe for a moment, then looked over at Daine. "Move on, outsiders," he rumbled, his voice hoarse and deep. "You have no business here."

"On the contrary," Jode said, skipping forward. "We were sent to . . . well, talk to the wind. Is that you? We have a gift."

Lei held up the staff.

The minotaur roared, and Daine had almost grabbed Jode before he realized that the creature was laughing.

"*You* would enter?" The minotaur snorted. "You think you can defeat me?"

Daine felt foolish challenging this juggernaut with his tiny dagger, but its keen edge had served him well. "Watch your tone. Size isn't everything. There's four of us to your one, and you're not even armed. So why don't you step aside?"

The monster fixed Daine with its inhuman eyes. "Don't threaten me, little human. I am appointed to guard this gate, and only I can open it. You face me or you do not pass. One person. No weapons. One chance."

Daine stepped back and turned to his companions. "What do you think?" he said quietly. "I know when I'm outmatched. Pierce?"

"I'm willing to try, Captain."

"No. I'll do it." It was Lei. The other three looked over, surprised.

"What are you talking about?"

"Jura said this person wanted to see *me*. He gave me the staff. For all we know, I *have* to do it."

Daine blinked. "Yes, but . . . " He glanced back as the minotaur lifted up the unconscious bugbear and threw him from the steps. "What are you going to do against *that*?"

"He said no weapons. I can handle that better than you can. Trust me, Daine. With all that I've been through the last two days, I'm going to enjoy this."

"Your uncle, your decision." Daine shrugged. "Jode, be ready to help her the instant she needs it."

The halfling nodded.

Lei turned and bowed to the minotaur. It watched her, its inhuman expression impossible to read. Handing the dark-wood staff to Pierce, Lei ran her fingers along the studs of her armor, murmuring quietly, then she produced a pinch of powdered stone from her pouch and rubbed it into the leather of her belt. Daine recognized the mystical significance of her actions, but he had no idea what enchantments she was weaving into her clothing.

After a few minutes, Lei's preparations were complete. She turned and walked toward the minotaur, pausing at the bottom of the steps. She stood straight and tall, her arms at her sides, and took one slow, deep breath.

"I wish to talk to the wind," she said.

The guardian nodded, then without warning he charged down the steps, a blur of black and gold.

Lei was no soldier. She had been assigned to Daine's unit to care for the warforged. By the rules of war, she was a non-combatant, safe from the danger of battle so long as she posed no threat to anyone involved. Most artificers and magewrights had relied entirely on this pledge to serve as their shield, but Lei's parents had not been so trusting. She was no warrior, but she'd been taught to defend herself with both magical and martial skill. To the others, the minotaur might be moving with blinding speed. But Lei had prepared for the fight, and to her enchanted eyes the beast was like a bull charging through three feet of mud. She barely moved, slipping just beyond his reach and turning as he rumbled past.

The minotaur turned to face her, and Lei raised her left hand. With a whispered word she activated the power stored within her glove, and a dark bolt lanced out to strike her foe. Shadows wreathed the minotaur, blue light tracing his muscles as the magic leached the energy from his sinews. But the minotaur was already in motion, and he slammed into Lei before she could slip out of the way. The golden studs of Lei's armor flared with light, and a shimmering field of translucent energy deflected much of the raw force of the blow—but the sheer momentum of the attack threw her to the ground.

Lei cursed as she struggled to her feet. Never start a fight. Never draw a blade. Her parents had taught her defense, but the first principle of defense was to avoid the fight. Challenging a minotaur . . . what would her mother say to such foolishness?

She hadn't hurt the minotaur, but she had weakened him, and he was acting with more caution. They circled for a moment, then Lei slipped forward and past him, coming up behind and planting a powerful kick where she thought his kidneys might be. But if the minotaur felt any pain, he didn't show it, and Lei had left herself open with the attack. Grunting, the beast slapped her with a powerful backhand blow. Her enchanted armor kept her on her feet, but for a moment the world went black, and when her vision cleared a monstrous fist was flying toward her face. Calling on every ounce of will, Lei dropped beneath the blow and slipped forward. Bringing her right hand up against her opponent's chest, she extended her mind, reaching into the glove and unlocking the power she'd bound within. The minotaur howled as a brilliant arc of electrical energy surged through his body. The beast dropped to his knees and offered no resistance as Lei put her foot to his throat and pushed him to the ground.

The smell of ozone and burned fur filled the air, and for a moment the only sound was the minotaur's labored breathing. Finally, he opened his eyes and looked up at her.

"You may enter," he said. There was a distinct *click,* and the door to the temple swung open a few inches.

"What of my friends?"

"You have earned . . . passage for all."

Lei nodded. "Then let's go." She looked over at Daine, and surprise spread over her face. "Daine!"

He turned around. They had been so focused on the battle that they had not heard the others approach. Over a dozen men spread out behind them, wearing the green and black of the Sharn Watch. Daine hadn't seen any watchmen during their earlier exploration of the district, and he had a sinking feeling this was no ordinary patrol. These men had the look of veteran soldiers, and the occasional spot of blood hinted at a recent clash with residents of the Gate. Four crossbows were leveled in their direction. Four halberdiers moved into flanking positions, and the four closest men carried iron cudgels.

The sergeant leveled his sword at Daine and said, "Lay down your arms! By the authority of the Lord Mayor of Sharn, I hereby place you under arrest for the heinous crime of murder!"

Jode looked up at Daine. "Well, I guess no one caught him."

CHAPTER 12

BRELAND
SHARN
Dravago 27, 996 YK

Daine studied the enemy and their surroundings, strategies flashing through his mind. None were good. The numbers were against them, Lei was unarmed, and all he had was his thrice-damned dagger. Even if they could fight, the guards were just doing their jobs, and resisting arrest would only make matters worse. For a moment Daine thought about running for the open door of the church, but they had no idea what was inside or any reason to believe they would be offered shelter against the law.

"Captain?" Pierce said quietly.

Daine knew that the 'forged could drop two of the archers in the first few seconds of battle. But it just wasn't enough.

There were no real alternatives. Slowly, Daine set his dagger on the ground and gestured for the others to follow suit. Guards surrounded them and bound their wrists, and they were led out of the district.

The guards were silent and tense, and the halberdiers and archers kept their weapons at the ready, as if they expected an attack to come at any moment. Maybe they did. Goblins glared from the shadows, and an ogre sneered at the guardsmen, revealing filthy fangs. The Watch was not welcome in Malleon's Gate, and only sheer numbers protected the patrol. Daine was impressed. Clearly this force had been dispatched to track them down and apprehend them only hours after the guard's death. Even in Metrol, Daine wouldn't have expected such a swift response. And with Sharn's sordid reputation, he had half-expected that the law wouldn't even try to solve the crime—though the fact that the victim was a guardsman probably had a great deal to do with the speed of the response.

They made it out of Malleon's Gate without incident, and the guards relaxed as they boarded a lift and rose up through the towers. Nothing could keep Jode quiet, and he'd managed to strike up a conversation with one of the guards as they were moving out of the district. Now that they were standing still, Daine picked up on the end of the conversation.

" . . . Carralag?" Jode said. "I've heard he's got quite a few tricks tucked away."

"He's a *gargoyle*," said his captor, a half-elf woman with short silvery hair and freckled cheeks. "It doesn't matter how tricky he is, he just doesn't have the wingspan to compete with a pegasus or hippogriff."

"*Daeras!* Don't talk to the prisoners!" The sergeant was almost as large as Pierce, and Daine guessed that he owed his gray complexion and flat nose to orcish blood. The half-elf nodded sullenly and turned away from Jode.

"We're going to Daggerwatch," Jode whispered, sidling up to Daine. Daggerwatch was the garrison district Jode had mentioned earlier.

"Great. So while I'm being boiled in oil, why don't you try to ask a few questions about Rasial."

"What's interesting is that the guard didn't know anything about the nature of our crime. She knew that the charge was murder, but she was instructed to apprehend you and anyone you might be traveling with. Let's face it: you're the killer."

"Thanks, Jode. Good to know you're standing at my side. Besides which, you stabbed the woman."

"And healed her," Jode pointed out. "But don't worry, I'm sure I can talk us through this. I was just thinking of Lei and Pierce. How could the Watch possibly hold them responsible?"

"*Silence!*" The sergeant sent Jode sprawling with a kick. Daine gritted his teeth but stood his ground—the last time he'd fought on a lift it had ended poorly, and the gray-skinned sergeant was looking for an excuse for further violence.

That excuse came from an unexpected quarter. As the sergeant turned toward Daine, there was a flash of movement. Lei's foot caught the back of the half-orc's knee and sent him sprawling to the ground. The guards knew nothing of the enchantments Lei had woven for her battle with the minotaur, and none were prepared for her blinding speed. She dove forward, stripped the rope from the hands of her captor, and rolled into a defensive crouch, raising her bound fists before her like a mace.

The sergeant rose to his feet and drew his blade. "I'll have your foot for that, Mourner trash!"

"Try me, brute," Lei hissed. "You saw that minotaur a minute ago? I did that with my bare hands. You touch my friends again and you'll be kissing cobblestones before you can blink."

The sergeant watched her through narrowed eyes, and Daine caught the hint of motion he made with his sword. The four archers readied themselves, moving along the perimeter and preparing to fire on a moment's notice. Pierce caught Daine's glance, and his thoughts were clear—for all her supernatural speed, Lei couldn't fight the guards alone. Either they acted together, or—

"Lei, stand down," Daine said firmly. "I'm the one you want here, grayskin. If you're going to take your anger out on someone, deal with me."

Lei remained in her crouch. Behind her, the archers were taking aim.

"Lei!"

Reluctantly, Lei lowered her arms. A guard took hold of her tether, but the others were taking no chances. Two of the archers kept their crossbows leveled at her back. The sergeant walked over, glared at Daine, then smashed him in the face with the pommel of his sword, knocking him to the ground. Glaring down, the half-orc spat at him and turned away. Slowly Daine rose to his feet and shuffled over towards Lei.

"I never thought you'd be the one to start a fight," he muttered, testing his teeth with his tongue.

"I never thought you'd be the one to stop me," she replied. He could see the anger in her eyes, but the archers still stood at the ready, fingers white on the stocks of their crossbows.

"I've fought too many fights that couldn't be won. I'm proud of what you did—now and earlier—but it's not the time. Let's see where this takes us."

She nodded, but she wouldn't meet his gaze.

The lift came to a stop, and they were escorted through the streets of Daggerwatch. Every district seemed to have its own flavor, and Daggerwatch was no exception. It had the atmosphere of a vast fortress. The walls were reinforced to resist siege weaponry, and guardsmen filled the streets. Compared to the lower districts and even Den'iyas, the streets were remarkably quiet. People spoke in lowered voices, and even the merchants refrained from hawking their wares. A pair of hippogriffs wheeled overhead, and Daine could see soldiers riding the beasts. Once Rasial Tann had been up there.

"It's quite clean, I'll give it that," Jode remarked. "I wonder who cleans up all the hippogriff shit."

A guard shoved him with the butt of a halberd.

They passed a large open square, containing a circle of pillories. A group of criminals were on display, heads and hands pinned in the wooden restraints. A few spectators were throwing refuse at prisoners, but even this behavior seemed rather quiet and reserved compared to what Daine had come to expect.

Daggerwatch was home to the local military as well as the Sharn Watch. Occasionally squads of Brelish soldiers passed by, some marching in strict formation, others off-duty and drifting. Daine was still wearing his Cyran uniform, and he was greeted with sneers and the occasional thrown stone.

They reached their destination. Daggerwatch Garrison was an impressive sight. The stone walls were two feet thick, studded with arrow slits and murder holes, and Daine could see a few archers watching them as they approached. There were deep scars in a few spots along the wall, as if acid or fire had eaten away at the rock—apparently the fortifications had been tested in the past. A massive stone hippogriff stood to either side of the gate, foreclaws raised and ready to strike. Daine wondered if the statues would come to life if there was an attack.

Entering the garrison, they were surrounded by even more guards. Steel manacles replaced their rope bonds—apparently the Sharn Watch was taking no chances.

The sergeant conferred with an administrator in black-and-green robes. The sergeant looked displeased with the news, but Daine couldn't hear the conversation. Eventually, he returned and spoke quietly with his men. The sergeant nodded to Daine. The next thing he knew, there was a splitting pain in the back of his head and everything went black.

❀ ❀ ❀ ❀ ❀ ❀ ❀ ❀

When his senses returned, he was lying on a hard stone floor. He opened his eyes, expecting to see the dim light of a prison cell. Instead he was surprised by bright illumination and a soft carpet beneath his head. His skull was still throbbing from where he'd been sapped, but no permanent damage seemed to have been done. Something seemed wrong, and then he realized—his manacles had been removed.

"Well, Daine. Who'd have thought we'd meet like this? Olladra's done you no favors, I see."

The voice was familiar, but in his dazed state Daine had trouble placing it. Rising to his knees, he struggled to take in his surroundings. By the granite floor and walls, he judged he was still inside the Daggerwatch garrison—perhaps an officer's chamber? A tapestry covered the wall in front of him, depicting the famous battle between the sentinel marshals of House Deneith and the Bandit King of the Whistling Wood. But the voice had come from his right. Daine shook the cobwebs from his head and turned to face the voice.

A man sat behind a beautiful desk of Aerenal densewood. The seal of Sharn dominated the wall behind the desk. Daine's vision was still slightly blurred, but he could see that the man was wearing the uniform of a captain. He squinted and the stranger's face came into focus. "Grazen?" he said, shocked. "Grazen d'Deneith?"

The captain laughed and stood up. "For a moment I thought the guards had done you permanent damage. Mourner soldiers aren't well liked in Daggerwatch." He walked around the desk and offered Daine a hand, pulling him to his feet. "But it's Grazen ir'Tala now."

Daine shook his head, trying to process this information. "What?"

"What can I say?" Grazen ran a hand through his golden-brown hair and smiled. "Love conquers all. I was a sentinel marshal back when we last saw each other, yes? I had an extended tour of duty in Sharn, pursuing a group of Lhazaar assassins. During my stay, I met a lovely young woman who just happened to be the sole heir of a wealthy estate, and after some thought, I decided to leave the house and settle in Sharn. It may sound like madness, I know, but I'm not the first to leave his house voluntarily."

Grazen pointed Daine toward a chair, then returned to his desk. Daine sat down, still absorbing the information. "But . . ."

"What am I doing here? Like I said, I had served a long tour of duty here. When he heard I was staying, Lord Commander Iyan was quite happy to offer me a commission. So here I am today. I have a lovely wife, a vast fortune, two beautiful children—albeit unmarked—and a position that offers me considerable authority and respect. I'm glad to see that you've managed to do as well for yourself."

Daine's head had cleared, but he chose not to respond to the barb.

"But you were always one for lost causes, weren't you, Daine? And look what it got you. According to Sergeant Holas, you didn't even have a sword when they apprehended you. I wonder what your grandfather would say about that?"

Daine clenched his fists but held his ground. "Let's get this over with, Grazen. I killed your man. I admit it. But it was an accident, and my companions had nothing to do with it."

"Ah, yes. Your little motley crew. You always knew how to

pick your companions. Speaking of which, have you seen Alina recently?"

Daine was caught off guard. "What?"

"Oh, she's here in Sharn. I just thought you might want to reminisce about old times. In any case, you're mistaken." Grazen smirked. "You haven't killed anyone."

He reached into a belt pouch and produced a platinum disk, which he tossed to Daine. The symbol of a feather was engraved on the surface, along with an assortment of mystical glyphs.

"Feather token. Only one use, but it's a lifesaver if you find yourself plummeting to your death. If you live on the upper levels and you can afford one, you're a fool not to—and Sergeant Lorrak is no fool. I suppose that I could have sent Lorrak to bring you in, but I hate to spoil a surprise. I'd stay out of Lorrak's way, if I were you. He may be alive, but he's certainly one to hold a grudge. And I understand you kept him from having a little fun."

"Yeah, fun," Daine said, thinking of the goblin girl. "Great crew you've got here. So the murder charge—you just made that up?"

"Would you have come if I'd just asked?"

"I don't know."

"At least you're honest. Something that's all too rare these days." He studied Daine carefully. "What would you say if I offered you a job, Daine? It wouldn't be easy, given that you were an officer for the enemy, but Cyre's gone now and it's not coming back. And I've got connections here. Feel like working for a winner for a change?"

"What's that got to do with you?"

Grazen laughed. "I've missed you, Daine. Well, I'll give you a few days to think about it. But a few words of advice: stay away from Alina. Stay out of trouble. And keep an eye out for Sergeant Lorrak. In light of our old friendship, I won't ask what you were doing in Malleon's Gate. But friendship or not, this is where my heart lies now. You haven't crossed any lines. Yet. But if you do, I'll be right there to bring you down."

"Thanks for the advice, Grazen. It's been great catching

up like this. Now if you don't mind, I'd like to get back to my *friends.*"

"Of course." He ran a finger over an alarm-stone on his desk, and two guards entered the room. "Minal, Dal, escort our guest back to his companions and see that his possessions are restored to him." He looked back at Daine. "Think about my offer, Daine. And my advice. It might be the only chance you have left to do the right thing."

Daine said nothing as the guards led him away.

❧ ❧ ❧ ❧ ❧ ❧ ❧

Jode, Pierce, and Lei were waiting for him in the atrium.

"Daine!" Lei called. "What's going on?"

"It was all a misunderstanding."

"You mean someone *did* catch him?" Jode said. A servant brought in their weapons and began to distribute them.

"Something like that, yeah." The servant reached him. She handed Daine his dagger and then gave him a longsword with a scabbard and harness of black leather. "This isn't mine," Daine said.

"Compliments of Captain Grazen," she replied. "He said you'd lost your own blade." It was a beautiful weapon, even in the scabbard.

Lei glanced at the weapon and frowned. "Daine, why . . . ?"

He followed her gaze and saw the eye-in-the-sun sigil of House Deneith engraved on the pommel, glittering in the light of the cold fire.

"It belonged to an old friend," he said. "Apparently he doesn't have a use for it any more." He considered handing it back to the servant, but a sword was a sword. Scowling, he buckled on the harness. "Now let's get out of here."

CHAPTER 13

BRELAND
SHARN

Dravago 27, 996 YK

Wearing a Cyran uniform cloak to a Brelish garrison wasn't one of Daine's better ideas—not that it was his plan. Even though they weren't in chains, Daine's uniform was drawing unwanted attention, and they moved swiftly through the streets towards the closest lift.

"I think it might be worthwhile to spend a few sovereigns on new clothes, Daine," Jode said.

Daine scowled. He knew Jode was right, but he hated the thought of setting aside the uniform. The war was over, and Cyre was no more, but as long as he wore the uniform, the nation still existed in his heart.

They walked most of the way in silence, each lost in his or her own thoughts. Pierce approached Daine and spoke quietly. "This situation troubles me, Captain."

"What is it?"

"You say that we were brought here because this watch captain knew who you were, that he wished to give you a warning."

And to gloat, Daine thought, but he kept it to himself. "Yes?"

"How did he know your identity? According to your story, the injured guard only saw you for a few minutes, and you never spoke your name. Yet this watch captain committed a significant force to apprehend you for what was apparently a nonexistent crime." It was just like Pierce to cut to the point of an issue. Many of the social aspects of human behavior were still an enigma to the warforged soldier. But he had fought for Cyre for almost thirty years, and his sense of tactics was at least as sharp as Daine's.

"You're right," Daine said, "and it seems as if they knew where to find us."

"Could you have been betrayed by our employer? This . . . Alina?"

Would she do something like that? Daine let his thoughts drift back, reflecting on his two years in her service. "I honestly don't know. I don't see what she would stand to gain."

"If you aren't certain this woman can be trusted, why are we working for her?"

"It's not that simple, Pierce. We're on our own now. Alina's offering a great deal of gold, and we need money if we're going to survive. I know it's not something you need to think about, but most of us need to eat and drink, and after years of that gruel I'd like to be able to eat something with some flavor. We need shelter and security. And I want to get *my* sword back!" His voice rose with the last sentence. He took a deep breath to calm his nerves.

"Is that so important?" Pierce asked. "The sword you have been given is of similar quality and design. It appears to be almost identical. Why do you need to reclaim your first sword?"

"It's not about function. That sword was a gift from my grandfather. It was the blade he carried into battle, and it's all I have left of him. It's the memory, not the weapon."

If Pierce had been human, he might have shrugged. As it was, he paused for a moment, then continued speaking. "If not Alina, what about Lei's Uncle Jura? It was his request that led us to Malleon's Gate. Could it have been a trap of some sort?"

"He would have known we were there, but I still don't see the motive. And the guard captain, Grazen, there's nothing I can see that would connect him to Jura. Perhaps it is just a coincidence."

"Perhaps." Pierce fell silent. His mithral-steel faceplate was impossible to read, as impassive as any statue or helmet.

They reached the lift a few minutes later. "Good riddance," the lift guard muttered when he saw Daine.

"I'm staying here," Jode announced as they got ready to board. "We still need to investigate Rasial, and we're already here."

"What—?" Daine began to protest, but Jode cut him off.

"You need to get out of here, now. As long as you're dressed like that you're a brawl waiting to happen, and Pierce is almost as bad." He counted out a few sovereigns. "Here, get new cloaks for both of you. Something nondescript. Brelish. Understood?"

Daine wasn't used to taking orders from the halfling, but he knew Jode was right.

"I'll see what I can find here," Jode said. "Why don't you go down to this Hareth's Folly and see what you can find out there?"

"What about the temple?" Lei interjected. "I beat down a minotaur and now we're going to forget about it?"

"I doubt it's going anywhere," Jode said. "We'll work our way down the tower and get back to it once we're back at the bottom. So, we meet back at the Manticore at, say, the seventh bell?"

Lei glanced at Daine. After a moment, he nodded. "Very well. But watch yourself."

"Of course," Jode said. "And Pierce? Make sure to trail back a little. When people are trying to have a nonchalant discussion . . . well, you attract too much attention."

"As you wish," Pierce said.

Jode produced a few more coins and tossed them to Lei. "Here. If you're going to be nosing around the taverns, you'll need to buy a drink or two."

"Now that's an idea I can get behind," muttered Daine.

❂ ❂ ❂ ❂ ❂ ❂ ❂

Each of the districts of Sharn was the size of a village or small town, and like any village or town, each had its own distinctive personality. Between the squalor of High Walls and Malleon's Gate, the cold militant atmosphere of Daggerwatch, the pretentious luxury of Dalan's Refuge, and the relentless good cheer of Den'iyas, Daine had seen more diversity than he had in years, but nothing prepared him for Hareth's Folly. Set halfway down the great tower of Dura, the Folly was a bizarre assortment of spires and small towers. Every building was completely different. Architectural styles, building materials, color schemes . . . nothing matched. A traditional Brelish tower of stone and mortar stood next to a gnarled spire of Aerenal densewood, which appeared to have been carved from the trunk of a single massive tree. A squat keep of red brick dominated a square covered with glittering silver sand. The sky was just as chaotic. The upper levels of the towers were connected by a tangle of bridges, a labyrinth of wood, stone, and rope. Flying creatures were darting in and around the towers. A winged stallion was playing a game of tag with a massive black-feathered owl, and a pair of Gold Wing guards passed overhead on hippogriff mounts.

"What madness is this?" Daine murmured.

"You may have answered your own question," Lei replied. "The architect was a man named Hareth ir'Talan, and 'mad' would be a polite way of describing him." She paused by the densewood tower, studying the irregular, crooked walls. "According to the stories, he wanted to have buildings reflecting all of the different nations in Galifar, so a visitor from any country would have a place that felt like home."

"Sounds reasonable enough, but . . . I know the elves of Aerenal use wood in most of their structures, but I never heard of them actually living in trees."

"They don't." Lei looked up at the higher branches of the tower. "When Hareth had constructed buildings for all of the different cultures in the Kingdom of Galifar . . . well, there was still room in the district. So he began looking to other cultures—Riedra, Adar, even the ruins in the Demon Wastes and Xen'drik. Eventually even this well ran dry, so he turned to the outer planes for inspiration. I believe this is his vision of what homes would look like in Lamannia, the Twilight Forest."

The outer planes were one of the greater mysteries of the world. The sages said there were thirteen planes—shadows of reality bound to different aspects of existence. Sages and wise women told fanciful stories about the nature of each plane—the endless battlefields of Shavarath, the brilliant crystalline landscape of Irian, the floating citadels of Syrania. As far as Daine was concerned, these descriptions were pure fantasy. He'd heard the legends of mighty wizards traveling to the outer realms, but until he met someone who had actually done it, Daine would treat the stories like any other fable. Still, there was no denying that there were forces that had an influence on the world. Daine could still remember when Eberron aligned with Shavarath in the midst of the Last War—the storms of whirling blades that erupted in the midst of battles, shredding the warriors of both sides in a terrifying whirlwind of blood. His grandfather had spoken of the last conjunction with Dolurrh, the Realm of the Dead, and how the soldiers that fell in battle simply refused to die. While these conjunctions were rare and temporary, there were places in the world where the touch of the outer planes was always felt. Sharn was one of these. The bond to the plane of Syrania enhanced the powers of flight, and this supported the spells that prevented the vast towers from falling. Lamannia was said to be the heart of the natural world. Studying the strange tree-tower, Daine could see how it might fit into such a place.

"The buildings, the bridges . . ." Lei continued. "Some say he was mad, but there are a few artificers in House Cannith who believe differently. My father believed that Hareth's Folly was designed according to a precise formula, that when the planes and moons come into a specific alignment, its true purpose will be revealed."

She fell silent, a hint of sorrow crossing her features. She rarely mentioned her parents. They had lived in the Cyran capital of Metrol, and Daine knew that they had both died in the war some ten years ago. Lei had never spoken of the circumstances of their deaths, and Daine had not wished to pry. He let her reflect in silence and examined the streets around them. The inhabitants of Hareth's Folly were almost as diverse as the buildings themselves. Daine could see travelers from every corner of Khorvaire who'd come to the Folly to participate in the games and spectacles of Sharn.

"Daine . . ." When Lei spoke again, her voice was soft and thoughtful. "Who gave you that sword?"

"A man named Grazen. An old friend, I told you."

"A member of House Deneith?"

"Yes."

"But . . . the soldiers of House Deneith give their allegiance to no nation. The house is founded on the principle of mercenary service. How could an heir of Deneith serve as an officer of the Sharn Watch?"

"He *was* in House Deneith. He left the house."

Lei's eyes widened. "You mean . . . he was excoriated? Like me?"

"I don't think so. I think he chose to leave of his own free will."

"I've heard of it happening, but . . . it's just hard for me to imagine."

"Really? Are the other members of your family such wonderful people? I could imagine getting tired of spending my life in the company of someone like Lord Jura."

Lei shook her head. "You can't understand, Daine. The house . . . it's more than just a family. It's the foundation of life. Being part of the house raises you above any nation, above any race. As a girl, I dreamed of the day that my mark would appear and allow me to be a part of the work of my house." She stopped walking, her eyes glistening and thoughts far away. "Kings come and go. It is the dragonmarked houses that have shaped Khorvaire. Look at what Cannith has done in the last century alone. We gave birth to a new *race.*" She broke off and took a deep breath.

Daine put his hand on her shoulder. "You don't have to be a part of a house to make a difference," he said. "There's the Twelve, the Arcane Congress—"

Lei pushed his hand aside, blinking back tears. "You don't understand! It's . . ." She reached up and rubbed the small of her back, just below her neck. Though it was usually covered, Daine knew that this was where her dragonmark was located. "It's what I was born for. It's who I am. How could anyone throw that away?"

Daine knew she didn't really want an answer, but he couldn't help it. "What about Jode?" he said. "How does he fit in with this?"

The question seemed to shock Lei out of her reverie. Jode made no efforts to conceal his dragonmark, yet he had never spoken of his connection to House Jorasco, the halfling house of Healing.

"I . . . I don't know. I tried to bring it up once before, but he changed the subject and I didn't want to press. He might have been expelled. But it's always possible that he's a foundling."

"What do you mean?"

The change in subject allowed Lei to fall back on her role as sage and lecturer, and they began walking again. "You know that the dragonmarks are bound to bloodlines, yes? Since the marks are tied to the family line of the house, they remain within the house. It's one reason people who bear a particular dragonmark often share similar physical traits. But when you have an . . . excoriate . . . he still carries the power of the mark and can pass it on to offspring. Thus it's possible for a child to be born outside the house and yet to possess the mark of the house. I think that's what you see with Jode—a man with the gift of Jorasco, but with no actual tie to the house."

"I'd think the house wouldn't approve of that—someone interfering with their monopoly on the mark. What's to stop a group of outsiders from starting a new house?"

"Well, that's more or less what has happened with the elves, though the split came from inside the house," Lei said. "But you're right, it's something that has always been discouraged. You have to understand, it's exceedingly rare for someone to be punished in this way. Uncle Jura is the only excoriate I've ever met. As Jode said before, they use to kill excoriates. Even after that practice was ended, excoriates were often castrated or . . . maimed. Since the rise of Galifar, these practices have been discouraged. Over the last few centuries, most of the houses passed rules allowing foundlings to apply for admittance into the house. Unless the parent was some sort of incarnate fiend, there's nothing to be gained by punishing the child."

"And yet we have Jode."

"Look, I don't know! Ask him."

Daine shook his head. "Better left alone."

They walked a little further. "You changed the subject," Lei said. "I still don't understand why your friend Grazen would leave the house. But given that he did . . . why would he keep that sword? And why give it to you?"

"Well . . ." Daine ran his fingers along the hilt of the sword. "You're right. The soldiers of Deneith cannot give their allegiance to any king or queen. Their loyalty belongs to the house first and paymaster second, whoever that may be. Apparently Grazen found something—or someone—who became more important to him than the house. I imagine he had to leave to be with her. So it's not like, well, what's happened to you. He may have wanted to keep the memory of his achievements within the house, so he kept the sword. As for why he gave it to me, I couldn't tell you. He knew I didn't have a sword." And wanted to rub my face in it, he thought. "This is a fine blade, and obviously I'll never be able to wield it without thinking of him." It was close enough to the truth, and Lei seemed to accept it.

Lei stopped again and looked at him critically. "You have a bit of the Deneith look, you know," she said. "The color of your hair, those dark blue eyes, even the shape of the eye . . . I don't know why I've never noticed it before."

Daine shrugged. "Perhaps there's a foundling in my family tree? I supposed it would explain why Grazen and I were such good friends."

Lei nodded. "I suppose it might, at that. Anyhow, we're here."

"What?"

Lei gestured at the building next to them. Daine had been so absorbed in the conversation that he hadn't been paying attention to their surroundings. He glanced over at their destination and blinked. The King of Fire was unlike any tavern he'd ever seen. A squat tower of black stone inlaid with sigils of gleaming brass, it seemed like it should be the fortress of an evil wizard plucked out of fey tales. But the square sign above the door had the unmistakable look of an inn post, bearing the image of a deck of playing cards with the King of Fire showing on the top. As he watched, a trio of drunken gnomes came staggering out of the building. All three of them needed to lean against the door to push it open.

"What is it?" Daine asked.

Lei had produced Alina's packet of parchments. "It's supposed to be the primary center for gambling in the tower—especially for betting on aerial sports, such as the Race of Eight Winds. Jode's thought was that we might be able to get information about Rasial from some of the patrons. As for the design, I imagine it was inspired by the stories of the fiery plane of Fernia. Are you ready to go in?"

Daine glanced around, looking for Pierce. Given his size and unusual appearance, the warforged soldier had a gift for concealment, and it took Daine a moment to pick him out against the shadows. He gave Pierce a "hold and watch" sign with his right hand, and Pierce nodded almost imperceptibly.

"All right," Daine said. "Let's see what we can find."

CHAPTER 14   BRELAND
SHARN
Dravago 27, 996 YK

The tables were on fire. The walls and floor of the King of Fire were the same black stone as the exterior. Mystical symbols were carved into the walls and inlaid with brass; set against the dark stone they almost seemed to be floating in midair. There were no torches, no chandeliers. The light came from the chairs and tables themselves. Half a dozen round tables, carved from darkwood and inscribed with the same symbols as the walls, were spread around the common room. Cold fire had been woven into the wood of the tables, and these insubstantial flames cast long shadows across the walls. People were laughing and talking, and the rattle of dice and flutter of shuffling cards filled the air.

"Welcome! What are you looking for?" The voice seemed to come from thin air, but as his eyes adjusted to the strange lighting, Daine realized that there was a slender halfling woman standing next to him. She had short dark hair and wore a black dress embroidered with the same symbols that could be seen on the walls.

"Can I get a flagon of korluaat?" he asked. He had developed a taste for the pitchy brew while serving with a troop of Darguul mercenaries.

Lei made a face, but the halfling nodded. "Oh, absolutely." Noticing Lei's expression, she said, "A lot of people think the Gargoyle has a strong chance this year, and we're expecting to

99

have a lot of goblins up from Malleon's Gate to get a closer view. Now, what can I get for you, dear?"

"Blackroot tal," Lei said.

"Very well. Take any open stool, and I'll be right back. I'm Kela. Just call if you need anything." As if in response, a burly half-orc bellowed her name from across the room and she scurried away.

They found an empty table and sat down. Daine found it difficult to set his hands down on the smoldering table. No heat flickered from the flames that covered the table, no crackle or smoke, but it was still difficult to overcome his instincts.

Lei had no such trouble. She set her elbows on the table and gazed into the silvery flames. She looked over at him, and there was sorrow in her eyes. "I remember my first lessons with eternal fire," she said, her voice distant. "My mother had woven the flame into the lining of a small wooden casket. I used to keep it by my bed, so I always had light at my side when the wind rose and the shadows seemed threatening . . ." Her voice drifted off.

Daine wanted to let her reminisce, to work through her emotions and her loss, but there simply wasn't time. "Lei . . ."

Her misty eyes cleared, and she looked up at him. "Yes?"

"We need information. We don't have enough money for bribes, and with Jode busy . . . well, you know I'm not a master of diplomacy."

"True enough."

"Thanks. Anyhow, without Jode, you'd better prepare a charmer."

Lei nodded. She pulled a small shard of quartz from her belt pouch and began to polish it with a piece of fox's fur, whispering quietly.

As Lei wove an enchantment into the stone, Daine examined the common room. A number of people played games of chance, but these appeared to be friendly contests, and from the stream of people moving to and fro, Daine gathered that there was a formal gaming hall farther in the building. The patrons of the King came from all races and nations. Glancing around the room Daine could see a gnome on a tall stool playing a round of sundown with an elderly man and a burly half-orc. A pair of shifters were dicing against a trio of Valenar elves. An elf woman cried out in triumph as she made a difficult roll, and one of her opponents bared long fangs in a frustrated snarl.

Daine's wandering gaze finally fixed on a woman who had just emerged from the inner hall. She was wrapped in a dark, flowing cloak, and only her face was visible. Even that was shadowed under a voluminous hood. What caught Daine's attention were her eyes—large and green, glowing like emeralds in the magical firelight. She held his gaze for a long moment, a hint of a smile playing over her lips. Then she looked away, and the spell was broken. She knelt and spoke to the innkeeper, then disappeared out the front door.

A moment later Kela arrived at their table, carrying their drinks. Lei was absorbed in her work and didn't look up when the mug of steaming tal was placed before her. Daine swirled the sludgy korluaat about in the tankard.

"What do we owe you?" he said.

"It's already been taken care of," the tiny innkeeper said.

"By . . . ?"

"The lady who just left. I saw you looking at her. I'm afraid I don't know her name. Kalashtar, I think."

Kalashtar. Daine had heard of the kalashtar but had never actually met one before. Tales said the kalashtar were possessed, that their ancestors were humans who had sold their bodies to ghosts or spirits from another plane. They were supposed to have unnatural powers over mortal minds. Of course, these same storytellers claimed House Cannith made the warforged by binding the spirits of the dead into shells of wood and metal, and that the dragonmarked houses had actual dragons hidden in their basements. Still, he could see how such stories could arise. Her gaze had been hypnotic. But she was gone, and it was a mystery for another day.

"If the korluaat is free, I've got a few crowns to spare," Daine said, tossing a coin in the air. "Perhaps you could help me do something about that."

"We aim to please, my lord," Kela said with a smile. "What's your pleasure?"

"I'm new to Sharn, and I'm intrigued by these races. 'Wind-chases,' is that right?"

"Indeed. If this is your first time to Sharn, I assure you after you've seen a windchase, then chariots, horses, and hounds will hold no interest."

"Well, I'm looking for a mentor, someone who can tell me how the game is played, who to keep an eye on, who's won in the past. I like to know what I'm getting into before I take risks. Anyone around who might help me with that?"

Kela nodded. "I expect that Dek will be happy to help you, for a few crowns. I'll see if he's free."

Daine tossed her a coin. She deftly caught it and threw it back to him.

"Save it for the games," she said with a smile, before disappearing into the crowd.

❦ ❦ ❦ ❦ ❦ ❦ ❦

A few minutes later, Daine approached them and sat down. Or so it seemed. "I hear you're interested in the races?" the new-comer said. While his face was a perfect mirror of Daine's, his voice was too high and he was dressed in loose brown clothing.

A changeling. Daine hated changelings.

"That's right," he said, placing a few crowns on the table. "But I've never liked talking to myself."

His twin passed a hand over the coins, and they vanished. "My apologies. Some people don't like to see their own faces." The pigment slowly ran out of his skin, and a white film spread across his eyes. His hair grew out, becoming fair and wispy. His facial features seemed to melt away, leaving only a hint of nose and lips. "It's the scar, isn't it? You're not comfortable with it yet?"

"Let's stick to the games," Daine said.

"Touchy. So why don't you tell me what you want to know, and we'll see what it's worth?"

Daine caught Lei's eye and blinked twice. She pulled out the polished quartz shard. "We don't have much to offer," she said shyly, "but we do have this." She held the stone out toward the changeling, and as he reached for it she muttered a swift triggering incantation. Patterns of light and mist seemed to swirl about in the depths of the stone. With some effort, Daine pulled his eyes away.

It was a calculated risk. If the charmer worked, Dek would think of Lei as an old friend. But if it failed and he realized what happened . . . at the very least, they'd be thrown out of the King of Fire. And changelings were known for their slippery minds. But they didn't have money to spare, and Daine needed to be able to trust the information they received.

The light faded. Lei left the stone on the table. Slowly, Dek picked up the crystal shard. He seemed slightly dazed. Lei caught Daine's eye and nodded slightly.

"I know it's not much, Dek, but I wanted you to have it," Lei said, putting her hand on that of the changeling. "Something to remember me by."

"Thank you," Dek said, and his voice was suddenly a mirror of hers. A swirl of coppery color ran through his hair, then faded away. "What . . . what was it you wanted to know again? I'm afraid I blacked out for a moment."

Lei asked questions about the aerial races of Sharn. Dek was only too happy to help his new best friend, and he told them all about the different sports—skyblade jousts, the windchasing routes that wound through the maze of spires, and the Race of Eight Winds, an ancient tradition dating back to the early days of Sharn.

"The race is incredibly important to the people of this tower," Dek explained. "Each district is associated with one of the eight beasts that can compete in the race. As the race draws near, you'll see the inhabitants of each district wearing the colors of their beast or showing their allegiance in other ways. There are feasts and games for weeks before and after the race. Of course, tempers grow high. There are long feuds based on past performance, and occasionally it turns into violence."

"I don't understand," Lei said. "How could a griffon possibly compete in a race against a hippogriff? The Hippogriff is far faster."

"There's more to the Race of Eight Winds than speed," Dek

explained. "The rider is allowed to carry a small crossbow and a quiver of quarrels coated with a weak venom—not enough to kill a creature, but strong enough to slow it down. And the beasts are allowed to use claw, tooth and beak. I've never seen the Griffon win the race, but one or two of the other contestants usually fall prey to its claws. The people of Precarious don't expect to win. They just want to see who the Griffon will take down. But while it was before my time, the Griffon *has* won the race before, and I'm sure it will again. The Windguard—the handlers, racers, and organizers—spend the time between races negotiating and scheming. The Griffon's services are bought with future favors, and eventually those all come due."

"But the faster beasts usually win?"

"Well, yes. It's often really a race between the Pegasus and the Hippogriff, with all the rest following in a pack. But I've seen some interesting things before. Many of the racing beasts are intelligent, after all. I've heard a rumor that the current owl is studying magic to enhance her speed with wizardry, though that seems a bit farfetched. The Gargoyle is a recent addition, replacing the bat. He's a surprisingly tricky beast, and the goblins love him. I wouldn't be surprised if he pulls it off one of these years."

"Lei," Daine whispered, "can we get to the point? We've got a dinner appointment."

She nodded. "This is fascinating information, Dek, but I was wondering if you could tell me about one of the riders—a human named Rasial Tann, who used to race with the Hippogriff?"

Dek thought for a moment, then his face brightened—literally. "Yes! Rasial! I remember him now. He started out doing the lesser windchases, aerial jousts in the Hollow Tower and the like. His first time in the Race of Eight winds was 991, I think, and he won the year after that. One of the finest hippogriff riders I've seen, and a good man by all accounts. Gold Wing guard, you know. Terrible loss for the Hippogriff. Ralus, their new rider, isn't nearly as good."

"New rider? What happened to Rasial?"

"Well, he had a series of accidents, the first of which cost him victory in the Race of Eight Winds. After the third death, he left for good."

"Death?"

"During the last race, it seemed that Rasial might bring home a second victory for the Hippogriff. He was neck to wing with the Pegasus rider, and closing in on the Hollow Tower. Then his mount died. Just like that. Rasial was almost killed. He broke free from the saddle with just enough time to use his token of the winds, but another moment and he would have been nothing but a stain."

"How did the Hippogriff die? Was it poison?"

"Well, the poisons used in the race are very weak. The goal is to give the rider a chance to slow down his enemies, not to kill them outright. Rasial's mount may have been hit—by the Gargoyle, I think—but the crossbow and bolts are presented to the racing authorities at the start of the game, and the riders are carefully searched for contraband before the race. Of course, there wasn't enough left of the body to do any sort of testing. But from what I've heard, according to Rasial his mount simply died without warning. Healthy one moment, dead the next."

Lei nodded.

"Even though no one knew exactly what happened, it seemed clear enough that it was the work of one of the other seven beasts, and the Hippogriff Windguard was investigating it. Then, a week later, Rasial lost another mount—this time during the Kelsa Chase, a race with far lower stakes. The exact same thing, only this time he couldn't get free in time. Luckily, it was a low altitude race, but he still broke his leg."

Daine noticed a motion near the wall. There was a rat in the shadows, watching him. Daine was surprised to see rats in a place as stylish as the King of Fire. There was a pair of dice on the table, and he slipped one into his palm. With a quick motion he threw the die at the rat, striking it dead center. The rodent squeaked and scampered out of sight. Smiling, Daine turned his attention back to the conversation.

"Were any of Rasial's opponents in this Kelsa race people who had ridden against him in Eight Winds?" Lei asked.

"Just one. Mulg Oranon, a hawk rider. But even the Hippogriff Windguard couldn't find anything suspicious."

"What happened next?"

"Rasial recovered from the injury, but he never returned to the races. There were rumors, but . . . well, it's better not to say."

Lei rubbed his hand. "Oh, come now, Dek. You know you can trust me."

"They say he got involved with the Tarkanans, which doesn't make any sense. He was a Gold Wing! But that's what I heard."

"Tarkanans?" Lei asked.

"A group of thieves and assassins. I don't know much about them and I don't want to. If you want someone dead by morning, the Tarkanans can make it happen. What Rasial could possibly have in common with those cutthroats, I couldn't tell you. As far as I know, he never killed anyone, even in his tenure with the Watch. But last I heard, he'd been seen in their company."

"Where could we find these Tarkanans, Dek?"

"Look. As a friend, I don't know what your interest is here, but you don't want to cross the Tarkanans. Whatever it is, just let it go."

"Don't worry, Dek. We'll be all right. Where can we find them?"

Dek shivered, and for a moment his features shook like jelly. "I don't know. Honest I don't. I follow the races. I'm not a thug. I've heard . . . I've heard they're somewhere in Dragon Towers, in the Central Plateau. But it's not worth it. There are some things better left alone."

"That's enough," Daine said, standing up. "We need to get moving, and we've got something to work with."

"Thank you so much, Dek," Lei said, with a brilliant smile. "I knew I could rely on you. If we ever can afford to put money on one of the races, we'll certainly come to you."

"Oh, my pleasure," Dek said. "Anything for a friend. Here, I suppose you'd better take these back." He tossed Daine the coins he'd been given earlier and smiled. "I'll see you around."

CHAPTER 15

BRELAND
SHARN
Dravago 27, 996 YK

Watching Daine and Lei enter the inn, Pierce clung to the scant shadows of the alley, his mithral plating blending into the darkness. He had been built to serve as a scout and skirmisher, and a talent for stealth had been forged into his soul. He held his great bow in one hand, an arrow at the ready. There was no sign of danger, but Pierce had been a soldier since the day he was born, and he never lowered his guard.

The city felt strange and unnatural to Pierce. He was twenty-eight years old, and he had spent his entire life on the battlefields of Cyre. Even after Cyre was destroyed, exploring the Mournland was much like fighting a war. Horrors far more dangerous than any Brelish soldier filled the devastated land. It was hard for him to conceive of a life without conflict, to look at the bustling street without evaluating the threat posed by each traveler. A part of him yearned for a sudden attack, an ambush, something that would justify his vigilance.

"Do you miss war so much?"

The voice was soft and warm, as was the hand that touched his shoulder.

During the siege of Felmar Valley, the Valenar elves had played games with the Cyran defenders, killing sentries and leaving the corpses standing at their posts. After a time, Pierce began playing a game of his own—making himself an inviting target, then bringing down any elf who thought he could approach undetected. He'd caught five would-be assassins this way, though he had a few arrow-marks from elves who'd wisely chosen not to play his game. But no one had ever come close enough to touch him without his noticing. Until now.

It was not in Pierce's nature to fear for his life. He was made to fight, and if he died in battle he would know that he had served his purpose. Rather than fear, he felt a deep sense of disappointment at his failure to spot this potential threat—and the need to regain the upper hand as quickly as possible. He turned to face the stranger and took a long step back, trying to get enough room to draw back his bow.

But even as he stepped away, the stranger moved forward, perfectly matching his stride. She wore a dark cloak with a deep hood, and she moved as silently and smoothly as a shadow, remaining inches from his chest.

Pierce was at a loss. This woman had taken no directly hostile action, and the folds of the cloak suggested her hands were empty. He was larger and presumably stronger than her. Should he drop the bow and lash out with a steel fist? Or was this some sort of misunderstanding?

"I suppose in battle the answers are always clear," she said.

Her voice was low and musical. Had Pierce been made from flesh and blood, it might have sent a shiver down his spine. As it was, he merely noted the clarity and enunciation, the unknown accent that suggested a homeland beyond the Five Nations.

"If you mean me no harm, back away slowly."

The woman took a few steps back. "My apologies," she said.

She looked up to meet his gaze, and her hood fell back far enough to reveal her pale skin and finely sculpted features. Green eyes glowed within a halo of black hair, and her lips twisted with the slightest hint of a smile. To Pierce's eyes she seemed human, though it was hard to tell for certain, with the shadows and the hood.

"I have little experience with your kind," she said. "I didn't mean to startle you."

"I was not startled," Pierce replied.

The stranger's smile widened ever so slightly, and Pierce

wondered why he felt the need to defend himself. He set down the bow and pulled his flail off of his back. The woman was unarmed, but still he felt the need to be prepared for battle.

"You didn't answer my question." If she felt threatened by the flail, she didn't show it.

"What do you want with me?" Pierce was used to dealing with allies and enemies. Abstract conversation was not something he'd had much time for on the battlefield. He'd listened to the lady and the captain argue with one another, and he enjoyed the healer's wordplay, but he wasn't used to being the target of such things.

"The answer to a question, nothing more. Do you have a place in a world without war?" Her eyes flickered down to encompass the flail. "Or are you just a weapon, worthless when there is no blood to be spilled?"

Pierce stared at her, trying to find the words to answer. It was not a new question. In fact, it was what he'd been asking himself before the stranger showed up. Did she know that?

Even as he searched for an answer, he caught the glimpse of motion in his peripheral vision, two figures stepping into the alley. The possible threat was a welcome release from the question, and he relaxed and let his reflexes take over, stepping back against the wall and setting the chain of his flail in motion. But there was no threat. Just Captain Daine and Lady Lei, exiting the tavern.

Captain Daine eyed the spinning flail, glanced at the bow on the ground, and his hand went to the hilt of his sword. "What's wrong?"

Pierce let the flail come to a stop. "Nothing, Captain. A misunderstanding. I was just . . ." He glanced toward the stranger, but she was nowhere to be seen. If he'd had eyelids, Pierce would have blinked in surprise. She had slipped away as smoothly as she had appeared. ". . . thinking," he finished.

The captain shrugged. "Let's get moving then. I'll fill you in along the way."

Pierce nodded. He returned his flail to its harness and picked up his bow, studying the empty alley. He listened to Daine's words, but his thoughts were far away.

The trip to the tavern had done one thing. It had taken Lei's mind off of her own misfortune. Lei was full of questions as the trio headed back to High Walls, while Pierce was, if anything, quieter than usual.

"Do you suppose these Tarkanans could have killed his hippogriffs? Maybe they'd been hired by one of these opposing beast groups, and he was trying to find out who was behind it."

"Possibly," Daine said. "That, or he knew who killed his mounts and thought that the Tarkanans could help him get revenge on the killers. I suppose that finding the Tarkanans is the next step."

"It sounds dangerous."

"This from the woman who fought three hundred warforged?"

"Do you have an army I don't know about?"

"Good point. Still, there's something that's bothering me."

"What's that?" Lei said. She was momentarily distracted by a small tower up the street. It appeared to be formed from overlapping steel plates.

"Alina implied that Rasial served her as a smuggler, bringing in contraband through the air. So if he was still flying, if he was still in Sharn, why'd he quit racing?"

"Perhaps he was still trying to find out who sabotaged his

earlier bouts," Lei said. "He didn't dare return until he'd identified his foe."

"It's possible," Daine said. "But . . . he was a member of the Sharn Watch! Why would he turn to a group of assassins instead of the forces of the law? Why would they have anything to do with him?"

"I don't know."

They walked a ways in silence, eventually reaching the lift. Three other people boarded the lift with them. Beggars by the look, dressed in worn cloaks and tatters. There was a muscular half-orc, a tall, lean man, and a young halfling woman. As the lift began to fall, something about the halfling caught Daine's eye. She was covered with dirt, and her cloak was torn wool. At a glance, she seemed like any of the hundreds of beggars Daine had seen over the years. But as he watched, a rat came crawling out of the folds of her cloak and climbed up toward her face. It chittered and squeaked, and she whispered quietly to it. Daine remembered the rat he'd seen in the King of Fire, and a chill ran down his spine.

Looking up, Daine saw that the thin man had moved closer to him. Beneath the hood of his cloak, the stranger's face was horribly disfigured, scarred by pustules and the ravages of disease. His robes carried a sweet odor of rot and decay.

He looked down at Daine and spoke in a deep, rasping voice, "You have information I require, Mourner."

The stranger seemed quite confident, considering that both he and his companions were completely unarmed. Daine put his hand on the hilt of his sword, making the motion as obvious as possible.

"And you are?"

"I am Bal of the House of Tarkanan, and you will tell me what I wish to know. Or you will not leave this lift alive."

"I guess that takes care of our next step," said Lei.

"Is this going to happen every time we get on a lift?" Daine said. "Because I may start taking the stairs." He drew his sword but kept the point to the side. "Now. Shall we start this conversation again?"

"I believe that we shall." Bal spun forward in a blur of

motion. Before Daine even realized what was happening, the rotting man smashed Daine's hand with a powerful kick. The sword went spinning through the air and came to a halt against the railing. Bal drew his cracked lips back from decaying teeth. "Shall we begin?"

Daine nodded. He cursed himself for underestimating his foe . . . but he could see the same overconfidence in Bal. "All right. Let's see if we can't shed some *light* on things."

Lei slipped her hand into her belt pouch, obviously catching Daine's signal. She pulled a golden sphere from her pouch and flung it between the halfling and the half-orc. Both cried out as a cloud of blinding golden particles engulfed them.

Pierce drew his long flail from his back. As he shook the chain free from the haft, he sent Daine's sword spinning across the lift with a well-placed kick. Daine knelt and caught the sword with his right hand, drawing his dagger with his left. He rose to his feet and leveled his sword at the chest of his foe.

"All right," said Daine. "Let's talk."

Bal came forward again, moving with eerie speed and grace. But this time Daine was prepared. He ducked out of the way and drew a long, shallow cut along his enemy's shin.

"You have no idea what you are dealing with," Bal hissed through gritted teeth. Slipping past Daine's guard as if he were a ghost, the rotting man pressed the palm of his right hand against Daine's throat.

Suddenly ice was flowing through Daine's blood. Chills ran along every nerve, and it was all that he could do to stay on his feet. He made a weak thrust, but Bal slipped under the blow. The next thing Daine knew, he was on the floor of the lift with Bal standing above him. The pain grew worse. He could see Pierce standing over the fallen body of the half-orc, with Lei and the rat girl beyond.

"Hold!" Bal called out, in a voice like a winter wind. "If I touch your friend again, he will die."

Lei froze. Pierce kept the chain of his flail spinning, forming a singing web of steel, but he did not strike. "Should I shatter your comrade's head," he said, "I suspect that he will also die." His voice was calm and collected.

There was a moment of tension that seemed to last for an eternity . . . and then Bal laughed, a long, dry rasp. "True enough." He stepped back. "I apologize for my uncalled-for aggression. Perhaps we can help each other."

Behind him, the half-orc moaned and brought a hand to his head.

Daine rose to his feet. He was dizzy and nauseous, but the pain seemed to be subsiding. "What do you want?" he growled.

"We are looking for Rasial. Zae"—he nodded toward the halfling, who was rubbing her eyes and glaring at Lei—"heard you mention him. I've never seen you before. How do you know him?"

The lift was approaching the ground. "I think I'd like to hear your story before I say much more. I know an inn not far from here. Can I offer you a cup of tal?"

Bal glanced at his comrades, the rat girl huddled in the corner and the warrior stretched out on the floor. "Perhaps that would be for the best."

❂ ❂ ❂ ◉ ❂ ❂ ❂

The half-orc, whom Bal called Korlan, split off from the group after they arrived in High Walls; apparently he had a personal errand to attend to. Zae and Bal accompanied the trio to the Manticore. The other patrons quickly dispersed once Bal entered the common room, though Daine couldn't say whether it was due to a sinister reputation or simply his diseased appearance. The innkeeper grumbled, but once Daine gave her a few crowns she quickly returned with a pot of steaming tal.

Little Zae ducked under a table and watched them. Two rats emerged from the folds of her cloak, and their movements mirrored her own.

"Chew this," Bal said, handing Daine a dried, leathery leaf. "It will help with the symptoms."

Daine considered the leaf and finally began to chew. The worst it could do was kill him, and with the way he was feeling that might be a relief. Though he hadn't gotten any worse since they'd left the lift, he was still feeling dizzy and weak.

"What did you do to me?" he asked.

Bal took a slow sip of tal, watching Daine closely. "The chilling touch is my inheritance. It is a gift that I share with Rasial Tarkanan."

"Tarkanan . . ." Lei breathed in sharply. "You're aberrants!" She pushed her chair back from the table.

"I am blessed, child of Cannith," Bal said. His voice was level, but his eyes glittered. "Shall we compare the power of our gifts?"

Zae giggled in the shadows of the table, her rats chittering beside her.

"Lei!" Daine barked. "Calm down! What are you talking about?"

Lei took a deep breath and pulled her chair back up to the table. "What do you know about the War of the Mark?"

Daine shrugged.

"Halas Tarkanan was the mightiest of the aberrant lords. When the pure lines sought to cleanse the darkness, it was Tarkanan who organized those who bore aberrant marks into an army."

Bal showed his teeth. " 'Cleanse the darkness.' A pleasant way to talk about murder."

Lei glared at him, and for a moment Daine thought she was about to draw a weapon. "The aberrant marks are dangerous to body and soul! Fire, darkness, death . . . these are not forces the living were meant to channel!"

"And yet we do. You fear what you cannot control. You build. I destroy."

"Enough!" said Daine. The pieces were beginning to come together. "You said we could help each other, Bal. What is it you want?"

"Rasial is one of us, and he's missing. He returned to the city two days ago, but in that time he hasn't been seen. We are concerned that he has placed himself in danger, and we wish to find him before he is harmed."

Daine wished Jode was around. Reading faces wasn't his specialty. "Why do you think he'd be in danger?"

"Rasial was working in the shadows. We know he wasn't telling us about some of his activities. We have our suspicions.

Which leads me to ask: Why are *you* looking for him?"

"We were hired by the Windguard of Daggerwatch. They want him back for the upcoming race, and no one knows where he went." Daine had spent the last ten minutes coming up with this story, and he cursed Jode for not being around. Lying was not something Daine did well.

"Daggerwatch?" Bal considered this. "So. The guardsmen of Daggerwatch hired a group of Mourners to do their work?"

Damn! Daine thought. If only they'd had time to buy new clothes. Lei spoke before he could answer. "I believe they gave us the job on my account," she said. "I may be from . . . the Mournland, but I am of Cannith first and foremost. And I am of an age to be betrothed. I believe the commander hoped to win my favor by offering this work to my friends. And to be honest, I believe that he enjoys ordering a former Cyran captain about like a paid dog."

Bal nodded slowly. "I suppose he might, at that. But Rasial won't be coming back to your employers. Rasial Tann is dead. He is Rasial Tarkanan now, and his place is with us."

"I understand," Daine said. "But surely you understand that the longer we continue the investigation, the longer we get paid. Perhaps we can help you. We're new in the city, and we could use a few friends. If we discover any more information, I'd be willing to pass it along—for the proper considerations."

There was a pause as Bal drank the last of his tal. Finally he set the mug down. "Very well, Mourner. Prove your worth. You can contact me through the Illian Apothecary in Dragon Towers."

He pushed back his chair and stood up. Beneath her table, Zae was carrying on a quiet, animated discussion with two rats and a mouse. In unison, the rodents disappeared into the folds of her cloak.

"Before you go," said Daine, "is there anything you can tell us that could help us find him?"

Bal paused. "I believe he was dealing with someone in this district. But I don't know who." He nodded to Zae, and they moved for the door. "Perhaps we'll meet again, Mourner. Next time, I'd think carefully before you draw your weapon."

Daine stared at him, face grim. "Next time, surprise won't be on your side."

The rotting man held his gaze for a moment then left without a word.

Dassi the innkeeper finally broke the long silence that followed. "Good to see the back of that one, General. I'm sure you saw worse in your day, but I certainly didn't like the looks of him. Why don't I get you another cup of tal, and you can tell us the story about the Olaran orphanage again?"

Daine nodded and smiled, though inside he was cursing all lying halflings.

❃ ❃ ❃ ❃ ❃ ❃ ❃

It was not long before Jode returned. The four retired to their room, and Daine recounted the events of the last two hours.

"Aberrant dragonmarks . . . interesting," Jode said, rubbing his own dragonmark thoughtfully.

"Disturbing," Lei said.

"There's one thing I don't understand about this," Daine said. "I've heard of aberrant dragonmarks before. But in the stories I've heard, the people with these black marks sour milk or scare dogs—that sort of thing. Killing with a touch is a far cry from making paint peel. How come I haven't heard about this before?"

"Most of the aberrants were wiped out over a thousand years ago," said Lei. "These days, they usually only appear when two people from different dragonmarked houses have a child together. Instead of possessing the mark of either house, the child may develop a warped, damaged mark—usually with a weak power or no power at all. The common theory is that the damaged mark reflects damage to the soul of the bearer, and those who bear aberrant marks often go mad, or so I've heard. That's why the dragonmarked houses aren't supposed to mingle their blood."

"Killing with a touch doesn't strike me as a weak power."

"I met a man with an aberrant mark once," Jode interjected.

"He had a chilling touch, much as you described. An unpleasant fellow, no question there. But I wouldn't think he'd have been able to take you down, Daine."

"I know." Lei paused and thought for a moment. "There is one other possibility . . . but it's just a legend."

Daine shrugged. "Tell me a story, then."

"The War of the Mark established the twelve dragonmarked houses that exist today. Supposedly, the houses came together to put an end to aberrant marks—to prevent crossbreeding and to destroy those already tainted by the darkness."

"So I've gathered."

"All we have to work with now is legend and hearsay. But according to the tales, the aberrant dragonmarks possessed by Lord Tarkanan and his allies were not weak, damaged marks. They could spread plagues, call fire from the sky, break the earth with tremors, and far worse. But the human mind and body were not made to channel these dark powers, and the marks drove their bearers to madness or caused them to grow ill and die."

"Which would explain the walking boil and the girl who spends more time talking to rats than people."

"It's just a theory." Lei paused, considering. "I've also heard of a substance called dragon's blood, which increases the power of a dragonmark for a brief period of time. I imagine it would work on an aberrant mark just as it would on a true mark."

"And don't forget Korlev," Jode said, referring to a sorcerer who had served with them for a few months during the war.

While he had no dragonmark, Korlev had learned to manipulate mystical energy to produce a wide range of effects. He claimed to be one of the "teeth of Eberron" and had been quite useful before the Valenar killed him.

Daine shook his head. "Fine. Maybe they're drug-addled aberrations. Maybe they're sorcerers. So just don't let them touch you. Let's focus on Rasial. Did you find anything useful, Jode?"

"Rasial was well liked. Honest, by all accounts. Had a real knack for working with hippogriffs, and a lot of friends in the local enclave of House Vadalis. Racing and flying were both passions of his. All in all, he was handsome, talented, popular—a rising star. Then he suffered those two accidents. A week later, he vanished. No one has seen him since."

"Hmm."

"With that said, there were a few guards who weren't telling the whole truth—and not the nicest bunch. Rasial may have been honest to begin with, but I think he's been dealing with these Tarkanans recently—probably to help hide his smuggling activities."

Daine nodded. "So the real question is why. Why does a successful, honest man throw away everything he has and turn to the other side of the law?"

"Maybe he didn't have a choice," Lei said. The others turned and looked at her. "Think about it, Jode. Dragonmarks . . . pure dragonmarks . . . don't appear at birth. They appear late in life, usually triggered by stress. If Rasial really had this chilling touch, what if it first manifested during the Race of Eight Winds? What if *he* killed his mount?"

Jode nodded. "He gets excited during the races, his mount dies . . . that would be a dilemma."

"He could have joined the Tarkanans to learn about his mark."

"And from the sound of it," Daine said, "once you sign up, you're in for life. But there are still a few loose ends. I don't think the Tarkanans know about the connection between Rasial and Alina, and we'd better keep it that way. But what was Rasial doing for Alina? Why did he betray her, and who is he dealing with now? What is he hiding from the Tarkanans? And where is he?"

"All good questions," Jode said. "But as I recall, we're supposed to meet Councilor Teral for dinner at the seventh bell."

"And?" Daine said.

Outside, the seventh bell rang. Jode smiled. "Shall we be off to dinner, Lord Daine?"

INTERLUDE

Korlan hated Sharn. He was a child of the deep swamps, and he missed the tranquility of his homeland—the nights spent alone with the sounds of shadowtoads, water, crickets, the wind in the rushes . . .

The towers of Sharn were unnatural, and the constant babble of voices was a constant assault on his ears. He hated the mobs of people; eyes everywhere he looked, watching him, shouting and squabbling, filling the air with noise and stench.

But the marshes were no longer his home. When he was ten, the mark had appeared, the fire flowed in his blood, threatening to consume his spirit if he did not grant it a release. In a moment of madness, he had killed his brother with a gout of fire that burst forth from his hands. That was all it took. He was driven from the Marches, tainted and touched by the Deep Wyrm, and if he returned to his family they would do their best to kill him. For a time he had wandered, feverish and dazed, through the western plains—and then the Tarkanans had found him and taught him to control his gift. He hated Sharn, but it was the home of his true family. It was the only place he would ever belong.

Korlan had the pink skin of a Brelander, but his muscular physique and fiery temper hinted at his inhuman ancestry, and oversized canine teeth protruded from his lips when he was angry. Today, his fangs were in full view. Bal had said that intimidation would be the best approach, and Korlan wanted to get this over with quickly, so he could return to his quiet room in Dragon Towers.

There was a guard in front of the tentflap. But Korlan had grown up hunting duskwisps, and it was a simple matter to slip through the shadows without being seen. A single powerful blow was all it took to send the guard to the ground in a crumpled heap.

His target was already waiting for him when he stepped inside the tent. The man appeared to be unarmed, but Korlan was well aware of how deceiving appearances could be. Korlan concentrated, and there was a moment of terrible pain as the blood in his veins burned with a terrible heat. He focused the pain on his palm, and flames flickered around his fingers.

"I am here for Rasial Tarkanan," Korlan said, glaring down at his enemy. "You will tell me where he is, and you will tell me what dealings you have had with him."

"I'm afraid I have other plans."

It was difficult to read the man's expression. His face was a horrid mask of raw, wet muscle, and his eyes were sunk deep within his sockets. If he was afraid of Korlan and the flames, he did not show it.

"It wasn't a request," Korlan said.

He couldn't unleash the full force of his burning hands without setting the tent alight, but he'd found that his fiery touch had a way of changing opinions, and he reached for the flayed man's shoulder.

The man moved with astonishing speed, darting down and slamming into Korlan. He was unnaturally strong for his size, and Korlan was thrown back against the side of the tent. Snarling, he rose to his feet, intending to release the full fire he held within. Bal had wanted answers, but there would be other sources.

But as he raised his burning hands, there was a blur before him. His enemy's tongue snapped out of his mouth, stretching across the space between them. Pain stabbed his throat, and as the tongue withdrew Korlan saw a vicious barb protruding from the tip. A cold chill spread across his body, numbing his nerves and extinguishing the flames. His legs refused to respond to his brain, and he fell. Within seconds he was completely paralyzed, unable to do anything but watch as his foe came toward him.

"I am pleased to see that Rasial's former friends are looking for him," the skinless man said. Korlan could not even cringe as the man produced a long knife. With one smooth motion the stranger cut open Korlan's jerkin, revealing his torso and the aberrant mark that covered his left breast. "Lovely."

The man smiled, revealing a mouth filled with bloody teeth. He stepped out of Korlan's field of vision. Korlan heard others enter the tent, but he couldn't turn his head to look.

"Take him below," the man said. He came back into view, leering at Korlan with his ruined face. "I'm afraid I have business elsewhere, but my associates will see that you are reunited with young Rasial. I thank you for your contribution to our cause."

CHAPTER 17

BRELAND
SHARN
Dravago 27, 996 YK

In the early days of Sharn, Togran Square had been a center for commerce. The tents of merchants from across Khorvaire and more exotic lands had filled the open plaza. The plaza was still filled with tents, but the richly decorated cloth had been replaced by patched oilskin. There were hundreds of Cyran refugees in the city, and many of them lived in this makeshift village. After the destruction of Cyre, Breland was the only nation that agreed to provide shelter to the refugees, and many Cyrans had made the long journey south in hopes of reconnecting with relatives that had been established in Sharn before the war. They'd arrived to find that Cyrans and other non-Brelish citizens had been relocated to the ghetto of High Walls and stripped of their livelihood. Like Daine, most of these refugees arrived in Sharn with only the clothes on their backs. In this tent town, nobles and peasants were all alike.

Dozens of people studied Daine as he made his way to the large black tent in the center of the square. Some nodded respectfully, but an equal number seemed sullen or even resentful.

"Not what I'd call a hero's welcome," Jode observed.

"Do you see any heroes?" Daine looked into the eyes of the angry refugees and wondered where they had been three years ago, what war had stolen from each of them. "We lost."

Jode wore his one piece of festive attire—a jaunty burgundy flat cap, embroidered with a spiderweb pattern portrayed in a rainbow of colors. In addition to adding a touch of flair to his drab military leather, the cap hid his dragonmark from view.

"It looks like all the good spaces have been taken," he said, studying the tents. "I was hoping to get a good view of one of the rubbish fires when we set up a tent of our own."

Jode was trying to make light of the situation, but he had a point. Unless they completed the job for Alina, they might be living in here in a week.

"If we must, we can pawn something else," Daine said. His dagger, Lei's pack . . . they had a few valuable items left, even if Daine hated the idea of putting these treasures at risk.

"You have to wonder, though," said Jode, "if we were to buy a tent of our own, what's to stop us from getting a black one? And if we did get a black tent, Councilor Teral couldn't tell people to come to the black tent. Do you think he'd do something about it?"

As it turned out, Teral's tent was difficult to miss. Color aside, it towered over the surrounding tents, and the flag of Cyre was flying from the central post. A squat, balding dwarf stood by the entrance. He bowed as they approached and opened the flap.

"Teral is expecting you," he said.

Cloth walls divided the interior into rooms. The entry chamber seemed to double as a dining hall and servants' quarters, and tattered bedrolls were stacked against the walls. A low, round table dominated the center of the room, and six people were already seated on the floor around it—Teral, an old half-elven woman with a child, two young men who appeared to be identical twins, and a woman in her thirties who wore a patch over one eye.

Councilor Teral rose to his feet and slowly made his way around the table, leaning on a gnarled cane.

"Ah, Captain Daine! You are welcome in my house."

Age and injury had both taken their toll on the former councilor. He favored his right foot, and the tip of a large, puckered scar could be seen at the left side of his throat. Despite these infirmities, he moved with calm confidence, and his voice was warm and soothing.

Jode stepped forward and bowed. "Truly, the honor is ours." He smiled as he rose. "But I have to ask. Should you really call it a house? 'Home' is certainly a broad term. I've seen homes that really were just holes in a wall, but somehow I've always thought that it wasn't a house if you could cut through the walls."

Daine reached down and grabbed Jode's collar, yanking him back. "I trust you remember Jode, my healer. As he said, it is we who are honored by the invitation, Lord ir'Soras."

"Please, Daine. Just Teral. I have no estates any more, and we are all equals in this community."

"Except your servants?" Jode said, as a young woman emerged from one of the flaps with bread for the table.

Daine gave him a rap on the head. "My apologies."

"No, it's a simple misunderstanding. There are no servants here. I am an old man, but there are those who respect what I have done for Cyre in the past and my attempts to unify the survivors today. I don't know what I would do without Olalia, Karris, and the others." He smiled at the young woman, who inclined her head and disappeared into the back of the tent. Despite Teral's reassurances, she did not speak, and she avoided eye contact with the visitors.

Teral shuffled back to the table and sat down. "Now please, join us and introduce yourselves. I try to dine with different people each night. Our people are all that remains of our proud nation, and we must come together if we are going to survive."

Daine sat next to Teral, and the other soldiers spread around the table. Pierce stood behind Daine. "I have no need of sustenance," he said. "I prefer to stand."

The other guests glanced at one another. "That's fine," Daine said. Bowing his head slightly, he continued, "This is my comrade Pierce, who served our nation as a scout and skirmisher. I am Daine, and until the tragedy I held the rank of captain in the southern command."

The one-eyed woman sitting to Teral's left smiled at that. She appeared to be slightly older than Daine. Her golden brown hair was tied back in a long ponytail that fell down to her hips. A maze of fine scars ran back to her torn right ear. She was dressed in a brown blouse and breeches, patched with green cloth. "And do you have a family name, Captain Daine?"

"I prefer Daine."

"Who wouldn't?"

Teral nodded toward the woman. "Greykell was also an officer of the southern command. Perhaps you know one another?"

Daine studied the woman. She grinned, and then it came to him. "The laughing wolf?"

"I prefer Greykell," she said, her smile widening. Born to one of the lesser noble families of Cyre, she was one of the few female captains in the southern command and was known for her brilliantly unorthodox strategies, dogged tenacity, and ability to inspire her troops. Some said she showed too much mercy to the enemy, but mercy had always been a Cyran virtue, and the Queen had praised her behavior. She rubbed her chin thoughtfully, studying Daine in turn. "Let's see. Daine. You fought on the Valenar front, didn't you? And what was it I'd heard? Before you joined the guard, you—?"

"Could I get something to drink?" Daine said. "I'm parched."

"My apologies," said Teral. "Olalia!" He clapped his hands and the server returned, carrying a clay pitcher. "I'm afraid we only have water, Captain. My table is a humble one."

"Company matters more than the mead," said Daine.

The serving girl carefully filled his cup with water. She seemed to be trembling slightly.

"Is something wrong?" he asked.

Teral touched the girl's arm and she flinched, almost dropping the pitcher. She made no sound.

"Olalia has suffered grievously these last few years. She lived in the village of Callol. Have you heard of it? It was captured by the Darguuls a little over two years ago, and she and her family were taken. After the disaster struck, she escaped into the ruins of Cyre, and I found her there when I was searching for survivors. It's been hard to tell what was done by the goblins and what happened to her in the Mournland. But I know she had to watch her brothers die, and . . ." He took her hand, but she kept her eyes down on the floor. "Show them, Olalia," he said gently.

Slowly, Olalia looked up. She pulled back her lips, and Jode gasped. Olalia's teeth and gums were sculpted from black marble. The two fair-haired twins sitting across the table laughed, but Greykell glared at them and they fell silent.

"What . . . ?" said Daine.

"Her mouth has been turned to stone," Teral explained. "Teeth, gums, tongue, and much of the muscle. She can open her mouth just enough to drink. Terrible, I know, but fascinating, don't you think?"

"How did this happen?" Daine said.

Olalia looked away and kept her silence. Her skin was even paler than Lei's, and she had short black hair and dark eyes. Strangely, Daine found himself thinking that her teeth matched her eyes.

"I don't know for certain," Teral said. "She can't speak, and as far as I know, she's illiterate. My thought was some sort of torture—cockatrice blood, activated through sorcery and dripped in the mouth. But it could have just been some effect of the Mournland itself."

Daine nodded. They had seen strange and terrible things during the time they spent in Cyre—far worse things than a stone tongue. She'd been lucky. "I'm sorry," he said to her. "But I'm glad that you're alive."

Olalia refused to meet his gaze.

"You may go," Teral said, and she returned to the kitchen without looking back.

There was a moment of silence following Olalia's departure, then Teral broke one of the loaves of bread and passed it around. "You'll see far worse sights here, I'm afraid," he said quietly. "Many of those caught in the wake of the Mourning suffered in some way—either in mind or body." His eyes dipped toward his injured leg and his scar. "I was one of the lucky ones."

"I think the Mourning is the best thing that could have happened to us," said one of the twins.

The two men across the table appeared to be identical. Both were humans, in their late twenties, dressed in identical drab green clothes. Lanky blond hair fell to their shoulders. But what caught Daine's attention were the speaker's eyes. They were the palest shade of blue he'd ever seen, and the man never blinked.

"And *I* think you're an idiot, Monan," Greykell said, striking the man above the nose with a well-placed chunk of bread.

"It's Hugal."

"No, it's not. You're just saying that because you think I can't tell the difference between you."

"Can you?" The man's smirk wavered.

"You'll never know, will you?"

Lei interrupted. "How could you possibly say that the destruction of our homeland has helped us?" She had grown increasingly moody as they'd pushed through the mobs of refugees to reach Teral's tent, and her voice was low and hard.

Monan smiled and made a mock bow while seated. "I was beginning to wonder if you could speak or if you were stone-mouthed too. I am Monan Desal, and this is my brother Hugal."

"I am Lei d—" Lei broke off, catching herself. She had removed her Cannith ring, and her dragonmark was hidden from view.

"Leida? A lovely name."

"Back off," Daine growled.

Lei flushed and glared at Daine before turning back to Monan. "You didn't answer my question. How could you possibly believe that the Mourning was a good thing?"

Monan was distracted by the arrival of the meal—tribex stew seasoned with selas leaves. Teral may have considered the meal humble fare, but after six months of tasteless gruel, it was a true delight. The twins pounced on the stew like starving men, and it was Teral who finally answered Lei's question.

"There are a few people in our community who believe that Cyre deserved its fate," he said.

Daine almost dropped his spoon. *"What?"*

"Hundreds of refugees live in High Walls, and each person has a different opinion. But the root of this argument is that Cyre was weak. Mishann was the rightful heir to the throne of Galifar. If she'd been more aggressive, she might have put down the rebellion before it came to war."

Greykell scowled. "In other words, she should have killed her brothers and sisters instead of trusting them to follow the laws and wishes of their father."

Monan looked up from his stew. "Well, they didn't, did they?"

Hugal laughed.

"Remind me, Monan, what you did during the war?"

Hugal stopped laughing and Monan looked away.

Greykell smirked, then looked back at Daine. "Speaking of the war, how long are you planning to wear that uniform?"

Daine flushed slightly, remembering his conversation with Jode earlier in the day. "Why? Was it so easy for you to abandon it?"

She shrugged. "Wearing a cloak or a pin doesn't change who you are. Cyre is still with us. But the nation is gone. The army is gone. All you're doing by wearing that cloak is angering the people you need as friends, and you should know better. You're encouraging a fight when we need to work for peace."

"This is a point that Greykell and I don't quite see eye to eye on," Teral said. "If we let go of our tradition, our unity, what do we have left?"

"What do we have now?" Greykell was still smiling, but her voice had taken a sharper tone. "Are we going to be the kingdom of tents? You've seen the Mournland. Cyre's not coming back. I don't like it any more then you do, but we should be trying to find good lives for our people here in Breland. We need to get our people out of High Walls, not rejoice in our isolation."

Monan broke in again. No, this time it was Hugal. "We're still a force to be reckoned with. What do you say, Captain? Do you believe the war is over?"

Is he serious? Daine didn't know what to say.

"No offense, Hugal," Jode said, "but how can you say otherwise? Let's be honest. We were losing the war. Even if every surviving Cyran could wield a weapon, you couldn't field an army capable of standing against Breland."

"Who said anything about an army?" Hugal's eyes glittered.

"What then?" Daine said.

"Have you *seen* the Mournland?" Hugal asked.

Greykell rolled her eye. Apparently she'd heard this before.

"I spent months searching for survivors," Daine replied. "Teral, you said you found the serving girl there, didn't you? That's one more survivor than we ever found."

Teral stared down into his water, his eyes distant. "There were more in the south, Daine. I myself was in Metrol when the Mourning came. I'll never forget that night."

"If you've seen it, you should know," Hugal said. "Cyre isn't dead. It's simply changed."

Daine thought back, remembering the corpses that wouldn't decay, the burning mist, the rain of blood. "I . . . suppose."

"We can't go back there," Hugal said. "The land can't support life. We know that. But it is still our homeland. It is our past—and perhaps our path to the future. There is power in Cyre. You've seen the wonders and horrors that lie beyond the mist. What if we can harness that power? How could anyone stand against us then?"

"And what would we do with such a weapon?" Greykell asked. "Olladra's teeth, Hugal! Our ancestors prided themselves on their skill and wisdom. Alone of the five nations, we held true to the dictates of Galifar. Would you spread the Mournland across the entire continent?"

"The throne of Galifar was ours by right. The others betrayed a thousand years of tradition, and our homeland paid the price. Do they deserve any better? How about you, Daine? Do you intend to let Cyre be forgotten?"

Daine considered. Eventually he said, "I will never forgive Wroann for her role in starting the war. I don't know if I can ever look at a Brelish soldier and see anything but an enemy. But Cyre always stood for peace and for wisdom. We fought to preserve our nation, not out of a desire for conquest or revenge. If we turn against that now . . . then we will be the ones who truly destroy Cyre."

There was a long pause, then Teral clapped his hands. "Well said, Captain."

Greykell nodded, and even Monan smiled.

Hugal inclined his head. "Indeed. I hope you'll pardon

my outburst. My brother and I enjoy taking the side of the Traveler, and sometimes I take things too far. Obviously it would be madness to spread the Mournland"—he smiled— "even if we could unlock the mysteries behind it."

Daine studied the twin carefully, looking for any signs of his true thoughts. Had he simply been arguing the side of discord? Greykell was also watching Hugal, and there was nothing but disgust in her eye.

The conversation eventually began again. Teral shared his memories of the court and the last noble queen of Cyre, whom he had advised in the final days of the war. The other two diners were an elderly half-elf named Sallea and her grandson, Solas. They said little during the meal. Sallea occasionally made comments in the language of the Valenar, and Daine concluded that she didn't speak the common tongue of Galifar. The boy was thin and sickly and picked at his stew. At one point he coughed, and Daine saw a spot of blood. Jode saw it too and quickly moved over to look at the boy.

"What is it, Jode?" Daine asked.

"Flameworms. Fairly advanced. It doesn't look good."

Sallea grabbed the child, pulling him away. Greykell frowned, and Teral nodded gravely. "He's not the first, I'm afraid. I know the main wells are clean, but we've lost a number of the children. I'll have Hulda take a look at him. She should be able to ease his pain."

Jode looked at Daine, a question in his eyes. Daine nodded. Jode removed the woolen cap he was wearing, revealing the blue and silver spread across his bald head.

Teral's eyes widened. "Is that . . . ?"

Jode spoke a few words in Sallea's language. Slowly, he pulled the boy away from her embrace and placed his palms on either side of the child's head. The people around the table fell silent, and all eyes were fixed on Jode. The blue of his dragonmark began to glow with an inner light. It only lasted a moment, but it seemed to stretch on far longer.

Jode released the boy's head, and the light from his mark faded. "It's going to take a few days for him to recover," he told Sallea. "But he'll live."

With that, the spell was broken, and everyone began to talk at once. Teral made his voice heard over the din. "Jold, did you just heal that boy?"

Jode nodded. "Yes. And it's *Jode*."

"So you are a member of House Jorasco?"

Jode shrugged. "I bear the Mark of Healing, but I owe allegiance to no house." He said this so easily that it seemed perfectly natural.

Greykell broke in. "This is outstanding! What are your limits? I can think of half a dozen sick children, and then there's Elymer—he's starting to go blind."

Jode looked back to Daine. This was why he'd hidden the mark to begin with, why he'd asked Daine before healing the child.

"I can only draw so much power before I need to rest," Jode said. "Fighting an infection is hard—harder than fighting a battle. You may have had healers in your other units, but most probably used dragonshards to focus their energy. I suppose I can try to treat the children, but I'll only be able to help one each day. And I can't do anything for this Elymer, I'm afraid. I just don't have that kind of power."

"Then I suppose . . ." Greykell tapped her eyepatch.

"I'm afraid not."

"Well, I'm getting used to it. But any sort of help you could provide to the community would be appreciated."

"Absolutely!" Teral echoed. "This is an unprecedented stroke of good fortune. I had no idea. A free dragonmark, right here in our midst!"

Daine glanced over at Lei, but she remained silent.

"And you, Daine?" Greykell pointed at his sword, with the blazing Eye of Deneith emblazoned on the pommel. "Do you carry the Mark of Sentinel?"

Thank you, Captain Grazen, Daine thought. "No," he said. "I lost my sword during our travels, and this is a gift from a friend."

For a time, the conversation turned to the powers and limitations of Jode's dragonmark. Teral was interested in what he could do. Could he restore Olalia's jaw? What sort of parasites could he destroy? Greykell was more interested in the immediate civic applications of his abilities, and Jode agreed to work with the local healer Hulda to try to identify and help those refugees with the most serious problems.

After the meal was done, Sallea thanked Jode again and took her grandson off to bed. One of the twins left—Daine couldn't remember which one it was. Looking across the table, he noticed that Lei and the other twin were still deep in conversation—a little too deep for his tastes.

"Monan," Daine said, "shouldn't you be going now?"

The man laughed—a sound Daine was beginning to hate. "It's Hugal." He put a hand on Lei's shoulder. "And it's been such a lovely conversation."

"We must be going," Daine said. "Lei, Jode . . ."

"One moment," Jode said. "Councilor Teral, if I may ask—you are fairly familiar with the comings and goings in High Walls, yes?"

Teral nodded. "Why do you ask?"

"Have you seen this man, by any chance?" Jode produced one of Alina's sketches, folded to hide the writing. He pushed it to the center of the table, and both Hugal and Teral examined it. "His name is Rasial."

"Is he Cyran?" Teral said, frowning.

"No. Brelish. But he had family in Cyre. One of his cousins served in our unit and died at Keldan Ridge. We just need to deliver a message."

Teral studied the parchment for a moment. "No, I'm afraid I can't help you."

Hugal just shook his head and laughed.

"He does look somewhat familiar," Greykell said. "Are you sure you haven't seen him, Hugal?" The twin shrugged. "Hmm. Perhaps it was Monan, then."

"Well, it was worth a try." Jode picked up the sheet of parchment and stood up. "Shall we, my friends?"

Greykell stood, and without warning she wrapped Daine in a crushing embrace. She had the strength of a bear. "Well met, Daine, Lei! Jode, I'll expect to see you tomorrow."

After he'd caught his breath, Daine nodded. "Good night,

Captain. And thank you again, Lord Teral. Let me know if we can be of service."

"Don't worry, Daine. I certainly shall."

The four soldiers gathered their belongings. The serving girl, Olalia, had emerged to clear the table, and Daine noticed that she was staring at Jode. Her marble teeth glittered in the torchlight, and then she disappeared behind a flap of cloth.

CHAPTER 18

BRELAND
SHARN
Dravago 27, 996 YK

Night had fallen long ago. Shadows stretched across the streets, punctuated by pools of light from the cold fire torches as they made their way back to the Manticore. Pierce had slung his bow across his back and was carrying his long flail. The chain swung slightly as he walked. He found the motion was relaxing, steady, predictable.

"It was nice to see a few friendly faces," Lei said.

"Some a little too friendly, if you ask me," Daine grumbled.

"I'm not so sure about that," Jode said.

"What do you mean?"

"Hugal . . . he'd seen Rasial before. I'm sure of it. I was watching him, and there was a definite reaction."

"Interesting," Daine said. "We'll track him down in the morning. Pierce, are you all right? You didn't say a word at dinner."

Pierce raised his flail, causing the chain to wind around the haft. "There seemed little to say, Captain. Though I wonder at Greykell's words. If she believes that it is a mistake for you to wear your uniform because it is a symbol of the war, what am I to do?" Pierce had been built to serve in the Cyran military, and the symbols of his service were engraved into his torso. "War is my purpose. If the world must forget the war, what place is there for me?"

Even the usually glib Jode had no answer to this.

"Your place is with us," Lei offered.

Pierce inclined his head, acknowledging the thought. But he wasn't so certain. He heard a stranger's words echoing in the back of his mind. *Are you just a weapon, worthless when there is no blood to be spilled?*

They followed the street around a tight curve as it followed the wall of the central tower. Around the bend, six people were spread across the street. In the dim light, they all appeared human, though their features were hidden by ragged cloaks and cowls. The man in the center pulled back his hood. It was Monan—or Hugal. Pierce had noticed that the two had a few unique quirks; Hugal seemed to speak more often and more quickly, and Monan had a tendency to fidget. Given time, he was confident he could distinguish between the two. But at a glance, he wasn't sure which one they were dealing with.

"I suppose we could have that talk now," Daine said.

The six figures rushed forward. Monan brandished a long knife, and one young woman had her hands outstretched like weapons. Pierce saw that her fingers were tipped with long, curved claws.

"Take them alive if you can!" Daine cried.

As Monan closed with Daine, the woman and another stranger charged Pierce. He raised his flail and dropped into combat consciousness, setting aside emotion and thought to rely on the battle instincts that were a part of his being.

Two foes.

A human male.

Middle-aged.

Overweight.

Features twisted in fury, but no visible weapons.

No signs of the mystical tools or components that distinguished an artificer or spellcaster.

That's one.

A human female.

Young.

Athletic.

Claws.

That's two.

Pierce did not question the presence of her talons. He simply evaluated the threat they presented. She was armed, and for the moment, she seemed the greater danger.

The captain had requested that they be taken alive. Pierce's flail was already ready and in hand, and even as the woman leapt forward he swung his weapon in a low arc. Wrapping the chain around her ankles, he gave a mighty pull. She fell back with a snarl, slamming her head against the street. Pierce was moving forward even as she fell, lashing out with the haft of the flail. But even as he struck her across the face, agony lashed across his shoulder.

In a split second he replayed the scene in his mind, reviewing the attack—

As he engaged the young woman, the older man had jerked his head forward and let loose with a stream of bile, a gout of acid that was now eating into the metal plating and composite material of Pierce's shoulder.

Pierce was no creature of flesh and blood. He did not cry out, but he still felt the pain, a terrible burning that warned him of the injury he had suffered.

Priorities had changed. The portly man was a threat after all, and it was impossible to guess what other powers he might possess. Pierce disentangle the flail's chain from the woman's legs and raised it as the acid-spitter charged.

His attacker took in a deep breath. Pierce crouched and pulled his flail back to strike. The man's mouth opened—

And he turned to stone.

One instant, the man was in motion. A second later, he was a granite statue. There were still flecks of bile on his lips, and the acid began to pit the stone.

The clawed woman was rising to her feet. Judging he had two or three seconds to spare, Pierce glanced over his shoulder. The lady Lei was on the ground, struggling with an old woman. From the strain on her face, it was clear that the crone was far stronger than she appeared. At the start of the battle, Pierce remembered seeing rags wrapped around the woman's hands. Now one of her hands was free, and Pierce caught sight of a blemish on her palm—a scar or tattoo that resembled a large reptilian eye.

"Pierce, watch out!" Lei called. "Don't look at her left hand!"

With the threat identified, his course of action was clear. The clawed woman had regained her feet and was charging him. Pierce hurled his flail at her. She dodged the clumsy attack with ease, but it bought Pierce enough time to turn and grapple with the crone, pinning her. Her strength was unnatural, but Pierce had muscles of steel and stone. As the taloned woman came forward, Pierce twisted, bringing the old woman's hand up like a shield, and a moment later, there was a second statue in the middle of the street, claws outstretched in a frozen frenzy.

"Assist the others!" Pierce called out to Lei. He struggled with the crone, and slowly brought her hands together. She hissed in fury and redoubled her struggle. He brought his massive metal foot down on one of her rag-wrapped feet. She gasped, her eyes widening in pain—and he forced her left palm up to her face. The old woman turned to stone, frozen forever as she stared at her own third eye.

❋ ❋ ❋ ❋ ❋ ❋ ❋

Daine couldn't bring himself to strike a fellow Cyran, no matter how strange these people seemed to be. Monan had no such scruples, and he slashed at Daine with his long knife. Daine parried the blade, but even as he did so a raking pain blazed across his back. He side-stepped away from Monan and turned. A filthy dwarf with a vicious light in his eyes was right behind him. There was blood on his hands, and vicious talons protruded from his fingertips and the strange, twisted musculature of his arms.

"Flame!" Daine cursed, dodging another of Monan's blows. "What are you people?"

Monan laughed, and both enemies charged. Gritting his teeth against the pain in his back, Daine held the dwarf at bay while lashing out with a powerful kick. He caught Monan in the chest and the twin staggered back, giving Daine a moment to focus on the dwarf. His foe moved with unnatural speed, smashing Daine's hand and knocking his sword from his hand. The dwarf pressed forward, lashing at Daine's legs with his claws.

Daine gasped and fell to one knee. While he hated the thought of striking one of his own, there was no choice. The dwarf would tear him apart. With his free hand, Daine reached out and grabbed the first thing he could—the beard of the feral dwarf. He yanked forward as hard as he could, and the unexpected indignity caught his foe off balance. Even as the dwarf slipped forward, Daine brought up his dagger and buried it in the dwarf's throat. With a gurgle, the dwarf staggered back, claws scrabbling ineffectively at the knife buried in his neck.

Even as Daine rose to his feet, Monan was upon him, and now Daine was completely disarmed. He leaped out of the path of Monan's blade and tried to spot his fallen sword. Monan continued to laugh, and the sound seemed to echo in Daine's head, an unnatural reverberation that drowned out all natural thought. His vision blurred, and it seemed as though there were a dozen Monans dancing before him.

A blade lashed out, and it was all he could do to catch it with his forearm, pain lancing through him. The blade flashed in the light of the cold fire, and through the drowning laughter Daine knew the end was near.

A shadow flew past. The statue of the old woman smashed into Monan, slamming him down to the ground with a crunch of bone. Struggling to stay on his feet, Daine saw Pierce approaching. The warforged had hurled his petrified foe at Monan.

As Daine's head began to clear, he grabbed Monan's fallen knife and put his foot on the twin's chest. Lei, Pierce, and Jode spread out around him.

"It's over, Monan," Daine said. "Tell me what this is about, and I'll get you to a healer."

Monan continued to cackle, but his mouth was full of blood. Daine slapped the man, hard. He grabbed Monan by the throat and brought the dagger into view. "Don't make me hurt you, Monan."

The twin laughed again, his voice a little weaker this time. "It's Hugal," he whispered, and then Daine's mind exploded.

Daine staggered back. Wave upon wave of alien thoughts assailed his mind. A lifetime of memories, an overwhelming flood of images and sensations were trying to burrow their way into his brain. He fell to his knees, trying to raise his own memories as a defense—his grandfather shouting at his father, that last time he'd seen Alina ten years ago, the attack at Whitehearth.

"I know my name!" he said, and for a moment he believed it.

CHAPTER 19

BRELAND
SHARN
Dravago 28, 996 YK

He was lying on a blanket in a bare, dusty room. A small man—a halfling—was sitting next to him. Somewhere, bells were ringing.

"Are you well?" the little man said.

Jode. This was Jode. Slowly, memories came back to him.

"Jode," he whispered. "You're all right."

Jode shrugged. "I'm fine. They didn't seem that interested in me. The man who came after me wasn't even armed, and after I put a knife through his knees he seemed happy to leave me alone. How about you? Can you remember what happened?"

"I . . . I think so."

"Apparently Monan—Hugal, whoever—destroyed his own mind, and you were caught in some sort of psychic backlash." Jode studied Daine intently. "If you don't mind my asking, can you tell me how we survived the final battle at Keldan Ridge?"

Keldan Ridge . . . "No," Daine answered eventually. "None of us can remember what happened."

"That's right," Jode said with a relieved smile. "Just checking."

"Did you find out what they were after?"

"I'm afraid not. All of the others died. Monan-Hugal is still alive, but he's not responding to anything."

"I see."

"It's worse," Jode said. "He's a changeling. He reverted to his true form after he collapsed."

140

"Changeling?"

"So it may have been Monan, it may have been Hugal, or it may not have been either of them. There's no way of knowing—until we find the other twin."

Daine rose up to a sitting position. "Are the others all right?"

"Olladra smiles. I've healed your back and Lei patched up Pierce. They're downstairs having breakfast. We thought it best to let you sleep as long as you needed."

Since the last thing he could remember was eating dinner, Daine was surprised to find that he was hungry. He looked around and found his clothes. "We should stay together from this point on. I don't know why we were attacked, but clearly something strange is going on in High Walls."

"Stranger than you think, Captain. But I think I'd better let Lei explain."

❋ ❋ ❋ ❋ ❋ ❋ ❋

"A basilisk's eye?"

"I think so." Lei was enjoying another bowl of the Manticore's legendary gruel. "Once she'd been petrified, it was safe to examine it. I think someone somehow embedded a basilisk's eye in the palm of her hand, keeping all the abilities of a true, living basilisk."

"So this wasn't the Tarkanans?"

"Assuming the people we met yesterday were telling the truth, there's nothing similar about the two. Bal's powers are based on the same principles as a dragonmark. These others . . . I've never seen anything like it."

"After you collapsed, that other captain—Greykell—showed up with a few members of the local militia. She took us to the healer, Hulda, along with the other bodies. There wasn't much room in her tent, so we brought you back here once we knew it was safe."

"With the exception of the changeling, Greykell knew who all of the attackers were," Jode said. "It could have been an act, but as far as I could tell, she really was surprised and disturbed by what she saw. She claimed to have no idea how or why they would do what they did."

"Well, we're getting to the how," Lei continued. "Those two with the claws? We extracted some sort of *creatures* from their arms. They looked like worms of some sort. Given the mental powers of the changeling, I think that these worms were linked to their minds somehow. It's possible their sinews were even controlling their behavior. In any case, I've heard of kalashtar adepts who can use the powers of their minds to reshape their bodies, and I think that's what this was. These worms increased their strength and speed and produced those claws. The petrification makes it impossible to tell, but I'm guessing that the old man who spat acid at Pierce had a similar graft—some monstrous organ implanted in his chest."

"So you're saying we're looking for a man with a deadly touch and we're being chased by people have been physically altered to spit acid and turn people to stone?"

"That's about right."

"Doesn't *anyone* use swords any more?" Daine slumped in his chair. "I'm beginning to miss the war."

"Greykell is keeping the changeling under watch in case he recovers," Jode said. "I need to go heal some of the local children, so if you want to talk to her about the people who attacked us, we can see what she knows."

"Clearly we need all the information we can get." Daine paused for a moment. "Do think that it could have simply been a random attack? That we were just in the wrong place at the wrong time? After all, they didn't ask for anything."

"I suppose. One the other hand, Monan did seem to recognize Rasial, and I can't help but wonder if the attack was related to the dinner conversation. Perhaps we were asking too many questions, and someone wanted you dead."

"Or maybe . . . " Lei said thoughtfully. "Maybe someone wanted *you* alive."

"What do you mean?" Jode said.

"You said it yourself, Jode. You're the only one they didn't try to kill, even after you injured your enemy. Perhaps they didn't expect the rest of us to last as long as we did. Once we were down, the attackers could have teamed up to subdue you."

"But what would they want with me?" Jode said.

"That is the question," Lei said.

"So where do we go from here?"

Daine tried to collect his thoughts. "To begin with, you don't go anywhere alone, especially in High Walls. Let's talk to Greykell and see what she knows about our attackers. After that . . . well, we still need to talk to the wind, whatever that means."

Lei clutched her forehead. "Sovereign Lords! I'd completely forgotten about that. Do you think we'll have to fight the guard again?"

"There's only one way to find out."

CHAPTER 20

Greykell met them at the Cyran infirmary in Togran Square. The floor of the tent was lined with pallets, and people of all ages were spread out across the floor. The smell of blood and gangrenous flesh was strong in the air, and moans and low cries filled the chamber. Most of the patients were veterans of the war. Some were recovering from physical injuries, but others were victims of magical attacks or the Mourning itself. One man was missing his right arm and leg. It seemed as though his right side had been transformed into wax and then exposed to tremendous heat. A young woman was sitting up and gesturing with her right hand, making the same complex gesture over and over again, but her eyes were vacant and blank. Greykell stood in the back of the tent, looking down at an immobile figure with dead-white skin and lank silver-gray hair—the changeling.

"Good to see you up and about, Daine," Greykell said, looking over at him. "So far, no signs of life from our friend here. Hulda took another look at him this morning. Unfortunately, it's hard to tell if he's just playing possum."

"I can try to do something about that," Lei said. Her ability to channel and weave magical energy was limited, but after a good night's rest she was ready to get back to work.

"Do it," Daine said.

Lei produced a small disk of polished red marble from her belt pouch. An eye was engraved into the surface, and Daine was reminded of the symbol on the pommel of his borrowed sword. Lei traced the lines of the eye, whispering incantations, and after a moment the eye began to glow in the wake of her touch.

A minute later, she was done. "Shall I?" she asked, looking at Daine. He nodded, and she held the stone above the changeling's head. She closed her eyes, reaching out to study the surface of the changeling's mind. Eventually, she opened her eyes again. "Nothing," she said. "He's completely empty. There are no thoughts left at all."

"Keep at it," Daine said. He turned to Greykell. "Jode told me that you knew the people who attacked us. Can you explain any of this?"

Greykell shook her head. "Not at all. Philan, the fat man—now the fat statue—just the other day he was out in the market telling the children stories of Cyre. Sarris, the woman with the claws, served as a scout under my command. Overzealous, maybe, but I never saw her claws before."

"Did they know each other?" Jode asked.

"Everyone here knows each other," Greykell said. "But did they spend much time together? Not that I know of."

"What about the other twin?" Daine said. "Have you found him?"

"Not yet. But Daine, you're dealing with a changeling. This may not have anything to do with Hugal and Monan. They could be as innocent as you or I."

"Or there may never have been a Hugal or Monan."

"My guess is that one has always been a changeling and the other is human," Jode said. "Changelings aren't inherently evil, but few people trust them."

"I can't imagine why," Daine said.

"They're just people, Daine. This Monan could have met Hugal at an early age. They took a liking to one another and decided to be 'brothers'. It's not that uncommon, from what I hear. I've heard that other changeling communities have a set of identities that they share, so you could have six changelings who take turns being Lei, Jode, or Daine."

"Or Hugal or Monan."

"Exactly."

Daine scowled. "So Greykell, you don't know anything about this, what these people were up to, or why they might have attacked us?"

"Well . . ." She pondered a moment before continuing. "If you assume it was Monan you were dealing with, there are a number of factors to consider. You are all members of the Cyran army, but so am I, and I haven't been attacked yet. Your companion has the Mark of Healing—speaking of which, Jode, would you mind helping Hulda over there? She's got four more cases of flameworm fever. And then there was that friend of yours from the sketch. I'm putting my money on one of the last two. So, seeing as I've taken it on myself to maintain order in High Walls, would you like to tell me what that's really about?"

"What do you mean?"

She tapped her good eye. "Only half-blind, Daine. Your Jode is a smooth talker, but I don't believe that 'second cousin' story for a minute. The way I see it, either Monan and his strange friends were working with this Rasial and were trying to protect him from you—or they want him dead, and you happened to be more convenient. You want to tell me about it? And while you're at it"—she turned to look at Lei, who was sitting quietly with her eyes closed—"you want to tell your friend here to stop trying to read my mind? If you've got questions, just ask."

Daine blushed and tapped Lei on the shoulder. She blinked and dropped the carved stone. "She's telling the truth," she said.

"I could have told you that for free," Greykell grumbled.

"All right, Captain Greykell," Daine said. "But I'm not comfortable talking here. Come back to our room at the Manticore and I'll tell you what we know."

Greykell grinned. "Sounds good. I've always wanted to try their gruel. I hear it's top notch."

Daine shrugged. "I don't know. I've had a lot of gruel in my day, and honestly, it's just fair."

◦ ◦ ◦ ◉ ◦ ◦ ◦

"Aberrant dragonmarks?" Greykell frowned. "As in, 'Eat your candied jask roots or the Lady of the Plague will steal you away in the middle of the night?'"

Daine nodded. "You said you'd seen Rasial talking to Hugal or Monan, right?"

"I think so . . . but it's just a vague memory. A discussion in the marketplace, maybe a week ago."

"That might be about right. Rasial was supposed to be transporting contraband goods for my employer. He returned with the goods two days ago but never made his delivery. I wonder if he was working another deal on the side."

"Or two," Jode commented. "The Tarkanans seemed eager to find him. It may just be family bonds, or there could be more to it."

"What was the delivery?"

"Some sort of rare dragonshards."

"But none of the attackers had dragonmarks," Greykell said. "What possible good could the shards do for them?"

"Different types of dragonmarks have different purposes," Lei explained. "These are Khyber dragonshards, and they can bind the energies of dragonmarks and other sources of magical power. Thinking about it, I can see the value. I don't know how, but someone seems to have woven unnatural abilities into these people, the same way I can place enchantments into objects. Perhaps these dragonshards can streamline the process. If the dragonshard was grown up and suspended in a liquid medium . . . I don't know. It's all theoretical. Is there a skilled artificer in the community, Greykell? Or possibly a transmuter?"

"Sure," Greykell said. "Old Jol, who lives in the tent with all the holes in it and wears his skillet as a hat." She snorted. "No, we don't have a skilled artificer around. Do you think the place would look such a mess if we did?"

"What about the woman with the basilisk eye in her palm? How'd that happen?"

"Well, Old Hila was a war widow—and lost both her sons in battle as well. I remember having dinner with her at Teral's a few months back. She was surprisingly energetic and spent most of the time complaining about Breland feeding us table scraps after destroying everything we have. I remember arguing the point with her. As I was saying last night, it's not going to do any good to hold onto that sort of anger."

"And then she turned you into stone?" Jode said.

"No. And I'm certain her hands were normal then. She's a seamstress. I remember seeing her with that bandage a few weeks ago, but I assumed that she'd cut herself in her work."

This troubled Daine. "So much for this being an effect of the Mourning. So you're saying that sometime over the last month, she had a basilisk's eye stuck in her palm?" He looked at Lei. "I know they say 'if you can buy it, you can buy it in Sharn,' but I didn't realize that extended to living body parts."

"I've never heard of such a thing, Daine."

"Hmm. What about that girl with the stone teeth? Could the two be related?"

"I wouldn't think so," said Lei. "I've never seen such a focused petrifying effect before."

"There's no connection," Greykell said. "I met Olalia the first time I had dinner with Teral, and that was almost four months ago. I think she really is a casualty of the Mourning. We've seen a lot of horrors come out of our homeland. There are at least six people in the infirmary in far worse condition than she is."

"Jode . . . you seem to be the expert on changelings," Daine said. "They reshape their own bodies, right? Could a changeling twist someone else's body . . . plant a basilisk's eye in Hila's hand?"

"No." Jode and Lei answered at the same time. They looked at each other, and Lei continued. "Changelings have a very limited ability to shift their appearance. A changeling couldn't even place a functioning eye in its own palm, let alone an eye with magical powers. It's like dragonmarks—a changeling can place the design on its skin, but it doesn't actually get the powers of the mark."

"All right." Daine rubbed his forehead. "Let's go over this one more time. We've got a group of people in Sharn with aberrant dragonmarks, which channel dangerous energies. One member of this group is a former guardsman, who can kill people with a touch. He starts working behind the back of his new friends. In the process, he begins dealing with either Hugal or Monan, who may or may not have been a changeling at the time. Monan—if it was Monan—has his own group of friends, the acid-spitting-extra-eye-and-claw club. We have dinner last night. Monan discovers that Jode has the Mark of Healing and that we are looking for Rasial. He proceeds to gather together a group of his friends and attacks us. Why?"

Lei spoke up. "Rasial might not have anything to do with it, actually. Clearly these people are twisting their bodies in unnatural ways. That's got to be dangerous work." She looked over at Greykell. "Have there been any mysterious deaths recently?"

"Disappearances, certainly . . . but it's not the safest place or time to be a Cyran."

"Implanting monstrous organs . . . I imagine that for every working basilisk eye you end up with a corpse. Whoever is doing this may simply have wanted Jode's services to keep their subjects alive. The real question is how many more of these people are out there. Did we encounter all of them last night, or are there more?"

"I imagine Hugal could tell us that," Daine said.

"We're looking for him," Greykell said. "The Sharn Watch tends to ignore us. Either we're not worth their time or they're afraid to enter the district. Believe what best suits your ego, but I've pulled together a few friends to help maintain order. We'll see if we can turn him up for you."

"Thank you, Captain Greykell."

"I told you, I'm done with that. And don't think I'm doing it for you. I just don't want anything happening to Jode while we've still got flameworm going around!" She laughed and struck Daine on the shoulder. "How about you? Any ideas?"

"Only one," Daine sighed. He looked over at Lei. "Ready to go back to Malleon's Gate?"

CHAPTER 21

BRELAND
SHARN
Dravago 28, 996 YK

The streets of Malleon's Gate were almost empty.
Goblins were nocturnal by nature, and the midmorning sun
fell on quiet streets and cracked cobblestones. The inhabitants
were beginning to stir as Daine and his allies passed through
the streets; a pair of goblin children peered out of a nest of
garbage and cloth, and a well-dressed bugbear poured the
contents of a chamberpot out of an upper window. A sweet
sound filled the air—a woman's voice raised in wordless song,
filling the air with joy and beauty. Almost unconsciously,
Daine began walking toward the sound, but after a few steps
he found that his leg was trapped. It was Jode, who had latched
onto his ankle.

"That would be a harpy," he said, as the ethereal sound continued. "Not your best choice for a lunch companion."

Pierce had put a hand on Lei's shoulder, preventing her
from following the sound. They listened to the enchanting
melody for a few moments, before it finally faded away. A harpy
took to the air from a nearby tower, a piece of dripping meat
in one hand.

Daine shook his head as they began to move again. "What are
creatures like that *doing* in a city anyway? Why hasn't the guard
done something about them?"

"You may see these creatures as monsters." Lei remarked,
"but many of them are as intelligent as you or I, and they're

just trying to survive like the rest of us." She had caught a toe on one of the uneven cobblestones, and was using the darkwood staff to take the weight off of her right foot. "She's found a place in this community, and I'd lay gold that she paid for her breakfast. Most of the more exotic monsters here are employed by House Tharashk, which sells their services and vouches for their behavior."

"Outside Malleon's Gate, maybe," Jode said. "But remember those statues we found yesterday? I'm going to guess that the laws of the land don't always apply in this district."

"It's possible. I was always told to stay out of the Gate, and I don't think the watch would care about the death of an innocent goblin."

"Hmm," Daine said. "What if those statues weren't the work of a medusa? We've just met someone who could turn people to stone."

"An interesting idea," said Jode. "But what would an old seamstress from Cyre gain from petrifying goblins?"

"What would she gain from petrifying Lei? Or me?"

"Well, she'd be able to buy your sword from the pawnbroker when you didn't reclaim it."

Daine touched his borrowed sword. "Don't remind me. Aureon knows I've considered killing you to get it back."

Jode flashed a disarming smile. In the distance, the harpy began to sing again. "You have to admit," he said, "It is a lovely sound."

"Lovely," Daine said, scowling.

❂ ❂ ❂ ⦿ ❂ ❂ ❂

An ogress was standing at the door to the temple. She wore a black skirt and a harness of black leather studded with brass spikes. Similar bands of spiked leather were wrapped around her massive, calloused fists. She was remarkably well groomed for an ogress, especially in Malleon's Gate. She seemed to have washed her dark hair at least once, and there was a surprising glint of intelligence in her eyes as she watched them approach.

"Well?" Lei murmured, as they came closer to the gate

guardian. "It looks like we're in for a fight after all. Think you can handle her?"

"I can't match her strength. Let's hope she doesn't know what to do with it." Daine steeled himself and stepped up to the ogress. To his surprise, she moved to the side and bowed her head slightly.

"She awaits." Her voice was gruff thunder, almost too rough to be understood. She struck the door with a leatherbound fist. There was an echoing boom, and the door swung open. Though the sun was high in the sky, the passage beyond was filled with shadow.

"Could you be more specific?" Jode said, peering up at her knees. "Does she have a name? Is she bigger than a bugbear?"

The ogress didn't even look down at him. "Enter and learn," she said. It wasn't a suggestion.

❧ ❧ ❧ ❧ ❧ ❧ ❧

The door swung closed after they passed under the arch, and the darkness was complete. Lei whispered a few words, and the golden studs on her armor burst into light.

From the outside, the building appeared to be a forgotten temple to the Sovereign Host, abandoned centuries ago and left to crack and crumble. In the light of Lei's glowing armor, it was easy to see why it had been abandoned. A few supporting beams had fallen from the ceiling, and the floor was choked with dust and rubble. The slit windows had been filled in with mortar.

"Somehow, I was expecting something a little grander," Jode said, looking around. "If you're going to bother to get your ogress to wash her hair, you'd think you'd dust your temple."

"Is it safe?" Daine wondered, looking up at the ceiling. "I'm going to be disappointed if we came all this way to get crushed by a falling stone."

"I think so," Lei said, squinting up into the darkness. "Though I wouldn't throw any stones."

A cool breeze blew through the room. Daine looked for the source, but he couldn't see any openings. Then he noticed a dim orange light at the far end of the hall—something set into the floor. "Over there. Let's go. Pierce, fall back and follow."

Pierce nocked an arrow to his string and held another in his palm. Daine drew sword and dagger, and Lei held the darkwood staff at the ready. Jode started whistling a cheerful Talentan tune but stopped when Daine glared at him.

"What?" he said. "You really think someone is going to set up an ambush by requiring Lei to fight a minotaur with her bare hands? I must admit, I never saw it coming." Daine continued to stare. "Fine," he sighed, drawing his stiletto. "Silent it is."

Lei whispered a word of power, and the magical light faded. In the new-fallen darkness, the glow at the end of the room was even more obvious. The three spread out in a semi-circle and moved forward, with Pierce following thirty steps behind. Daine began to hear a low bubbling, the sound of thick, boiling liquid. The source of the sound was also the source of the light. It appeared to be a pool of molten metal, almost ten feet across. As they drew close, they could feel the heat and smell the fire. Nine stone altars were spread in a circle around the fiery pool, one for each of the lords of the Sovereign Host. The largest of the altars lay directly before them. It was of red granite and engraved with the hammer sigil of Onatar, Lord of Fire and Forge. A large crack ran down the center of the altar, splitting the hammer in two.

"What a fiendish trap!" Jode whispered. "They know we'll never be able to resist leaping into the pool."

Daine sighed and lowered his sword.

"You're already caught in the fire."

It took a moment for the words to register in Daine's ears. He was reminded of the harpy's song; it was pure beauty distilled into sound, unearthly and inhuman.

The voice came from directly in front of them, and suddenly Daine noticed the vast black shadow crouched atop the broken altar of Onatar. Had it always been there? Or had it appeared with the sound of the voice? The figure moved forward, and it was revealed by the light of the molten pool.

A sphinx.

She had the body of a great black cat, with the neck and head of a beautiful elf-maiden, though if the head had been on a humanoid body, she'd have been nine feet tall to match the scale. Her skin was flawless cream, her eyes glittering gold. Her long hair was midnight black, dropping down and mingling with the vast raven's wings folded on her back. The black of her fur and hair was striped with bands of brilliant orange, and these seemed to glow in the dim light. When she shifted, the stripes rippled like flame. She wore three chains around her neck—one of gold, one of silver, and one of black adamantine—and they, too, glittered in the light of the glowing pool.

Daine was struck speechless. He'd seen strange creatures before. Some of the beasts they'd fought in the Mournland would haunt his nightmares for the rest of his life. But he'd never encountered anything with the raw presence and the pure sense of inhuman majesty as the sphinx. Those golden eyes seemed to probe within him, then she spoke again. It was an impressive sight, but Daine found uneasy suspicion warring against his sense of wonder.

"Lei. Daine, Jode. Have no fear. Come in peace, and you will be safe. Come forward, Pierce. I am Flamewind, and I have been expecting you."

Struggling to find his voice, Daine said, "How could you know we were coming?"

"Calm yourself." Her voice was so hypnotic that this was almost a command. "Destiny is like a flame."

"It consumes and destroys anything it touches?" Jode said. Unlike Daine and the others, Jode was not affected by the majesty of the sphinx.

"Be careful what you suggest," the sphinx said. "Your fate can certainly consume you, and bring about great destruction. But the greater the flame, the more light it sheds, and the farther away it can be seen. I saw your fires burning in the Mournland. I watched as you approached, and I arranged for you to be here today."

"And if we'd decided not to come?" Daine said.

Flamewind smiled and said nothing.

"So, we didn't have a choice. Is that what you're trying to say?"

"No. You have choice. You have power. But you do not always see the forces that move you. Why did you come this morning?"

"Well, we tried to visit you yesterday, but the watch showed up."

"Why?"

"An old friend wanted to see me."

"Why?"

"I don't know. To warn me, I suppose."

"And how did he know to find you here, in a place the watch does not watch?"

"I don't know! Are you going to answer any questions, or do you just ask them?"

Flamewind turned her head, her golden eyes catching the light of the pool. "You will find out the answers in time. For now, you must ask yourself the questions. I am not the only one who can see your flames. Others are watching, and they are shaping your path. The death of Hadran d'Cannith, the presence of your friend Alina . . . these are not accidents. Beware coincidence."

Lei stepped forward, and now it was her eyes that burned in the darkness. "You know who killed Hadran? Tell me!"

Flamewind reared up and spread her wings. Golden feathers were hidden within the black, and for a moment she seemed to be surrounded by flame. "You killed him, Lei. Those watching you have plans for you, and a life with Hadran was not what they wished."

"They? They *who?*"

The sphinx settled onto her haunches, folding her wings again. "I cannot say. I see your fires, but we who watch are hidden in the shadows. I will tell you this. All of your troubles are tied to your past, to who you are, and those who have come before. Your fate is linked to your family—your parents and your brothers."

"My parents are dead," Lei said, "and I have no brothers."

"You carry the legacy of your line, and you have already met one of your brothers. You must forget your house and focus on your family."

"Stop! *Stop!*" Lei cried. "Take your stick and leave us alone!" She hurled the darkwood staff at Flamewind. The staff froze in mid-air, then slowly drifted back to Lei and fell at her feet.

"The staff was never mine," Flamewind said. "I simply arranged for it to come to you. There is little I can do for you. Accept this gift."

Pierce walked up behind Lei. He picked up the staff and put his other hand on her shoulder. Flamewind smiled slightly. "Your friends will rely on your strength in days to come, Pierce," she said. "But even you do not know your true strength."

"What do you mean?" Pierce said. Even Lei looked puzzled.

"Do you know what your purpose is, Pierce?"

"I was designed to serve as a light infantry scout and support unit, specializing in stealth and reconnaissance."

"That is what you were told. That is what you have done. But it is far from the truth. You too must learn about your family."

Pierce's metal faceplate was incapable of expression. "I have no family. I was forged in the workshops of Cyre."

"By whom?"

"I do not know."

"If you wish to know your purpose, that is where you must begin."

"What about me?" Jode said. "Do I have mysterious family issues as well?"

Flamewind looked down at the little halfling. "You know your family, Jode. And you know who you are. What matters are the choices that you will make in the next few hours. There is a key that only you can find, hidden between two stone that only you can move. You must find it alone, but you will pay a terrible price to do so. You have the power to end the suffering of others, but you will need to sacrifice all that you have."

"Why are you doing this?" Daine said. "If you know so much about our destinies, why the riddles? Why not just tell us what you know?"

The sphinx looked at Daine and smiled. "What answer do you wish to hear, Daine with no family name? That I am bound by divine and arcane laws and have told you all that I can? That I have told you what you need to know to fulfill your purpose in this world? Or that I have my own plans, and I am shaping your destiny as much as any of the others who watch?"

"Which is true?"

"Which will you believe?"

"I suppose you have a mysterious riddle for me?"

Flamewind looked at him. "You have turned your back on your past, Daine. You sold your family sword long before Jode did. You will need to take up that sword again."

"One sword's as good as another."

"You don't believe that. The wielder determines the value of the sword. If you will not use what you have, you will never succeed."

Daine said nothing. Her eyes glittered as she continued.

"You will have lost far more than your sword by the time the sun has set. You must make peace with the shadows if you are to survive. Enemies are all around you, and the deepest darkness is hidden within the light."

"Do you have any more parables, or are we done here?"

"Just one more. There will come a time when you will be asked to give away your closest friend. Be careful. You will have to carry the consequences for the rest of your life."

"And you already know what I'll decide?"

"Of course. But you haven't decided yet." Flamewind smiled one last time. "I have said all that I can say—or all that I will say. Now go. Your enemies await."

She spread her wings and took to the air, disappearing into the shadows of the dome. Daine looked up after her, but she was nowhere to be seen.

CHAPTER 22

BRELAND
SHARN
Dravago 28, 996 YK

Well, that certainly cleared things up." Daine said, kicking a piece of rubble. When they'd left the temple, the ogress was nowhere to be seen. However, the people of Malleon's Gate were beginning to stir. Bands of goblins were setting off for the workhouses, and up the street a few bugbears were wrestling on a stoop. "Lei and Pierce are supposed to go have a family reunion, you should start turning over stones, and I should get ready to suffer a big loss. And we've got three days to sort all this out before we're out on the street."

"I don't know," Jode said. "I thought it was worth doing. When's the last time *you* saw a sphinx? I wonder if she participates in the races."

Lei had taken the darkwood staff from Pierce, and they had been walking in silence. Now she spoke again, though her thoughts seemed distant. "I don't think so. Back when I was studying in Sharn, I remember hearing a story about a Morgrave expedition bringing a sphinx to the city."

"Where'd she come from?" Jode asked. "Droaam?"

"Xen'drik, I think."

Xen'drik was a continent to the south, a land of secrets and mysteries. Daine had never been there, but he knew it was said to be the homeland of the elves, and the home of an ancient civilization of giants that had been destroyed millennia before the rise of humanity.

"A group of explorers found her in the jungles," Lei continued, "or she found them, depending on how you look at it. As I heard the story, the sphinx said she'd been waiting for the explorers and that she would be returning to Sharn with them. They took her along because you don't meet a sphinx every day. Supposedly she was hidden away at the university, talking to sages about Xen'drik. No one ever said anything about a temple in Malleon's Gate. That I know for certain."

"So do you think that we should give any weight to this?" Daine asked.

"I don't know. She knew we were here. She knew who we were. And Uncle Jura seemed to take her seriously, for whatever reason."

"The ogress wasn't there when we left," Jode said.

"Yes, I think we all noticed that," Daine said.

"I was just wondering if you'd ever seen a female minotaur before. Is it easy to tell the genders apart?"

"I don't know. Why?"

"Never mind. I'm sure it's nothing."

Daine began to protest, then he looked down the street and the words died in his throat. Three hobgoblin warriors were spread out across the street, all wearing the spiked leather armor common to Darguun. Stealing a glance over his shoulder, he saw a bugbear and two more hobgoblins stepping out into the street behind them.

"Hold," he said quietly. His comrades paused in mid stride, and they formed a loose circle to guard their backs. *"Tsash ghaal'dar!"* Daine called out, hailing them in the Goblin tongue. "Strength to your arms."

The hobgoblins seemed slightly surprised to hear their own language. One of the warriors in front stepped forward. Hobgoblins stood between the tiny goblins and massive bugbears in height and build. While they lacked the inhuman strength of the bugbears, hobgoblins were tough and quick. This wasn't one of the largest hobgoblins Daine had dealt with, but he moved with a sinister grace. He had striped his black armor with streaks of crimson. An odd design, but that wasn't what disturbed Daine. The hobgoblin carried a heavy chain studded with spikes. A chainmaster. Daine cursed under his breath. He had fought Darguul chainmasters before, and they weren't pleasant memories.

"What brings you to this place, outsider?" said the hobgoblin.

"I could ask the same, chainmaster," Daine said, continuing to speak in Goblin. He had served with Darguuls both before and after he'd joined the army of Cyre, and he could tell that these five were looking for a fight. But there were many ways he could make it difficult for them. "This is not the land of the Ghaal'dar. What brings you to a city of men?"

"Your failure, homeless one. With your land destroyed, the other humans have called a halt to battle. There is no war to the north, and so we have come here. Perhaps you can pay for the mistakes of your country."

Daine felt his anger growing. "Who failed first? Our greatest mistake was trusting the honor of the Ghaal'dar. Your ancestors were paid to protect the nation of Cyre, and you turned on those who trusted you."

The hobgoblin bared his teeth and set the end of his chain whirling. But as Daine had hoped, the other warriors held back. Daine had made this an argument between the two of them, a contest of honor. One way or another, the leader needed to prove himself against Daine before the others would support him.

"It was always our land," the chainmaster said. "Your kind stole it long ago. Our king has reclaimed what was ours by right!"

The other warriors nodded, but Daine had anticipated this response. "My ancestors claimed this land with fire and sword, and the Ghaal'dar fled before them. Is treachery the only way you can win it back?"

The hobgoblin hissed and sent his chain spinning forward, but Daine was ready. In one move, he leaped up and over the chain and lunged for the hobgoblin, blades in hand. Stepping backward to keep Daine at a distance, the hobgoblin shifted his grip and the chain came whirling out again, catching Daine's sword and pulling it free. But Daine had fought chainmasters before, and he'd expected this move. Sword now gone, he lashed out with his dagger, and the adamantine blade sliced through the steel links as if they were cloth. A second slash scattered spiked links across the street, leaving the warrior holding a tiny scrap of chain.

Daine raised the point of the dagger and kept it in line with the hobgoblin as he knelt to recover his longsword, pulling it free from the entangling chain.

"I hope this time you will have the honor to admit your defeat," said Daine, smiling.

Perhaps it was the smile that did it. Perhaps he'd overestimated the honor of the Ghaal'dar hobgoblins. Whatever the case, Daine realized he'd pushed things too far. The hobgoblin flung the remnants of his shattered chain, and as Daine side-stepped away, his opponent drew a jagged broadsword.

"Shaarat'kor!" he cried. This goaded his companions into action. The warriors began to circle Daine and his allies, searching for an opening.

"Stand ready!" Daine said, sliding into guard and waiting for the charge.

But the attack never came. A high female voice called out in Goblin, interrupting the battle. "Leave him alone, Jhaakat! Leave him be unless you plan to drink your own blood!"

The hobgoblin hissed, but he paused and looked over his shoulder to the source of the source of the voice. Daine stole a glance as well and blinked in surprise. The speaker was the goblin girl he'd met on the lift from Deni'yas—the thief who had stolen his purse.

"Begone, girl!" the hobgoblin snapped. "This is business of the Ghaal'dar. No place for cityfolk who have long lost touch with our ways."

"You are in *my* home, Jhaakat, and you do not know *our* ways. We know better than to drink poisoned korluaat, but I've seen a number of you Darguuls make that mistake. Besides, the Stone Eye wants to see him. Perhaps *you'd* like to explain the delay?"

Jhaakat looked askance at that. The other hobgoblins lowered their weapons and took a step back. "Fine," said the hobgoblin.

"Take him." He looked at Daine, spat at the ground, then turned and walked away.

"Daine," Lei whispered. "As someone who doesn't speak Goblin, would you tell me what is going on?"

"I'm still trying to figure that out," he said. He looked over to the little girl. "It seems that there's more to you than meets the eye," he said in the common tongue of Galifar. "I suppose I should thank you for helping us. I'm not in the habit of being rescued by thieves."

Looking at her now, it was clear that the girl had been playing a role on the lift. Daine remembered hearing that the short-lived goblinoids matured faster than humans, and clearly the girl's wide-eyed "I just wanted to see the sky" burbling had been an act. He'd been thinking of her as a child of six, but her level gaze had the focus of a young adult.

"You saved me on the lift," she said in the tongue of Galifar. Her voice was so childish and sweet that it was difficult to take her seriously. "And you did give me all that money. It was the least I could do."

"I didn't exactly *give* you that money."

"I know . . . but you had it just hanging there. And I know *you* saw me." She looked at Jode, who grinned. "I thought you just didn't want to give it to me in front of the guards."

"What did you just do?" Lei asked. "Who are you?"

The girl studied Lei carefully. "I'm Rhazala. Those mean Darguuls sleep at my father's hostel, so they know better than to cross me. And I told them someone important wants to see you."

Daine nodded. "Well, thanks, Rhazala. Since I imagine you don't have the money any more, I guess we'll just have to call it even and be on our way."

"You can't do that!"

"Why not?"

"I told you. Someone important wants to see you."

"You weren't just making that up?"

"You don't joke about the Stone Eye. If you don't come, I don't know what he'll do to me."

Daine sighed and looked at the other three. "Well, I suppose

we can take a few more minutes before following up on all of
our other leads. What do you think?"

There were general nods of assent.

He turned back to Rhazala. "Fine. Lead on."

❋ ❋ ❋ ❋ ❋ ❋ ❋

The people of Malleon's Gate seemed to know Rhazala.
Many waved as the goblin girl passed by. Others looked away
or studiously ignored the girl and her traveling companions.
As they continued deeper into the district, they began to see
more statues—a hobgoblin warrior in full armor, his flail
broken off halfway up the handle; an angry bugbear with
one arm missing; a pair of goblins encrusted with mildew
and mold.

"I'll give you one guess as to what old 'Stone Eye' is," Jode
murmured, touching his eye and then pointing to one of the
statues.

"A medusa, you think?" Daine frowned. "But the girl said
'he.' "

"You listen to too many stories. Where do you think little
medusas come from? Phoenix eggs?"

"Wonderful."

Rhazala stopped at an old, run-down building—a tavern
with boards over the windows, seemingly abandoned for
centuries. There were two doors, one sized for goblins,
gnomes, and halflings, and the other large enough to admit
an ogre. The girl tapped out a complex pattern of knocks on
the larger door, and a moment later it slid open. Rhazala
stepped inside and motioned for them to follow.

The door guards were tall, powerful humanoids covered
with shaggy, spotted fur. Their heads featured long canine
ears, glowing green eyes, and long snouts filled with sharp
teeth. Gnolls, Daine guessed, though he'd never actually seen
one before. Gnolls were natives of the land of Droaam to the
west. Droaam was the home of harpies and trolls, and according to bedtime stories these were the least of its terrors. The
last werewolves were said to lurk in the depths of the forests
of Droaam, and the barren Byeshk Mountains were home to

medusas, basilisks, and other horrible creatures. A gnoll might be a match for a bugbear, if not as bright, and the presence of the gnolls hinted at greater horrors that might lie deeper in the building.

Rhazala exchanged a few words with the door guards, speaking in a language he didn't know. After an exchange of snarls and grunts, she led them deeper into the old inn. The common room of the inn had been transformed into a barracks. Gnolls, goblins, and even a few ogres were sitting on pallets spread around the room, sharpening weapons and sharing stories or jokes. Rhalaza led them through the common room and the kitchen, back to what must have once been the innkeeper's quarters. A lone figure stood before a small shrine constructed from strange, inhuman bones. The stranger, shrouded in a long, hooded cloak of green wool, was facing away from them. The back of the hood seemed to shift slightly as they entered, and despite the raucous chatter from the common room, Daine heard a *hiss*.

"Lord Kasslak?" Rhazala said. "I've brought them."

The stranger rose and turned around. His hood was pulled down to cover his eyes and upper face, but Jode had clearly guessed correctly. Where Kasslak's skin was exposed, it was covered with coppery scales, and a few vipers were peering out of the depths of the hood. Daine and the others dropped their eyes, and Daine's hand went to the hilt of his sword.

"There is no need to draw your sword. I mean you no harm . . . at this time," the medusa said. His voice was smooth and sibilant.

Can he see through the eyes of his snakes? Daine wondered. He'd never really considered the relationship between a medusa and its mane of serpents.

"Glad to hear it," Daine said.

"Please, be seated." The medusa gestured at the chairs scattered around the room. "I am Kasslak. I'm afraid I don't know your names."

Daine sat down. "I'm Daine, and my companions are Lei, Jode, and Pierce."

"A pleasure," Kasslak said, dipping his hooded head.

"Rhazala, you may stay, but please close the door." He walked over to a desk set against the northern wall and idly shifted a few sheets of parchment while he talked. "Sharn was built by the hands of the goblins, and Malleon's Gate has been their home for centuries. The goblins have long been mistreated by humanity and its cousins, but nonetheless, a balance had been struck. That changed with the rise of Darguun, as the larger and more powerful goblinoids emerged from their mountain fortresses to spread across the land. The Darguuls have their own traditions, and over the last few decades the balance of power has been lost."

"And where do medusas fit into this history lesson?" Daine asked. "I'm no sage, but I didn't think that you were part of the same family tree."

"Patience." A serpent peered around the cowl and hissed softly. "As the Darguuls have come from the east, we of Droaam have come from the west. Since before the age of Galifar we have been seen as monsters, and in truth, our history has been one of violence and bloodshed. But this has changed over the last century. As war tore your nations apart, the Daughters of Sora Kell called us together, uniting the warlords under one banner. The Daughters saw great promise in commerce with your kind, and indeed, many of your people sought our warriors for their strength in battle."

Daine could attest to this. While he'd mainly fought in the south, he'd heard tales of ogre irregulars fighting along the western front, and they hadn't been pleasant stories.

"But we have much to offer besides our power in battle. The Daughters have sent us east to work with your dragonmarked houses and forge new bonds between our nations."

"Does this involve us somehow?"

Two snakes hissed this time, but Kasslak's voice was as smooth and emotionless as ever. "Ogres, trolls, hobgoblins, bugbears . . . there is fire in the blood of these races, and conflict is in their nature. But it does not serve our purposes to fight one another. The Sharn Watch has long left this area alone, but someone needs to maintain order. This is my role. Should there be trouble in the district, I wish to know the source of it and if I can put an end to it."

Daine began to see what was going on. "Well, that's kind of you. And don't think we don't appreciate it. But those Darguuls were just looking for trouble. I don't think there's anything unusual there."

"Nor do I. But the Sharn Watch came into the district in search of you—the first time in three years that they've set foot in the Gate. And I understand that you entered the broken temple. Yet here you are . . . alive."

"That's a surprise?"

"I see you know little about the history of our home. That may explain why you went to the temple to begin with. In any case, I would like to know your business with the Watch, and whether we should be expecting them to return. I also wish to know why you entered the broken temple, and how you survived the experience."

"And I'd like a magic ring that grants wishes," Daine said.

The medusa's snakes hissed angrily, but the goblin girl laughed. Kasslak stood and walked toward Daine. "You are refusing to answer?"

Daine took a deep breath then stood and faced Kasslak, all too aware of the deadly gaze hidden behind a flimsy hood. "It's good that you're trying to keep this place under control, and I'm glad I didn't have to sully my blade with hobgoblin blood back on the street. But I can't answer your questions. I don't know why the Watch broke the rules and came in here after me. I'd tell you if I did. As for what happened in the temple . . . it sounds to me like you should know better than to ask."

There was a long pause. Daine could almost feel the medusa's eyes locked onto him from beneath the green hood, and he wondered if he could draw his sword and strike before Kasslak could pull back his hood. Then the medusa let out his breath in a long hiss. "You may go. Rhazala will see you safely to the edge."

Daine turned to the door then paused. "Kasslak . . ." he said. "Do you keep basilisks?"

"Basilisks are dangerous creatures," the medusa said. "What use would I have for one?"

"I was just wondering if a basilisk might have disappeared around three weeks ago," Daine said. "Or at least, one of its eyes. Anyhow, if you want to talk about it, I suggest you drop by the Manticore in High Walls. We won't be coming back here again."

CHAPTER 23

BRELAND
SHARN
Dravago 28, 996 YK

Rhazala led the way through the streets of Malleon's Gate. As before the inhabitants gave her a wide berth. Clearly she was known to be an emissary of the medusa, and Daine wondered what she had done to earn her place in his band. It was still difficult to take her seriously. Half the time she was skipping through the streets, and the other half she was singing nonsense songs in Goblin. But having seen her at the brawl, Daine wondered how much of this was part of her pose.

They passed a group of goblins painting gargoyle silhouettes onto strips of gray cloth. "It's for Eight Winds," Rhazala explained, tapping a band of gray cloth wrapped around her wrist. "Carralag *will* win this year. Wait and see."

Jode was cheerful as always, and he chattered away with the girl, discussing the Race of Eight Winds and the history of the Bat and the Gargoyle. But Daine was still frustrated by his encounter with the medusa, and he had no interest in hearing the tricks the Gargoyle might use against the Griffon or Pegasus. This fire still burned when they reached the gates of the district, and he nodded curtly to the goblin and headed off to the streets of Oldkeep. Without speaking to the others, he led them into the first tavern he saw, a grimy dive with an upside-down griffon above the door.

"Do you still have any silver?" he growled to Jode.

Jode threw him a sovereign. Daine slapped the coin down on the bar. "I don't care what it is, as long as it's strong," he said.

The bartender grunted, and Daine turned and made his way to a filthy table. The others followed him. Jode and Lei sat down. Pierce continued to stand; being made of steel, stone, and wood he was immune to the effects of fatigue, and he generally preferred to remain ready for action. Having studied their surroundings, Pierce held his flail in one hand. The chain was still wrapped around the haft, but clearly he felt that it was best to be prepared.

"You're in a charming mood today," Jode said to Daine. "I expected you to be interested in the aerial archery discussion. It sounds like we could have used a squad of gargoyle archers a year ago."

"But we didn't have any, did we? And now all those soldiers are dead."

The bartender brought over a few mugs filled with some foul Marcher brew. Daine took a deep swallow. Lei sniffed her mug and pushed it away.

"And this is news?" Jode said. "I would hope that there's something more recent bringing you down."

"Fine." Daine drained his mug in one long draught then slammed it down on the table. He took Lei's rejected flagon. "Why are we doing this? Why are we here?"

"On Eberron?"

Daine glared at him. "In Sharn. Working for Alina. Talking about weather and wind with thrice-damned goblin *thieves!*"

"Oh, Rhazala's a good girl. Reminds me of myself at that age." Jode took a sip and winced. "Except for the orange skin, of course. But really, Daine, where else should we be? Cyre isn't coming back, and there are probably as many Cyrans in Sharn as there are anywhere else in Khorvaire. Working for Alina . . . where else can we make that kind of money? If you don't like it, then do something to help the refugees. Give them the money we get from Alina. I'm sure that Greykell could put it to good use. Or here's an idea—figure out who's turning Cyran refugees into monsters and do something about it. Crazy, hmm?"

Daine looked down into the drink and scowled. "And what's Alina got to do with this?"

Jode nodded. "This is about *your* family, isn't it?"

Lei had been studying the grimy patrons of the tavern, but at this she looked up. "What do you mean?"

"Quiet, Jode," Daine growled.

"You heard what the sphinx said about your past. I think she had a point."

"What are you talking about?" Lei said.

"I don't think Daine's ready to talk about it," Jode said. "Let's just say that we crossed paths some time before we joined the army, and there are some issues I think our captain needs to deal with."

Lei looked over at Daine, but he just scowled. "Look," she said, "I don't care what this is about, but we don't have anywhere else to go. You know what? I'd like to live in a place that isn't filled with lice. And do you think I like that gruel just because I can make it? This isn't how I expected to live my life. The future I should have had has been stolen from me, as well, so get over it. Let's do what we need to do to get this gold. If you want to give your share to the refugees, then do so. Cyre wasn't my home, and I don't have a family any more. And I'm sick of suffering for both of them."

Behind them, Pierce remained silent and still.

"I see it's good moods all around," Jode said. "The joy at this table is overwhelming. But you're right. We won't get anything accomplished by drinking except to pour away what little money we have. So what more do we have to work with?"

Daine closed his eyes and took a deep breath. Jode was right, of course. "Fine. We have the freaks in High Walls, who appear to have been created—through magic, I assume. Perhaps it's voluntary. Perhaps not. And a changeling is involved."

"I doubt that means anything," Lei said. "There's no huge changeling conspiracy. It's easy to mistrust them, but changelings are individuals just like us. They aren't some faceless mob."

"Except for the part about being faceless," Jode pointed out.

"And how can you be so certain there's no conspiracy? Unless *you're* a changeling . . ."

Lei glared at him. "As I recall, you were the one who said changelings weren't inherently evil."

Jode shrugged. "Just taking the side of the Traveler. Are you sure it was me you were talking to this morning?"

Daine opened his eyes. "Shut up, Jode. We know three things about the freaks we fought last night. One was a changeling, another had received her . . . "gift" within the last few weeks, and there's a good chance they had some sort of dealing with our friend Rasial."

"All true," Jode said.

"What we don't know is what Rasial would be doing with a group of monster makers." He drained the last of his drink and stood up. "Drink up. We're going to talk to Alina."

Jode eyed the mug. "I think I'll pass on the drink. I'd just as soon be on my toes when talking with her."

"Suit yourself."

❧ ❧ ❧ ❧ ❧ ❧ ❧

"Do you suppose we need to make an appointment?" Daine said, as the lift pulled up to Den'iyas.

"I'm sure she already knows we're coming," Jode said.

"If she knows so much, what does she need us for, anyway?"

"An excellent question."

"Is there anything more I should know before meeting this Alina?" Lei's curiosity had overcome her general malaise, and it was hard to stay gloomy amidst the pleasant surroundings of the gnome enclave.

"She likes to play games," Jode said. "If she talks to you, bear that in mind. She'll try to provoke you, and she'll pretend to know more than she does."

"Why?"

Jode shrugged. "It's part of Zil culture. The gnomes have always fought with words instead of swords. The more she knows about you—how you react, how she can manipulate you—the stronger her position."

"Better not to speak at all," said Daine.

Lei nodded. "Is she dangerous?"

Who isn't? Daine thought, remembering her description of Rasial. "Without question," he said. "She's extremely wealthy, and you can be certain she has wards and other magical defenses spread around her lair."

"And bodyguards, I imagine," Jode put in. "Alina likes bodyguards."

Lei shot Daine an inquiring glance, and he took a deep breath before continuing. "She's a wizard of some talent, though I couldn't tell you exactly how powerful she is. Just be careful. Don't push her."

"I wasn't planning on it."

"Good."

The gnome gardener smiled and bowed courteously at their approach, and a moment later the secret passage beneath the garden stood revealed. "Lady Lyrris is expecting you," he said.

"See?" said Jode.

Daine shook his head.

They descended through the passage and soon found themselves in the mirrored room. Daine noticed that the long "window" now displayed an entirely different view than it had before. Unless his eyes deceived him, they were looking down over Malleon's Gate. Alina stood by the window, a golden spyglass in her hand. Today she wore a gown of green and gold, the patterns of which bore an uncanny resemblance to Lei's heirloom armor. She turned toward them with a brilliant smile.

"Welcome back, Daine, Jode." She made a sweeping gesture. "Please, sit." She walked over to Lei, and looked up at her; Daine always forgot just how small Alina actually was. "I am Alina Lorridan Lyrris. And you must be Lei d'Cannith?"

"Just Lei."

"Of course. My apologies. A cup of blackroot tal, perhaps?"

"Leave her alone, Alina," Daine said. "We came here for a reason."

"You've run out of money?"

"That, too," said Jode.

"I'm listening."

"I don't know what sort of game you're playing," said Daine.

"You obviously know more than we do. It's hard to imagine that you couldn't find Rasial without us."

Alina looked back out the window. "I know it's hard to believe, but my powers are limited." Daine shot a glance at Jode. Such an admission of weakness was very uncharacteristic of her—and thus, highly suspect. "I believe that you've already encountered other members of House Tarkanan?"

"Yes. So you did know about Rasial's connection to the Tarkanans?"

"Of course." She turned to face him and tapped her hand. "I told you not to let Rasial touch you, if you recall. That's why I haven't been able to employ my usual sources. The balance of power in the city is shifting. There are a number of old, established forces that have been part of Sharn since the first towers were built. But new powers have arrived in the wake of the war—myself among them. Now it is a game of alliance and subterfuge, to see if the newcomers can set roots and dislodge the old, established trees."

"I never thought of you as a gardener, Alina."

"I have a knack for making things grow. You of all people should know that."

"And where do the Tarkanans fit into your garden?"

"At the moment, the Tarkanans have remained neutral in this struggle. I doubt they would be pleased to know that Rasial had been working for me. But even so, if something had to be done about him I didn't want it to be traced back to me. I can't afford to have the Tarkanans as enemies . . . yet."

"Why didn't you mention this before?"

"There are things I simply can't say, Daine."

Daine was surprised to see Jode's shocked expression; this was more or less what he'd expected Alina to say.

"I knew you'd encounter the Tarkanans," Alina continued. "The less you knew about the situation, the more natural your reaction would be—and the less chance of their recognizing the connection. At this point, I think you're safe enough from them. You made quite an impression."

"So what about our freakish friends in High Walls? What do you know about that?"

"You know that I hate to admit my own limitations, but until yesterday, I knew nothing whatsoever. I have a few contacts in High Walls, so I've heard about the corpses. Do you know why you were attacked?"

Was she telling the truth? Daine wondered. Alina was as unreadable as always. Her features might have been carved from white marble.

"I had hoped that you could tell us," Daine said. "I think your friend Rasial had dealings with them."

"Ah."

"Ah, indeed. You know more about your stolen shards than we do, and more about magic than I ever will. Do you have any idea why a cackling changeling and a woman with a new eye on her hand would want your shards?"

Alina paused, her eyes distant. She sat down and reached behind her chair, producing a glass of shimmering light. She took a thoughtful sip. "I don't know."

"Really? Or is this another of those things you 'can't say?'"

Alina looked up at him, her eyes cold and hard. Daine held up a hand in apology. Remember who you're dealing with. "I'm sorry. It's been a long day, and we're barely at the first bell. But we're running out of leads, Alina. Anything would help."

She nodded. "I don't know . . . but it's possible. The dragonshards are ideally suited to holding certain types of magical energy. In theory, if you charged the stone then ground it to powder and infused it into a liquid form . . ."

"That's exactly what I was thinking!" Lei said. Alina glanced at her, and she looked away.

"I can't say exactly what would happen," said Alina. "I've never acquired stones of this caliber before, which is why I was trying to acquire this batch. But in theory, if you were trying to induce a magical transformation and you weren't concerned with the possible side effects on the subjects . . . yes, the shards might be extremely valuable to your monster makers."

Daine nodded. "So what are they worth? How much do you think they paid Rasial?"

"You've worked with me before, Daine," Alina said. "I think

that Rasial knows better than to cross me for something so petty as gold."

"He was willing to cross the Tarkanans to work with you," Jode commented.

"True, but I don't think Rasial has ever really seen himself as a Tarkanan. They base their membership on those miserable dragonmarks, and Rasial hates his mark, useful as it is. They may punish him for working behind their backs, but they won't kill him or do anything worse. Now, our relationship . . . as I said, he wouldn't betray me for money."

"It's possible they have some sort of leverage over him, that he didn't have a choice in the matter," said Daine. "If they are interested in the shards, I'd say that the odds are good that he's already passed them along."

"Agreed." Alina swirled the liquid light about in her long glass. "Rasial is a secondary concern, Daine. I want my shards back. If you are correct and these makers-of-monsters already have the shards, I want to know what they plan to do with them—or what they've already done. *That* is what I'm paying four hundred dragons for—the shards themselves, or whatever is left of them. Rasial can rot."

"Any ideas on where to look? Our leads came to nothing."

Jode looked thoughtful, but it was Alina who eventually spoke. "You're sure that the people who attacked you were all Cyrans?"

"Absolutely. Well, except for the changeling."

Alina pondered. "Whoever is making these . . . aberrations would need to include space for the patient to recover—not to mention binding tables and a system to preserve living elements. You couldn't do this in a tent or a single room. If your people really are operating out of High Walls, I would think the only place they'd be able to fit such a workplace would be down below, in the Cogs."

"What might we expect to run into if we find more of them?"

"I couldn't say. The basilisk eye is quite ingenious. I've never met anyone who could accomplish such a transfer. If that level of skill can be relied upon . . . well, a harpy would be a good source for wings—and perhaps you could even find a way to steal its voice. The breath of a dragon, a unicorn's horn, the shroud of a displacer beast . . . a fascinating concept, really. They say changelings are the children of humans and doppelgangers. Can you be certain your changeling was born that way?"

Lei frowned. "It's possible, but I still don't see—"

"You are from the House of Making, Lady d'Cannith," Alina said. "You weave magic into stone and metal. Your enemy—our enemy—seems to do the same with flesh and bone. You may wish to find out why, how, and who. And I might pay you for this information. If there is a new player on the board, I should wish to know about it—and all the more reason for using you, my outsiders. But for now, I want my dragonshards. I suggest you act quickly. If these people are performing magical experiments, it may soon be too late to recover them." She produced a small purse, which she threw to Jode. "I think you'd better keep this one, Jode."

The halfling nodded.

"Now please get on with it. Time is running out." She walked over to one of the mirrors. A moment later she passed through and disappeared.

❋ ❋ ❋ ❋ ❋ ❋ ❋ ❋

"She didn't seem so bad," Lei said. A gnomish child ran past them, twirling a hoop of cold fire.

"Did you notice the new bird? The purple one?" Daine remarked to Jode.

Jode nodded. "Q'barran nutcatcher, I think. Very exotic."

"So?" said Lei.

"Oh, nothing."

"There's something I need to do," Jode said, and Daine was surprised by his serious tone. "I had a thought while I was listening to Alina, and . . . well, it's something I need to do alone. I'll meet you at the Manticore at the third bell."

"No," said Daine. "It's not safe, especially if those . . . *things* were after you. What's on your mind?"

Jode shook his head. "This is something I have to do myself.

You need to trust me."

"Trust isn't the issue."

"After all we've been through, you know I can handle myself alone. I'll stay out of sight."

"We don't know how many more of these freaks are out there, what they look like, or what they can do. I'm sorry, Jode, but—"

"Dasei!" Lei shouted. A moment later, she was running through the crowd.

"Dolurrh," Daine cursed. "Come on! Quickly!" He dove through the crowd after her. As he ran he slipped his dagger out of its sheath, holding the blade close against his forearm.

"Dasei d'Cannith!" Lei called, still running. She came to a small plaza and grabbed hold of a woman in a green robe, her short red hair partially hidden by a headdress of gold and silk. "Dasei! Thank Olladra! You don't know how glad I am to see you."

The woman turned to face Lei, and her face was cold. It was just then that Daine noticed. Pierce had followed him, but Jode was nowhere to be seen.

Daine turned to Pierce. "Find Jode. Quickly. If you can't, head back to the Manticore, and we'll see you there."

Pierce sprinted away, and Daine turned his attention back to Lei and the stranger. She was slightly younger than Lei, and there was no questioning her wealth. Her beautiful green gown was made from Zil dreamsilk, sprinkled with gold and platinum threads that recalled the patterns of the stars in the sky. A rainbow of gems adorned her golden headdress, scattering the light into a thousand shards. She was staring disdainfully at Lei, and she did not speak.

Then Lei hit her.

This was no elegant slap. Lei had been in the battlefield for years, and although she was part of the support corps, she'd been in more than one brawl. The blow caught Dasei completely by surprise. The woman staggered back, nearly knocking over a display of fine hats. A stream of blood trickled from her nose, and her eyes were full of fury. Rising again, she reached into one of her billowing sleeves and produced a crystal-tipped wand of black oak and leveled the slender rod at Lei.

Daine knew he couldn't reach Dasei in time to stop her from releasing the spell, but he charged anyway. Better late than never.

He needn't have worried. In the split-second it had taken Dasei to draw the wand, Lei was already in motion, spinning the darkwood staff. A low, sweeping blow caught Dasei just behind her left knee. She howled in pain and collapsed. A second blow smashed her hand and sent the wand flying. Daine snatched it out of the air and tucked it into his belt.

Lei stood over the fallen woman, the darkwood staff leveled at her throat. Surely it was a trick of the light, but it seemed to Daine that the face carved into the shaft of the staff was smiling a little wider than usual. Lei's expression was grim.

"Lei, what are you doing?" he said.

"Stay out of this, Daine."

Her opponent glared at Lei from the ground, clutching her bruised fingers.

"I have endured more pain in the last three days than you have in your entire life, Dasei." Lei flicked her staff toward Dasei's face, pulling back at the last minute. The injured woman flinched and cried out. "Perhaps it's time to change that."

"Lei?" said Daine, and he took a careful step forward. Was it the staff making Lei act this way? Could it have done something to her?

"I said *stay out of this!*" she snapped. She set the tip of her staff against Dasei's throat. "I'm adapting. I'll survive. But to have you—*you!*—not even speak to me . . ." She pressed on Dasei's throat, pushing her back. "If you think I'll put up with that, you don't know me as well as I thought." She drew back the staff, and the woman gasped. "Now, let's try this again. Dasei d'Cannith, you don't know how glad I am to see you."

For a moment, Dasei held Lei's gaze, and Daine could see the same fire in her eyes that he'd seen in Lei so many times before. Then it went out, and she looked down at the ground. "You shouldn't be here, Lei. Just go."

"And where should I go, cousin?"

"Dolurrh for all I care!" Dasei glared up at her. "You're not my cousin anymore. You have no place in the family or Sharn."

"I think that I can live with two of those three." Lei's voice was calmer, and she lowered the staff. "But I'd just as soon our final conversation didn't end in the street." She held out her hand. "Get up. Surely you can find it in your heart to buy a last meal for your departing cousin?"

Dasei said nothing, but she took the hand and let Lei pull her to her feet.

"Lead on," said Lei. "As this may be my last meal with a member of House Cannith, I'll trust to your generosity." As Dasei led them to a waterhouse, Lei looked back at Daine. "Where are Pierce and Jode?"

"Jode vanished on some errand. I sent Pierce after him. What's going on here?" He nodded toward Dasei. "That was a rather . . . surprising display back there."

"As I recall, you're the one who throws dwarves off lifts. I'm not allowed to express my anger?"

"It just didn't seem like you."

Lei looked down at the ground for a moment. "I know. I shouldn't have hit her. It's just . . . after our history, I couldn't believe she was standing by this excoriate claim." She shook her head and smiled slightly. "Did you see her expression when she hit the ground? I may have lost my family fortune, but that's a memory I'll treasure."

Daine chuckled and slid his dagger back into its sheath. "There is that. And speaking of priceless, it looks like it's time for lunch."

❦ ❦ ❦ ❦ ❦ ❦ ❦

The waterhouse drew a wealthy crowd. At a table in the corner, a Mrorian banker was entertaining a group of dwarves and gnome merchants with a colorful story about the relative values of sovereigns, crowns, and golden galifars, and a burst of laughter echoed throughout the room.

Daine sniffed his mug. "Gnomes. It's one thing to have the innkeeper water down the ale, but only a gnome could get people to pay even more for straight water."

Dasei rolled her eyes.

"It's not just water," Lei explained. "It's infused with various herbs, and the mug itself is made from fragrant clay to add to the overall aesthetic experience."

"Right. So our little friends say. But have you tried it yet?"

He took a long pull. "If you ask me, you're paying good gold for water in a smelly mug."

Lei shrugged. "Which is why Dasei is paying. So, cousin, are you ready to talk?"

There were daggers in Dasei's stare, but she had regained her composure. "And if I'm not? Do you plan to start another brawl?"

"Is that why you chose a restaurant where they hold weapons at the door?"

Dasei looked away.

Lei looked down at the table. "Das, I'm sorry. I shouldn't have done it. But the last few days have been very difficult. Put yourself in my position."

"How can I?"

"How can *I*? This whole mess is still a mystery to me. What have I done to deserve this?"

Dasei's expression softened. "You mean you really don't know?"

"Why would I lie? I've been fighting in the war for the last three years. I spent the last five months digging through the wreckage of my homeland. It's been over half a year since I've even seen another member of the house, and he was just a supply courier. How could I have betrayed the house? When could I have done it?"

Their meals arrived, drifting through the air in the hands of an invisible servitor. Daine had been dreaming about a bloody piece of meat, but it turned out that the specialty of the waterhouse was bread, which was just as exotic and carefully prepared as the water.

"I . . . I don't know," said Dasei "You weren't the only one to be ousted, and I didn't press for details. These last few months have been difficult for everyone."

"I think my difficult tops your difficult."

"You don't understand." Dasei drained her mug and set it down hard; a moment later, it was snatched away by an invisible servant. "You grew up in Cyre. Metrol was the heart of the house, and it was the council that held us all together. These last few months . . . it's been chaos, Lei. Supply lines have been shattered. Business is uncertain. They're saying that the Council of Thronehold may outlaw the use of warforged—or at least their creation. Half the barons want to lead the next council, while the other half don't even want a council. There's been hoarding of goods and materials, even some talk of sabotage within the house."

"What's this have to do with me?"

"Merrix is one of the aspiring leaders. He's been trying to purge the house. He says he's removing traitors and enemies of the house, but he may just be flexing his muscles."

"I still don't understand. How am I an enemy of the house? Doesn't he have to justify this to someone?"

Dasei nodded. "He had to explain his case to the regional arbiters, yes. I don't know the answer, but I do have a little information you may not have. Among other things, you're not the only person he's driven from the house."

"I'd gathered that."

"What you may not know is that two of the others he excoriated were your parents, Aleisa and Talin."

"What? But . . . they're dead!"

"Apparently he's not taking any chances. Perhaps your fate is linked to theirs. He may have simply accused your entire family."

Lei finished her water and slammed the mug down on the table. Daine was surprised that it survived the experience. Looking around, she grabbed his half-full mug and took another swallow. Daine put his hand on her shoulder.

"Blaming the dead is always easier than challenging the living," he said gently. "It sounds to me like this Merrix is just trying to make the best of a bad situation, and he's willing to sacrifice the memory of your family to improve his own situation."

Lei blinked back tears, but her voice was steady. "What were *they* accused of, Dasei?"

"I don't know. I told you, they only gave names, not reasons. With all the upheaval, it didn't seem like the time to ask questions. Although . . ." She shifted uncomfortably, rubbing her bruised fingers.

"What?"

"You're not going to hit me again, are you?"

"What were you going to say?"

"Do you know what happened to Cyre?"

"I told you we spent the last six months there. I've seen it. It's
. . . more disturbing that you can imagine."

"I've heard." Dasei looked around and lowered here voice.
"But what I meant was, do you know what caused it?"

"Does anyone?"

"That's the question of the hour. A lot of people are blaming
House Cannith. It's common knowledge that the house had a
strong presence in the region, and the magewrights and sages
are still trying to make sense of it. I don't know for certain,
but I think that Baron Merrix has claimed that your family was
involved in some way."

Lei leaped to her feet and her chair crashed to the floor.
Daine was up and had grabbed her arm before she had a chance
to strike the blow.

"I'm just telling you what I heard!" Dasei cringed against her
seat. The fire in her eyes had gone out again.

Lei pulled against Daine's arm, but he held fast. She stopped
and took a deep breath, closing her eyes. She exhaled slowly
then opened her eyes again. Daine let go of her arm.

"I take it you weren't involved in the Mourning, then?"
Dasei said.

"I was *there*. It's a miracle I survived at all. And even I don't
know what happened."

"So how can you be certain that your parents—"

Daine grabbed Lei's arm again, before she could wind back
for another blow.

Dasei raised her hands defensively. "Look, Lei, I'm not saying that they did anything wrong. I'm just asking—"

"I think you've said enough, Lady d'Cannith." Daine pulled
Lei out of her chair. "I thank you for the"—he gestured at the
remnants of bread and water—"meal, but I think we should go
our separate ways now."

Dasei nodded, and her relief was easy to see. "I'll settle the
cost."

Lei seemed calm, but Daine kept hold of her hand. "Shall we depart, my lady?"

✻ ✻ ✻ ✹ ✻ ✻ ✻

Lei whirled her staff and struck at the air, venting her anger on flies and shadows. While he'd sooner have seen her happy, Daine actually preferred the angry Lei to the distant, emotionally drained Lei he'd been living with the last few days.

"She was only repeating what she'd heard," Daine said.

"I know. It just makes me angry. How could anyone think that we—that they—could do such a horrible thing?"

"Someone did it."

"Really?" She stopped and turned to face him. "Then why haven't they done it again? There's nothing to prove that any human agency was involved. Perhaps some sort of epic conjunction of the planes opened a gateway to Kythri."

"Covering an entire nation?"

"Well, we don't know, do we? You used to follow the Silver Flame, right? How do you know it wasn't the work of one of those fiends bound by the Flame?"

"Maybe because they're *bound* by the Flame?"

She glared at him. "You know what I'm saying. There's nothing proving that humans had anything to do with it—let alone House Cannith, and certainly not my parents."

"Well . . ." Daine began walking again.

Lei followed on his heels. "Well, what?"

"Do you remember our last battle at Keldan Ridge?"

"How could I forget?"

"We never did find out who those 'forged were fighting for."

"So?"

"Come on, Lei. An army of strange warforged? You know as well as I do that they don't build themselves, and they weren't wearing any insignia. What were they doing in Cyre? And then there's the stormship. Someone had devoted a tremendous amount of resources to protecting that area. What was going on there?"

Lei looked away. "You're thinking of Whitehearth, aren't you?"

"Can you blame me?"

Lei sighed and shook her head. They had reached the lift. Surprisingly, it was empty. "I know. You've got no reason to trust my—er, House Cannith. But I refuse to believe that my parents had anything to do with this."

"What *did* they do during the war?"

"They spent most of their lives working on the warforged. They worked with Aaren d'Cannith on the first true warforged thirty-one years ago. It's a long story, but we weren't that close at the end. It's my fault, I suppose."

"Hmm. What was it the sphinx said? 'You must forget your house and focus on your family?' "

Lei nodded, thoughtfully. They stopped at the next district, and a patrol of the Watch came aboard. "You're right. But how could I—"

"Well, well!" The harsh voice came from behind them, ringing out as the lift began to descend.

Daine turned. There were four halberdiers blocking the gate of the lift. Standing before them was a dwarf—Sergeant Lorrak, whom Daine had thrown off a lift.

This lift.

"Looking to get to the ground, boy?" the dwarf said. "I know a faster way."

Jode made his way through the streets of Daggerwatch. Where yesterday the streets had been calm and quiet, today the garrison district was thronged with people. Beggars, soldiers, and many others lined the wide streets, waiting for something. Jode made his way through the crowd, but given his small stature, it was quite a challenge. He squeezed through a jungle of shifting legs and feet, dodging boots and kicks. After a few minutes, he felt the need to escape from the chaos, if only of a moment. Passing by a large storm drain, he considered a moment then crawled into the hole.

The tunnel was three feet across, and the walls were crusted with dirt and mold. Insects scurried into the shadows, and the stench of rot filled the air. The passage dropped down nearly six feet before ending in a metal grate. It was the perfect sanctuary for a curious halfling, and that's exactly what Jode found there.

The self-appointed guardian of the grate was a ragged halfling, who would have seemed more at home in High Walls or Malleon's Gate than a respectable garrison district. His profession was clear. A few scraps of cloth and leather lay at his feet—the remains of purses and pouches sliced apart with a deft hand and sharp blade. Most of his dark hair was gathered in a thick braid that fell down his back. A smaller plait of hair fell along his left cheek. His eyes were bright, and so was the blade of the curved dagger he held in his hands.

"Jhola'tanda!" Jode called. The stranger's plait was the mark of a Talentan scout, and Jode hailed him in the Halfling tongue. This salutation could be interpreted many different ways, depending on the relationship between the speakers and the time of day. Under these circumstances, it could be generally translated as, "Greetings, one who is not my brother in blood but yet might become one in friendship."

The stranger studied him then blew on his blade—a symbolic preparation for battle. "This is my ground, orasca." His voice was high and raspy. In this place, the word orasca meant "one who seeks to steal my livelihood" or "lizard-meat seller"—or in the case of a dispute between lizard-vendors, both.

Jode held up his empty hands. "I have no interest in crowns and copper," he said. "I simply sought shelter from the gorlan'tor." The term meant "stampede" or more literally "thundering herd of pea-brained creatures that a just deity should never have made so huge."

The stranger smiled slightly at that but kept his blade at the ready.

"I am Jode, and I ask forgiveness for the intrusion," he dropped to one knee and laid both his hands on the steel grate. "I ask for your protection as I pass across your land." By tradition, this was a polite way of saying, "I'm harmless, but follow me if you want to make sure."

The other halfling considered for a long moment, then finally tucked his blade into his belt and held out his hand. "I am Moresco, and I give you welcome for the length of your stay." He helped Jode to his feet. "So you weren't expecting the carnival then?"

"Carnival?"

"The Carnival of Shadows has come to town. It will soon pass by on its way to the Talain Coliseum. The crowds have gathered to watch the opening parade, and it is good hunting for my swift blade."

The Carnival of Shadows! The elves of House Phiarlan were known across the length of Khorvaire as the finest actors and entertainers in the land, and the Carnival of Shadows was a jewel in their crown. A blend of magic, skills honed over the course of centuries, beasts, and exotic entertainers drawn from across Eberron . . . the wonders of the carnival were a thing of legend.

Even as Jode absorbed this information, the crowd cheered. Apparently the parade had just come into view. He sighed. "Normally, I would be overjoyed to see such a spectacle, but I imagine it will make my travels even more difficult." He glanced thoughtfully down at the metal grate. "I don't suppose that you know any secret paths that pass beneath the street and the many feet above?"

Moresco gave him an appraising glance. "Where do you wish to travel?"

"The Daggerwatch Garrison."

Moresco raised an eyebrow, but Jode simply smiled and shrugged. Outside the tunnel, some sort of exotic beast gave an eerie, fluting cry.

"I may know a path that would be safe to travel, but you must act quickly if you wish to make use of it. Tell me what you have to offer in exchange for my secret knowledge."

"Would that I had my treasures on my person," Jode said. "But all of my possessions were wrongfully taken from me by a zealous watchman. I was contacted by an honest sergeant—a rarer beast than any you may seen in the carnival, I imagine—who has promised to return them to me. Escort me to the garrison, and I can offer you a ruby the size of your nose or a targath charm that will protect you from disease and infection."

Moresco considered the offer with narrowed eyes, than nodded. "Very well, I will show you the path. But we travel above the streets, not below." The sound of drums and elven pipes drifted down from outside. Moresco cocked his head then grabbed one of the rungs on the wall of the drain shaft. "Follow me. Quick and close."

They emerged into a sea of sound and motion. Jode had heard stories of the Carnival of Shadows, but he was not prepared for what lay beyond the drain. Sharn was infused with the magic of Syrania, energy that enhanced all powers of flight, and the parade presented wonders that could be shown in no other city.

Through the forest of people, he saw acrobats dancing between floating platforms—miniature citadels of crystal and stone, each carved to resemble one of the royal palaces of Khorvaire. As the performers tumbled through the air, glowing figures darted after them. Ghosts? Illusions? From the ground, it was impossible to tell. Hidden musicians wove webs of melody that were so dazzling and hypnotic that Jode almost missed seeing the manticore that soared overhead. Then he saw the men suspended forty feet above the street on massive stilts decorated to resemble the towers of Sharn. Perched atop their stilts, the walkers wore costumes patterned after the racing beasts of Eight Winds. Jode could see a griffon, a hippogriff, and a pegasus, and he assumed that others would follow.

"Quickly now!" Moresco said. The halfling had his knife in his hand, and he tucked it between his teeth.

They darted between boots and squeezed past shins, slowly making their way to the street itself. As they reached the very edge of the crowd a massive stilt came down right in front of them, and Moresco leaped onto it. Jode held his breath and jumped, digging his fingers and toes into the cloth and papier-mâché surrounding the massive pole. A moment later they were rising up through the air.

Moresco used his knife to carve tiny handholds into the stilt, then passed the knife down to Jode. "Hold on!" he called.

It was a dizzying way to travel, but a surprisingly swift one. Initially, Jode feared they would be noticed and caught, but apparently the halflings were light enough so as not to throw the stiltwalker off-balance—that or some magic in the stilts prevented disruption. As for the crowds, most were too busy watching the show in the sky to look at the halflings down near the earth. Those few who noticed simply pointed and laughed.

Minutes passed. Jode's arms felt as if they were on fire, and his stomach rose in his throat with every sweeping stride. Faces blurred and swarmed around him, and the dizzying music of the pipes flowed through his mind, drowning out the murmur and roar of the crowds. At long last the stone hippogriffs flanking the garrison gate came into view.

As they swept by the gates, the two halflings leaped off of the stilts. The guards were keeping the area before the gates clear of crowds, and the two tumbled across the cobblestones and came to a stop at the foot of a puzzled officer of the Watch. Jode stood and brushed himself off. His knee ached, and he foresaw many bruises in his future.

"Tanda!" cried Moresco. "Let us fetch your many treasures, then find a suitable hole to celebrate our adventure."

But as he had expected, Jode saw an avaricious gleam in the eyes of the cutpurse. He had no doubt as to what sort of welcome would await him in the suitable hole—or what Moresco would have done if he'd known that Jode was carrying a purse full of gold. He reached into the folds of his clothing and slipped a few golden galifars out of the hidden purse.

"I'm afraid my treasures are lost forever, and this is the end of our journeys together, orasca." He tossed the coins at Moresco. Surprised as he was, the rogue deftly caught the glittering gold. "I suggest you be on your way, before I tell these good guardsmen about the work you've been doing of late."

Moresco glared at him, but he had more gold than when the journey began. After a moment he spit on the back of a finger and flung the spittle at Jode, then disappeared into the crowd.

Jode watched him go, and then turned back to the guard at the gate.

"I need to speak with Captain Grazen," he said.

CHAPTER 26

BRELAND
SHARN
Dravago 28, 996 YK

Daine considered the odds. The lift itself was a broad disk surrounded by a low metal rail. Two of the halberdiers were blocking the gateway, while the other two were moving to either side. He cursed himself for not considering this possibility. The dwarf had been patrolling in the area of the Den'iyas lift the other day, and it was probably his regular beat.

Daine caught Lei's eye and cast a glance over his shoulder. They backed up to the railing. At least they couldn't be surrounded that way.

"Lorrak, right?" said Daine. "You're looking . . . alive."

The dwarf grinned, which wasn't a pleasant sight. "That's one thing we have in common." He was carrying a cudgel of heavy bronzewood, and he tapped it against the palm of his left hand. "But I think it looks better on me."

Lei rolled her eyes. "Sergeant. You don't like Cyrans. That's fine. But you're an officer of the law. Am I actually supposed to believe that you're going to push me off of a lift? Arrah's blade, if that's part of your job, what do you do to get a promotion?"

If Lorrak was affected by the speech, he hid it well. *We need Jode,* Daine thought. *If Jode were here, he'd already have convinced the sergeant to buy us a meal.*

"My duty is to protect the people of Sharn," Lorrak said. "The oath doesn't say anything about Mourner scum. There's

191

too many of you here already, and it's common knowledge that half of you are mad. If I told people you jumped off the edge, they'd probably believe me. Now, you hurt me . . . ? That's another story. Killing a guardsman is bad enough, but a Mourner killing an officer? If you were lucky, you'd be brought in by the guards before the mobs got to you."

Lorrak nodded to his men, and the halberdiers at the sides of the lift began to move forward.

Daine studied the dwarf. This was no idle threat. If the two guards at the gate didn't join in the fight immediately, he and Lei might have a chance. Daine had held his own against Lorrak the day before, but the sergeant was right. Even if they defeated the guards, things would only get worse. There was only one solution.

As the guards closed in, he turned to Lei and charged. He slammed into her, wrapping his arms around her. She was staggered by the blow and knocked off balance. He lifted her up and threw himself at the railing. His hip stung as his leg scraped against the top of the rail, and then they were falling, plummeting down the half-mile drop between the lift and the lowest streets of Sharn.

❧ ❧ ❧ ❧ ❧ ❧ ❧

Lei struggled as they fell. She was shouting, but the roaring of the wind drowned out the words. As the ground rushed up at them, Daine wondered if he'd made a mistake.

And then they stopped falling.

For a moment, they seemed to be standing still, then Daine realized they were still drifting down, slowly as a leaf falling from a tree.

Lei stopped struggling, taken aback by the change in velocity. "Daine?" she said.

"Yes?"

"Why aren't we dead now?"

"Feather token. Something Captain Grazen gave me. It's a charm they sell in the markets. Easy to see why people buy them. Only one use, though."

"And he just *gave* it to you?"

"Yes. When he was explaining how Lorrak survived the fall."

They were almost to the streets. No one seemed to be paying them any attention. Apparently, the citizens of Sharn were used to having people fall from the sky.

"And when you were jumping off the lift, did it ever occur to you that he might have actually given you the charm Lorrak used with its magic drained?"

"No."

"Next time, I think I'd rather take my chances with the dwarf."

They drifted the rest of the way in silence.

CHAPTER 27

BRELAND
SHARN
Dravago 28, 996 YK

Pierce stalked the streets of High Walls. He had lost
Jode at the lift. He had hoped to pick up the halfling's trail in
the lower districts, but his gift for tracking in the wild was proving to be of little use in the city. Following the captain's orders,
he was returning to the Manticore, and after last night's fight,
he was treating the district as hostile territory. Every shadow was
a potential ambush, every passerby a possible enemy. In a way,
he found this a relaxing exercise. The battle they'd fought last
evening had been a release, a chance to serve his true purpose.
But at the same time, it had been deeply disturbing. The people
they had fought were Cyrans, the people he had spent his life
defending. Old allies were now enemies, old friends had betrayed them . . . nothing made sense anymore. He missed the
war, when life had been clear—defend your friends, kill the
enemy, and do your best not to die. Questions easy. Answers
clear. Not anymore.

So far he had stood by the captain. For all that his purpose
was to defend Cyre, Pierce did not have the same sense of
nationalism he had seen in many of his fellow soldiers. Most
of his old comrades came from families that had lived in Cyre
for generations. Many had lost loved ones or relatives in the
centuries of war. They fought out of a burning desire for vengeance against Breland or Karrnath, seeking to repay their
losses with blood. But Pierce had no family history. For that

matter, he had no blood. Borders on a map, the concept of a nation . . . these things were meaningless to him. What mattered was the shape of a face, the distinctive sound of a Cyran accent. And what mattered most were his fellow soldiers, those few who had survived. Cyre might be destroyed, but Daine, Lei, Jode . . . they were his nation, his country. But what use was he to them, if the war was truly over?

Although these inner issues troubled his spirit, Pierce never let his concentration falter. A cloaked figure had been following Pierce for some distance. The stranger was making an effort to remain unseen, slipping into doorways and shadows. With his peripheral glances, Pierce had seen no weapons, but he could take no chances. A sense of calm settled over him, and the doubts of a moment ago evaporated. Issues of war and peace were no longer relevant. The lines of battle were drawn, and it was time for action.

Pierce was holding his bow, and he nocked an arrow as he walked, calculating that he could loose approximately four shots before the pursuer could close. But this was a city street, not a war zone, the events of last night not withstanding. There were bystanders about—Cyran refugees mostly. He couldn't risk the chance of a stray arrow. Pierce released the tension on his bowstring and slipped into the next alley, disappearing in a pool of shadows.

A moment later the stranger appeared, features hidden beneath a ragged oilskin cloak. The hooded figure slid into the alley, looking cautiously from side to side. It moved with the grace of a predator, but even a predator can fall prey to a superior hunter.

Pierce melted out of the shadows behind the stalker. He had dropped his bow and drawn his flail, and with one smooth motion he wrapped the chain around the stranger's neck. One hand was on the ironshod haft of the weapon; the other gripped the chain, just below the spiked steel ball.

"If you present any sort of threat, I will snap your neck," Pierce said. "Is that understood?"

"I have no need of breath, brother," The voice was low and feminine . . . and distinctly warforged. "And if it had been my intention to present a threat, we would not be having this conversation."

After a moment's consideration, Pierce let the stalker go. He loosened the flail and pulled the weapon away from her neck but kept the chain loose and ready to strike. She turned to face him, keeping her hands in sight.

Feminine warforged were an oddity. The 'forged were fundamentally inorganic, and while body designs varied slightly based on the duties of the warforged, functionality was the first concern. Pierce had never met a warforged that had a feminine appearance, but he had met one other 'forged with a female voice and personality. Perhaps the magewrights who built the warforged thought it was a better match for her military specialty—or perhaps it was just a quirk of an isolated female artificer who wanted to put her mark on the warforged she created. This 'forged was smaller than Pierce and lightly built. In some ways, she reminded Pierce of Lei. She'd done a remarkable job of hiding her armored body beneath loose clothing and her cloak. A cowl and woolen scarf hid her face, and even Pierce had taken her for a refugee bundled up against the frequent rain. But there was no mistaking the feeling of the metal and wood that had scraped against the chain of his flail when he'd circled her throat.

"What do you want?" he said, setting the chain of his flail spinning slowly. "And why do you call me brother?"

Her voice was as cool and impassive as his own. If she felt threatened by the flail, she didn't show it. "We share the same parents. We were born in the same womb. Does that not make us siblings?"

"We are not creatures of flesh and blood. Two swords made by the same smith are not brother and sister."

"If they could speak, they might say differently."

She pulled the scarf down from her face, revealing mithral features coated in dark blue enamel. Her faceplate was the standard model used for the Cyran warforged, scaled to her slight frame. Aside from the color, it was a perfect match to Pierce's own face.

"Believe as you will," he said. "My weapon has never spoken to me. What is it you want?"

"The question is what *you* want, why you remain among these creatures of flesh?"

"I was built to defend Cyrans, and I continue to do so." Something about the stranger made Pierce uncomfortable. The female voice was odd enough, and in spite of her empty hands he couldn't shake the feeling that she was dangerous.

"You were built to serve. You are a sword, bought and paid for. But unlike a sword, you have a voice. You can choose your destiny, and now is the time to choose. Even now, the war comes to a close. Ambassadors and princes hammer out treaties. Once they settle their differences, what do you think they will do with us? Who wants to look at a sword while trying to celebrate peace?"

Pierce remembered the words of the sphinx, the mention of his family. Was this what she'd meant? "Do you know who created me?" he asked.

"One human or another. Does it matter? Which does a sword have more in common with—another blade or the smith who forged it?"

"Perhaps it's not the metal, but the motive," he said. "A smith may not pass his blood to his creations, but he shapes them with his dreams."

"And have you ever had a dream?" She stepped forward, and Pierce moved back to maintain the distance between them. "For a creature of flesh, a dream is a trivial thing, an idle fantasy that comes in the night. We never sleep. But there are those of use who share a dream, one forged from courage and desire. Join us. Help us forge a new future, a place for our people."

"I have a place," Pierce said. He slid his flail across his back and reached down for his long bow.

The warforged inclined her head. "Very well. But consider my words—and I suggest you keep them to yourself. When peace finally falls, is the sword anyone's friend?" She drew her scarf up across her features. "We'll meet again."

She stepped back into the street, and in a moment she was gone. Her skills were impressive. Clearly she'd wanted Pierce to spot her when she'd been following him, and he wondered if she'd been spying on him at other times.

As he walked on to the Manticore, he thought about what she'd said. Was she right? Was this the family Flamewind had spoken of? Or did the sphinx have something more specific in mind—the purpose of two swords forged by the same hand, and not merely made at the same forge?

But these thoughts did not trouble him for long. He was warforged. His companions had need of him. Studying the crowds for any signs of Jode, he continued down the streets of High Walls.

INTERLUDE

What did he want?

She could hear the sounds coming from his mouth, but she couldn't understand them. The sounds were distorted fragments, robbed of context or meaning. Even his face . . . she found it difficult to look at him, to study him long enough to read his expressions. Last night she'd dreamed of the skinless man and his master, that they had taken her down below and changed her again. But maybe it wasn't a dream. Had she been back in the pit? And if so, what had he done? Had he eaten her memories of language? Could she relearn the meaning of these words if she kept tried hard enough? Or was it her ears? Were her ears still her own, or had they been taken away? What could he want with her ears? How much more would he take before he finally let her die?

The man was still talking. She looked down at him and shook her head. Did he want the skinless man? She put her hand to one of her cheeks and pulled at the skin, miming the action of a blade with the other.

Clearly he couldn't understand what she was trying to say. She held her fingers up around her mouth and wiggled them, but he didn't seem to understand that either.

Suddenly he tapped his forehead. A thought? He spoke again, but the words were just as meaningless as before. She shook her head. He beckoned to her, indicating that she should sit down. Gingerly, she did so—she rarely sat during the day.

Why was he doing this? What did he want?

He touched his mouth with his forefinger then made a turning gesture with his thumb and forefinger. She tried to study his face for clues, but as she did all of his features seemed to slip away, leaving her looking at a pure smooth slate. She winced and looked away, and as she did his features reappeared. It had to be her, she thought. One more change. One more thing that they'd taken away from her.

The visitor spoke again. She thought there was a twinge of frustration in his nonsense words, but she couldn't say for certain. What happened next surprised her. He reached out and touched her face. His hands were soft and gentle, and they slowly drifted across her lips.

"Welcome," a voice said.

She could understand! She knew these words! Then she saw the fear in the stranger's eyes and realized who it was that had spoken.

The skinless man had come into the room. His hood was thrown back, revealing the raw muscle that covered his face. "I wasn't expecting visitors," he said, "but this is a most welcome surprise."

The visitor said something in return, but his words were still a chaotic blur of sound.

"I'd be happy to explain," her master said, slowly moving closer. "But there are better places for it. You'll come with me, I trust?"

She couldn't let it happen. She pushed the visitor as hard as she could, and he went staggering for the door. But he seemed to understand, and as soon as he caught his balance he ran.

But it wasn't enough. The skinless man cracked his arm like a whip, and a tentacle of flesh flew forth from his sleeve. The glistening tendril wrapped around the visitor's ankles and pulled him to the floor. Her master called out, and one of the claws came through the door. There was a brief struggle, but the outcome was never in doubt.

"Take him below," her master said.

The claw threw him over her shoulder and carried him off.

The skinless man turned to face her, his mad eyes glittering in their deep sockets. "And you . . . I suppose I'll have to think of something new for you."

His laughter echoed in her ears as he turned to follow the claw.

The common room of the Manticore was nearly empty. Dassi the innkeeper had provided Daine, Pierce, and Lei with a battered deck of cards, and they'd been playing three stones for the length of a bell.

"He's an hour late," Lei said, crossing the king of fire with the alchemist.

"So?" Daine said. After a moment's thought, he picked up the alchemist of fire and replaced it with one of his water cards. "Jode's dealt with Darguuls, Valenar warriors, agents of the Citadel. What are you afraid of?"

"Well, for a start, most basilisks have two eyes. So who's got the other one?"

"Good point."

"Where did he go, anyway?"

"It must have been something Alina said. I remember he had a strange look on his face at one point . . . Aureon's blood! I can't remember what it was."

"Could he have gone back to see her?" Lei drew a card.

"It is unlikely," Pierce said. "I was able to follow him for a short time, and he moved directly to a lift. It departed before I reached it, and by the time it returned the trail was impossible to follow." It seemed to Daine that Pierce had been slightly distant since they met up at the Manticore, but as always it was difficult to read the moods of the warforged.

"Do you think that he came back here?" Lei asked.

"There's no way to know, my lady."

"I'm not a Cannith anymore, Pierce," Lei said. "I don't have a title."

"You will always be *my* lady," the warforged said.

Lei smiled. "At least I still have that." She considered her cards and then looked up. "You know, I've never actually asked you, Pierce, when were you constructed?"

"I was part of the second legion, my lady, forged in the nine hundred and sixty-eighth year of the kingdom."

"That's when I was born!" she said. "The second legion . . . so Aaren d'Cannith himself would have worked on you."

"I never learned the names of my creators," Pierce said. "Is this of interest?"

"I don't know. The sphinx asked you about it, didn't she? Maybe that's what she meant when she asked about your parents."

"I suppose. And have you had any insight about your brothers?"

"No, that still doesn't make any sense."

"And I still haven't lost anything," Daine pointed out. "Perhaps she was just playing games."

"It's certainly possible," Lei said. "But what are the stakes? Who's she playing against?"

"Three stones is normally played for silver," Pierce said. "And yet we are playing with no coins. Is the satisfaction of victory not sufficient reward?" He drew and then started a cascade, covering the board with water cards. The others sighed and threw down their cards.

❀ ❀ ❀ ❀ ❀ ❀ ❀

Greykell showed up as the fifth bell was ringing. "Well met, my friends!" she said, driving the air from Daine's chest with a powerful embrace. She went around the table, hugging each of them in turn. "And have you had a productive day?"

"No one's tried to kill us for an hour," Daine said. "Any news on Hugal?"

"You mean Monan? No, not yet, I'm afraid. That's why I stopped by. I'm still going through my rounds, and I have a few more places to check. Obviously I could use your support, but I also thought it would be a chance for you to meet more of our people."

Daine shrugged and set down his cards. "Why not? The only reason I haven't lost all of my money to Pierce is because I didn't have any to begin with."

"Come by the militia tent tomorrow night," Greykell said, slapping Pierce on the shoulder. "We're always looking for a few good players, and I assure you, my imaginary money is every bit as good as Daine's."

"I think I'll stay here," Lei said. "There's an alchemical formula I've been trying to perfect, and I want to take another look at the information we have about the stolen shards."

"Oh, come along," Greykell said, pulling the smaller woman up and out of her chair. "The splendor of High Walls awaits you!"

After a little more encouragement, Lei agreed to join the expedition. Pierce agreed as well, stringing his massive bow.

"There are still many dangers in this area," he said. "I believe it is best if we remain together."

"That's the spirit!" Greykell said. She studied the markings on Pierce's torso plating. "Second legion, right? 'Sword and Steel. We Stand As One.'"

"That was the motto of the legion, yes. Most of the legion was dispersed among the human units. I rarely fought alongside my own kind."

Greykell smiled and shrugged. "Well, stand as one with us humans." She turned to the others. "Now let's go looking for your evil twin."

❂ ❂ ❂ ❂ ❂ ❂ ❂

Although Cyran refugees made up the vast bulk of the population of High Walls, people of many nationalities had found their way into the district. During the height of the war, High Walls had served as a prison in all but name, a place where people of questionable loyalty could be concentrated into a single location. As they wandered through the maze of alleys surrounding the district, Greykell stopped frequently to check on the various families and clans that lived in the decrepit old buildings. A Lhazaar patriarch insisted that they taste his cold fish stew, and a former siege engineer from Karrnath eagerly discussed the science of fortifications with Lei. Greykell seemed to know everyone in the district, and everyone they met wanted to talk. Time passed in a blur of war stories, local gossip, and health problems. Greykell celebrated the triumphs and sympathized with the misfortunes. Often she was able to solve the problems of the most miserable. One man knew of openings in one of the foundries beneath the city. Another had lost his job because of a bigoted Brelish foreman. It soon became clear why Greykell had asked Lei to come along. She'd picked up on Lei's skill as an artificer and convinced her to fix broken tools and furniture. She wove a web of connections across the community, and Daine was impressed by her knowledge and charisma.

But there was no sign of Hugal.

"Did you actually expect to find Hugal in there?" Daine said. They'd just emerged from a tenement inhabited by a mixed family of orcs and humans from the Shadow Marches.

"No," Greykell admitted cheerfully. "But you never know with changelings, do you? I'm just following my usual path. I believe the most likely place to find your friend is up ahead."

"Do you do this every day?" Lei asked.

"More or less. When I arrived, there was a lot of tension in High Walls. The Karrns hated the Thranes, they both hated the Cyrans, and everyone hated the Lhazaarites. That's still there, though most of the people conceal it around me to be polite. People don't change in a day, but progress is being made. The war is over. And more importantly, we're not Cyrans and Karrns any more. If this is where we're going to stay, then we need to start thinking of ourselves as the people of Sharn."

"I don't see the Brelanders welcoming you with open arms."

"I didn't say citizens of Breland. I said people of Sharn. I'm not asking you to forget Cyre, Daine. I just want you to put the welfare of your neighbors ahead of a nation you'll never see again."

Daine frowned. There was some sense to what she said, but he'd spent the last ten years fighting Brelanders and Karrns, and it was hard to let that anger go in a day. And despite the months he spent in the Mournlands, it was hard to accept that Cyre truly was gone forever.

"And what does Councilor Teral think about this?" he asked.

"Teral and I don't always see eye to eye, but he's done a great deal to hold the community together. He brought a large number of survivors out of the Mournland, and it was his gold that paid for many of the tents in the square. If you ask me, it doesn't do us any good to pretend that Cyre will return. But Ambassador Jairen agrees with Teral." She shrugged.

"Jairen? You mean we still have an ambassador?"

Greykell nodded. "With so many Cyran refugees in the city, the mayor decided to allow the embassy to remain open. It doesn't have any real power, but they've been helping people find work, track down family members . . . that sort of thing. More or less what I do every day. They're just dealing with Karrnath itself instead of the families of Karrn veterans."

"Hmm."

Greykell stopped walking for a moment. "All right, this is our final stop. Watch your step."

They were standing outside an old tenement building. The door had been torn from its hinges and was nowhere to be seen, and most of the windows were covered with boards.

"You think this is where we'll find Hugal?" Daine said, reaching for his sword.

Greykell caught his hand and pushed the blade back into its sheath. "Maybe. But what I meant was 'watch your step.' The floors on some of the upper levels have been known to give way. How are you with structural engineering, Lei?"

Lei shrugged.

"They call this place Dolurrh's Doorstep," Greykell said, leading them through the shattered doorframe. "It's one of the oldest Cyran enclaves in the district. A tent in the square would be safer, but the people here have their own sense of community. You'll see."

The hallway reeked of sweat and urine. There was an emaciated old woman dressed in a rotting robe stretched out on the
floor of the atrium, and for a moment Daine thought she was
dead. When she turned to look at them, her eyes were glazed
and staring.

"Dreamlily," Greykell whispered. "Aureon only knows how
the people here afford it." She walked over to the old woman
and pulled her to her feet. "Syllia," Greykell said. "Why don't
I take you back to your family?"

The old woman gazed at Greykell without recognition. "I'm
comfortable," she said in a cracked, reedy voice. "Nothing
touches me here."

Daine glanced at Lei, who shrugged. He wondered if Jode
could do anything for the woman. He doubted it. The power of
Jode's dragonmark had little effect on mental afflictions.

"Come along, Syllia," Greykell said, taking her arm. "Let's
get you home."

"You're always willing to lend a hand, aren't you?"

Daine turned to face the new voice. Three people had just
come in from the street. The speaker was a massive man, almost as large as Pierce. Daine guessed he had some orc blood
in his veins, though it didn't show on his features. All three
were dressed in stained and ragged clothing, and the leader
was carrying a club of polished wood.

"We take care of our own," he said, and his deep voice was
alive with anger.

He gestured and one of his companions came forward—a
shifter, her fur filthy and matted, her fangs showing signs
of rot and decay. She pulled Syllia away from Greykell and
dragged her down the hall.

"Doras!" Greykell said cheerfully. "Just the person I wanted
to see." She walked to the angry man as if to give him a hug, but
Doras moved his cudgel between them.

"I've told you before," he said. "I don't want you here." He
glared at Daine and spat at his feet. "Or your pathetic lapdogs."

Daine moved forward, but Greykell stopped him.

"Is there a problem?" Daine snapped.

Doras pushed Greykell aside and stepped up to Daine. He

was at least four inches taller than Daine, and heavily muscled. Contempt surrounded him like a cloud.

"Yes, there is a problem. Our homeland has been destroyed. Our world could be coming to an end. And you, soldier—you who failed in your sworn duty to protect our people—dare to come into my home and pretend you can help us now?" He looked over at Greykell. "You and your kind had your chance to protect the people. Instead, your little war destroyed our land. And you think you can make it better by helping a man get a job making swords for Brelish soldiers? You disgust me."

"And where were you when my men were dying on the Brel-ish border?" Daine said. Greykell kept her hand on his arm, holding him back.

"I was tending the fields that fed your armies. And I never failed in my duty. Can you say the same?"

The third man—a lean half-elf with terrible burns across much of his exposed flesh—stepped forward. "We trusted you, soldier," he said. "And this . . . this is what you did for me. The end is coming. And you bloodthirsty fools opened the door."

Greykell moved in front of Daine, raising her hands. "Fine. You're right. We should have won the war. But what does this anger get you, Doras? Where will it take you?"

For a moment, Daine thought Doras was going to hit her; his knuckles whitened against his club. Finally, he loosened his grip. "What do you want? I told you I never wanted to see you here."

"I'm looking for someone," Greykell said. "I'm sure you remember Hugal? Or Monan? Either one will do."

"I haven't seen either in over a day," Doras said, his eyes narrowed. "Why? Have you found them work as street per-formers?"

"Actually, you'd be surprised," Greykell said. "I think they'd have a real knack for it. But I was wondering . . . did they have any friends? Other people who haven't been seen recently?"

"No. There are no friends here. Only survivors."

Greykell rolled her eyes. "Life is miserable and hard. You've lost everything. I hear you. And you know what? I've lost every-thing too. But whatever you may think, it's *not* the end of the world. We just need to let go of the past and embrace the future. To begin again."

"Very inspiring. But have you been to the ruins of Cyre? Have you seen what the war has left behind? If you'd seen what I've seen, you'd understand. We've seen the end, and it's only just beginning."

"Well, it's always a pleasure, Doras. If you don't want to see us here, I suppose we had best be on our way. Just one more thing. Do you know old Hila, the seamstress? Has she ever come around?"

Doras's eyes were as cold as stones. "No."

"Great!" Greykell took Daine's arm and pulled him out to the street. "And please, do something for Syllia, will you? She can't keep on like this."

Doras said nothing.

❀ ❀ ❀ ◉ ❀ ❀ ❀

"So what did you think?"

Night had fallen, and Greykell was leading the way back to the Manticore.

"Do you think that man is working with Hugal?" Lei asked.

"It's possible that Doras *is* Hugal," Greykell said. "Changelings, remember? But truthfully, I don't know what to think. I've known Doras for a few months now. He has a loud voice, and the people of Dolurrh's Door adore him . . . but I don't know. He likes to provoke, but I've never actually seen him take the first swing in a fight—and he seemed to have both his hands."

"I wish Jode had been there," Daine said. "He's got an amazing sense of people."

Greykell shrugged. "Well, he certainly seemed suspicious. I just didn't think that it was going to help to press the discussion. I'd rather try to go back sometime when he isn't around, sometime when we can take your Jode with us."

Daine nodded.

"Well, I'm dining with the Sorans in the square tonight," Greykell said. "One of the benefits of being a professional busybody. There's almost always someone having a meal somewhere. The Manticore is just around the bend. I'll catch up with you tomorrow!" She hugged them each in turn and then disappeared down one of the dark sidestreets.

The group turned the corner, and the Manticore came into view. A familiar figure was sitting on the doorstep—Hugal or Monan, Daine didn't know, but it was one of them for certain. In an instant, Daine's blades were in his hands. His companions paused, curious, but did not draw their weapons.

"Hello, Daine," the twin said. "It seems we have some unfinished business."

CHAPTER 29

BRELAND
SHARN
Dravago 28, 996 YK

"Take him down!" Daine cried to Pierce, but the war-forged didn't raise his bow. In fact, he didn't move at all.

"I'm afraid that this is between you and I, Daine," the twin said, standing up and walking toward him. "Your friends can't help you."

Turning to Lei, Daine saw that her body was completely rigid, her face devoid of expression. "What have you done to them?" he said, taking up a guard stance.

"It's Monan, actually. I was lying last night. Greykell was right. We like doing that just to confuse people."

He seemed unconcerned with Daine's glittering blades. And with good reason. As Monan approached, Daine made a long lunge with his sword. The blow should have pierced Monan's heart, but the twin moved with astonishing speed, swatting the blade aside with the palm of his left hand. Before Daine could react, Monan grabbed the blade with his left hand and struck at the hilt with his right, knocking it from Daine's grasp.

While he was surprised by the changeling's speed, Daine's reflexes were honed by a lifetime of training. Even as he lost his sword, Daine thrust with his dagger. Monan struck the point of the dagger with the palm of his hand, and the blade—which could cut through steel as easily as cheese—came to a dead stop.

"You still don't understand, do you?" Monan said. Daine managed to step back before the changeling could grab hold of

211

the dagger. "None of this is really happening. Not physically."

"What are you talking about?"

Monan smirked, the sadistic smile of a predator toying with his prey. "When you defeated my allies last night, I cast my spirit into your mind. This"—he gestured around them—"is dream and memory. Even now, you're drooling on the cobblestones. In a few moments I'll have disposed of you once and for all. I'll use your body for as long as it suits my needs, and then I'll leave you to rot in some madhouse."

"You're lying."

"Am I?" Monan reached behind his back, and when his hand came back into view there was a sword in it—one Daine recognized in an instant. "Look what I've found here. Remember this, Daine? A gift from your grandfather. And look what you did to it."

It had been a long time since Daine had really stopped to look at his grandfather's sword—the damage to the blade and hilt, both intentional and accidental. He glanced at the blade, and in that moment, everything changed. He was in the courtyard of the family estate in Metrol. For a moment, it seemed he was a child again; the walls and doors towered over him. Then he realized that he had not changed. The buildings were simply oversized, scaled to the perceptions of a boy. His grandfather towered over him, tarnished sword in hand.

"Look what you've done," he said, his voice filled with disappointment. "I believed in you. I knew you would uphold the legacy and the honor of my blood. And see what you have done with it."

"Clever," Daine said. "But I've fought your kind before."

He made a quick thrust, dipping beneath the expected parry and darting forward, trying to close the distance between them. But even as he moved forward, his enemy slipped back. It was like trying to hit a ghost. The creature wearing his grandfather's face laughed and raised his family sword.

"I've spent all day in your memories, Daine," the changeling said. "I know how you fight. But it hardly matters. You can't kill me with the idea of a sword. At best, you can force me into the shadows for a few more hours."

Now it was Monan's turn to go on the offensive, and even his movements were those of Daine's grandfather, who had taught Daine the fundamental principles of defense. But this was a mistake. Dailan had been a master swordsman, one of the best in Khorvaire. Daine remembered those practice sessions as vividly as his last conversation with his father. Combining his memories of the past with the skills he had acquired in the intervening years, it was a simple matter to block each blow.

"You may be able to hold me off, Monan, but you can't beat me with my own memories," Daine said.

He was growing suspicious. Monan seemed surprisingly eager to talk about the situation. The changeling might be telling the truth, but he could just as easily be lying, trying to demoralize his foe.

"Perhaps I don't need to win," Monan said. "Perhaps I just need to wait. Every minute you're trapped, my power grows. Soon I'll depart, and I'll take your body with me. But don't worry, you'll have all of your memories to keep you company. Soon enough, you'll be no more than a memory yourself."

Perhaps Monan was telling the truth; perhaps not, but the taunts were taking a toll on Daine. With every passing moment, he felt more detached, distant. It was becoming difficult to think, but he had to try. He launched a series of lightning-swift blows at the changeling, but his foe didn't parry. He simply avoided. Each warrior knew the other's fighting style perfectly.

And then Daine had an idea.

He was facing a deadly, highly skilled opponent. He only had one weapon left, and it was both his last defense and his only chance against his enemy. Every lesson he'd been taught, every instinct he had, told him that the dagger was his last hope.

He threw it away.

Monan was preparing for another pass when Daine hurled the dagger. Daine's real grandfather might have been able to block the blade, but Daine had never thrown a weapon in their practice sessions, and he never would have thrown the weapon in real life. In all of Daine's memories—the memories Monan was using against him—there was no precedent for such an act.

The blade caught Monan in the center of his throat. He sat down hard, and the mask of Daine's grandfather slipped away, revealing the almost featureless face of the changeling. His sword fell to the floor and vanished as his hands rose up, trying to grab hold of the hilt of the adamantine blade. But he didn't have the energy, and his hands fell back to the floor.

"Only . . . temporary . . . " he whispered, gazing into Daine's eyes.

Monan faded away, and the world went with him.

∂ ∂ ∂ ∂ ⊙ ∂ ∂ ∂

Daine woke on one of the pallets in their room in the Manticore. Lei was sitting by his side, holding a glittering crystal in her hand.

"Lei?" he whispered.

She looked over at him, and a smile spread over her face. "Daine! Thank the Sovereigns!"

"They didn't have anything to do with it," he muttered. "What . . . happened?" His head was muzzy, and he was having to force thoughts through the haze.

Pierce's voice came from above and behind him. "You collapsed, just outside the Manticore. We brought you inside."

"I was searching for outside influences," Lei explained, indicating the crystal in her hand. "But I can't sense anything. Do you remember what happened?"

"It's Monan. He's inside my mind. I've got to find a way to drive him out and quickly. If what he said is true, it's only a matter of time before he regains his strength and tries again."

Lei frowned. "A priest, then? They say that the adepts of the Silver Flame are masters of exorcism."

"No!" Daine shook his head. "No priests. Besides, this isn't a demon or fiend. It's . . . I don't know. His memories . . . thoughts. But I'm not talking to a priest of the Flame."

Lei shrugged. "Fine. So do you have an idea of your own?"

Daine pondered for a moment then rose to his feet and picked up his swordbelt. "Perhaps I do." He buckled on the belt and grabbed his chain mail shirt. "Where's Jode?"

"He still hasn't arrived," Pierce said.

That stopped him for a moment. "What time is it?"

"The seventh bell just rang," Lei replied.

"I'll be back by ten."

"Where are you going?"

"Following a hunch."

"And what happens if you faint in the middle of hunch-hunting?"

"Then I guess Jode won't be the only one missing."

Lei blocked his path. "Daine, you were the one demanding we stay together."

"This is something I need to do alone. Trust me. I'll be back soon." He pushed her aside and threw on his cloak as he walked out the door.

CHAPTER 30

BRELAND
SHARN
Dravago 28, 996 YK

The King of Fire came alive at night, and the common room was considerably more crowded than it had been before. Gamblers and revelers packed the burning tables packed, and it took Daine a few moments to locate the host. He exchanged a few words with the little halfling and slipped one of his few remaining coins into the man's tiny palm. In exchange, he received a wink and directions to a table in the inner hall.

On his last trip, Daine had remained in the common room for the whole time, but the gaming hall was the true heart of the King of Fire. The decoration was similar to the outer room—black marble with brass fixtures, darkwood tables that burned with cold fire. Eight massive brass pillars were also enchanted with cold fire, and these spread a flickering light across the entire chamber. Over a dozen long tables were spread throughout the room, and Daine saw a vast array of gambling equipment—cards, dice of all shapes, illusory battlefields, and far more. At the center of the chamber, a score of people were gathered around a circular scrying mirror set into the floor, shouting encouragement to a pair of jousting hippogriffs. As Daine passed the mirror, one of the riders was knocked from his mount, and a roar went through the crowd. For a moment, he seemed to hear Monan's voice, whispering just behind him: *What's your hurry? Why not stop, watch the games, enjoy yourself while you still can?*

The table he was looking for was small and dark, one of the only ones not lit by inner fire. Wrapped in the shadows at the corner of the room, it was currently home to only two people—a gnome dealer standing on a small pedestal and the woman Daine was searching for. She was still wearing her dark cloak, and her body was almost invisible in the deep shadows of the room. But she'd lowered the hood, revealing a flood of inky black hair.

Daine walked over to the table. As he approached, the woman turned to look at him. Her green eyes seemed to burn with the reflected light from the room. Her features were unnaturally perfect, her pale skin smooth and unblemished, and the lines of chin, cheek, and nose all in perfect proportion. He'd seen marble statues with more blemishes. Yet, as beautiful as she was, there was something alien about such perfection, something . . . inhuman.

The barest hint of a smile played across her lips. "We meet again." Her voice was soft and musical, set in such a tone to carry over the tumult.

"Well, you bought me a drink last time. The least I can do is return the favor."

This time, Daine could have sworn her emerald eyes actually *glowed* in the shadows of the room. "And a man of courtesy and manners. I sensed it when we first met."

"Yes, well . . . there is only one obstacle to this plan, and that's my complete lack of coin."

She shrugged. As with her smile, the motion was minimal, almost invisible, yet still intensely expressive. "Among my people, we believe the thought is what matters most."

"As a matter of fact, I wanted to talk to you about that."

The gnome *harrumphed*, tapping his fingers on his cards. The woman indicated the empty seat next to her. "Sit, then. Play a round."

"If I had the gold to gamble, my lady, you can be assured I'd first have repaid your hospitality."

She set five sovereigns and a golden galifar on the table in front of him. "Luck has been with me tonight. Indulge my hospitality a little longer." She paused, sizing him up with her smoldering eyes. "My name is Lakashtai."

Daine shrugged. "As you wish. Though I must warn you that I've seen little in the way of luck these past few days." He sat. "I'm Daine."

She extended a hand and he clasped it, bowing briefly from his chair. He accepted the cards the dealer pushed his way.

"War is not my vocation, but you are wearing the badge of the Cyran army, yes?"

"I've been told that it's time to buy a new cloak."

"I understand. My people were born in the wake of a terrible war, and we have carried the scars of that conflict for thousands of years." She studied her cards and then set out a foundation of earth. The dealer had revealed a single card—the king of fire.

Daine's luck had held true to form, and his hand was mixed and useless. He set down an earth card of his own. "Pardon my asking, but . . . you're kalashtar, aren't you?"

She gave the ghost of a nod. "Yes. There is no shame in the question."

"You're the first kalashtar I've ever met. I'm afraid I know little about your people."

The fractional shrug appeared again, the barest shifting of delicate shoulders beneath the flowing cloak. "We are raised to hold our secrets. Most of my kindred rarely leave the isolated communities they create for themselves, hiding in the shadows of the great cities."

"Forgive me for being blunt, but what is it that makes a kalashtar? You look human to me." He drew two cards.

"I'll trust that was intended as a compliment." She crossed her cards with the alchemist of earth and placed another coin on the table. "We are human, more or less. What defines the kalashtar is a matter of mind and soul. It's difficult to explain in few words, but I share my body with a spirit from the region of dreams. As with you and Cyre, this spirit has been driven from its home. Now it can only exist by spreading its essence through my soul and those of my sisters."

"So you have an . . . extra spirit sharing your mind?"

"It's not that simple. Ashtai is a part of me, but I cannot

speak to her directly. She moves within my soul, shaping my thoughts and emotions in subtle ways. Why do you ask?"

"Well . . . I *do* have an extra spirit sharing my mind. Uninvited and very unwanted. And if he's telling the truth, he's planning to drive me out of my mind. I was hoping you might have a friend who'd know how to deal with this sort of thing."

Lakashtai's lovely eyes widened. "A mind wraith? You shouldn't be wasting time." She set down her remaining cards, revealing all three dragons. "Add it to my credit, Talaran," she said, standing up. She didn't even bother looking at the dealer's cards. "Come with me, Daine. Quickly. And don't worry about the loss." She nodded at his unrevealed cards. "I'm still ahead for the night."

CHAPTER 31

BRELAND
SHARN
Dravago 25, 996 YK

Noise and music filled the air as Lei and Pierce rose into the heights of Sharn. Lei studied the other passengers on the lift. After her recent experience with Sergeant Lorrak, she was happy not to see any guards, but the other travelers were a colorful lot. Three drunken men howled with laughter—scions of noble families from the look of their fine clothing. A bard of House Phiarlan toyed with a set of fine pipes; his doublet and breeches were covered with darkweave ribbons, so it seemed as if the night itself clung to him. A muscular Karrn woman wearing leather armor and the scars of many battles kept her back to the railing. She had a greatsword strapped to her back and an ironshod club in one hand, and there was a fresh bruise on her right cheek. Lei guessed that the woman was returning from a fight in one of the pits. Menthis Towers was the hub of Sharn's entertainment industry, from the brothels and battle pits of the lower ward to the theaters and museums of the highest towers. Staring down the inner tower, Lei seemed to be looking into a well filled with stars—hundreds of eternal torches glittering on the levels below as revelers traveled from one amusement to another.

Lei had used a simple cosmetic charm to prepare Pierce and herself to mingle with the elite citizens of Sharn. While she was still wearing her armor, the green leather was smooth and polished, and the golden rivets on her jerkin gleamed like jewels.

Pierce was buffed to a mirror finish. For all that he was a simple soldier, he looked fit to serve in a king's honor guard.

"We should return to High Walls, my lady," Pierce said. "We could continue the search for Hugal . . . or Jode."

"We already covered the entire district with Greykell," Lei replied. "If there was anything to find, we'd have seen it already. Besides, it's getting dark. After what happened last night, I can't say I want to wander around the streets of High Walls on our own. If Daine can follow his hunches, I'm going to follow mine."

"You have a plan, then?"

"I'm still working on that part," Lei said. "But don't forget I'm the one who's been to the city before. I've let my concerns with my house cloud my judgment. I have other friends in Sharn. Acquaintances, at the least. It's time to catch up with a few of them."

"As you wish."

"Give me your bow. No one's going to attack us in Upper Menthis, and you already stand out like a troll in the court of Metrol."

"My lady, it is unwise to limit our defensive options."

"Pierce, trust me. You're a Cyran warforged. It's like Greykell said. Walking around with a weapon in your hand, you present a challenge to the guards. It's one thing if you're skulking in the shadows, but that's not what I have in mind."

A human might have shrugged or sighed. Seeing the futility of further argument, Pierce handed his bow to Lei, who stowed it away in the depths of her pack.

"And the flail."

"My lady—"

"I told you, Pierce. Up here our best defense is to look harmless." She held out her hand. "As long as you follow my lead, everything will be fine. Don't worry. You'll get it back before we return to the lower wards."

"Very well." He pulled the weapon from its harness and handed it over.

"Thank you. Now, I think the best idea is for you to play the role of a house servant. Remember that pompous ass Domo

at Round Wind? I know it's not what you were designed for,
but the war's over and servants are something the people here
understand."

"What about a bodyguard?"

Pierce's tone seemed slightly stiff, and Lei gave him a curious
glance. Had she insulted him? "Fine. You can be my bodyguard. But I'm still keeping the flail out of sight. It's just a little
too . . . well, blunt for this crowd."

Eventually the lift came to a stop at an open-air district, a
network of platforms and bridges bound to the massive central
towers. Lei led Pierce off of the lift and onto a quiet street.
It was a residential neighborhood, filled with orderly rows of
wood-and-plaster houses. Most of these homes were identical,
painted white and trimmed in brown. But here and there a few
trellises were covered with Eldeen rainbow ivy, creating living
murals of vivid color.

"They call this area Ivy Towers," Lei said. "Many of the stu-
dents and scholars of Morgrave University make their homes
here. The university itself is just around the ring."

"And who are we visiting?"

"A friend of mine, Lailin Calis. We spent a year at Arcanix
together. I've never had much luck with augurs, but I'd feel
foolish if I didn't at least talk to him. Hopefully he's still here.
And Pierce? I hate to ask, but if there was ever a time to lay on
the 'my lady,' this would be it."

"As you wish, my lady."

They continued down the quiet street. A patrol of the Watch
passed by with only the slightest glance at Pierce. A turn of the
corner, and they came to a house covered with myriad shades
of blue ivy.

"This would be his," Lei said. She stepped up to the door but
paused even as her hand went for the bell-pull.

"What is it, my lady?"

"There's a note tucked into the door," Lei said, pulling it
from the frame. "And it's addressed to me." Cautiously unfolding the paper, she read:

Dearest Lei,

I'm sorry that I cannot be here to greet you in person, but I am attending a gathering on Pride of the Storm. I hope that you can join me there. I will tell Lord Dantian to expect you and your companion. Any skycoach can bring you up to the yacht at Dantian's expense. Such arrangements are typical for his gatherings. I hope to see you soon.

Yours,

Lailin

"Apparently we're expected," Lei said, handing the note to Pierce. He read it somberly.

"Impressive," he said. "But I admit to some concern. An augur would need to inquire specifically about you to gain such information, would he not?"

Lei shrugged. "The sphinx said that we could be seen from far away. I guess she's not the only one who sensed my arrival."

"Hence my concern. May I have my weapons back, my lady?"

"Please, Pierce," Lei said. "We've been invited aboard a Lyrandar lord's yacht. Even if I gave you the weapons, they'd be confiscated at the door."

"So you intend to accept this invitation? What possible purpose could it serve?"

"Let's see . . . first, if Lailin is such a talented diviner, who knows what else he could tell us? At the least, he might be able to track down Jode or this Rasial."

"True," Pierce said.

"Second, I don't know how long we'll be in Sharn. As I see it, we could use all the contacts we can get, and this is an excellent opportunity to mingle with a class of people we normally would never see."

Pierce said nothing.

"And finally, you're talking to a woman who's been living on gruel and water for six months—and army rations before that. *You* may not eat, but if you think I'm going to pass up a chance to dine with one of the wealthiest men in Sharn, you're mistaken." She grinned. "Now let's find a coach."

❂ ❂ ❂ ❂ ❂ ❂ ❂

Menthis was a center of entertainment and nightlife, so they had little trouble catching the attention of a skycoach—a slender vessel apparently designed for gnomes and halflings. Lei was comfortable enough, but Pierce could barely fit in the ship.

"Don't worry, lady," the coachman said. An elderly halfling with long gray hair, he spoke with a strong Talentan accent. "I'll take things slowly. Keep the big 'un from falling."

Lei smiled. "My thanks, sir. We are expected at the *Pride of the Storm*. Do you know of it?"

"Ei," the halfling said, nodding. Lei took that as an affirmative. "Guests of the Lyrandar, yes?"

"That's correct," Lei said, wondering if it was true.

The Mark of Storm gave House Lyrandar power over wind and water, and the heirs of the house had dominated the shipping trade for centuries. In recent decades, an alliance between Cannith, Lyrandar, and the gnomish shipwrights of Zilargo had resulted in the creation of the first true skyship. Propelled by the power of bound elemental spirits, these airships had revolutionized trade and transportation and proved to be a powerful weapon of war, but the bound spirits were difficult to control, and only a stormchild could command their absolute loyalty. It was unlikely that the Lyrandars knew of her excoriate status, but she couldn't lie about it, and she had no idea how the House of Storm would treat an expelled Maker.

The halfling did not ask for payment—apparently Lailin was as good as his word. The skycoach rose up to the highest spires of Menthis. They were almost a mile above the ground, and Lei's head swam as she looked down at the world below and tried to pick out the spires of High Walls far, far below. Winds whipped at her hair and shoulders, but the coachman was as good as his world and took the ascent slowly. Lei gripped the rails and gritted her teeth, waiting for the ordeal to pass.

Moments later they completed their circuit of the towers, and Lei gasped at the sight that lay before them. The flying ships she had seen before were small transports or weapons platforms, like the stormship they had fought at Keldan Ridge. *Pride of the Storm* was in an entirely different class. It was a galleon, easily one of the largest ships she had seen on land or air. House Lyrandar used the kraken as its sigil, and the stern of the ship was carved in the shape of a vast kraken. The effect was astonishingly lifelike, as if the great beast was in the process of devouring the ship. The kraken was stained black, while the bow and midships were carved from pure white wood. Four silver lightning bolts adorned the bow. Most of the kraken's tentacles were carved along the side of the ship, but four arched out around, over, and under it, and these wooden beams supported the elemental rings that kept the ship afloat. Where most skyships were supported by a single ring of bound elementals, this vessel had two—a swirling belt of roiling clouds and a smaller ring of pure fire. Lei guessed that the bound air supported the ship while the fire elementals provided motive force. Staring into the flames, she wondered just how fast the galleon could move.

The skycoach came to a halt over the foredeck of the skyship. A servant in Lyrandar livery approached.

"Your name, my lady?" he called out.

Curiously, despite the altitude, there was no wind over the deck. Whether it was an aspect of the elemental binding or the power of the ship's captain, the howling winds spared the deck of the *Pride*.

"My name is Lei. I come as a guest of Lailin Calis, and I am accompanied by my servant."

The servant studied a sheaf of parchment then brought up a small footstool to help her disembark. He extended his hand, a smile on his face. "You are expected, Lady Lei. Welcome to the *Pride of the Storm*."

CHAPTER 32

BRELAND
SHARN
Dravago 28, 996 YK

As they left the King of Fire, Lakashtai drew up her hood, hiding her face in deep shadow. "Tell me everything," she said. "How did this begin? What do you know of this hostile spirit?"

"My companions and I were attacked last night on the streets of High Walls. It seemed like a simple mugging, but the leader had this strange laugh that seemed to get into my head, making it difficult to concentrate. After we'd brought down his allies, he . . . well, I don't know what he did, exactly. I was over-whelmed with this rush of thoughts and emotions, as if he were pouring his entire life into me. Then we both blacked out."

"This was almost twenty-four hours ago?"

"Yes."

"We should have privacy, but this will have to do."

They'd come to a building that was apparently an inn. Like many of the structures in the Folly, it was one of the strangest buildings Daine had ever seen. The walls seemed to be made of thick crystal, and the torches inside the building spread a glowing radiance across the entire structure. There were no windows, though in a sense the entire building was one large window. Daine could see people moving about inside, though the distorting effect of the thick crystal walls obscured details.

Stepping inside, they found that the entire building was

made of crystal. The surface of the floors was rough, providing traction and a high degree of opacity, but floors, walls, ceiling . . . all were solid glass. Daine wondered how such a thing could ever be constructed—undoubtedly Lei would know. The furnishings were standard wood and brass, and would have been at home in any Brelish farmhold. Somehow, the presence of such mundane furnishings only enhanced the bizarre nature of the architecture.

A young man with long white hair approached them as they entered. At first he seemed to be wearing a simple white shirt and a pair of brown breeches, but as he came closer Daine say a faint motion in the air around him, and realized the man was also wearing a greatcoat woven from invisible cloth.

"Welcome to the Glass House, travelers," the host said. "If you have come for the evening meal, we are serving the finest ghostfish in Sharn this evening, along with—"

"A room is all we require," Lakashtai said. She produced a platinum coin that would have bought a month's stay in the Manticore. "Time is of the essence."

The host's eyes gleamed and the coin quickly vanished. "Please, follow me, travelers."

The walls were made of glass, but the doors were rough wood, and they almost seemed to be floating amidst the firelit crystal. The room itself was surprisingly sparse, though Daine imagined what Lei might say if she heard that he'd been in a room with a real bed. Embedded in the wall was an everbright lantern with a shutter to hide the light from sleeping eyes.

"Lie down," Lakashtai commanded. Her words were a song, but there was iron behind the music. She drew her hood away from her face. "Continue your story. What became of the man who attacked you?"

"He fell into a coma, then about an hour ago I thought I saw him on the street. But apparently, I'd passed out and the encounter was all in my mind. We fought and I managed to defeat him, but I doubt the trick I used would work a second time."

"The physical conflict is only a metaphor," Lakashtai said. "But you are correct. The longer the spirit stays within you, the more power it will gain and the harder it will be to overcome. You cannot resist it forever."

Daine nodded glumly. "I figured as much. Is there anything that can be done?"

"I have a . . . friend who can help you," Lakashtai said. "If you are willing, she can reach your mind and attempt to excise the foreign spirit. It's dangerous, but . . ."

"What choice do I have?" Daine said. "So, what's the price of my freedom? I've told you I don't have coin to spare. I'd have to sell my sword to pay back the price of this room, and it isn't even my sword."

Lakashtai raised his chin with a finger and stared into his eyes. Her skin was smooth and slightly cold, and as before her gaze was deep and hypnotic. She released him and looked away.

"My people were engaged in spiritual warfare long before the rise of Galifar—before your Cyre ever existed. You cannot put a price on a soul. I will help you because I can." She looked back at him. "All I ask is that if I should need your help in the future, you remember what I have done for you."

"Very well." Daine didn't like the thought of being indebted to anyone, and the situation was unfolding with remarkable speed. But he could feel Monan's power growing, could hear the changeling's voice whispering in the back of his mind, and he felt flashes of emotion that had nothing to do with his own desires. "What do I do?"

"Lie back. Let your thoughts wander. By now, your enemy will be gathering his power, preparing for his next attack. Don't try to resist. Whatever happens, whatever threat he presents, don't fight back. Let my friend handle everything."

She leaned in close to him, and for a moment Daine thought she was going to kiss him. Instead, she touched her forehead to his. Her eyes filled his field of view, and her scent filled his mind—strange and exotic, yet somehow intimately familiar, an old friend he had forgotten.

"Let go," she said, and he fell into her eyes.

* * * * * * *

"So here we are again."

He was outside the Manticore, and Monan's voice rang through the air. The changeling was leaning against the door of the inn.

Daine said nothing.

"Your grandfather was a poor choice," said Monan, walking toward him. "Perhaps he was a professional soldier, but you were used to fighting him, and that was my mistake. But there are so many weapons I can use against you."

The surroundings changed, and Daine found himself in a luxurious manor—Alina Lyrris' estate in Metrol, which Daine hadn't seen for eight years. The floors were covered with soft bearskin, the air filled with the scent of cinnamon and rich perfumes. Daine knew what Monan was trying to do, and he expected to hear Alina's voice next. But it was Lei who appeared nearby.

"Now, what do you suppose I would think if I knew about this?" Lei said. "I never thought you were capable of such things, Daine. But neither did you, did you? Does it still trouble you? Or has the war burned the shame from your system?"

She came closer, and Daine saw a glint of metal in her hand. A knife? Instinct brought his hand to the hilt of his sword, but memory weighted down his thoughts. Why fight it? Despite his best efforts, what difference had he made over the last eight years? Cyre was gone and he was working for Alina again. What was the point?

But even as he let go of his sword, even as Lei came closer, he felt a *presence*, something fundamentally . . . other.

Look away, Daine. Close your eyes.

The thoughts came from within his own mind, yet he knew they were Lakashtai's. Even as he glanced away, he saw a shadow falling over the false Lei, saw a look of pure terror on her face. He closed his eyes. There was a horrible, gurgling scream . . . and no matter how hard he tried to ignore it, it was still Lei's voice. It was a sound that would haunt his dreams for years to come.

When Daine opened his eyes, he was lying on a soft bed in a room of glowing crystal. He felt no trace of Monan in his mind, and Lakashtai was nowhere to be seen. A small shard of green crystal was on the bed next to him. He picked it up. It was cool to the touch, and for a moment he felt the touch of kalashtar fingers on his hand.

He slipped the crystal into his belt pouch, picked up his cloak, and left the glowing room for the dark streets below.

CHAPTER 33

BRELAND
SHARN
Dravago 28, 996 YK

The sun had set over Sharn, but the towers were alive with light. Lei looked over the railing and was stunned by the sight. The spires of the tallest towers were the playgrounds of the wealthy. Buildings of crystal and gold glittered in the light of magical fire. She could see a long pool of water atop one tower and a grove of ancient trees atop another—private pieces of nature hidden amidst the city. Looking down the length of the tower was a lesson in architectural style. Every few hundred feet structures and materials changed, as each tower and ward reflected the traditions of a different era or culture.

There was no shortage of light on the deck of the *Pride of the Storm*. The ship's railings were studded with crystal shards charged with cold fire. But these tiny torches were over-shadowed by the enormous ring of elemental fire wrapped around the waist of the ship, the light from this belt of flame almost a match for the sun itself. There were a dozen Lyrandar servants scattered around the deck, polishing the railings and performing other forms of maintenance. But there were also a few guests, and after taking Lei's pack the chief servant led Lei and Pierce to the small knot of guests—one of which was a massive owl—standing midship beneath the flaming arch.

"Master Calis?" the servant said. "Your guest has arrived."

Lailin Callis was an enormous man, at least in girth. His

long beard was dyed in various shades of blue, matching the swirling patterns of his loose robes. "Lei!" he bellowed, charging forward and embracing her. The small group of people watched him go with looks of mild bemusement. "What a wonderful surprise."

"Surprise?" Lei said, breaking free and gasping for breath. "From your note, it seemed a matter of fate."

Lailin's face split in a massive grin. "Yes, well, that's because you didn't see the note I left last night—or this afternoon."

"What do you mean?"

"A friend told me you were in town and would be coming to visit, but I had no idea when you might arrive. I've been leaving notes for you every time I leave the house."

Lei smiled. "And my companion?"

"As if you would be traveling alone, my dear!" Lailin studied Pierce with a curious eye. "Although I must admit, I rather expected you to be in the company of a handsome young man. No offense meant."

"None taken," Pierce rumbled.

"And here I thought you'd finally unlocked the secrets of the stars and moons, Lailin. Nonetheless, I thank you for making me feel welcome. After what we've been through recently, it's wonderful to have a chance to socialize."

"And on that note," he said as he led Lei and Pierce to the small group. He made a brief round of introductions of various merchants, and finally turned to the owl. "Allow me to introduce my companion of the moment. Master Hu'ur'hnn makes his home in the Bazaar of Middle Dura. Without question, he is one of the cleverest birds I have ever crossed wits with."

"Too kind, Lailin," Hu'ur'hnn said. Standing almost nine feet tall from the tips of his talons to his tufted horns, Hu'ur'hnn was a the largest owl Lei had ever seen, covered with gray-black feathers. He regarded Lei with yellow eyes the size of small saucers. "Lei, it is? And would you be House of Cannith, my lady?" His voice was strange and inhuman—deep, fluting tones twisted to form words.

Lailin caught Lei's eye and spoke before she could answer. "Hu'ur'hnn used to be a windchaser in the sporting events of

Dura. I've forgotten. Did you ever actually win a match, old owl?"

The owl rotated his head to face Lailin, a slightly disconcerting effect. "Indeed, this is well known. Difficult for the owl to race the Pegasus, but not impossible with proper plans and arrangements. My people admire such effort."

"Your people?" Lei said. "Are there really so many owls in Sharn?"

"Less than a dozen. Mine are the people of the Bazaar, merchants and others who know the value of word and wit. It took diplomacy to overcome the Griffon and the Hippogriff. Now those same gifts are used in the service of Dura. But as to you . . ."

"I should probably introduce Lei to our host, Hu'ur'hnn. It's her first time aboard the *Pride*, you know."

"Very well." The owl bobbed his head. "Perhaps we shall talk later, lady."

Lailin took Lei's arm and led her to a set of stairs. Pierce followed behind. "A fascinating fellow, Hu'ur'hnn, but he's a hunter by nature. I didn't think he'd latch onto your house so quickly."

"So what do *you* know of my situation, Lailin? And who told you I was in Sharn to begin with."

"Her name is Flamewind."

"The *sphinx?*" Lei tried to imagine Lailin fighting a minotaur barehanded and failed completely.

"Yes, that's her. She spends a certain amount of time at Morgrave University."

This was what Lei had heard in the first stories of the sphinx. "Talking about Xen'drik?"

"Yes."

Lei wondered why Flamewind maintained two homes. The temple in Malleon's Gate was a fairly elaborate stage, if she could just be found in the Morgrave Library. But then again, many mystical powers were linked to specific locations. If Flamewind was a true oracle, perhaps she channeled some hidden power in the temple to obtain the knowledge of the future and the past.

"What did she tell you?"

"That you were in Sharn, no longer part of House Cannith, and that you would be visiting in the future. She's never spoken to me before. I've seen her certainly, but we've never spoken. I've heard she eats people who ask her stupid questions, and I've never felt like taking that chance."

"Food for thought."

"Well, exactly."

They descended a large, spiral staircase into an elaborate ballroom. Both the staircase and the room below were massive in scale, and Lei imagined that they had been designed to accommodate large guests like Hu'ur'hnn or an ogre servant. The ceilings were at least twenty feet high, and Lei wondered if the chamber was making use of two decks. Light fell from glittering chandeliers, each crystal shard enchanted with its own spell of light. Lei was impressed. All magic had its price, and clearly expense was not a concern for the heirs of Lyrandar.

"Thank you for not mentioning my disgrace to the owl," Lei said. She saw a long table filled with food and started toward it.

"Well, if it's what I think, I know you're not allowed to lie about it. But if you'd like . . . well, a friend who simply hasn't heard the news and mistakenly misreports things, that's no crime. If you'd like to be a lady for the night, I'd be happy to assist."

She smiled. "You're kind, Lailin. But you know . . . I'm ready. Perhaps I'm curious to see what will happen. Just let me get some food before you start making introductions. If I'm going to be thrown off the ship, I'd rather it was on a full stomach."

"A woman after my own heart," Lailin said, taking a plate. "The blackspiced dragonhawk is excellent, but you simply must try the fish; You'll never get fish as fresh as at a Lyrandar feast. I think the deepscale trout were brought in from the Thunder Sea mere hours ago." He helped himself to a generous portion of the trout, along with a salad made from watercress and other Marcher staples.

After Lei had filled her plate, Lailin led her over to another table where a few others were already seated. "Lord Alais, do you mind if we join you?"

"Not at all." The speaker was in his middle years, but lean and handsome. He rose and pulled out a chair for Lei. "And who is your charming companion, Lailin?"

"My name is Lei, my lord," she replied. "Former heir of the House of Making, now finding my own way in the world."

It was interesting to watch the man's reaction. There were dozens of physical traits that distinguished the dragonmarked bloodlines—a certain shade of hair or eye, curve of cheek, slant of nose. Each house had thousands of members, and these traits were many and varied. But Lei had paid close attention to the subject in her schooling, and she was fairly certain this man wasn't an heir himself. This was why she'd chosen him as her test subject. For an instant, his eyes widened in surprise, then they narrowed, and she could see his interest growing. He took her proffered hand, brushing her fingers with dry lips as he gazed into her eyes.

"I am Alais ir'Lantar," he said, "and I have the honor of being one of the ambassadors from the nation of Aundair. I hope you will not consider the question rude, but do you possess the Mark of Making?"

Lei considered this for a moment but saw no harm in the question. "I do."

"Fascinating," Alais said. "And what brings you to Sharn?"

Lei brushed her fingers across her armor. "I learned the ways of artifice and enchantment as a child. . . ."

"And truly, you are one of the most gifted enchantresses I have ever set eyes upon, magic or no."

Lei wanted to roll her eyes, but she resisted the urge. She'd been in the field for so long that she'd almost forgotten the ways of the court, the constant interplay of simpering flattery. She smiled and cast her eyes to the floor. "Like many members of my house, I served in the support corps during the war. My home was in Metrol, and—"

"I understand," Alais said, putting his hand over hers. "Truly, the destruction of Cyre is a tragedy that has affected us all deeply. At Arcanix, we have the greatest mystical minds of the age studying the disaster, trying to unlock its secrets and ensure that it never happens again. Perhaps you would be interested in a seat on the Arcane Congress?"

The offer took Lei by surprise, but then she caught scent of where he was going. "My lord, that's most generous of you, but I did not realize that Aundair was providing shelter for the refugees of the war."

"We are a small country, and we do not have the resources of Breland. Otherwise, I can assure you we would be doing everything in our power to help the scattered people of Cyre. But I have no doubt that the queen would make a special exception in your case, in light of the many difficulties you have overcome—not to mention your loss of status within your own house."

"Truly, your offer is most kind." Lei was curious to see how far this would go. "Yet with the destruction of my home, I find myself without the means to travel. Even shelter itself has been a difficulty."

Alais opened his mouth to speak but was distracted by the arrival of a servant. The young girl whispered in his ear, and he sighed. "I am afraid I must depart, my lady," he said, pushing back his chair and rising from the table. "But why don't you stop by the embassy of Aundair in Dragon Towers? I am certain that we could find a way to alleviate your current difficulties." He smiled.

"I thank you, Lord Alais. Perhaps I shall."

Alais bowed and departed, and Lailin glanced at her with a raised eyebrow.

"I do not trust him, my lady," said Pierce, who had continued to stand behind her chair throughout the conversation. His eyes followed the departing ambassador.

"Nor do I, Pierce."

"You wouldn't want a seat on the Arcane Congress, Lei?" Lailin said. "After our time in Arcanix, it might feel like home."

"It's a pretty offer. But who knows what the truth would be when I arrived in Aundair? It didn't occur to me at first, but I suppose . . . I am an heir to the Mark of Making, with knowledge of the techniques of House Cannith. But I am no longer protected by my house. It wouldn't surprise me if Lord Alais is dreaming about a new Aundarian bloodline carrying the Mark of Making—starting with me."

"That seems a little far-fetched," Lailin said. "If it was that simple, why hasn't it happened before?"

"I didn't say it was simple—or even that it was possible—just that it's what I think the ambassador had in mind. People are rarely forced out of the house, and there is always the hope that you might be reinstated. My Uncle Jura was the only excoriate I've ever met, and I know he's hoping to return to the family. So loyalty plays a role. More importantly . . . I don't think the barons would allow it to happen."

"What do you mean?"

"Just that. If the house truly thought an excoriate could present a threat to the purity of the bloodline . . . I've certainly met a few purists who would do whatever they considered necessary to stop it—and that could go a long ways."

"So your life is in danger, then?" Lailin asked.

"Not if I play by the rules. I'm sure Lord Alais would be happy to protect me—in exchange for my cooperation, of course. But . . . I still don't know why I've been expelled or if there's a chance for me to return. And for all that I'd like to smash the barons' faces, I still believe in the ideals of my family. I'll wait to see what happens." She paused, thoughtfully. "Of course, I am sitting at a table with a gifted augur. Perhaps you'd care to give me some advice?"

Lailin rubbed his blue beard. "Well . . . I don't have to be an augur to see financial ruin in my future if I start giving my friends free advice."

"Oh, please," she said playfully. "At least tell me if I should follow up on this business with Alais. If I become a wealthy lady of Arcanix, I promise to find a place for you there."

He rolled his eyes. "Oh, very well." He reached into a leather pouch and produced a set of flat blue stones. He spread them across the surface of the table. Each stone was a slightly different color, and they formed a mesmerizing mosaic. "So what will happen if you accept Alais's invitation?"

He stared at the stones, drumming his fingers on the table and humming to himself. Each diviner had his own method for seeing into the mists of time.

After a minute he stopped, looked over at her, and shook his head. "I think you're right. I can't tell if the threat comes from Aundair or your own house, but misfortune would certainly follow."

"I guess we won't be teaching together at Arcanix, then."

"That's all right. I still have my hopes set on Morgrave University. I can see myself teaching at some point in the future, though from the image I see in the stones, I need to lose a little weight first."

Lei took another bite of the excellent deepscale trout "In that case, attending these parties can't be helping your cause."

"Too true. In any case, as long as I have the stones spread out, I may as well make use of them. Is there anything else I can do for you?"

"Well, actually . . . I'm looking for a friend of mine, a halfling named Jode. Can you tell me where to find him?"

Pierce spoke up from behind them. "Not to intrude, my lady, but if you have confidence in master Lailin's talents, should we not ask about Rasial Tann?"

"Right, good thinking. We're also looking for a man named Rasial Tann. For a friend."

"Well," Lailin said. "This is certainly a more complicated question. But let me see what I can do with it. Where are Jode and Rasial, and how can you find them?" He fixed his gaze on the stones and began tapping his fingers again. This time the process took longer, and near the end he closed his eyes for almost a minute.

Finally he stopped humming and tapping and took a deep breath. "It's difficult to see," he said. "But I think that your Jode and Rasial are actually together right now. And you will be reunited tonight."

"Well, good for Jode," Lei murmured. "I guess he had a good lead after all."

"It would seem so," Pierce said. "If this augury is to be trusted."

"Pardon my companion, Lailin. He's never had much faith in such things."

"All is forgiven." Lailin gathered up the stones. "Shall we see what Lyrandar has to offer in the way of dessert?"

Even as Lei rose, she noticed a group of people walking toward them. The man in the lead was dressed in martial style, four silver lightning bolts adorned his black leather jerkin, and a blue cloak draped his shoulders. His pure white hair and slightly pointed ears hinted at his half-elven blood. As new to Sharn as she was, it was a simple matter for Lei to guess who this was.

She curtsied gracefully as he approached. Pierce moved up to stand by her side. "Lord Dantian, I thank you for your hospitality." Her words were carefully chosen. She didn't like his demeanor, so reminding him that she was a guest seemed a wise move.

"You are Lei, formerly of House Cannith?" Dantian's tone was cold, his blue-green eyes unreadable.

"I have that honor."

"I am afraid that I must ask you to leave my ship."

Lei spotted Dasei d'Cannith across the room, and the situation became clear. "My lord, I am sorry to hear this. The hospitality of House Lyrandar is legendary. After my long journey, I had hoped to discover the truth to the legends. But"—she sighed—"I suppose that I have."

Dantian stiffened but did not swerve from his course. "Your presence is causing discomfort to my other guests, and I am afraid that I must put the needs of the group above those of a single guest—especially one in such reduced circumstances." He gestured, and two armed men in Lyrandar livery stepped forward. "My guards will escort you and your servant to the foredeck. Kadran will see to it that your belongings are returned and that you have transportation to . . ." He raised an eyebrow. "High Walls, I believe?"

A small crowd had gathered to observe the scene, and a chuckle ran through the masses at this.

"That's very kind of you, Lord Dantian," Lei replied. "It's good to know that House Lyrandar drives its guests home when it drives them away."

Lailin rose to join her, but Lei pushed him back down. "There's no need for you to get involved in this," she said quietly. "Thank you for the help. Pierce, let's go."

❀ ❀ ❀ ❀ ❀ ❀ ❀

The guards led them up the stairs and out onto the main deck. The guests who had been talking beneath the rings had left, and the deck was deserted. Lei looked up at the rings of fire and clouds, and for a moment her thoughts were lost in the swirling steam.

"Look out!" Pierce's voice tore her from her reverie.

The warning came in the nick of time, and she threw herself forward just as she felt the point of the blade touching her back. Spinning around, she saw Pierce facing the two guards who had drawn their blades.

The shorter guard was carrying two daggers. He was the one who'd tried to stab her and failed. He cursed. "Deal with the 'forged! I'll finish her."

Pierce moved forward in a blur of motion. He grabbed the smaller man, pinning his arms with a grip of steel. But before he could crush the breath from his foe, the second guard stepped up. This man was tall and lanky. While he had a short-sword in his right hand, it was the left that he brought to bear, laying his palm on Pierce's back. The warforged stiffened, let go of his victim, and staggered back a step or two, obviously in great pain. But he'd bought Lei a few moments, and she'd put them to good use. Both guards were wearing chainmail, and as they struggled with Pierce, she'd whispered to the metal of their armor and swords, recalling the heat of the shaping forge. Even as the man with the dagger turned to her, the links of his armor began to glow. He cried out in agony as the searing heat from his daggers raised blisters on his hands. Dropping the weapons, he tore at his armor, trying to tear free before his clothes caught fire.

The other guard had escaped the effects of the enchantment, but he had problems of his own. Pierce was back on his feet, and for all that he was unarmed, his fists were stone and steel. Even as the lanky man made a quick thrust at Pierce, the warforged knocked the blade aside and landed a powerful blow on his jaw. Blood spattered across the deck and the man staggered back.

Lei stepped up to join Pierce, ready to strike. But when their opponent rose to his feet, he turned away and raced for the railing. Pierce charged after him, but too late. The scrawny guard leaped the rail in a single bound and went tumbling over the edge.

Even as Pierce peered over the edge, more Lyrandar guardsmen were running toward them. Within seconds, a half-dozen swordsmen and a pair of crossbowmen had surrounded them.

"Don't move!" the sergeant cried, his face livid.

Lei just stood, her hands facing out, as the chief servant came running from the foredeck. The smell of burned flesh filled the air. The dagger-wielding guard had succumbed to the terrible heat and was either unconscious or dead.

"What is going on?" the chief servant cried.

"You tell me," Lei said coolly. "This man and his companion just tried to kill me. If that's what you have planned for me, then let's get it over quickly."

The burned man was lying face down, and the chief servant turned the body over. Lei was surprised. His features were nothing like the man who had attacked her. The servant studied the corpse for a moment.

"Sergeant, do you know who this man is?"

"No. Never saw him before."

The chief servant looked back at Lei, and his expression was grim. "You have the apologies of the house, my lady, and I assure you that we will look into this matter immediately."

"If you'd like my assistance, I—"

"You and your servant are to leave immediately. A skycoach is waiting at the foredeck, along with your belongings."

"But—"

"This is a matter for the house. You must leave. Now."

The guards raised their weapons again, ready to act if ordered. It was clear she had no friends here.

"Very well."

❖ ❖ ❖ ◉ ❖ ❖ ❖

The coachman was an unusually dour gnome who had no interest in conversation. He stayed completely silent, keeping his hand on the tiller as they sailed down through the night air to the glittering spires below.

This gave Lei the time to focus on Pierce. Laying her hands on his armor, she reached within, tracing the magical web that gave him life. The web was damaged, and in places it had snapped entirely. Physically, Pierce seemed perfectly healthy, but to the eyes of an artificer, it was clear how close he had come to being destroyed. Drawing on the energy of her own spirit, Lei reinforced the threads, patching those that had been cut.

"I don't like this," she said. "Only another artificer could do this much damage. He resisted my heating charm, as well."

"But he did turn to his sword after the first attack, my lady," Pierce said. "Perhaps the power had been placed within him by another and he was only releasing what he'd been given to hold."

"All we really know is that we know nothing. The man who came after me had a glamour concealing his features, so we can assume that Lord Dantian didn't know about it. He wasn't a changeling, though, and nothing about him indicated any sort of connection to our friends in High Walls. As for the other one . . . given my recent experiences with Daine, while it's possible he chose death over facing you, I imagine he had a feather charm."

"Could this have been arranged by a member of your own house, my lady? Your cousin Dasei—"

"Doesn't have the skill or the courage to do this on her own. I don't know. We need to be careful, Pierce."

"High Walls, lady. The Manticore." The gnome's voice was a mixture of boredom and despair. He brought the coach to a stop just outside the inn, and they clambered out. The instant they had cleared the boat, he rose back into the air.

"Eager to be on his way, I guess," Lei said.

"Pierce! Lei!"

It was Daine. He came running down the street toward them, and before they could respond, he wrapped Lei in a powerful embrace.

"Daine?" she said.

Instantly, he let go and took a step back. Even in the dim light, she could see the flush rising on his cheeks.

"Sorry," he said. "It's been . . . well, it's been a strange few hours. Was that a skycoach? Where have you *been?*"

"That's a long story," she said.

"Then you can tell it inside. I don't know about you, but I still haven't had any sort of dinner. Let's see what wonders Dassi has to offer."

The common room of the Manticore was filled with the smell of the evening meal, and Lei thanked the sovereigns she'd been able to dine with the Lyrandars. Dassi was serving a thin stew with string meat that Lei guessed to be some sort of lizard—and none too fresh from the smell. Looking around the room, she saw no sign of Jode. But another tiny figure standing in a dark corner caught her eye.

"Rhazala?" said Daine, following Lei's gaze.

"There you are," the goblin girl said. "I thought I might have heards you wrong this morning when you said the place." While it was difficult for her to avoid being adorable, her voice was level and grim. "You need to come with me. Now."

"Why?" Obviously Daine had trouble placing his trust in a girl who'd picked his pocket just two days before.

"You must come and see." Rhazala said. "It is about your friend. The little one."

"What?" Lei broke in. "Where is he?"

"Come and see," Rhazala said. She darted out the door of the inn and they followed.

Chapter 34

BRELAND
SHARN
Dravago 28, 996 YK

Rhazala wouldn't speak as she slipped through the shadows. She dismissed any questions with a wave of her hand. "Quiet and quick," she said. "Enemies about."

While Daine didn't trust the goblin, the previous night had proven that there was danger lurking on the streets of High Walls. He drew his dagger, concealing the dark blade against his forearm. Pierce retrieved his bow from Lei's pack and put an arrow to string. Lei drew the darkwood staff out of the depths of her pack.

Rhazala led them through a winding labyrinth of alleys. The streets grew narrower and narrower, and there were fewer and fewer bystanders to be seen. Eventually the alley came to a dead end. A steel door was set into the final wall, but there were no signs of any sort of lock or handle. An arcane seal, Daine thought. No mere thief could open this door, for there was no lock to pick. The door was sealed with pure magical energy. Before Daine could say anything, Rhazala barked a short phrase in a harsh, rasping tongue and traced a complex pattern on the front of the door. Sparkling light followed in the wake of her finger, and a moment later the door swung open.

Daine exchanged a glance with Lei. Rhazala had already proven herself to be a talented pickpocket. She seemed to have a gift for sorcery as well. He wondered how old the girl actually was and how she'd developed her skills.

The steel door opened into a small, bare chamber. The only feature was a hatch on the floor. Rhazala lifted this trapdoor, revealing a long tunnel that dropped down into utter darkness. Rungs had been carved into the stone wall; at was impossible to see how far they extended.

"Down!" said Rhazala.

"Wait," Daine said. "Just because you can see in the dark doesn't mean the rest of us can. Lei, a little light?"

Lei brushed her fingers across her armor, and the studs began to radiate a golden glow.

"Captain," Pierce said, studying the passage, "I will be unable to shift position within this tunnel. My presence may be a hindrance."

He was right. Daine would have a hard time fitting into the tunnel. For Pierce, it would be all but impossible.

"If you need me with you, I could—"

"No, that's fine," Daine said. "Stay here. Hold this position until the ninth bell, if you can hear it from here. If we haven't returned by then, go back to the Manticore."

Pierce nodded and stepped out into the alley, an arrow to his bowstring and a second tucked between his fingers. He calmly sighted down the alley and waited for an enemy to appear.

"Quickly!" Rhazala hissed. She had already started down the tunnel.

Daine looked at Lei, then back at the tunnel. Sheathing his dagger, he climbed into the tunnel and began his descent. Lei dropped her staff into one of the unnaturally large pockets of her pack and followed close behind.

❦ ❦ ❦ ❦ ❦ ❦ ❦

The tunnel seemed to go on forever.

"Where are we going, Rhazala?" Daine asked.

"Down."

"I noticed that."

"Cogs. Sewers. Undercity beneath Sharn."

"Ah." Now they were getting somewhere. The Cogs had been mentioned frequently during their earlier travels with Greykell. Many of Sharn's largest and least attractive industries were located beneath the city. Workhouses, tanneries, and foundries lay buried in the subterranean Cogs. The sewers were even further below, and some said that there were ancient ruins hidden even below the sewers.

"Many passages to the depths were built long ago. Forgotten now, but the quiet folk remember."

"And would you care to tell me what we're doing down here?"

"You must see."

"*What* must we see?" Lei said from below.

"You will see."

"Oh, I see."

"No, you *will* see," Daine corrected.

"Hush," Rhazala said. "Many dangers lurk below. No time for laughter."

They continued the descent in silence.

❁ ❁ ❁ ❁ ❁ ❁ ❁

The stench was appalling. A stream of sewage and wastewater flowed down the center of the tunnel, and the walls were crusted with mold and filth. Lei's armor was the only source of light, and swarms of insects and other vermin scurried away from the circle of illumination.

"Interesting," Lei said, examining the design of the roof. "I've heard a lot about the design. Sharn's the largest city in Khorvaire, and the towers make traditional systems of plumbing difficulty to implement."

"And the water is served in mugs of scented clay," Daine said.

"*Hush,*" Rhazala said. "Almost there, but very dangerous."

"Are all goblins such worriers?" Daine said. "There's no one anywhere to be seen."

A gray ooze exploded out of the water in front of him.

Wastewater dripped off of the creature as it dove for Daine. It was long and narrow, a strip of dull gray protoplasm almost ten feet in length. It slammed into Daine, and he staggered back against the wall. He threw himself to the side just in time to avoid being caught in the coils of the monster.

The creature snapped at him again, but this time he was

ready. Darting beneath the tendril, he thrust his sword into the slimy mass. It felt like stabbing a bag filled with mud, but the creature pulled back.

"Doraashka!" the goblin called out. "Gray eater! Look to your blade! It burns!"

Daine's eyes dropped to his sword, and he cursed. The blade was pitted and scarred, as if it had been exposed to powerful acid. A lesser blade might have been destroyed with a single stroke. The odds were poor that his sword would survive another attack.

Daine saw Lei about to strike the ooze with her staff.

"Lei, stop!"

She paused, puzzled, and the creature struck, throwing him across the hallway. His left shoulder ached, and the acid began to eat away at cloak and armor.

"It's covered with acid! We can't hit it!" Daine rolled forward, dodging the next blow and rising to his feet in one fluid motion. He tried not to think about the sewage soaking his clothes.

"So what do we do?" Lei shrieked.

He remembered the wand he'd taken from Dasei d'Cannith. He still had it, tucked in his belt. The Cannith heir must have forgotten about it in the chaos.

"Lei, catch!" he cried, tossing the shard-encrusted wooden wand to Lei.

She caught the wand, but even as she did, the ooze caught Daine. The gray tentacle wrapped around his torso, constricting with terrible strength. He cried out in pain as a few drops of acid seeped below his armor.

Daine didn't see what Lei did, but there was a brilliant flash of light. The creature spasmed, tightening its grip, and now the acid was burning his arms and chest.

"Lei . . ." he gasped.

There was another flash of light, and the pressure was gone. The ooze collapsed, dissolving and flowing away into the water. Daine collapsed, gasping, on the floor. His chainmail byrnie was ruined, and his cloak had been eaten away. *I guess I'll be buying a new cloak after all,* he thought, wincing from the acid burns.

"Just sit still," Lei said. She drew a bloodstone shard out of her pouch and whispered to it, weaving an enchantment to neutralize the acid and heal the burns. It wasn't as quick or efficient as Jode's healing touch, but Daine breathed a sigh of relief as a relaxing numbness spread across his chest.

"You destroyed a gray eater!" Rhazala said, and for an instant she was a child again. "I've only seen it done once before."

"What *was* it?" Daine said, slowly getting to his feat and examining his sword.

"Part of the sewer system, I think," Lei said. "I told you it was fascinating. A living system for dissolving and disposing of the garbage that gets sent down here."

"It's always a race to find the true treasures before the doraashka arrives," Rhazala said. "I hope we're not too late. Come, quickly!"

She raced down the tunnel, and they followed as quickly as they could.

❂ ❂ ❂ ◉ ❂ ❂ ❂

A few minutes later they came to the midden heap.

It was a cavernous chamber. The walls and arched ceiling stretched far beyond the dim light of Lei's armor. Filthy water flowed around their feet, carrying waste down the passage they'd come from. Ahead of them was the heap.

Daine had never seen so much garbage in one place. It was a mountain of filth and rotting material mixed with various scraps and damaged goods. As they walked forward, a cascade of rotten vegetables fell from the ceiling. Daine couldn't see the roof, but it seemed that there were a series of chutes that channeled waste down from the city.

The heap was teaming with rats and insects, but the vermin had competition. Goblins. At least a dozen were crawling through the garbage, sifting through the refuse and looking for anything of value. Daine noticed a few more goblins standing near the entrances of the chamber, armed with makeshift clubs and spears. He imagined that these were scouts, watching for "gray eaters" or other dangers.

Rhazala approached one of the scouts. Speaking in the guttural tongue of the goblins, she said, "Are they still safe?"

248

The man nodded.

"Pay him," Rhazala said to Daine.

"What?"

"Pay him. They mine the garbage to survive. He has something you must see. Pay him."

"Look," Daine said. "I appreciate that you may actually be trying to help us. But I don't have any money. Everything I had was stolen by a goblin who looked remarkably like you. So if you want me to pay him with my own coins . . . I'm afraid you've got them."

Rhazala watched Daine carefully, then her hand darted into her robes, and when it emerged she was holding a double crown. She tossed it to the sentinel without saying a word, and he led them deeper into the chamber.

As they moved to the center of the chamber the water grew deeper, coming up to the hips of the little goblins. Slowly, they made their way around the massive garbage heap.

And that's when they saw the bodies.

There were four corpses lined up along the midden heap. Their bodies were bloated from exposure to water, and they were in varying states of decomposition. The first was a dwarf, whom Daine didn't recognize. The second was Jode.

Lei cried out and sloshed forward through the water. Daine found himself at a loss. For a moment he couldn't move, couldn't think. He'd lost soldiers before—even friends—but this was *Jode*. He couldn't imagine a world without him.

Lei knelt by the corpse and gasped. Daine made his legs move and staggered forward. Jode's skull had been caved in. Very little was left of the back of his head.

"Who . . . ?" Lei said, her voice muted. She turned to look at Daine. *"Why?"*

Daine was still in a daze. "I told him," he said, more to himself than to Lei. "I told him not to go."

"Last night they wanted him alive!" Lei cried. "Who would do this?"

Daine turned away. He couldn't look at the corpse any more. "When was he found?" he said.

"Around the sixth bell," said Rhazala, glancing over at the

scout for confirmation. He nodded. "They found all four of them together. It's rare for flesh to escape the notice of the doraashka, so they were not in the water for long. I thought you should know. I liked the little one."

All four together? Did Jode go to meet these people? Daine walked over to the bodies. Lei was wiping the filth off of Jode's skin and clothes. Daine still couldn't bear the site of his best friend's face, so he turned to examine the remaining two corpses.

Once again, he found himself at a loss for words.

He knew both of these people. One was Korlan, the half-orc he'd met in the company of Bal Tarkanan, and the other was Rasial Tann.

CHAPTER 35

BRELAND
SHARN
Dravago 28, 996 YK

It was hard to focus with Jode's body lying there, but Daine had to push on. He knelt to examine the bodies. He was no expert, but Rasial's corpse seemed to be in worse condition than the others. Perhaps he'd died before the others. All the bodies had the same sort of massive head injuries as Jode—the backs of their skulls shattered, probably with a mace or a club. The skull cavity was almost completely empty. Rasial had a series of light, raking cuts along his chest—claw marks, most likely, and not deep enough to be lethal. The head wounds were the only ones that seemed significant. Daine searched the bodies, but neither was carrying anything. He turned back to the goblin scout.

"Did this one have any possessions?"

The goblin shook his head.

"Are you certain? I can get you gold, if you have what I'm looking for."

The mention of gold lit a fire in the goblin's eyes, but he shook his head again. "He had nothing."

Daine cursed. He walked over to Lei. "Let's get out of here, Lei. We need to take him back to the surface."

Lei said nothing. Her eyes were wide as she looked down at Jode.

"What is it?"

"Daine, his dragonmark . . . it's missing."

She was right. The Mark of Healing had been spread across Jode's head, a proud symbol of his magical gift. Despite the terrible wound, it was easy to see. The mark was no longer there.

"How is that possible?" Daine said. "Is it not really him?"

Lei examined the body more closely, studying the forehead. "I don't know, but dragonmarks don't disappear after death. They don't disappear *ever*." She ran her hand across his face. "I'd like to believe this is some trick, but I don't think so." A tear ran down her cheek as she looked at Daine. "The sphinx said you'd suffer a loss today, Daine. She didn't say we all would."

Daine closed his eyes and took a deep breath. "We'll find out who did this, Lei. We'll make them pay. But right now, we have to keep moving. We'll mourn him when he's been avenged."

She nodded, though her face was still a mask of sorrow. "I know."

"We need to find a way to carry him. Here." He took off the remnants of his ruined cloak. "Use this."

"What about the others?"

"We can't take them all. Worry about Jode."

Lei nodded and wrapped Jode in the cloak. She whispered to the cloth.

"What are you doing?" he asked.

"Weaving an enchantment. It will keep his body from decomposing."

Leaving her to her business, Daine turned to Rhazala. "Are you or your friends here looking to make a few more coins?"

"Always!" the girl said cheerfully.

"Then go to the Illian Apothecary in . . . Dragon Towers, I think. You want to talk to a man named Bal. Tell him you've found the corpses of two of his friends."

"That we will do. But what of you? You claim to have no coin, then you offer gold for stolen goods."

"I can get more money. Possibly a lot more. If you'll help us, you and your friends will get your reward."

Rhazala and the scout had a hushed exchange. Rhazala turned back to Daine and nodded. "I will help you. If you need the quiet folk, I know where to find them."

252

"Good. I want to talk to whoever found these bodies. I need to see where they were found."

"You'll be wanting Hazg," said the goblin scout. "I'll fetch that one." He waded away into the murky depths.

"Daine!" Lei called.

He turned back to her. She'd stripped the wet rags off of Rasial and was studying his naked body.

"What are you *doing?*" he said.

"He doesn't have a mark either, Daine."

"What do you mean?"

"According to Bal, their powers come from aberrant dragon-marks. Rasial was supposed to be able to kill with a touch. So . . . where's his mark?"

"Hmm. Any more ideas?"

"Perhaps. I need to get back to the Manticore."

"What about Jode? Is he . . . ready?"

Lei grimaced and indicated the cloth-wrapped bundle at the foot of the heap. "I'll need your help."

Daine waded through the sewage and picked up the body of his friend. Lei took off her pack and opened it. A length of cord defined the size of the opening into the central compartment of the pack. Loosening the cord, she pulled at the mouth of the opening, creating a funnel-like cone. "I think he'll fit," she said. She extended the opening toward Daine.

Looking into the opening was like staring into deep, black water. Daine could sense something there, but he could see nothing. Blinking back tears, Daine pushed Jode's body through the opening. There was a slight sensation of resistance, as if he was pushing the corpse through mud, then it was gone and so was Jode.

Lei tightened the cord and buckled the pack.

❂ ❂ ❂ ❂ ❂ ❂ ❂

Hazg was a surly goblin with patchy hair and flaking gray skin. He spoke little but moved with surprising speed along the slippery stone. He took them up one of the routing tunnels that brought waste into the central chamber. About two hundred feet down the passage, a large chunk of rock had fallen from the ceiling. Hazg stopped and perched on the stone.

"Here," he croaked, his voice rough and raspy. "The stone's a recent falling. Things been getting caught. Bodies was here."

"My thanks, Hazg," Daine said.

"Not wanting thanks." He rubbed thumb and forefinger together.

Daine glanced at Rhazala. She pouted and finally produced a crown for Hzag, who scampered back down the tunnel.

"When do *I* get more money?" Rhazala asked.

"Why? Have you already spent all mine?"

Rhazala showed no signs of shame. "You shouldn't have made it so easy. Someone else would have taken it if I hadn't. You're lucky. If not for me, who'd be paying the quiet folk now?"

Daine decided not to argue the point. "Where does the waste in this tunnel come from?"

Rhazala looked around and spotted a few worn markings on the wall. "High Walls and Khyber's Gate."

"Two districts through this one tunnel?"

"Khyber's Gate is *under* High Walls," Rhazala said. She used her hands to indicate multiple levels. "It's like the Cogs, but there's not really any business there. Just rat's markets and people fearing the light. It's wider than High Walls, and it goes deeper than even here, down to old places where even the quiet folk won't go."

"And where's the nearest passage to the surface?"

"Not far. Want to go?"

Daine thought for a moment. "Do you know where it comes out?"

"No, but someone does, I'm sure. Shall I find out?"

"Show us the way back first. Then find out and meet us at the Manticore in two hours. If it turns out to be dangerous, we'll want Pierce along. I'll have your gold, I hope."

"If you have the gold, I'll have your information," Rhazala said, beaming.

"Lead on, then."

✦ ✦ ✦ ✦ ✦ ✦ ✦

The tenth bell was ringing when they returned to the streets of High Walls. Rhazala had stayed below to investigate the tunnels.

"How are you going to pay her?" Lei asked.

"Let me handle that. What was your thought on the missing dragonmark?"

"I should examine Jode and see what he can tell me. I'll need to make a divining rod. I should warn you, though, I can't do many more infusions tonight."

Daine nodded. "I know. We'll need to be careful. But I'll never be able to sleep until we've done all we can."

Sorrow crossed Lei's face. "I don't know if I'll be able to sleep in any case. It's . . . I keep trying to forget about it, to think that he'll be waiting for us at the Manticore."

Daine put his hand on her shoulder. "Don't give up hope. If anyone could find a way to swindle the Keeper of Souls, it would be Jode."

She nodded, but she had no cheerful words.

Pierce was waiting in the common room when they arrived. "Ca—uh, General Daine, my lady Lei. I have seen no signs of Jode, and Mistress Dassi says that he did not return in our absence." He paused. "What became of your armor and clothing, captain?"

Daine and Lei looked at one another. "Jode is dead, Pierce."

"I don't understand."

"That's what the goblin needed to show us. She found Jode's body down in the sewers."

Pierce was silent for a moment. "Was he attacked by our enemies from yesterday evening?"

"It seems likely. The sewer was fed from High Walls. But we don't know how they found him or why they killed him. Yesterday they seemed to want him alive."

"Perhaps he did not have what they were looking for."

"Perhaps." Lei said.

Pierce was silent again. His metal face gave no hint of his emotions. Finally he said "There is no war here. This death has no purpose."

"That may be where you're wrong," Lei said. "One of you, help me back to our room."

"Pierce, go with her. I have something else to attend to."

"Yes, Captain."

Once Lei and Pierce had left, Daine found the innkeeper, Dassi. "Where's the nearest message station?"

"Halfstone Street in Black Arch, General." She smiled sweetly. "Has there been any progress on establishing your credit?"

"Perhaps," he said. "I'll tell you when I get back."

❀ ❀ ❀ ❀ ❀ ❀ ❀

Black Arch housed the garrison of Tavick's Landing. It was the most austere district Daine had been in yet. Located on the ground and close to the gates of Sharn, it was even more heavily fortified than Daggerwatch. It didn't take long for Daine to find what he was looking for—the crest of House Sivis, hanging from a gilded board over a large black door.

Even late at night, the message station was a bustle of activity. Gnomes were scurrying about and the air was full of whispers. One entire wall was covered with bookshelves, filled with identical black leather tomes. The opposite side of the room was dominated by three marble busts on high pedestals. The busts had the features of elderly, sagacious gnomes, with faceted dragonshards in place of eyes. Two gnomes sat by each bust, each holding a quill and book. Occasionally the gnomes would talk to the statue, but most of the time they seemed to sit and listen, furiously scribbling notes in their books. There were a few more chairs by the door. A woman wearing the courier's badge of House Orien was fast asleep in one chair, while a messenger in the livery of the Sharn Watch sat in another.

The message stations of House Sivis were the backbone of long-distance communication in Khorvaire. While they called it the Mark of Scribing, the dragonmark of House Sivis related to all forms of communication. By speaking to the stone figure, a gnome could send a message across the continent. It was far from instantaneous but still far faster than any human or beast. When the message reached the intended speaking stone, a gnome at the stone station would copy it down, either holding it for pickup or passing it to a courier for local delivery. Daine had heard that House Sivis had developed its own language just for sending and recording messages. It wouldn't surprise him. The gnomes were obsessed with the security of their system.

Daine approached the gnome spokesman. "Good evening, sir!" the gnome said cheerfully. "Are you sending or receiving?"

"Sending," Daine said, "though there is a complication."

The gnome raised bushy eyebrows and waited for Daine to continue.

"I need to send the message at the recipient's expense."

"Well, sir, there are a few nations that have made such arrangements with the house, but unless you are an accredited member of the court in question, I'm afraid that I cannot—"

"The message is for Alina Lorridan Lyrris."

"And what is it you wished to say?" The speaker produced a parchment and quill and smiled.

❧ ❧ ❧ ❧ ❧ ❧ ❧

Back at the Manticore, Pierce set Jode's body on one of the ragged pallets. He studied the terrible wound that had shattered his comrade's head.

"Whoever did this must be punished," he rumbled.

Lei was rummaging through her backpack, pulling out mystical charms and sheafs of parchment. "I never knew you to have a sense of vengeance, Pierce."

"This is not a matter of vengeance, my lady. This is war, and war is my purpose."

She nodded. "Then let it be mine, as well."

She saw a minotaur falling at her touch, a warforged soldier collapsing into pieces, and for that moment, pure hatred chased away all sorrow. The moment passed, and she was left in the squalid room with her charms and her papers and the corpse of her friend. She sighed, determined to hold back her tears.

Lei spread her tools around the pallet. She took a wooden rod and whispered to it, weaving a minor spell of divination. When this task was completed, she found a flat shard of black crystal and etched the symbol of a skull into its surface. She set the stone disk aside.

"What are you doing, my lady?" Pierce asked.

Lei picked up the rod. "First, I'm going to examine him more closely and search for any sort of mystical energies. Then we'll see what he can tell us."

She ran her fingers across the rod, activating the enchantment she'd placed within. Slowly, carefully, she passed the rod along the body.

"There is residual magical energy here—ever so faint, but definitely there." She studied the shattered skull more closely, then gagged, dropping the wand.

"My lady?" Pierce said, moving to take her shoulders.

"I'm . . . I'm all right," she said, returning to her feet. "It's . . ." She knelt again. Steeling herself, she examined the wound more closely.

"What is it?"

"This injury . . . it's not what it appears." Lei picked up a small glowing crystal, illuminating the jagged edge of the wound. "Look. This was caused by one or two powerful blows with a large, blunt implement."

"Yes?" Pierce said.

"But beneath, it looks as if his brain was removed before this injury occurred. There's no trace of brain matter against the inside of the skull."

"Why would someone do such a thing?"

"I don't know, but it means he was dead before the crushing blow, that someone was trying to cover up that first injury. I can only assume that the killers were trying to hide the subtle wound with this savage blow." She shivered and picked up the disk of black crystal. "Let's see if Jode can tell us."

"How could he do that?"

Lei positioned the disk on what remained of Jode's forehead. "The enchantment I've woven within this stone will let us speak with Jode, if only for a few minutes. It's . . . not really him, just the traces of his spirit left behind. But he should be able to tell us what happened—at least, as much as he knew before . . ."

Lei was trying to hold things together, to focus on this as an academic challenge, but this was her friend, and she knew this was the last time she would ever speak to him. Pierce put his hand on her shoulder, and for a moment she clung to his arm, squeezing the cold metal as hard as she could. Then she took a deep breath and let go, moving back to the corpse.

She touched the stone disk and unlocked the energies with a whisper and a thought. "Jode," she said quietly. "Tell us who did this to you."

The silence was absolute.

"Jode," she repeated. "Tell us what was done to you."

Nothing.

"Jode!" she screamed, though she knew he could not hear. *"Jode!"*

A moment later Pierce was holding her, gently shaking her. "Be calm, my lady. Your enchantment has failed, that is all. Be calm."

Lei shook her head, touching the stone. She could feel the mystical energies still running through it. "No. No, that's not it. He's gone, Pierce. There's nothing there at all. It's all gone."

She grabbed hold of Pierce and clung to him, and her tears began to flow.

"They didn't just take his mark," she whispered. "They destroyed him completely."

CHAPTER 36

BRELAND
SHARN
Dravago 28, 996 YK

It was almost the eleventh bell by the time Daine returned to the Manticore. Pierce had draped the ruined cloak
over Jode's body. Lei was studying sheets of parchment, her eyes
still red with tears.

Daine sat down on the empty pallet and removed the shreds
of his chainmail shirt. "What have you found?"

"His mark *was* removed," Lei said. "Moreover, I think it
was removed with these." She pushed a sheet of parchment
across the floor. It was the description of the deep dragonshards Alina wished to have returned. "The other day I told
you that such a shard might be able to bind the energies of a
dragonmark, to create some sort of defense against a mark.
I think someone managed to take that one step further.
They drew out his mark, his spirit, everything that defined
his mystical identity." Briefly, she recounted the results of
her autopsy.

Daine drew his dagger while she was talking and slowly
carved grooves in the floor. When she mentioned the missing brain he slammed the dagger down, the adamantine blade
passing through wood as if it were paper. He ground his teeth
and pulled the dagger from the floor. He'd seen so many die
over the past two years, and right now there was no time for sorrow or fury. He took a deep breath and set down the dagger. He
drew his acid-scarred sword and laid it next to his armor.

"I need restoration. We may have a battle soon, and I don't want this shattering the moment it strikes steel."

Lei nodded and picked up the sword. As she ran her fingers along the blade, the metal began to flow and reform. Within moments it had been restored to its original condition. Then she turned to the armor.

"I'm going to have to stretch the metal to make do," she said. "It won't be as strong as it was before."

"Whatever you need to do," Daine said.

There was a knock on the door.

It was still too early for Rhazala to show up. Daine snatched his restored sword and rolled over to the door. Remaining in a low crouch, he indicated that Pierce should open the door. As soon as there was enough space, his hand was through the opening, the point of his blade poised at the belly of their visitor.

A human woman stood on the other side of the door. She was dressed in black leather and wool and carried a large satchel. The courier's crest of House Orien was emblazoned above her heart. She didn't flinch or blink. Apparently she was used to suspicious clients.

"You would be Daine?" she said.

"That's me."

Daine stood up. He lowered his sword but not his guard. He had been expecting a courier, but after Jode's death he couldn't be sure of anything.

The courier's eyes flicked down to take in the Deneith symbol at the pommel of Daine's sword, and she nodded. Apparently that had been mentioned as an identifying feature. She produced two objects from her satchel—a small leather pouch and a sealed letter—both of which she handed to Daine. Opening the pouch, Daine dug out a double crown and pressed it into her palm. A moment later she had vanished.

"What was that?"

Lei said. She had just finished with Daine's armor. The links were thinner than they had been, but at least it would cover his torso.

"Orien courier from Alina." He shook the pouch. "We've

got a purse of silver sovereigns. That should help buy the time of the goblins. I guess we'd better pay off Dassi as well." He broke the seal on the letter and unfolded the parchment; the message was written in an elegant, flowing script.

With the passing of my former employee, you are to find the goods that he was carrying, regardless of what shape they may take. As these goods may be removed from the city, if you cannot resolve this matter within two days I shall have to consider our new partnership to be a failure, which would be a tragedy for both of us. Good luck.

"Anything?" said Lei.

"Not really. Alina wants the shards, 'regardless of what shape they may take,' and if we can't settle the matter in a few days, she may get . . . upset."

"And this is a concern?"

"She's hired us for this job because she needs outsiders. I don't think that the same restrictions would apply to disposing of ineffectual employees."

"I see."

"You said you're about done for the day, right?"

Lei nodded. "I could perform minor repairs, but that's about it. I need rest."

"What about that wand—the one that destroyed that thing in the sewer?"

Lei reached into one of the side pocket of her pack and produced the wand. She tapped the row of dragonshards running along the shaft. "Lightning discharge, powered by the embedded shards. But it's drained. It's going to take time for the energy to build up again."

"So if we're looking for a fight," said Daine, "we should wait until morning." He paused, thinking. "A lot will depend on what we find out from Rhazala. For now . . . empty out your pack, Lei. I want to see what else we've got available."

"All of it?"

"Yes."

She shrugged. It took a few minutes to pull everything out. Daine had forgotten how large the central compartment really was. But his memory had been correct, and he smiled. "All right, Lei. Here's what I want you to do."

❦ ❦ ❦ ❦ ❦ ❦ ❦

Ten minutes later, Pierce, Rhazala, and Daine were back on the streets of High Walls. The goblin and the warforged flowed across the streets like shadows. Despite his bulk, Pierce had been built for reconnaissance, and he moved with a fluid grace the bulkier warforged warriors couldn't match. Next to his companions, Daine felt clumsy and loud, as if he were a bear hunting in the company of panthers.

After five minutes Rhazala came to a stop. "Somewhere near the center," she said, pointing.

"You're sure?" Daine said.

"Yes, yes. The tunnel comes up underneath. Runs through Khyber's Gate, just like the tunnel of waste and water. And a bad place it is below there. The quiet folk have lost scouts in that region before. Usually they lose to eaters or the red jackals, but there are worse things in Khyber's Gate, and I believe this is where at least one may live. The quiet folk, they won't go near to it."

"Very well. Good job, Rhazala. Here's your payment."

He had tied the pouch of coins around his neck, but when he reached up he found it was gone. Turning, he saw that Rhazala was holding it out to him. She showed him the two sovereigns in her left hand.

"I only took for my services," she said smugly. "This time."

Daine sighed and took the purse. Rhazala smiled and bowed, and a moment later she was gone. Daine blinked. Was her disappearance the work of her skill and his own exhaustion, or was magic involved? Whatever the answer, she was nowhere to be seen.

Daine shook his head. "Let's go, Pierce. I don't want to take this any further without daylight on our side, and I could use a good night's rest."

"As you wish, Captain."

The two began walking back towards the Manticore. Daine studied his warforged companion for a moment. "You all right, Pierce?"

"Captain?"

Daine gestured vaguely. "Well, with Jode . . . you know, it's just got me thinking about the troop. You've served with me since I first accepted my commission. You've been everything a commander could ask for in a soldier, and you've never let me down. You've followed my every order without question, and I've come to rely on that."

"I am gratified to hear that, sir."

"But . . . we're not in the army anymore, Pierce. I'm not your captain anymore. I'm just your companion, your friend."

"I understand, but I am most comfortable operating under a military chain of command. You had a life before you entered the Cyran army. I did not. I was forged with the knowledge of war burned into my mind, and I was on the front lines within a week of my . . . birth, if you can call it that. War is in my nature, and it will always be part of how I view the world. As long as you will have me, you will always be my captain."

"You served in the guard more than four times as long as I did. Don't you feel that you should be the one in charge?"

"You don't understand, Captain. Humans are born without a purpose. You must find your path in life. I was made to accomplish a specific task, and I have always known the nature of that task. I was not made to lead, and I have no desire to try."

Daine shrugged. "Fair enough. But Pierce . . . humans often think they know what they're supposed to do with their lives, and they aren't always right. Just because someone's told you what your purpose is supposed to be . . . are you sure it's the truth?"

"I was born of design. I was made to excel at a specific task, and I would never be able to be as successful in another field. Is there a point to this discussion?"

"I was just thinking about the sphinx again. She said that you don't know your purpose yet."

"It seemed to me that you gave little credence to her words."

"I didn't—at the time But now . . ." Daine shook his head. "After what we've seen tonight, I can't help but wonder about the other things she said."

Pierce remained as impassive as ever. "If I have another purpose, it may become clear in time. Until then, I am content."

"Very well. But Pierce, you don't talk much. I understand if you just don't have much to say. But if there is ever anything I can do, I want you to tell me."

"As you wish."

Daine studied Pierce, but the warforged had no expression to read. Daine still felt that there was something that Pierce wasn't talking about. Perhaps it was Jode's death. Daine had sent Pierce to watch Jode, and the warforged might be blaming himself for the death of their friend. I'll just have to watch and wait, Daine decided.

The first bell of the new day was ringing when they returned to the Manticore. Daine was exhausted. It had been a long day, and the coming dawn promised to be even more dangerous. The thought of bed—even a wretched pallet on the floor—called out to him.

At this hour, Daine assumed that the common room of the Manticore would be empty, but he was mistaken. A single man was sitting at one of the tables, watching the door and drinking from a chipped mug. As Daine and Pierce entered the room, the visitor set down his mug and rose from his chair.

"It's about time you arrived, Daine. And what trouble have you been getting into now?"

It was Grazen ir'Tala, Captain of the Sharn Watch.

CHAPTER 37

BRELAND
SHARN
Nymm 1, 996 YK

Grazen ir'Tala was dressed for battle. In place of the green and black leather of the Sharn Watch, Grazen wore a beautiful chainmail shirt. The links were coated with black enamel, and it was so finely crafted that it made no sound as Grazen rose from his chair. If anything, the armor seemed to absorb the sounds of his movement. Grazen wore a belt of black leather, and like Daine, he was armed with a longsword and dagger. Beneath his armor, he wore a black silk doublet and breeches, with gloves and boots of dark leather. His flowing darkweave cloak was darkness given solid form. He was a vision of elegance in the squalid surroundings of the Manticore, but his hand was on the hilt of his sword, and Daine knew how quick and deadly that blade could be.

"Captain Grazen, what an unexpected surprise," Daine said. "What brings you to our humble home so late? Or is it now considered early?"

Pierce still had his bow in his hands. If it came to it, Daine knew that Pierce could aim and loose an arrow before Grazen could close the distance between them. But he still wasn't sure what to make of Grazen's presence. Were they going to be arrested again?

Grazen looked at Pierce, obviously evaluating the threat posed by the warforged archer. Finally he sat down again. "Join me, won't you?" he said, gesturing at a stool across the table.

"I brought a skin of Iltrayan down with me, along with a good loaf of bread and a few strips of smoked tribex. I don't imagine you've had many feasts in this charming little inn. As I recall, you always enjoyed a good Iltrayan."

Daine studied Grazen carefully. Finally he turned to Pierce. "Why don't you check on Lei? I can handle this."

"As you wish."

After Pierce had disappeared up the staircase, Daine pulled out the stool and sat down. Grazen produced another mug and placed a sack upon the table. As promised, it contained bread, cheese, and a skin of the finest wine Daine had tasted in five years. For a few minutes, Daine focused entirely on the food. He knew Grazen would get to the point sooner or later, and finally he did.

"I know what you've been doing, Daine."

"Then you're one step ahead of me." Daine tore off another chunk of bread and looked at it. "Have you ever been to one of those gnome restaurants where all they serve is bread and water?" He placed a strip of smoked tribex on the bread and took a large bite, chewing thoughtfully.

Grazen watched him and said nothing.

"So tell me," Daine said. "What have I been doing?"

"Working for Alina Lyrris."

"What could ever drive me to do that?"

"That's the question. After all your years of service to Cyre, are you going to become a mercenary now? My sword suits you better than I thought."

Daine's fingers tightened around his mug. "Watch your words, my friend."

"And what sort of friend would I be if I did? I offered you a job, Daine, a chance to work for the Watch. The pay might not be much, but it would be an honest living."

"From what I've heard of Sharn, there's little honest about the Watch."

Now it was Grazen's turn to scowl.

"Besides, I served *Cyre*. I spent the last six years fighting Brelanders. What could possibly bring me to risk my life defending them?"

"What could possibly bring you to work for Lyrris?"

"I asked you first."

Grazen drained his mug and set it down. "Fine. Let me talk straight with you, Daine. Out of respect for the friendship we had in the past, if nothing else. Whatever Alina has you searching for. When you find it, I want you to bring it to me."

"I don't know what—"

"I'm willing to match whatever she's paying you. I've come into quite a fortune through my marriage, and I can do it. Whatever it is. Whatever the price."

"I don't understand. Why would you be interested?"

"Because whatever it is she wants . . . I don't want her to have it. Do you need a better reason?"

"Grazen, look. Even if I was working for Alina—"

"Don't lie to me, Daine. You were never very good at it, and I hate to see you lying for her."

Daine closed his eyes and took a deep breath. "Fine. So I'm working for Alina. I made a deal, Grazen. I agreed to do a job. Are you asking me to break my word? I thought you believed in honoring commitments."

"Does Alina?"

"I've never known her to go back on her word. But I've certainly seen what she does to those who betray her."

"Daine, you're on the wrong side here."

"And you're on the right side?"

"I'm not on *anyone's* side. I'm just trying to offer you a way out."

Daine pondered this for a moment. "Do you remember my friend Jode?"

"The halfling?"

"Yes." He looked straight into Grazen's eyes. "He's dead. I think he was killed by Alina's enemies. Tell me. Do you think the Sharn Watch would hunt down the killers of a halfling refugee murdered beneath the city?"

For a moment, Grazen met his gaze, then he looked away. "No."

"I'm not doing this for Alina. I've lost my homeland. I've lost the war. Now I've lost my best friend. I may be about to lose my life. But I'm *not* going to lose my honor. I made a promise, and I'll see it through."

Grazen stood up. "Very well. But consider my offer—and think about what your promise might cost you. You don't want me as an enemy, Daine."

"You're right. I don't."

"Then I hope you'll make the right decision."

"We'll see."

Grazen slowly walked towards the door. "You can keep the rest of the wine. For old times' sake."

Daine nodded, and Grazen stepped out into the dark streets of High Walls. Daine poured another mug of Iltryan wine and sat in the shadows of the empty room, thinking about Jode and the promises he'd made.

But eventually, the wineskin was empty. Picking up the sack of food, Daine walked upstairs to the waiting arms of sleep.

INTERLUDE

No light broke in the depths of the sewers, no source of illumination, yet somehow the darkness did not hinder his sight. Shades of gray and blue painted the world, but he could still make out every detail of his surroundings—the murky water lapping at his feet, the vast mountain of waste towering before him, and the four bodies stretched out at the foot of the hill, now without the slightest sign of rot or decay.

"It's a sad sight, isn't it?"

The voice was a shock. Daine spun, the motion sending a splash of water across the waves. There was Jode, perched on the wreckage of an old stool, looking every bit as alive as he had last morning.

"Jode? But you're . . ." He looked back at the midden heap. The corpse was still there, its peaceful expression belying the ghastly wound across the back of its skull.

"Dead? Perhaps. Perhaps not." He inclined his head, tapping the faintly glowing dragonmark spread across his scalp. "You didn't find my mark, Daine, so how do you know you found me? What really defined *me*?" He smiled and hopped down off his perch. "Water's a bit deep here," he said, wading over to where Daine stood. He looked down at the corpse. "Tell me, Daine, where am I in that? Can you see me in that corpse?"

"No."

270

"There you have it. You said it yourself. If anyone could find a way to swindle the Keeper of Souls, it would be Jode. So why are you so worried about me? Now come on, let's get out of the water."

Jode waded over to one of the sewer tunnels and climbed up to walk on the raised edge.

"This is a dream," Daine said, slowly following. "It's all in my imagination."

"Just because it's a dream doesn't mean it's in your imagination," Jode said. "Have you ever considered that your imagination might have been drawn into the dream?"

"What do you mean?"

"What if the dream doesn't stop when you wake up?" As Jode spoke, the hallway in front of them began to collapse. Then Daine realized it was actually being reformed—a row of massive stone teeth were rising from both floor and ceiling. A moment later the hallway was blocked by this devilish black-marble grin. "What would it do while you were awake?"

Daine spun around, but a second row of teeth had sealed the hallway behind them.

"Perhaps it just doesn't want to let you go."

Daine kicked at the giant teeth. They seemed solid as any stone, and pain flared up his ankle.

Jode walked in front of him. "That's always been your problem, Daine. Always trying to use anger as an answer. Sometimes you have to look within."

Jode reached into his own mouth and pulled out a long key cut from white marble. He fit the key in a gap between the teeth. It clicked, and a grinding sound filled the chamber as the teeth retracted.

"What do you already know? And what are you really looking for?"

The world revealed behind the stone teeth was not the sewer hallway that they had seen before. Instead, they were in the midst of a masked ball. Dozens of dancers whirled about, elaborate costumes concealing face and form. Daine recognized this place. It was Alina's mirrored hall in the city of Metrol. The arched ceiling of the ballroom rose far above him, and chandeliers of pale blue light floated in the air like constellations. Every surface was reflective and every dancer was broken into a hundred different images. But something was wrong. He cast no reflection in any of the mirrors. And Jode . . . the images of Jode were those of the bloody corpse. As for the dancers . . . their reflections were of the soldiers who'd fought for him in the war. Saerath, Lynna, Cadrian, even Jholeg the goblin, all watching him from the walls as they moved in the endless dance.

"You're trapped by the past," Jode said. "You tried to destroy your shame by becoming a hero, but your righteous cause brought only blood and death."

Daine tried to answer but found that he could not speak. Then across the hall he saw a pale young woman with coppery hair bound above her head, dancing alone with her reflections. Her backless green gown revealed the dragonmark of Making, set just beneath the base of her neck. There was no doubt in his mind that it was Lei. He pushed through the crowd, trying to reach her, but it was like wading through a muddy swamp. He could barely move his feet, and dancers were constantly darting in front of him. When he tried to push them aside, they turned to stone, becoming even greater obstacles to his path.

The woman in green slipped further and further ahead of him. She reached the hallway that led to Alina's private workshop. She paused and looked back at him, and it was Lei, but something was wrong—her eyes. The irises were large and violet and stood out like stars amidst the tones of blue and gray. She smiled and disappeared around the corner.

Finally, Daine reached the hallway, but Lei was nowhere to be seen. Instead, another Daine was standing there: He was younger, more arrogant, impatient for action. The watchful eye emblem of House Deneith glittered on the pommel of his sword. "Looking for someone, old man?"

"Lei . . . ?"

"You're a threat to those you care about, old man. You sacrificed your family for your country. You failed to save your country, and then you failed to save your friend. You even lost your grandfather's sword."

"Jode pawned it, and now I don't even know who he pawned it to!"

"Do you always make excuses to yourself?"

"You're not me."

"And who are you?"

Daine drew his sword—Grazen's sword. His mirror-image laughed. "It is a poor man who relies on another man's blade." Then he took up a guard position, and said in a bored tone, "Lady Lyrris has declared this section of the manor to be off limits to her guests. If you'd like to survive the evening, I suggest you go back the way you came."

Daine leaped forward with a lightning thrust that should have speared his double through the knee. But his enemy swept the blow aside with a sweeping parry. He barely blocked the lazy riposte that followed, and his blade hummed from the impact.

"You're fighting yourself, Daine," his double said. He countered an attempted double-thrust, nearly sweeping the sword from Daine's grip with a circular parry. "But you've thrown away your past, and you have yet to embrace the future."

The younger Daine moved with lightning speed, and an arc of steel caught the flat of Daine's blade, which shivered and shattered into a dozen pieces. A second later, the point was at Daine's throat.

"Ask yourself," the double said. "Who are you really? What do you want in this world? Find out quickly. You may not have much time left."

His features shifted until he wasn't Daine at all: He was Monan. With a wild laugh, he drove his blade home. There was a sharp, terrible pain, and Daine couldn't breathe. He was falling, and the last thing he heard was Jode's voice.

"There are some things I can't say."

Darkness. . . .

CHAPTER 38

BRELAND
SHARN
Nymm 1, 996 YK

Daine jerked upright. The light of morning was struggling through the thick layer of dust on the windows. Lei was still sleeping on the pallet beside him. Jode's body had been wrapped up in the preserving cloak and was set against the wall. Daine climbed out of bed and touched the cloth-wrapped bundle. There was no movement.

"There are some things I can't say," Daine murmured.

"Captain?"

Daine jerked upright and spun around. It was only Pierce, but it took a moment for Daine to recover from the shock.

Lei stirred. "Mmm?"

"I know you were built as a scout, Pierce, but *try* to make more noise first thing in the morning, will you?"

"I will do my best. You appear agitated."

"Bad dreams. I suppose it's to be expected when you're sleeping in the same room with the body of your best friend."

"I wouldn't know." The warforged did not sleep or dream.

* * * * * * *

A few galifars had secured the room at the Manticore for another week and also convinced Dassi to produce a heartier meal for the general and his men. The morning's gruel was supplemented with red sugar and sagal powder, and she was able to produce three small hardboiled eggs and a pitcher of

274

tribex milk. When Daine returned to the room, Lei was fully awake.

"Here," he said, setting the platter on the ground. "I think they're lizard eggs, but anything solid sounds good to me."

Lei shrugged. She picked up one of the eggs and cracked its green speckled shell.

"Do you need more sleep?" he asked.

"No," she said. "I'm fine."

"And the work?"

"You've got two. I had to break up the third. And it's a hasty job. I can't promise how long the enchantments will hold."

"Well, two is better than none." He tried the gruel. "Hmm. Not bad, once you add the sagal. Remind me to get you some of that next time we're in the field."

Lei said nothing. Here eyes were still on Jode.

Daine sighed, embarrassed by his own attempts at levity. "Let's get started. When we arrived in Sharn, Alina Lyrris hired us to find her dragonshards, which had been stolen by Rasial, her courier. Rasial, once a city guard and windchaser, left the guard shortly after developing an aberrant dragon-mark, which may or may not have been responsible for his racing accidents."

"Such a mark could also jeopardize his social standing and would be the source of considerable pain and suffering," Lei said.

Daine nodded. "But even though he was adopted by a group of people who shared his . . . affliction, he didn't seem to fit in with them. They believed he was working behind their backs. We know he was. Working with Alina and someone in High Walls—possibly Hugal or Monan."

"Daine, we know all this," Lei said. "Why are you—"

"Just thinking out loud," he replied. "Bear with me. Three nights ago, Rasial brings a shipment of contraband shards in, but he fails to deliver them to Alina. He's our first corpse. The next day, the Tarkanans send a half-orc looking for Rasial—in High Walls—and he ends up as our second corpse. Yesterday, Jode disappears, for reasons unknown, and is"—he paused, swallowing his emotion—"also killed. Finally, we have the fourth body, which we know nothing about. All of these bodies were dumped in the sewers beneath High Walls. At least three of the four should have had dragonmarks, but none of them did. What am I missing?"

"If the marks were removed, I think the dragonshards Rasial was carrying were the key, though I'm still not sure how this could be done," Lei said.

"We were attacked by a group of humans that had been somehow altered and enhanced," Pierce said. "They appeared to want to capture Jode alive."

"True," Daine said. "However, the leader of the group was a changeling. At this point, we don't know if his 'twin brother' is a human or a changeling, but he remains at large."

"As for Jode," Lei said, "if they can remove dragonmarks, they may have needed him alive in order to extract his dragonmark. We know nothing about the process involved."

"True. What about Rasial?"

"Well . . ." Lei said. "Perhaps he just wanted to find a way to get rid of his aberrant dragonmark, in the hopes that he could go back to his old life. He met someone who promised they could help him—if he obtained the shards. Though I imagine he didn't expect to be killed in the process."

"It does explain why there's only been a few deaths so far."

"If they really are stealing the power of a mark . . . well, the Mark of Healing would be a very important one to have for this sort of work. And a small, disorganized group like these Tarkanans would make easier prey than the great houses. Being outcasts, they can't even go to the law for assistance."

"All right," Daine said. "Assuming this is correct, the next question is: Who was Rasial dealing with?"

"If you accept that the person dealing with Rasial was the same person who wanted to kidnap Jode, we're dealing with Hugal or Monan."

Daine nodded. "What else do we know about the two of them?"

"They lived at the tenement called Dolurrh's Doorstep. According to that man Doras, they had few friends, but I would say that his testimony could be considered untrustworthy at best. Although . . . at dinner, what was it Hugal said about the destruction of Cyre?"

Pierce answered. "He suggested that the destruction of Cyre would provide a weapon that could be used against the rest of the world."

"That's right," said Daine. "Supposedly, he was in Cyre when the disaster came. Even though we searched for months and never found any survivors."

"Also, that old seamstress with the eye in her palm . . . that happened recently, so it wasn't a result of the Mournlands."

"So we still have some unanswered questions. But this much seems clear. Rasial made a deal with Hugal and his unnatural friends. They took his shards, took his mark, and killed him. They did the same thing to the Tarkanan half-orc, then they got Jode. But how? Why did Jode put himself at risk?"

Lei considered. "Well, he left right after we'd seen Alina. Before that, we'd spoken with the medusa and the sphinx."

"What was it the sphinx said to him?"

Again, it was Pierce's memory that came to their aid. "She emphasized urgency, then she said, 'There is a key that only you can find, hidden between two stones that only you can move. You must find it alone, but you will pay a terrible price to do so.'"

"So presumably he determined the location of this key and believed he had to act alone." Daine rubbed his chin thoughtfully.

"Didn't you say that he reacted to something Alina said?" Lei asked.

The images from his dream came flashing back, and Daine struck his forehead. "Of course! 'There are things I cannot say.'"

"I don't understand," Pierce said.

"Who have we met in the last two days who can't speak?"

"Yes!" Lei said. "That girl—Olassia?"

"Olalia," Pierce said, "whose mouth had been turned to stone."

"Exactly." Daine said. "Councilor Teral found her in the ruins of Cyre—along with Hugal and Monan. While the twins were at dinner, she seemed terrified. She must know the truth about the twins, but she couldn't speak because her jaws have been petrified. The secret—*the key*—is trapped between two stones."

"Then the sphinx was mistaken," Lei said. "He went alone, just like she said, but he was still killed."

"She did say that he would 'pay a terrible price,' " Pierce pointed out.

"Who knows what the sphinx wanted? Why didn't she just say 'go talk to the woman with the stone teeth?' I'll never trust an oracle." Daine shook his head. "There's one last piece to this. The closest tunnel that connects the sewers to the surface comes out in Togran Square where the tent town is. Alina said that whoever was performing these mystical operations probably has a base underground, possibly in this Khyber's Gate."

"How do we proceed?" Pierce asked.

"We find Olalia. If we find Councilor Teral, we explain the situation to him. But we go in carefully. Yesterday, Jode was stolen from us. Today, we're going to make the thieves pay for what they've done." Daine drew his dagger and slammed it into the floor. "Today, we finish this."

A light drizzle misted the air and soaked the streets as Lei and Daine made their way down the streets of High Walls.

"You're sure Pierce will be all right?" Daine said.

"We've done this before, Daine. He knows what to do." Lei sighed. "Do you suppose we should talk to Greykell about this?"

"Let's just get Olalia. Greykell and Teral . . . ? We take that as it comes."

"Very well."

The tenth bell or morning had rung, and Togran Square was unusually quiet. Those refugees with jobs had made their way to the workhouses and foundries, and most of those who remained were sleeping or gathered around communal cooking points, preparing the morning meal. Daine had lost his cloak in the sewers, but his chainmail shirt and the sword at his belt still drew attention. Back at the Manticore, Daine had borrowed some bootblack from Dassi the innkeeper and used it to cover the Deneith symbol on his sword. He was tired of the unwanted attention he received for bearing the sigil of the dragonmarked house.

Daine and Lei made their way through the maze of tents to the large black canopy in the center. The dwarf doorman stood at the opening flap. "What do you want?" he asked.

"We're looking for Olalia," Daine said.

"Councilor Teral is not accustomed to receiving guests at this hour," the dwarf said. "He'll be making his rounds later. See him then."

"We're not looking for Councilor Teral. We want to see the girl Olalia, his servant."

"You want to see the Councilor's servant, you see the Councilor first."

"Can't you just ask—?" Lei began.

"I know my duties, lady," the dwarf said.

"So do I," Daine said.

All the anger and frustration that had been building since Jode's death burst. Daine slammed his right elbow into the dwarf's nose, forcing him back into the tent. Daine darted in after him. The dwarf flailed wildly, but a sweeping kick from Daine knocked the guard off his feet. A moment later Daine had a knee on the guard's chest and punched him again and again until he stopped moving.

Lei slipped in behind him. "How are you going to explain that to Teral?" she said, looking at the battered guard.

Daine looked away, embarrassed by the moment of frenzy. "If we expose a conspiracy of monsters in the community, I'd hope he'd overlook a few bruises."

They were standing in the entry chamber where they'd eaten dinner with Teral. Only now, bedrolls were scattered across the floor. Six people had been sleeping in the chamber, but all had since departed. Daine dragged the dwarf on top of a blanket.

There was a rustle of fabric and the inner door of the tent opened. Daine tensed and prepared for action, but it was Olalia. Her eyes widened as she saw Daine and the fallen guard.

Daine stood and held out his hands in a gesture of peace, then gave a quick nod to Lei.

"Olalia, it's all right," he said. "We're not here to hurt you."

Behind him, Lei began to make mystical gestures over a crystal shard, weaving a minor enchantment into the gem. Daine slowly approached Olalia.

"We just want to talk. Everything will be all right now."

The girl watched Daine fearfully, her stone teeth shining out between half-parted lips. She didn't run, but there was no sign of understanding in her eyes.

"Calm down," Daine said gently. "Nothing will hurt you. Just wait. Lei is going to help you talk to us."

"I'm ready, Daine," Lei said. The crystal in her hand glowed faintly.

"Olalia," Daine said. "Have you seen our friend Jode, the halfling"—he gestured with his hand to indicate Jode's small size—"recently?" He watched Olalia's emotionless face, then glanced over at Lei. "Anything?"

"I don't think she can understand you," Lei said. "She's afraid. Wait! She remembers you and Jode from the dinner. I think she's afraid that what happened to Jode will happen to you."

Daine turned back to the girl. "What happened, Olalia? Who harmed our friend?"

"Daine?" Counselor Teral entered the room, leaning on a cane and holding a mug of tal in his hand. "What are you doing here? And Lei, yes? Is something wrong?"

Daine caught Lei's eyes and flicked a glance at Olalia. Lei blinked once.

Daine walked over to Teral. "Councilor, last night my friend Jode was killed, and I believe Olalia knows who did it."

Teral waved his hand dismissively. "Preposterous. Olalia couldn't harm a soul. She—" He broke off, noticing the unconscious guard. "What is this?"

"We need to finish talking to her, Councilor. This mystery threatens us all. Including you."

The old man glared at Daine. "You presume too much, Captain. Beating and questioning my servants. Leave now."

"Teral, you need to listen to me. Something terrible is hidden in High Walls. Hugal and Monan were not what they seemed."

"I have had enough of this, Captain!"

Olalia whimpered. Lei had been concealing the glowing crystal in her hand. She flung it away as hard as she could.

"Lei, what—?"

"Daine, it's *him*."

Daine looked at Teral. The councilor laughed. "I see. You were watching Olalia's thoughts while you talked to me. Oh, very good."

Daine's sword was in his hand in an instant, the point leveled at Teral's throat. "What are you talking about?"

Lei winced and clutched her head, as if the visions she'd drawn from Olalia's mind was causing her pain. "Inside . . . it's *inside*."

"I hope you don't mind, Daine," Teral said, his voice growing colder. "But I've just invited a few friends to join us."

Hugal emerged from the rear of the tent. Two more people walked through the front flap—a young boy with a feral expression and a middle-aged man whose left arm had been severed at the elbow.

"If they come any closer, you'll be dead," Daine warned. He flicked the point of his sword across the old man's throat, drawing a spot of blood. Across the room, Lei drew her dagger and set her back against the wall of the tent. Her face twisted in a rictus of pain, but whatever was bother her, she seemed to be fighting it and winning.

"I think not," said Teral.

There was a flash of movement, followed by a cold pain at Daine's throat. He fell to the floor, every muscle refusing to respond. The councilor kicked his sword out of his hand.

"I'm so glad you left your warforged friend behind," Teral said, retracting his long, barbed tongue. "He would have proved more difficult to deal with." As he spoke, Daine saw that the puckered scar at his throat was *opening*. A layer of raw muscle oozed out of the wound, flowing over Teral's flesh like a second skin. Within seconds Teral seemed to have doubled in mass. He threw aside his cane and turned to face Lei, glaring at her from eyes newly sunken in deep fleshy sockets. "Now, whatever shall we do about you?"

"I'm not afraid of you, monster," Lei said. Her voice was calm, and she held her dagger in a throwing grip.

The young boy *hissed*, and in the instant Lei glanced at him Teral was in motion. His left arm whipped forward and a long tentacle of flesh lashed out of his sleeve, catching Lei's wrist and jerking the dagger from her hand. A second later, he had his right hand around her throat.

"Lei . . ." Teral said, as she gasped for air. He studied the color of her hair and skin. "An artificer, it seems—and from Cyre." Then he noticed the bare circle on her finger where her house signet had been. "Could it be?" He *sniffed* the air around her, like a hound searching for a scent. Finally he lifted her off the ground with one hand, turned her back toward him, and with his other hand he brushed aside her hair, revealing the tip of the Mark of Making rising above her collar.

Daine raged within, but he couldn't move. He watched helplessly as Teral stabbed Lei with his venomous tongue and let her fall to the ground.

"Fortune shines on us again, my brothers," Teral said, raising his bloody, pulsing arms above his head. "Another true mark is ours for the taking. The call has gone out. The master awaits. Hugal, take her below."

"And this one?" Long claws had sprouted from the boy's right hand, and he ran these talons along Daine's throat.

"Take him as well. Why waste blood and brain? One way or the other, he will serve our master."

CHAPTER 40

BRELAND
SHARN
Nymm 1, 996 YK

Daine woke in chains. His arms were stretched pain-
fully above his head, bound by steel manacles and suspended by
a hook in the hard stone wall. His legs were unbound, but his
feet barely touched the floor below. The air was full of liquid
noise—a hypnotic mélange of bubbling, flowing sounds. But
the stench ruined any calming effects that the sounds might
have. Sulfur, burning flesh, and exotic spices mixed together
to form a horrible, overwhelming scent.

Daine opened his eyes, just far enough to peer at his surroundings. The chamber was dim, and it took a moment
for his eyes to adjust to the darkness. He was in a long stone
chamber with arched ceilings that disappeared into shadow.
There were no windows, and Daine guessed they were deep
underground. Beyond the cloying odor, the air had the same
stale scent as the sewers below Sharn. This must be Khyber's
Gate, he thought.

The room came into focus, and he could see tanks and tools
lined up along the walls to his left and right. Strange objects
floated in vats of luminescent liquid, but he was too far away to
make out details. He spotted Lei's pack lying on the floor a few
feet away from him, but there was no sign of his sword.

Then he saw Lei. A table was in the center of the chamber.
In the dim light, he hadn't seen it at first. The surface was
curved and covered with opalescent enamel, and the reflected

light of the glowing fluid glittered on the dark surface. Lei lay spreadeagled on top of the table, arms and legs pinned by heavy manacles. A few odd objects were scattered about—vials of fluid, knives of various shapes and sizes, and . . . a handful of crystals. *I wonder if those are Alina's shards,* Daine thought.

"There's no point in pretending to be unconscious, Captain Daine. I heard the shift in your breathing."

Teral's voice came out of the shadows to Daine's right. Wrapped in his armor of flesh, Teral's voice was deeper and had a horrible wet rasp. Teral stepped into the light. He had changed into a loose cloak, and he glared at Daine with a terrible grin on his raw, bloody face.

Daine raised his head and looked Teral in the eye. He could see Hugal and a few other shadowy figures lurking in the darkness. Hugal was wearing Daine's sword. He caught Daine's eye and giggled.

"What *happened* to you, Teral? What have you done?"

Teral moved with astonishing speed. Daine never saw the slap that slammed his head back against the wall.

"Mind your tone, Daine, or I might take your tongue . . . or worse. I've pushed Olalia about as far as I can. Perhaps you should be my next toy."

Daine glared at Teral. He could feel a trickle of blood where his right cheek had grazed the wall.

"It is not a question of what I *did*, Daine. It is a question of what was done to me. I was saved. You wandered the Mournland for months. In that time, did you ever find any survivors?"

"We found nothing that could be saved."

"Yet I came to Sharn with over a hundred, myself included." He glared up at Daine, his eyes crazed behind his horrible mask of flesh. "I was there on the night of the Mourning, Daine. I saw the mists with my own eyes. I could never explain it to you. It was . . . pure, transcendent beauty, land and life reshaped without regard for mercy or reason. It was over in a moment. I was still alive, but I could not move. I could only lie there, feeling my body slowly shifting from life to death. No sovereign lord came to defend me. No Silver Flame shielded my soul. But at the last moment, when the light had gone from my eyes, *they* found me. *They* pulled me back from death, filling me"—he ran a hand across the ghastly layer of muscle that covered his skin—"with new life. Together we found others. Their mortality burned out of them by the Mourning, they were vessels waiting to be filled by the power from below."

Daine glanced at Lei, hoping she would stir. He needed to buy more time. "I see that the power from below bought you a nice home here in the sewers."

Teral hissed, and his barbed tongue flickered into view for a moment. "There are forces in the deeper darkness that you can't begin to understand. The world could have been theirs in ages past, and it will be in the days to come. The Mourning is the first sign of their return. Through our war, we destroyed our nation. Through our magic, we broke the world itself. Now the children of madness are returning, and this time all will fall before them."

"Sure," Daine said. "I can see it. I mean, there's a hundred of you, right? Aside from the ones we killed, of course. That's an unstoppable army, no question."

A second slap slammed his head against the wall. "This is only the beginning," Teral said. "Our numbers grow every day. Our master can reshape body and mind, granting gifts or stripping strength away."

Daine remembered the old woman with the basilisk's eye, who had been fully human only a few weeks earlier. He saw movement in the vats of liquid and wondered what they contained—and how long he could avoid finding out.

"You will see," Teral said, gripping Daine's chin with one moist hand and staring into his eyes. "You have strength. Yes. I think you shall serve at my side once your mind has been properly . . . adjusted."

A chill ran down Daine's spine, but he kept talking. "So by day you fan the anger of the Cyran refugees, and by night you turn them into monsters?"

"My master gives us the power to act on our anger, Daine. He allows us to take our rightful place in the new age that lies ahead."

"And Jode?"

"The powers of your companion will be most useful—as will the gifts of the young lady," Teral said, glancing back at the unconscious Lei. "All flesh is as clay in the hands of my master. He strips the powers away from the beasts of earth and air and grafts these powers to our flesh. Now, at last, the gifts of the dragons are ours for the taking. He gestured to the far end of the room, where Daine could just make out a shelf of flasks and clay vials. "With the power of the binding stones, the dragon's mark can be stripped from this weak human flesh. Once it has been concentrated into this purest form, it is only a matter of time until that power is mine."

It is time, Daine thought, then he frowned. Time for what?

"He approaches," Teral whispered.

❧ ❧ ❧ ◉ ❧ ❧ ❧

Lei heard voices, but she couldn't make out the words. She couldn't move, even to open her eyes.

Where was she?

Lying down, that much she could tell. The sound of water was all around her, and there was a horrible smell—yet one that seemed strangely familiar.

How quickly we forget, she thought. Or did she? Why would she have thought such a thing?

Her body was tilted, her head lower than her feet, and the blood was pounding in her forehead. The surface beneath her was cool and smooth. She could see vague, flickering illumination to either side of her, as if light was shining through water. She could almost hear a voice in the distance, calling her name . . . or was that just another stray thought?

A figure moved into the light, blurred and indistinct. "All is well, my dear," said the figure. It was Hadran. His hand touched her forehead, brushing the hair back from her face. Her vision was still blurry, but she could see him in her mind, proud and stately in his robes of blue and gold. His gray mustaches were carefully waxed, and he pulled at one as he smiled at her. "There is much to be done, but you're safe now."

Hadran picked up a tall, thin urn and poured the contents out next to her. Due to the curved surface and the tilt of the table, the fluid gathered at the back of her head and the small of her back. It was cold, and a tingling sensation spread across her skin.

She tried to speak, but her mouth still wouldn't move. How could this be?

"There are many mysteries in the world," Hadran said, squeezing her shoulder comfortingly. He poured the contents of a second beaker into the basin, and the tingling increased to a sharper sting. "Only the mad can understand them all, for they have gone beyond understanding. Relax, my love."

Despite the pain at her neck, Hadran's words were soothing, and she began to drift. But then the image of Councilor Teral flashed through her mind, his skinless armor wet with blood.

I do not take orders from excoriates. You have no place here. Those had been Domo's words. Domo the warforged. Hadran's warforged.

The thought brought her back to her senses, but she still couldn't open her eyes or move her limbs.

Hadran still had a hand on her shoulder. He was spreading an object across her chest. Jewelery? A necklace? "Let it go," he said soothingly. "All is forgotten. All is forgiven. You are finally home, and nothing else matters."

Someone was combing her hair, straightening it and tugging at it with a dozen small brushes.

The pain across her back was becoming more specific, concentrated into distinct points, as if a dozen small needles were pushing slowly into her flesh. The light before her eyes faded until it was the barest flickering of firelight.

The image of fire brought new thoughts. Fire . . . flame . . . Flamewind the sphinx, and her words—

You killed him, Lei. Those watching you have plans for you, and a life with Hadran was not what they wished.

A surge of anger rushed through her, and she managed to lift her head a little. This couldn't be real! Hadran is dead!

"Lei! Lei, let it go!" It was Daine. He caught her head between his hands and pushed her back down into the cold, into the stinging. Small rocks had been scattered across the surface of the table—or were they on her skin? It was so hard to tell. Daine's fingers continued to brush gently against her forehead, driving away the pain. "It's all over, Lei," he said, massaging her scalp. "Forget your fears. We're together, and—"

"Lei! Wake up NOW!" It was Daine's voice again, but louder and urgent. For a moment she was on the battlefield of Cyre, with blood and steel all around, and in that instant she followed the command without thought. She opened her eyes.

It was not a hand that she had felt on her forehead. It was a tentacle. Her first sight was of slick, purple skin, a round mouth lined with needle teeth, and deep black eyes with glowing golden pupils. Four tentacles ringed the vicious mouth of the creature that was bending over her, and they were carefully holding her head in place. She could see a barbed, razor-sharp tongue emerging as the mouth, descending toward her forehead, and with every ounce of strength she possessed she threw her head to the side.

She broke free of the confining tentacles. The piercing tongue scraped against the side of her head but failed to penetrate her skull. Hissing, the figure stepped back.

At first, she thought she was still dreaming. Silhouetted against the light, her enemy seemed to be a man—tall, thin, and regal. He wore a cyan robe of rich brocade, covered with swirling, interlocking lines of golden thread. But his head was a violet nightmare, powerful tentacles writhing around the lamprey mouth.

Stinging thoughts will send our work awry, she thought—

No, it thought. It was almost impossible to separate the alien thoughts from her own. She could sense its aggravation at the delay in its work.

Enforced tranquility drains the derivations of shadows. Release your fears. Embrace your fate.

Her head was beginning to clear, and she could feel her limbs again. It felt as if the icy liquid had eaten through the back of her clothing and tiny crystals had formed along her skin. She raised her head and stared into the creature's inhuman eyes.

Go to Dolurrh, she thought.

Xoriat, it returned, naming the Plane of Madness. *We must ride the imperfect mind.*

It moved in, bending over her, the steel manacles pinning her in place. The suckers on the beast's four tentacles latched onto the sides of her head. There was no chance of breaking free now.

Release your thoughts. Embrace eternity in me.

The piercing tongue stabbed down.

CHAPTER 41

BRELAND
SHARN
Nymm 1, 996 YK

Lord Chyrassk," Teral whispered, and he and his comrades prostrated themselves. Daine watched in horror as the hideous being entered the room. The creature did not speak, but the tendrils around its mouth twitched, and Daine could *feel* its satisfaction as if it were his own.

Chyrassk strode across the chamber to the table where Lei was bound and began to fill the basin in the table with glowing fluids.

"Lei!" Daine cried.

The gaunt figure continued its preparations, adjusting the fluids in the basin and arranging crystals around Lei's body. Occasionally it would stroke her forehead with one of the tentacles around its mouth.

"Lei!"

No response.

Even from across the room, Daine could feel the creature's power, the mental force that was holding Lei entranced. Its presence was overwhelming. It was as if he were seeing through the thing's glowing golden eyes, as if he were preparing to drain Lei's very life. Daine could almost taste Lei's brain, both the delicious flesh and the far more exquisite memories within. He knew that the instant she died, her essence—her spirit, her dragonmark, all that she was—would be drawn away, captured in crystal and ready to be processed. The sensation passed, and Daine's thoughts were his own again.

Teral was cackling and chittering to himself, rubbing his hands together. "Mine soon," he muttered. "Her soul mine, yes, mine."

Curiosity overcame Daine's horror and he spoke. "But why? Why would that monster share power with you?"

Teral's eyes were mad and gleaming, and Daine wasn't sure the councilor even knew he was speaking. "Chyrassk is a child of madness, an emissary of the age to come," Teral said, his eyes gleaming. "He feeds on thoughts and minds, but he is not of this world, and he cannot devour a human soul. But I have no such limitations. Chyrassk will consume her flesh, but her spirit will be mine. Yes."

Lei moved slightly as the mind flayer caught her head with its tendrils. Daine could stand no more.

"Lei!" he cried, putting every ounce of energy into his voice. "Wake up *now!*"

It worked. Teral drew in a sharp breath as Lei jerked her head to the side, pulling free of the monster's grip. The creature paused, and Daine could feel its frustration. A restless mind was less savory for the devourer. Again, its thoughts flooded through his mind, and he could see Lei's face as Chyrassk darted in for a second attack.

"Kazha zar!" Lei cried.

The air rippled, and Lei vanished. Chryassk's piercing tongue whipped through empty air. The enchantment Lei had woven into her glove could only be used once and its range was limited, but it was enough. Slipping through space and time, Lei reappeared an instant later in the dark corner of the room, standing over her pack.

Surprised as he was, Teral recovered quickly. But Daine knew what enchantments Lei had prepared, and he was already in motion. Calling on every ounce of strength, he pulled himself up, straining against the chains, and lashed out with his legs, catching Teral by the throat and hurling him to the ground.

"Do it!" he called to Lei.

Daine's blow had stunned Teral, but only for a moment.

He was already rising to his feet. Chyrassk spun to face them, its anger a stabbing pain in their minds, and Hugal and the others were sprinting across the hall, claws and blades glittering in the faint light.

A moment was all Lei needed.

Grabbing her pack, she threw open the central compartment, folding out the cloth funnel that allowed her to fit large objects into the extradimensional pocket.

"Now!" she cried.

Pierce emerged, his massive bow in hand, and loosed an arrow the moment he cleared the portal. The feral boy charging Lei fell with an arrow through his knee.

But Pierce was not alone. Two smaller warforged, swift-moving scouts with swords fused to their arms, darted through the portal in his wake. Lei and Daine had found three of these 'forged damaged and inert in the ruins of Cyre, and Lei had been carrying them with her for months. Last night, she had finally managed to get two of them working. They were battered and worn, and Lei's enchantments would not hold for long, but for the moment they could fight.

They charged Councilor Teral. The warped councilor was unnaturally swift and strong, but two warforged were a challenge for any warrior, and being made from metal and wood, the 'forged were immune to Teral's paralytic venom. Teral hissed and cursed, dodging a blade and planting a powerful kick in the stomach of one of the scouts.

Once the 'forged were released, Lei rummaged in the side pocket of the pack. Daine had worn his sword to Teral's tent, but the rest of their weapons were hidden in the magical pack, ready to be retrieved as necessary.

The altered humans were the lesser threat. The deadliest foe was Chyrassk. Now that Lei was on her feet and fully conscious, she recognized the creature from her studies—an illithid, a mindflayer, devourer of hope. These were the commanders of the armies of Xoriat, the Plane of Madness. It was said they had come to Eberron thousands of years in the past, in an extra-planar invasion that had devastated the empires of that age. An ancient order of druids had driven them and their armies into the depths of the earth, sealing them in the caverns of Khyber. Clearly those ancient bonds had grown weak if the flayers were preying on the surface once more.

Although it could consume a human brain in a matter of seconds, the greatest weapon of the illithid was its telepathic power. Even as Lei was rummaging for their weapons, Chyrassk unleashed a devastating mental shockwave. From Hugal to Daine, the creatures in the room gasped and twitched, their minds caught in the storm of conflicting thoughts. The one-armed man next to Hugal fell to the floor sobbing, and Hugal himself clutched at his head, his face a rictus of pain.

Lei struggled with the flood of emotions. Her mind was a blur—despair, hopelessness, and pain sought to overwhelm any sort of conscious thought. But she fought it. She clung to the memories of her companions—Jode's laughter, Daine striding through the burning field at Keldan Ridge, the calm and gentle voice of Pierce. She remembered the challenges they had faced together, the forces they had overcome, and knew she could not falter now.

As suddenly as it had begun, the assault was over. The warforged were largely unaffected by the mental assault, as was Teral. Daine had withstood the attack, but his face was pale, his eyes haunted.

"Pierce!" he cried, his voice trembling. "Engage . . . leader . . . now!"

Pierce responded instantly. Dropping his bow, he charged Chyrassk, drawing his long flail as he ran. The mindflayer hissed, and a bolt of pure mental force engulfed Pierce. Even the inhuman consciousness of the warforged was not enough to shield him from its effects. But while the blow would have reduced a human to drooling catatonia, Pierce was only momentarily dazed. Within seconds he had reached Chyrassk, and the mindflayer barely avoided the first sweeping blow of the flail.

"Daine!" Lei called.

She threw his adamantine dagger through the air. It was a good throw, but he barely managed to catch it with one manacled hand. And not a moment too soon. Hugal had recovered, and he leveled a sweeping blow at Daine with his own sword. Daine flung himself to the side, but he couldn't move fast enough, and the Deneith blade raked his ribs. Hugal cackled.

He wasn't laughing for long. Lei produced the wand she'd stolen from her cousin, and she flung a crackling bolt of energy at Huhal. But the man seemed to have eyes in the side of his head, and he moved with unnatural speed. The lightning flew over him as he ducked and spun. Righting himself, he ran for Lei.

The distraction was enough. Gripping his chains with his left hand and bracing against the wall with his feet, Daine pulled himself up and slashed at the length of loose chain above his right wrist. No metal could stand against an adamantine edge, and the chain parted as if it were simple rope. Daine fell to the floor, his sore muscles causing him to cry out in pain. But there was no time to indulge the agony. Hugal had backed Lei into the corner of the room, and the wand was no match for the sword.

With a length of chain dangling from his left wrist, Daine charged for Hugal. He lashed out with the chain, but his foe turned, slipping under Daine's attack with unnatural ease.

"You're no match for me, Daine," Hugal said with a laugh. He spun out of the path of Daine's dagger, and for a moment Daine was looking right at the tip of Lei's wand. A second later, Hugal's blade raked across Daine's back even as he turned. "I have extra eyes inside my mind. I can read your every move."

"Really?"

Daine caught Lei's eyes, and flicked a glance towards the floor. He went on the defensive, but no matter what he did, Hugal managed to dart past his blade. It was as if Hugal's sword was made of mist. Every time he tried to parry, Hugal slipped around or over his blade, drawing another tiny cut. None of the blows were severe, but the pain and blood loss were beginning to take their toll.

Lei had already pulled the darkwood staff from the backpack, and as Hugal made another lunge at Daine she grabbed the staff and made a spinning strike at Hugal's knees. Once again he reacted with inhuman reflexes, leaping to avoid a blow he shouldn't even have seen. But a moment's distraction was all Daine needed. A shining arc of dark adamantine cut through the air, and Hugal was left with a hilt and an inch of blade.

"Won't your friend have something to say about that?" Lei asked Daine as she struck at Hugal's legs.

"I never needed a dragonmark's sword," Daine replied. "How do you want to end this, Hugal?"

"I've got a few ideas," Hugal said.

He moved in a blur, catching Daine off guard. He flung the useless hilt at Daine's face then sent him tumbling to the ground with a swift, sweeping kick. Continuing the same motion he spun to face Lei, catching the staff in both hands. He raised his foot to kick her in the stomach—

—and then he screamed.

Black thorns had grown out of the shaft of the staff, and they pierced right through his hands. The twisted thorns pinned his hands to the staff, and the agony seemed to be precluding any conscious thought. He and Lei struggled over the staff, but Lei could shift her grip for superior leverage, and Hugal was weakened by pain, blood flowing from his pierced palms. He whimpered but still refused to surrender.

Daine snatched up the dagger. For a moment he hesitated. He had never liked stabbing a man in the back. But he had been a soldier for six years and a swordsman for many more, and he was covered in his own blood. This had to end now. He planted the point of his dagger in the back of Hugal's neck and leaned in, putting his full weight behind it. With barely a cry, Hugal collapsed to the floor. His dead weight almost pulled the staff from Lei's hands, but the black thorns vanished and the staff slipped free.

Even as Daine caught his breath, a crash came from behind him and an armored arm skidded along the floor. He turned to see Teral surrounded by the wreckage of the two scouts. The councilor's robe was slashed and torn, and he was covered with bloody gashes. Despite his injuries, he faced Daine and Lei without fear.

"You can put an end to this, Teral," Daine said.

He crouched and prepared for the attack, slowly spinning

the chain attached to his left wrist. Lei was whispering behind him, and he knew that she needed time to complete whatever enchantment she was weaving.

"I intend to." Teral hissed and licked at a wide gash that split the back of one hand. "Your blades have no power over me."

Indeed, as Daine watched, he saw that the wounds in Teral's fleshy armor were slowly healing.

"I'm impressed," Daine said. "Does that work with a severed head?"

Teral sneered. "What are you fighting for, Daine? You have no country. All that you have worked for has been destroyed. Join us. Let the world share that pain." He moved closer, and a fleshy tentacle drifted out from under his left sleeve and coiled above his hand, a blind cobra waiting to strike.

"You're right," Daine said. "My home has been destroyed, but that's not all I have. I still have my friends. And you took one from me." He rushed forward, and a lightning swift slash with his dagger severed the hovering tentacle.

Teral howled with rage. But even as Daine braced for the attack, Lei was moving. Her staff lashed out, catching Teral dead in the chest. The councilor stopped in his tracks, screaming in pain. To Daine's astonishment, he saw that Teral's unnatural armor had pulled back from the point of Lei's blow.

"Come on!" she cried.

They charged. Teral had regained his balance. Moving inhumanly fast, he snatched up the leg of one of the shattered 'forged scouts and flung it at Lei. It caught her full in the chest and she fell. Daine kept moving, and with one smooth motion he struck the bare patch in Teral's armor. There was a slight resistance as the dagger pierced flesh, scraped between the ribs, then it slid in the councilor's chest up to the hilt.

Teral howled. He grabbed Daine by the throat and lifted him off of the ground. Blood was streaming from Teral's mouth and down his chest, but his strength was inhuman. His hand was crushing Daine's throat, the world began to fade—

And then Teral's head exploded.

Pierce had come up behind Teral and brought the full force

of his flail on the councilor's skull. Teral instantly turned to dead weight, dragging Daine to the ground. Even in death his grip was strong, and Daine struggled to pry the grasping fingers from his throat.

"Pierce . . ." he gasped. For a moment, relief washed over him. Then he realized Chyrassk was nowhere to be seen.

With one curt kick, Pierce knocked Teral's body aside, then planted his steel foot on Daine's chest, slamming him back to the ground. Without a word, Pierce raised his flail for another killing blow.

CHAPTER 42 BRELAND
SHARN
Nymm 1, 996 YK

Lei groaned. The coppery taste of blood filled her mouth, and her head was a throbbing anvil. Gripping the staff, she forced herself to her feet, trying to ignore the pain in her ribs. She found her footing just in time to see Pierce shatter Teral's skull. But as she moved forward, Pierce knocked Daine to the ground and pulled back for a second swing.

It was clear to her in an instant. As difficult as it was to influence the thoughts of a warforged, it was not impossible. Chyrassk must have found a way to twist Pierce's perceptions. Pierce had struck Teral first, and Lei surmised he was seeing everyone as enemies. If so—she prayed she was right—at least Pierce wasn't under Chyrassk's direct control. If that were the case, she knew beyond doubt that she and Daine were both dead.

Lei lunged forward and put her hand on his chest. She concentrated and time seemed to stand still. Pierce became the center of all her senses, the rest of the world fading away as his binding web of energy came into view. She sharpened her focus, trying to find some way to sense what Chyrassk had done, to break his mental hold. Her talent was with mending metal and stone, not thought and spirit, but desperation drove her to act on pure instinct, and she pushed deeper and deeper. But there was nothing to be done, and for all that time seemed frozen she knew that she only had moments to act. Filled with remorse, she hardened her thoughts and struck at the heart of the web, the light that gave Pierce life.

And her world exploded.

For a moment she thought she had gone mad. Pierce's lifeweb had replicated, and she was looking at four different variations of the same pattern. Then she realized that changes were being made, that someone else was thinking with her mind and making minor adjustments to each of the four webs, discussing the shifts with another whose thoughts she couldn't feel. She couldn't hold onto any of the words. It was as if she forgot them the moment she heard them. But there was a sense of self, a recognition, and she realized these were the thoughts of her mother, preserved in the very essence of Pierce since the moment of his creation. In that instant, that mere fraction of an indrawn breath, she knew what Pierce had been built for.

And just as suddenly, she was back in the material world, falling to her knees. Pierce stood stock still for a second, wavered, then collapsed. Lei retched, both from the pain in her ribs and head and the horrible ache in her mind. The memories were already fading, and she could no longer remember exactly what it was she had seen. But she knew that her parents had built Pierce the same year that she was born, and looking down at the fallen warforged, she wondered if she had killed her brother.

❀ ❀ ❀ ❀ ❀ ❀ ❀

Daine struggled to his feet. Lei was looking down at Pierce's inert form. "Is he dead?" he said, reaching out and putting his hand on her shoulder.

"I . . . don't know." Lei wiped at her face, brushing aside the mingled blood, tears, and bile. "I tried. I tried to destroy him. I had to. But something . . . something happened."

Her words were lost in a new round of tears. Daine didn't know what she was dealing with, but he didn't have the time to find out.

"Lei," he said. "We need to keep moving. That thing, Chyrassk, it must have fled while we were fighting Teral. We need to find it. We have to finish this. If Teral was telling the truth, there are dozens of those warped warriors up above. We need to destroy Chyrassk before it can reach them. Otherwise, all of this—Pierce, Jode—it's been for nothing."

Lei had a gift for turning grief into anger, and it came to her aid now. In her mind she saw the monster leaning over her, its piercing tongue descending to devour her brain. She imagined Jode suffering the same treatment, and fire burned in her blood. She blinked away her tears and nodded.

Daine led the way. He was weak from loss of blood, but he ran as fast as he could. Before long they emerged from the long room. Identical hallways stretched left and right.

"Which way?" Lei said.

Pierce had always been the tracker for the unit, but Daine had had to hone his senses in his first career. "There," he said, pointing. A few patches of green-black blood could be seen along the floor to the left. "It looks like Pierce managed to get in a few good blows before Chyrassk overwhelmed him."

They ran down the dark corridor. The cold fire torches were few and far between, and the air was damp and cold. The hall twisted and turned. It was ideally suited to an ambush, so Daine was hardly surprised when one finally came.

Daine turned a corner and found two Cyran refugees—a half-elf woman and a scarred, elderly man—waiting for them. The moment Daine came into view, the woman began to sing. Her voice was the sweetest sound Daine had ever heard, a music beyond mere words. For a moment he forgot the devourer of minds, Teral, the old man. The world vanished in the purity of the sound. But a moment later the sound came to an abrupt end—just as the old man was leaping at Daine, a mouth full of needle teeth descending towards Daine's throat. Instinct was all that saved him. He sidestepped the attack and planted his dagger between his enemy's ribs. The warped man hissed, clawing at Daine, but he did not possess the vitality of Teral, and a moment later he collapsed to the floor.

Pulling his dagger free, Daine found Lei in battle with the woman. Even as he turned to face them, Lei delivered a powerful blow to the throat, and the half-elf fell.

"Harpy's voice," Lei said, looking at the unconscious woman. "Lead on."

They passed a few open portals, but the trail of inhuman blood continued on down the hall. Through the open arches, Daine caught a glimpse of a room filled with stone slabs. A barracks? Crypt?

At last, the hall came to an end. Stepping into the final chamber, Daine had to catch his breath.

A labyrinth of steel catwalks was suspended above pools of glowing fluids, a kaleidoscope of colors and scents. A hot wave of air washed over Daine as he stepped onto the catwalk, and the sweet, cloying scent filled him with dizziness. He almost lost his balance, but he managed to pull himself together just in time. The catwalks were barely three feet across, and there was no railing. Any loss of composure would result in a fall into the churning reservoir that lay below.

Daine took the lead, and the two of them slowly walked down the first catwalk. There were no torches in the chamber, and the only light came from the bubbling pools thirty feet below. Daine couldn't see any sign of Chyrassk, but there was a patch of oily green blood on the catwalk ahead. As far as he could tell, there were no other exits from the room.

"Lei, what do you make of this?" he whispered.

As his eyes adjusted to the light, he could see that there were a series of chains and pulleys fixed to the ceiling. Some of these were supporting the catwalks. But others descended into the pools below.

Lei peered over the edge, studying one of the pools. "I think it's some sort of incubator. Look where the chain is touching the surface? There's some sort of casket down there. I think that people have been lowered into these pools."

"But why?"

"Think about it. Teral and his followers had those things grafted to their bodies. We know that it's something they were continuing to do here. The container at the end of that chain may hold some sort of creature waiting to be grafted to a human host—or it may be the human subject, recovering from the experience."

"That's great," Daine said. "So each of these chains is attached to a monster-to-be? What do we do about that?"

"Cut the chains?"

"I suppose there's not much choice."

Daine looked down at the catwalk, studying the way the steel segments were joined together. He felt a growing sense of satisfaction. Just a few more steps . . .

"Lei! Move!" he cried, charging forward and shoving her with all his might. Caught completely by surprise, she tumbled forward. Nearing the edge of a catwalk, she managed to stop her movement by plunging her staff through a gap in the floor of the platform.

"Dolurrh!" she swore. "What do you think—"

A tremendous crash struck behind her, and she spun around. The catwalk that they'd been standing on a moment earlier had dropped to the floor of the chamber. The suspending chains had come undone, and Daine had barely pushed them onto the next segment in time.

"Chyrassk is here," Daine said. "I can feel him."

Lei studied the supporting chains and drew the lightning wand. "I think this platform is stable, but now we're cut off from the exit."

Daine watched the shadows. He could feel a presence, a gloating thought in the back of his mind. *Two have no hope*, he thought. *Best to end it quickly.* They were his thoughts, pure and natural, and for a moment he shifted his balance and prepared to throw himself to the floor.

Only Lei stopped him, holding him back with the darkwood staff. "Daine, what are you *doing?*"

"I was . . . I . . . don't know," he said. "It . . . was . . . I . . . *there!*"

Chyrassk stepped out from the shadows. Its slick skin glistened in the light of the pools, its golden eyes gleaming in the shadows. Chyrassk was less than thirty feet away, but it was on a different catwalk, and at a quick glance it was impossible to see how to reach it. It raised a hand in their direction.

Fall and be done.

Once again Daine was caught in a storm of savage thoughts,

a mental tumult that drowned out all conscious reasoning. He staggered in the wake of the mental blast—then the pain was gone. There was a sound, faint but clear, that seemed to surround him and drive the madness away. It took him a moment to realize what it was.

Lei's staff was singing. The tiny darkwood face was fully animated. Its voice was faint but clear. Daine could feel Chyrassk's fury, and again the storm of chaotic thoughts lashed, only to scatter against the barrier of song. Daine glanced at Lei, but she seemed as surprised as he was.

Daine didn't like the darkwood staff. There was too much they didn't know about it. The sphinx had wanted Lei to have it, but it still seemed possible that Flamewind had sent Jode to his death—or at least set him on the path that killed him. And when it had sprouted thorns to catch Hugal's hands . . .

What was it? What did it want?

It was too dangerous. He needed to get rid of it. He'd find a way to deal with the mindflayer, but he needed to be able to trust the people at his side. How could he know that this thing wasn't manipulating Lei's mind? He still had the long chain attached to his wrist, and he lashed out with it.

❀ ❀ ❀ ❀ ❀ ❀ ❀

Lei was just as surprised as Daine when her staff began to sing. It was clear that it had hidden powers, but with the chaos of the last few days she hadn't had time to study it properly. Was it actually sentient? As expressive as the tiny face was, it was entirely possible that the powers of the staff were triggered by certain events. The song seemed to be shielding both of the from Chyrassk's attack, but for how long? Lei knew she had to act.

"What do we do?" she said. She glanced over at Daine—and jerked back, just in time to avoid the blow of the chain. Dropping the wand, she took up a defensive posture. "What are you *doing?*"

"Get rid of the staff, Lei," Daine said, moving toward her. She stepped back, but there was little room to maneuver on the narrow catwalk. "Throw it over the edge. It's done something to you, and we can't take any chances."

"Don't be ridiculous! It's the only reason we're still standing!"

"It's manipulating you, Lei! If you won't get rid of it, I will."

Daine lashed out again. Lei managed to turn the edge of the blade with the staff, but Daine's dagger drew a long furrow against the shaft. For a moment, the song took on a pained note.

It's Chyrassk, Lei realized. The mindflayer was standing, unmoving, on the catwalk across the chamber. Chyrassk must be amplifying Daine's fears and suspicions and using them to control him. If I drop the staff, we're both defenseless.

"Daine, stop! What happens once the staff is destroyed?"

Daine was still weak from his injuries, and that was the only reason she'd been able to avoid his attacks as long as she had. But now he was moving in, trying to grab the staff with his free hand, and she was running out of room to retreat.

Calling on desperate reserves of willpower, Lei reached out with her mind. Her armor was a family heirloom, designed to hold temporary enchantments. While it normally took a significant period of time to weave an enchantment, she could weave minor effects into her armor swiftly, though it was just as much of a drain on her energy as crafting a longer, more powerful enchantment.

As Daine came forward, she whispered a word of power and leaped forward. The golden studs of her armor seemed to pull her into the air. It wasn't full flight, but she could ignore much of the pull of gravity, and she sailed over Daine's head. She landed on the platform behind him. Turning around, she gave him a quick shove with the staff. He staggered and almost tumbled off the edge of the platform.

"Damn it, Lei, are you trying to kill me?" Daine cried. He spun around, and now there was real fury in his eyes.

What can I do? She thought. In his weakened condition, it was possible that she could knock Daine off the catwalk. Then what? But if she let Daine destroy the staff, they'd both be helpless.

Daine charged again. Lei leaped a second time, but she had underestimated him. This time he was ready for her, and as Lei sailed overhead his chain wrapped around her ankle and she landed hard, barely staying atop the catwalk. Daine faced her, and his expression was grim.

"No more running, Lei. Can't you see what it's done to your mind? Or is it too late to save you?" He paused for a moment, as if listening to inner voices. "Either you throw the staff below or I'll have to kill you. It's the only way . . . the only way to be sure. It's for your own good."

She could hear the uncertainty in Daine's voice, but clearly Chyrassk's desires were worming their way to the foreground. He was shifting his weight, preparing to charge, and this time he would probably kill her.

Lei didn't think her injured leg would take the strain of another jump, but Daine was still off-balance himself. If she timed it right, she might be able to trip him as he approached. He would certainly fall into the toxic fluid below, but she would live and she'd still have the staff to protect her.

But she couldn't do it. She'd already sacrificed Pierce. She couldn't hurt Daine, no matter the cost. She closed her eyes and waited for the blow to fall.

❖ ❖ ❖ ❖ ❖ ❖ ❖

Even as Daine began his charge, there was a blur of motion at the entrance of the chamber—a massive steel shadow emerging into the light. Pierce raised his bow, drew the string back, and loosed. There was the whisper of an arrow in flight, and Chyrassk cried out—a weird ululating wail.

Daine froze, confused, as the mindflayer's mental focus faltered. Had he really been about to *attack* Lei?

Pierce continued loosing, smooth and deadly. Arrow after arrow slammed into Chyrassk, and Daine could *feel* its fury. It lashed out with its thoughts, trying to crush Pierce's mind once and for all, but the warforged fought with stoic determination. The next arrow pierced one of Chyrassk's gold-flecked eyes. There was a terrible cry, a burst of pure pain that threatened to split Daine's head—and then Chyrassk tumbled from the catwalk, disappearing into the vat of bubbling vitriol that lay far below. Lei and Daine peered down, looking for any sign of movement. But aside from a brief trail of blood, which quickly faded, there was nothing. Chyrassk was gone.

Daine knelt beside Lei and held her tightly. Her leg was still bleeding and she winced in pain, but she smiled. "Pierce . . ." she whispered.

"Pierce!" Daine called. "Are you all right?"

"I am functional, though damaged," Pierce replied as he approached them. "I remember little after I first engaged that creature."

"You arrived just in time, and that's all that matters."

"No," said Pierce. "There is more. I believe . . . while I was incapacitated, I believe I had a dream."

"Dream?" Lei said, weakly. She had pushed herself to the edge of her limits, and she was fading fast. Daine noticed that the darkwood staff was no longer singing, and that the face was again frozen in wood.

INTERLUDE

Going somewhere?"

Lei's ribs were a single, massive ache. Every ounce of energy was gone. Even opening her eyes seemed not worth the effort. She was stretched out on a cold stone slab, but she was so exhausted that the discomfort seemed minimal.

But there was something . . . something important. The voice. She knew that voice.

She forced her eyes open. Her father was standing next to her, leaning over her and glancing at a sheet of parchment, as if he was comparing what he saw to notes on a schematic.

"Back now? Good."

He made a note on the parchment. His expression and his tone were completely neutral—so much like the last time she'd seen him. But something was different. His hair. The color was richer and deeper than she'd ever seen it, the copper catching the light to burn with an inner fire. And his skin . . . it was free of lines.

She tried to speak, but she didn't even have the energy to open her mouth. Her father seemed to notice her discomfort.

"Don't struggle. There's still work to be done."

A young woman stepped into her field of view. "How is she?"

"She'll be fine, Aleisa. I don't think any permanent damage was done."

Aleisa? Her mother? But this woman looked younger than Lei herself.

"And the others?" The pair turned away from her. She could see that there were a few other slabs in the chamber. A warforged soldier, each distinctly different from the others, was stretched out on top of each slab. Her parents were studying the figure on the next slab over, less than three feet away. No matter how hard she struggled, Lei couldn't move, but from where she was she could still see. It was Pierce.

"The work continues apace," her father said. "It was a traumatic experience for both of them, but the safeguards served their purpose. If anything, it may have helped to prepare this one for the task that lies ahead."

"Good," the woman said. She turned around and studied Lei, running her hand along her daughter's cheek. "Don't worry," she said gently. "You're doing fine. You're doing everything you're supposed to do."

"I'm afraid a few adjustments will need to be made," her father said. He had produced a few exotic tools—a long, narrow blade studded with dragonshards, and a pair of delicate silver tongs. "I imagine it will be painful for her."

The woman stroked Lei's cheek again, staring into her eyes, then she rose and turned her back on her daughter. "Do what you must," she said, her voice cool. "I need to check on the others."

Aleisa walked out of Lei's field of view. Her father moved in. Raising the tongs and the razor-sharp blade, he brought the point up until it was level with her right eye.

And then he pushed.

Lei sat up. Daine had been half-dozing, but the sudden motion jarred him to consciousness.

"Lei! Lei, are you all right?" He reached out and took her hand.

Lei looked from side to side. Daine was sitting next to her, and Pierce was to her left. The sight of Pierce brought an involuntary whimper from her throat. His impassive metal face brought back the image of her dream and the blinding pain in her eye.

"Can you speak, my lady?" Pierce said, his voice deep and calm.

"I can." Her ribs still ached with a dull, throbbing pain, but her energy was returning. She raised an arm, touching her forehead and her cheeks. "Where are we?"

It looked like a room in a small and comfortable inn—a considerable step up from the Manticore. There was a pillow beneath her head, and while the pallet beneath her was hardly remarkable, it was the softest thing she'd slept on in at least three years.

"It's a Jorasco house," Daine said. The Jorasco halflings were masters of the healing arts, and every large city had at least one Jorasco enclave. "We couldn't rouse you, and we still had some money left over from Alina's last advance."

While her ribs still ached, after she'd had a moment to

collect her senses, Lei realized that her legs felt fine. She pulled back the blankets. There wasn't even a mark where Daine had stabbed her."

"I . . . wanted that dealt with quickly," Daine said, somewhat sheepishly. "I didn't want you to have to limp around town because of me."

The thought of Jorasco's healing touch brought back other memories. "Jode?"

"He's gone, Lei. It wasn't a dream. He's not coming back."

Lei nodded. Her head was quickly clearing, but she felt empty inside. What had been a dream? She looked over at Pierce and started to reach out to touch him, but at the last moment she drew her hand back. "Are you all right?"

"I have fully recovered," Pierce said. "I am grateful for your actions. Whatever the risk, I would not wish to be responsible for the death of a friend."

I thought I was going to kill you, she thought, but she did not say it aloud.

"I do feel . . . different, however," Pierce continued. "I cannot explain it, exactly. My senses seem sharper, my movements more precise. May I ask what you did when you stopped me?"

"I don't really know, Pierce. I just reached within you, hoping to find some way to slow you down. I'm still not sure what the mindflayer was doing before I escaped. I was exposed to a number of different alchemical substances, and my memories are somewhat unclear."

Pierce nodded. "It appears to have worked out for the best, and all in all it was an interesting experience."

"What about Chyrassk?"

"I inflicted significant injuries on the creature in our initial encounter," Pierce said. "At least six of my arrows struck home in the second encounter. I believe that it was dead by the time it fell."

"If not, I'm guessing the fall finished the job—or whatever that liquid was that it fell into." Daine said. "We took a few minutes to cut the chains supporting those incubation chambers. Chyrassk never resurfaced, and I didn't feel its presence in my mind. I think we finished it off."

"What else?"

Daine frowned. "Well, we smashed the tanks and destroyed everything we could. No one will be making new monsters down there any time soon. But I'm still worried about what Teral said. If he really did come to Sharn with a hundred followers—not to mention those created by Chyrassk over the last two months— that means that there are dozens out there we haven't seen. I've mentioned it to Greykell, but most of the grafts seemed to be easily concealable. And we don't even know that all of Teral's followers settled in High Walls. I don't know. I imagine they'll be keeping a low profile, but I don't like thinking about what horrors might still be hidden in High Walls."

A stout, middle-aged halfling entered the room, the griffon badge of Jorasco on the breast of his brown robe. He was carrying a small tray bearing a bowl of clear broth and a mug of pungent milian tal.

"Ah, you're awake. Good."

He set the tray down by the bed and climbed up on a footstool to examine her. The Mark of Healing could be seen poking up from the collar of his robes, and once again Lei's thoughts drifted back to Jode. The healer touched a finger to her forehead, and she felt a slight tingle.

"You're doing just fine," the little man said. He pressed the tal into her hand. "Drink, now." He looked back to Daine. "I still can't tell you exactly what happened, but she's making an excellent recovery. With a few more days of rest, she'll be as healthy as she's ever been."

"Thank you, Suold."

"The pleasure is mine. I would imagine it's safe for her to move about at this point. If you would like to remain here for a few more days, you can settle things with Asdren out front." The halfling bowed, then trotted out the door.

"I'm fine, Daine," Lei said. "So don't tell me that I'm confined to bed."

"Drink your tal," Daine said. "Personally, I think the rest would do you good, but if you don't want to stay here, I'm not about to make it an order. It's up to you." He stood up. "But now that you're conscious, I need to make our final delivery to

Alina before she comes to the conclusion that we failed."

Lei drained the cup of bitter tal and pushed herself out of bed. He legs were a little stiff and she felt momentarily light-headed, but it quickly passed. "I'm coming with you."

"What?" Daine said. "Why do you want to do that? I'd avoid Alina, if I had the choice."

"I can't just stay here. Especially here. Not after what happened to Jode. Your healer said I was healthy."

"He also said you needed a few more days of rest."

She gave him a look. "And you'd lie here drinking broth if you were in my boots?" She took a few steps forward, gingerly at first. "Where are my goods?"

Daine produced her pack from under his chair, and she began to sort through it. She pulled out her leather jerkin. She hadn't noticed in the battle, but the alchemical bath had eaten through the upper back. She sighed. She could repair it, but it would take time. She pulled out the darkwood staff and frowned.

"Did you do this?" she asked Daine.

When she'd last seen it, the staff had been marred by a half-dozen deep gouges. In places Daine's blade had almost split the shaft in two. But those marks were gone. It was in perfect condition, even to the polished finish.

Daine shook his head. "I haven't touched it, other than putting it in your bag." He scowled. "That squid may have used it to get inside my head. I'll tell you now. I don't like that staff, Lei. There's too much we don't know. What it can do, why the sphinx wanted you to have it . . . maybe you *should* get rid of it."

Lei set her weight against the staff. It might have been her imagination, but she suddenly felt better—a little stronger, a little more alert. "Don't be stupid," she said. "Without the staff, we wouldn't have survived long enough for Pierce to finish Chyrassk. Once we have a little more time, I'll sit down with it. I'm sure that I can unlock its secrets."

"Fine." Daine shrugged. "Come if you want, but let's get this done quickly."

❦ ❦ ❦ ❦ ❦ ❦ ❦

After Daine settled accounts with the Jorascos, they made their way to the lift in silence. As they rose into the sky, Daine turned to Lei. "About what happened down there, Lei . . . ."

"You weren't in control of yourself. Neither was Pierce."

"I know, but it felt so real . . . as if they were my thoughts. I can't help but wonder if there was some part of me that could have resisted, that should have known."

Lei put her hand on his arm. "Daine, it's not your fault. If not for the staff, I would have been just as vulnerable. It wasn't you."

He closed his eyes for a moment then looked back at her. "It wasn't just the staff, Lei." He sighed. "You've known me for a few years, but there's a lot you don't know. What I did before I joined the Cyran Guard, how it is I know Alina. I've always kept a certain distance between us, and I hope, when I explain, that you'll understand why."

She watched him silently.

"But now . . . now we need to determine what happens next. If Alina pays us—"

"Is this in doubt?" Pierce asked.

"Probably not," Daine said, "But with Alina I don't think you can be certain of anything. The question is, what do we do with the gold? Where do we go from here?"

The question hung in the air. Lei had been banned from her house, her betrothed was dead. Pierce had been built for battle, to fight in a war that had ended. And everything Daine had fought for had come to an end on the Day of Mourning.

Daine turned to face his two comrades. "If Alina pays us, we could go anywhere. But where do you want to go? Lei, if you want to get away from here, I understand."

Lei shook her head. "No. If this Merrix has issues with me, that's his problem. I rather like the idea of living the good life under his nose. Show him I'm not going to crawl under a rock and die just because he's cut me off."

Daine nodded. "Pierce, how about you?"

"There is little that I need in this world, Captain. I have no interest in this gold, but I wish to remain with the two of you. For that reason, I hope that you will stay together."

"Which brings me back to my past. Before I joined the guard, I—"

"All the lifts in Sharn, and he comes to mine."

By now, Sergeant Lorrak's gravelly voice was a familiar sound. Daine turned. The dwarf watchman was standing by the gate of the lift with a pair of halberdiers.

"I see your little fall didn't knock any sense into you," Lorrak said.

Daine walked over to the dwarf. The halberdiers lowered their weapons, but Lorrak stopped them with a gesture. "How long is this going to go on, Lorrak?"

"Why, Mourner? Do you have somewhere to go?"

"My name is Daine, Sergeant." He dropped to one knee, to look the dwarf directly in the eye. "And you know what? I don't have anywhere to go. My homeland was destroyed. Your king invited my people to come here. And here I am."

Lorrak stared at him, saying nothing.

"We're not at war anymore, Sergeant. I'm not going anywhere. As a matter of fact, I imagine I'll be taking this lift on a regular basis. If you'd like, we can take turns throwing each other off. I believe it's your turn. But I'm guessing those feather tokens add up on a watchman's salary. I know they will for a refugee."

Lorrak stayed silent, but there was a twitch at the corner of his mouth.

"I didn't mean to throw you off the lift that first time we met," Daine continued.. "You charged me. And you know what? You were right. That girl did rob me. I hope you were just trying to scare her. I don't like the idea of guards murdering anyone, criminal or not. But I owe you an apology, Sergeant. So can we start this over again, one soldier to another?"

The dwarf stared at him for a long while. Finally he nodded. "All right, Mour— uh, Daine." He didn't smile. "We've both been over that edge once now. You mind your business, and I'll leave you be. But I don't want to see any trouble on my watch. Interfere with my work again, and I will have your head, Grazen be damned."

"Fair enough." Daine stood and walked back over to his friends. A moment later, the lift arrived at Den'iyas.

Alina was waiting for them in the room of mir-
rors. Today she was dressed in a gown of black and gold, with
amethyst-tipped rods tucked through her golden hair. Daine
idly wondered if these were pure decoration or if they might be
magic wands. It would be just like Alina to wear a mystic arsenal
as a form of decoration.

"I trust you come to me with results, Daine?" she said. There
was a silver-scaled serpent wrapped around her left wrist, and
she idly scratched its chin. She wore a platinum ring on each
finger, each one set with a different gemstone or dragonshard.
"Or is this yet another plea for gold?"

Daine reached into his belt pouch and produced a small
cloth bag. He set it down on the table and slid it toward her. "I
believe this is what you sent us to find."

Alina held her wrist up to her hair, and the tiny viper
slithered off her arm to coil around one of her long hair
rods. She picked up the bag and carefully spread its contents
out across the table. There were two large chunks of dark
crystal lined with deep blue veins, a host of smaller shards;
and two glass vials, corked and sealed with lead. The vials
were filled with a shadowy fluid, and the lid of each vial was
marked with a complex symbol—similar to a dragonmark, but
matching none of the twelve known marks.

Alina picked up one of the vials and examined it carefully.

"The people who stole your goods and killed Rasial had developed a process to remove dragonmarks," Daine explained. "That's supposed to be the essence of the dragonmark—at least, an aberrant dragonmark. I have no idea what you're supposed to do with it. Since the people who'd stolen it hadn't done anything with it, it may well be dangerous."

"Fascinating," said Alina. She glanced over at Daine. "And the tools they used in this extraction procedure?"

"It was a rough fight, Alina. We were almost all killed, and I'm afraid the workshop was destroyed in the battle. You said to recover whatever was left of your shards. You didn't say anything about limiting property damage in the process."

Alina shrugged. "I'm sure there was nothing that could be done. A tragic loss, however." She studied the vial more closely. "I suppose that this battle occurred after your visit to Councilor Teral's tent in High Walls?"

"It's good to know you're keeping an eye on us."

Alina smiled. "I always like to watch my investments. You know that."

"If you've been keeping such a close watch on us, I suppose you already know about Jode."

Alina set the vial down and placed a hand over her heart. "Yes. Daine, I am sorry. He will not soon be forgotten, and I can only give thanks that the rest of you survived the experience." She glanced down at the two dark vials. "What intrigues me is the fact that these villains preserved these aberrant dragonmarks but let Jode's mark slip through their fingers." She glanced up at Daine, her violet eyes cold in her otherwise perfect mask of sympathy. "Surely a fool could see how valuable the essence of such a mark might be."

Daine said nothing, and Lei spoke on his behalf. "There could be any number of explanations," she said. "Perhaps the process hadn't been perfected and they failed to capture the mark. Perhaps they already put it to use, though I still don't know how you'd apply it."

Alina studied Lei, and for a moment she said nothing. Lei found the experience disturbing. Alina was the size of a human child, but it was hard to reconcile that with her elegance and intelligence. From the way Daine acted around her, it was clear that Alina was dangerous, but Lei still hadn't learned what made her such a threat.

Finally Alina spoke. "True. That is ever the way with magical experimentation, and I suppose that it's for the best. If someone did find a reliable way to remove and transfer the powers of a dragonmark, what would happen to our civilization? Certainly, if I could buy a dragonmark, I would, and I'm certain I'm not alone. As you've already seen, there are those who would be more than willing to kill to obtain the power." She smiled at Lei. "How lucky for you, my dear, that the workshop was destroyed."

Daine shivered. He knew that Alina's minions would be searching through the wreckage beneath High Walls before the day was done. He hoped he and Pierce had done enough damage to render the workshop useless—though somehow, remembering the inhuman thoughts that had flowed through his mind, Daine thought the technique might require the touch of the mindflayer.

"In any case, you have completed your task, and at a terrible cost. How would you like to receive your payment? In coin? Jewels? A letter of credit?"

"Actually, Alina, I have a favor to ask."

Alina's eyes glittered in the light of the amethyst fire. "A favor? Well. What can I do for you, Daine?"

"I imagine that when it comes to matters of business, you have a few connections in the city."

"Indeed."

"Well, I was wondering if you'd take a portion of our payment and help us purchase property in Sharn."

Alina arched a perfect eyebrow. "A piece of the tower? A costly proposition."

"I'm interested in a place in High Walls."

Alina's face was as expressionless as ever, but Daine could *feel* her sneer. "Well, yes, that I could arrange. Do you want a hole in the wall or something vaguely bearable?"

Now Daine could feel Lei's stare. "Bearable. As good as we can get. No lice."

"A tall order in High Walls," Alina said. "But one I can accomplish." She considered for a moment, then reached through one of the mirrored walls. When her hand emerged, she was holding a small casket. She handed it to Lei. "A respectable home will be expensive, even in High Walls. But here, my lady Lei, a hundred platinum dragons for you and your friends. Hopefully you can find some little luxury amidst the squalor your captain has chosen for you."

Lei took the casket but said nothing.

"And as for you, Daine, I'm sure that you can imagine my surprise when I found an heirloom sword in the hands of a pawnbroker. I was even more surprised by the condition it was in. The pommel had been badly damaged. I had it restored to its original condition, and I thought that you might want it back."

She reached into the mirror again and pulled out a long sword. Daine's sword. But it was almost unrecognizable. The blade had been sharpened and polished to a mirror finish, but what drew the eye was the hilt. When he had served in the guard, the pommel of Daine's sword had been worn down, devoid of any detail. Now the hilt was as polished as the blade, and the pommel was glittering black and silver, engraved with the watchful eye of House Deneith.

"I'm sure that your grandfather would be proud to see it back in your hands," said Alina, smiling slightly.

Daine took the sword without a word. Lei and Pierce looked at him, but it was clear from his expression that this was not the time to ask questions.

"It will take a few days to locate an appropriate property," Alina said. "I'll arrange for rooms at the Silver Tree for the interim. It's just down Prospers Street."

"We still have our room at the Manticore," Daine said.

"Daine," Alina said reprovingly. "Won't you allow your companions a chance to see the best that Sharn has to offer before you settle down in the depths? Enjoy a few days of luxury, at least. Consider it a gift."

"I told you before, Alina . . ." Daine paused and turned away. He looked at Lei. "Fine. We'll be leaving, then."

"I'll be in touch when I've located your new home. And I was very pleased with the way you handled yourselves. All of you. I'm sure I'll have more work for you soon. Until then . . ." She gestured, and the mirrored door drifted open. "You know the way out."

❦ ❦ ❦ ❦ ❦ ❦ ❦

" 'I'm sure I'll have more work for you soon.' " Daine fumed as they made their way through the relentless cheer of the streets of Den'iyas. "Whether you like it or not."

Lei caught him by the arm and pulled him to a halt. "High Walls?"

He looked away. "You said you were willing to stay in the city for a time. I thought we'd be able to get the most for our gold in High Walls."

"I told you before, Daine. Cyre was your home, not mine. I only lived there."

"You were born in Cyre, Lei. You fought at our side. Your parents died there."

For a moment, there was a flash of real anger and he thought he might have pushed her too far. "And *you!*" she said. "How do you explain this?" She slapped the pommel of his sword. "Is there something we should know, Daine *with no name?*"

"Do we need to have this conversation in the street?"

"I want answers. *Now.*"

"Fine," Daine said. "I was born into House Deneith. My father is General Doran d'Deneith of the Blademark. This is my grandfather's blade, and yes, I removed the sigil when I joined the Cyran Guard."

"Do you have—?"

"The Mark of Sentinel? No. I failed the Test of Siberys, much to the disgust of my father."

Lei looked away, embarrassed.

"But that was only one of many disappointments and far from the worst. You see, I *cared.* I wanted to believe in what I was fighting for, to believe that I was actually serving a noble cause. But when your family business is built on selling your sword for gold, caring is a crime. You fight for anyone with the gold, and you do whatever you're ordered to do."

His tone had become more intense with each sentence. Lei still wouldn't meet his gaze.

"For a time, I played the part of the good son. I served a wealthy client of the house, and I did whatever was asked of me. I saw things—and *did* things—that will haunt my dreams until the day I die. Finally I couldn't stand it anymore. I renounced my birthright and turned to something I did believe in—the nation of Cyre, the nation that had sheltered me since I was a child, whose values I admire to this day. Perhaps I wasn't born a citizen of Cyre. But in my few years of service, I learned more about morality and friendship than I ever did as a child of Deneith."

"Daine . . ."

He took a deep breath. "And the irony? Look what it got me. I threw away my inheritance for a land now dead. It seems my father was right after all. Live for the moment. Take your satisfaction from the work, not the master."

"Daine, enough!" He just looked at her. "Fine. I didn't know. Obviously I have a lot to learn—and obviously, you've been keeping a lot of secrets from us."

Now it was Daine who looked away.

"But what does this have to do with now? With a life in High Walls?"

"Greykell was right. Cyre is gone, and we need to move on. And I admit it, you deserve better than you've received these last few years."

"I know that."

"But High Walls still feels as close to home as we'll find here. I know it's not what you're used to, Lei, but a hundred dragons won't buy a mansion in the clouds."

Lei sighed but acknowledged the point.

"I don't know what happens next. I was fighting for a cause, and that cause is gone. I'm a soldier. I'm not some sort of refugee caregiver. I'm not going to start wandering around like Greykell, helping people find work."

"But . . . ?"

"I don't know," Daine said. "Teral was a strong figure in the community; I'm sure there's going to be chaos with him gone."

"Greykell can handle it."

"Possibly. But what about Teral's other followers? I'm not going to become a caretaker, and I'm not asking you to help. But I am a soldier, and if I can help to protect these people, I will."

"I was created to protect the people of Cyre," Pierce rumbled. "I will join you."

"This wouldn't be a constant commitment, Lei," Daine said. "But we'd be there if Greykell and her militia needed help. In the meantime, we look for other work. Look for something to believe in. For a cause worth fighting for."

Lei pondered for a moment. "Why do I hear Jode when you're speaking?"

Daine thought about Jode, about the halfling who let a young goblin steal their gold. "Because you know he'd say the same thing."

"Fine," Lei said. "But I'm sick of sleeping on moldy, hard pallets. We've got a hundred dragons to spend: I expect a good bed."

"As you wish."

"And I never want to see a bowl of gruel again."

"No complaints here."

"Well then, let's get back to the Manticore. If we give her some gold, do you suppose Dassi can get some real meat for dinner? After gruel, lizard is next on my list of forbidden foods."

Lei linked arms with Pierce and Daine, and they walked to the lift that would take them home.

❋ ❋ ❋ ❋ ❋ ❋ ❋

Later that night, Daine excused himself and returned to the dusty room. Rummaging through his pack, he found the leather-wrapped bundle he'd hidden that morning and carefully unwrapped it. Inside there was a small bottle made from thick crystal and sealed with lead. The fluid inside was a luminous blue, and the mark pressed into the seal was as familiar to him as a friend's face—the Mark of Healing, the mark of Jode.

For a few minutes he sat alone in the dark, holding the bottle and staring into the glow. Finally, he wrapped the bottle up and placed it back in his pack.

"Good night, old friend," he whispered.

EPILOGUE

The room was full of shadows. Sunlight streamed through the solitary octagonal window, but this light had no power over the darkness. The shadows pooled in the corners of the room, and inky tendrils drifted across the room, obscuring the intricate sigils carved into the floor.

A woman stood by the window, and the shadows clung to her feet like petulant hounds. Though the room was quite warm, the woman kept her long cloak wrapped closely around her body, and her face was hidden by a deep hood. Silently, she stood by the window and stared at the world below, at the district of High Walls almost three thousand feet beneath her. The wind was a constant presence, whistling and howling through the open window. But no matter how powerful these gusts became, they had no effect on the misty shadows that clung to the corners of the chamber or the deep hood that hid the lady's face.

"Report," she said. Her voice was a velvet purr—smooth and quiet, yet resonating throughout the chamber.

The man hesitated, surprised. He had just entered the room, and the lady's back was turned. He had a gift for moving quietly, and with the sound of the wind whistling through the chamber, it seemed impossible for her to have heard his approach.

She turned around, her eyes gleaming in the depths of her hood. "Captain?" she said with a smile.

Captain Grazen inclined his head respectfully. "The workshop has been destroyed, and the mindflayer is dead. The damage was extensive, and we couldn't find anything of value."

"I doubt Chyrassk is dead, Grazen," she said. She lowered a hand toward the floor, and a tendril of mist reached up to embrace it. "It is difficult to kill a child of Xoriat, and Daine lacks the knowledge such a task would require. But its power is broken for the moment. With its tools destroyed and its chief agent slain, I imagine that it will be some time before Chyrassk shows itself again."

"You aren't concerned?" Grazen was visibly relieved.

"Not at all. Chyrassk served its purpose—as have my friends in the House of Cannith. The only issue is Flamewind and whether they will make sense of her riddles before it is too late."

"Why haven't you eliminated the sphinx, if she poses a threat?"

Green eyes gleamed in the shadows, and for a moment Grazen thought he had overstepped his bounds. But the lady answered. "Until I know what power Flamewind serves, direct action is unwise. But I am not concerned. Everything goes according to my plans. Lei has been driven from her house. Jode is dead. Pierce is beginning to awaken to his true potential. And Daine . . ." The dark mist swirled around her feet as she smiled. "The game has been in motion for longer than you can imagine, Grazen. Now the endgame begins. Keep an eye on Daine and his companions. Soon it will be time to put them into play."

She dismissed him with a gesture, and Grazen left the room, running from the shadows and searching for the light.

Appendix I:

A Guide to the World of Eberron

Excerpts from *Eberron: A World in the Shadow of War*
by Jhanor Jastalan Dolas, Provost of Korranberg

The oldest myths say that our world was born in war, born of the struggle between the first dragons. The Seren Tablets describe this battle, how the dark wyrm Khyber tore her brother Siberys into pieces before being bound within the coils of her sister Eberron.

In these enlightened times, we can see this as metaphor. Looking to the sky, it is easy to understand how the ancients could see the ring of Siberys as a great gold dragon stretching across the horizon. Eberron is the world on which we walk, the mother of all that is natural. Khyber is the darkness that lies beneath the surface of the soil, giving birth to horrors that haunt the night and things that should not be. Today, we may consider ourselves too wise to believe in such tales, but the ancients believed that Eberron was formed from magic and from war—and these forces have certainly shaped the world in which we live in today.

Magical energy is all around us, invisible and unknown. It is a force we are slowly learning to control. The wizard can draw on this power to reshape reality with a gesture and an incantation. The priestess calls on gods to work magic on her behalf. The artificer crafts tools that can produce the same effects as either. And then there are the dragonmarked, who carry mystic power in their very blood. As we have learned to control the powers of magic, we have created many wonders that have changed the world in which we live. There was a time when a journey from one edge of Khorvaire to the other would take months. Today the lightning rail and the airship allow the wealthy to traverse the continent in comfort and safety. The message stones of House Sivis send words across the world with the speed of the wind. Communication, entertainment, the healing arts . . . magic touches them all.

Over the course of the last century, we have created horrors far worse than any monster of legend. We have harnessed the power of fire and storm and turned them against our enemies. We have given birth to an army of living weapons. And in so doing we have destroyed the heart of our realm. Chroniclers are calling the recent conflict "The Last War," claiming—or at the very least hoping—that no one who has seen the destruction could thirst for war ever again. Perhaps they are correct. Surely, if we continue to toy with powers that we do not understand, with forces that can destroy an entire nation, our next war will be our last.

Khorvaire, Galifar, and the Last War

Though much of this world remains shrouded in mystery, scholars have kept records for thousands of years and many other secrets have been unlocked through exploration. The continent of Sarlona gave birth to humanity, but for the last millennium the people of Riedra, that continent's largest nation, have restricted contact with the outside world. Tales say that Xen'drik was once home to a civilization of giants who possessed mystical secrets far beyond anything known in the modern age, but this society vanished tens of thousands of years ago. The dragons reputed to live in Argonnessen, if they exist at all, hide their secrets. To date no one has penetrated the interior of this dark continent and returned to tell the tale.

Only one continent is known to us—Khorvaire. Human and elf, dwarf and gnome, we all have our homes here. According to the legends, many of these races traveled to this land—human settlers from Sarlona, dwarves from the frozen north, elves from Xen'drik by way of the isle of Aerenal. Though they were last to arrive, it was humanity that reshaped Khorvaire in its own image. Those who opposed the humans were conquered or driven from their lands. In time, one man managed to unite the budding human nations with sword and word—King Galifar I, founder of a kingdom that would last almost nine hundred years.

Galifar had five children, and he divided his kingdom into five provinces, one for each of his heirs. Each region had its own customs and strengths, and these would continue to develop over time. Aundair was renowned for wisdom, both mundane knowledge and the study of the mystical arts. The people of Karrnath were known for stoic temperaments and military skill. Breland was a center for innovation in philosophy and industry. Thrane soon became the seat of the Church of the Silver Flame, and its people were devoted to this altruistic religion. Cyre was the heart of the kingdom, a center of art and culture. While there were other outposts of culture in Khorvaire—the gnomes of Zilargo, the people of the Shadow Marches, the Lhazaar Pirates—the provinces were seen as the primary repository of civilization and culture. Collectively they were referred to as the Five Nations, and this phrase became so engrained in the psyche of the kingdom that it remains in use to this day, even though Cyre is no more.

The Kingdom of Galifar worked hand in hand with the dragonmarked houses, and for centuries civilization flourished across Khorvaire—until the death of King Jarot in 894 YK.

In accordance with the customs laid down by the first king, Jarot's children had been appointed as governors of the Five Nations. As the eldest child and governor of Cyre, Lady Mishann d'Wyrnarn was the rightful heir to the throne of the Five Nations. According to the ancient laws, her brothers and sisters were to step down from their posts and install Mishann's children as governors.

It was a precarious system, and there had been upheavals before—times when a governor refused to relinquish control. But a rightful heir to the throne had never had to contend with three rebellious siblings, as Mishann did. Lord Thalin of Thrane, Lady Wroanne of Breland, and Lord Kaius of Karrnath rose together to challenge Mishann and the traditions of Galifar. When Mishann fought for her claim, the three governors broke from the old throne, declaring themselves kings and queens. The Last War had begun.

The war lasted for over a century—far longer than the alliance of the three rebel rulers. Over the course of the conflict alliances shifted more often than the sands of the Blade Desert. Cultures long held in check by the power of Galifar shook off the yoke of old. Aundair was shattered by an internal rebellion. The strange creatures of Droaam rose up to declare their own nation. The goblinoids came down from the Seawall Mountains to claim the kingdom of Darguun. The elf mercenaries brought in to fight the war seized a territory of their own, creating the nation of Valenar. But even as the old kingdom crumbled, many advances were made. War encourages innovation, and across Khorvaire wizards and artificers crafted new tools of destruction. Greatest among these were the spellworkers of House Cannith, and their greatest creations were the warforged, tireless soldiers of steel and stone, born with the skill of elite soldiers and able to fight without rest or food. The first warforged soldiers were produced in 965YK, and today each of the Five Nations has its own army of armored warforged. Some question the morality of this practice, for the warforged seem to have the sentience of living creatures, and priests still debate the question of the warforged soul. But most generals see the warforged as weapons. They may be able to think and to speak, but they are tools to be used, nothing more.

Today it seems that the war is finally coming to an end. At the time of this writing, ambassadors have gathered at the isle of Thronehold, and while the conflict continues on the borders, the thirst for bloodshed has surely dimmed. All it took was the destruction of Cyre, the heart of the ancient kingdom. No one knows what force was unleashed in Cyre in 994 YK, and many would say that is the primary reason the nations now discuss the terms of treaty—fear, pure and simple. Was House Cannith working on a weapon in the depths of Cyre, something that went horribly wrong? Or was the devastation the result of the aggregation of magic used in the battles—a slow building of energies that finally reached a breaking point? Is it something that can happen again, and what nation will be next?

The kingdom of Galifar is no more, and even if a treaty of Thronehold brings peace, we can never recover what has been lost. The fertile realm of Cyre has been transformed into a warped wasteland, a place filled with all manner of unnatural horrors. Survivors have taken to calling this region the Mournland. Only time will tell if there is a way to reclaim this lost land—or if the destruction of Cyre is a harbinger of what lies ahead for all of Khorvaire.

The Currency of Galifar

In the modern age, merchants have begun to use letters of credit to handle large transactions, drawing on the reserves of the dwarf banks of the Mror Holds. But most day to day transactions are dealt with through the use of coins made from precious metal. Once all coins were minted under the authority of the King of Galifar. With the collapse of the old kingdom, each of the Five Nations began to mint its own currency, as did the Mror bankers. However, while the designs imprinted on these coins vary based on the source, each of these forces has continued to use the same metals, weights, and denominations set forth in the days of Galifar, maintaining a simple standard for commerce across Khorvaire.

The **crown** is made from copper and traditionally depicts the crown of Galifar on one face. The crown is the lowest denomination of coin minted under the rule of Galifar. Ten crowns are worth one sovereign.

The **sovereign** is made from silver and bears the face of a living or recent ruler. An unskilled laborer can expect to earn a sovereign for a day's work. Ten sovereigns are worth one golden galifar.

The **galifar** is made from gold. It bears the image of Galifar I, the founder of the old kingdom. Ten golden galifars are worth one platinum dragon.

The **dragon** is minted from platinum and bears the image of one of the dragons of legend. With a value of one hundred sovereigns, these coins are used only by the wealthiest citizens of Khorvaire, and the average peasant may never see such a coin.

There are a number of other coins in circulation, such as the double crown of Breland or the silver throne of Cyre, which has a value of five sovereigns. However, all of the major nations make use of the four basic coins described above.

To summarize the values: 1000 copper crowns = 100 silver sovereigns = 10 golden galifars = 1 platinum dragon.

The Calendar of Galifar

The most common method of marking time is the calendar established by King Galifar III. The calendar tracks the years since the kingdom was founded, using the abbreviation YK. The week is divided into seven days; there are four weeks to a month and twelve months to a year. Despite the fall of Galifar, the nations of Khorvaire have continued to use this calendar.

The seven days of the week, from the first day to the seventh, are Sul, Mol, Zol, Wir, Zor, Far, Sar.

The twelve months are named after the twelve moons that orbit the world. The twelve are Zarantyr (mid-winter), Olarune (late winter), Therendor (early spring), Eyre (mid-spring), Dravago (late spring), Nymm (early summer), Lharvion (mid-summer), Barrakas (late summer), Rhaan (early autumn), Sypheros (mid-autumn), Aryth (late autumn), and Vult (early winter).

King Jarot ir'Wynarn died on Therendor 12, 894 YK. The Day of Mourning—the mysterious event that destroyed the nation of Cyre—occurred almost exactly a century later, on Olarune 20 994 YK.

The Dragonmarked

Dragonmarks are one of the greatest mysteries of the age, and they have had a tremendous impact on the cultures of Khorvaire. A dragonmark is a design that appears on the skin, similar in appearance to a complex tattoo. The bearer of a dragonmark can call on the powers of this mark to perform a specific act of magic. Twelve different dragonmarks are now known to exist, each bound to a particular bloodline.

Over the course of two thousand years, these families have evolved into powerful dynasties. When Galifar I laid the foundation of his kingdom, he set severe limits on the dragonmarked houses to prevent them from becoming a threat to his realm. Aside from House Deneith, the houses are prohibited from maintaining armies or holding an office of the crown. But while the houses may have limited military might, they have developed considerable economic power and an infrastructure stretching across the length of Khorvaire. With the collapse of the kingdom of Galifar, many believe that the dragonmarked houses are now the greatest power in the land, and that the mercantile and magical power of the houses is a deadlier weapon than the armies of the Five Nations.

Although the dragonmarked families have no ties to the royal lines of Galifar, out of respect for their power and wealth, the heirs of a dragonmarked house are generally accorded the title of "lord" or "lady." The leader of the regional enclave of a house holds the title of "baron." Those who possess a dragonmark may add the suffix d' to the house name. Thus, Baron Merrix d'Cannith carries the Mark of Making, while Lord Heldoran Cannith does not.

With the sole exception of the Mark of Finding, each dragonmark can only be passed to members of a specific race. Heirs of a house are forbidden from breeding with members of other dragonmarked bloodlines, as this is said to produce aberrant dragonmarks.

The size of a dragonmark determines its power. A bearer of the smallest Mark of Healing might be able to mend a minor wound, while the bearer of a larger mark might be able to cure disease or negate the effects of poisons. The abilities of a mark can be enhanced using a specially designed dragonshard focus, allowing a healer to use his power many times each day.

Currently there are thirteen dragonmark houses.

House Cannith carries the Mark of Making. The artificers and magewrights of House Cannith are responsible for most of the magical innovations of the past millennia. The house made tremendous profits during the Last War through sales of arms and armor, including warforged soldiers. However, the leaders of the house were based in Cyre and died in the Mourning. As a result, House Cannith is suffering from internal strife as the barons struggle for control. The heirs of House Cannith are human.

House Deneith carries the Mark of Sentinel, which grants powers related to personal protection. The Blademark of House Deneith is the most respected mercenary force in Khorvaire, while the Defender's Guild provides bodyguards to anyone who can pay. The Sentinel Marshals are law enforcers with the authority to pursue criminals across the nations of Khorvaire. The house has a hard-earned reputation for neutrality, and a Deneith guard can be trusted to protect his charge or fight for his employee regardless of his personal feelings. The heirs of House Deneith are human.

House Ghallanda carries the Mark of Hospitality, which allows its bearers to provide shelter and sustenance. The mark first appeared among the nomadic halflings of the Talenta Plains, but the Ghallanda line has spread throughout Khorvaire and dominates the inn and tavern trade in the Five Nations.

House Jorasco carries the Mark of Healing. House Jorasco has established houses of healing in all of the major cities of Khorvaire, and during the war many nations hired Jorasco heirs to accompany their soldiers into battle. The heirs of House Jorasco are halflings.

House Kundarak carries the Mark of Warding. This mark allows its bearers to lay magical alarms and traps. By combining the powers of its mark with the vast mineral wealth of the Ironroot Mountains, House Kundarak has established itself as the greatest bank of Khorvaire. Only dwarves can hold the Mark of Warding.

House Lyrandar carries the Mark of Storm. This grants power over wind and weather, and in addition to selling their services as raincallers the Lyrandar have long dominated the shipping trade. A recent alliance with House Cannith allowed the Lyrandar to produce elemental airships. Only a storm heir can control the elemental that provides propulsion for one of these flying vessels. The ships themselves are rare and expensive, but already the airship is beginning to revolutionize transportation in Khorvaire. The heirs of the Mark of Storm are half-elves.

House Medani carries the Mark of Detection, whose bearers can sense hidden threats. Medani is a small house that sells its services to nobles and others in need of security. Where House Deneith specializes in physical protection, House Medani defends its charges from subtle attacks—poison, magic, and other hidden threats. The heirs of House Medani are half-elves.

House Orien carries the Mark of Passage, providing powers of motion—speed, flight, and even teleportation. Members of the house serve as couriers and scouts. Orien also dominates the trade of ground transportation, including mundane caravans and the elementally charged lightning rail, a form of swift transport that links the major cities of Khorvaire. The heirs of House Orien are human.

House Phiarlan carries the Mark of Shadow, which holds powers of illusion, deception, and scrying. The house has turned these powers to the art of entertainment, and the skills of actors, musicians, and acrobats of Phiarlan are legendary. However, there are rumors that the house is involved in espionage, using its powers of shadow to move unseen and spy upon the unwary. The heirs of House Phiarlan are elves.

House Sivis carries the Mark of Scribing, with power over the written and spoken word. The gnomes of House Sivis are renowned as translators, barristers, scribes, and mediators, but their greatest achievement is the network of message stones. Imbued with precious dragonshards, these stones can carry the words of an heir across great distances, and this system is the key to long-distance communication in Khorvaire.

House Tharashk carries the Mark of Finding. Heirs of the house serve as prospectors, bounty hunters, and inquisitives, using the powers of the mark to find things that are lost or hidden. Tharashk is a young house that has recently emerged from the Shadow Marches. The house includes humans, orcs, and their halfbreed offspring. Both humans and halfbreeds can manifest the mark.

House Thuranni first appeared in 972 YK, when a group of elves split off from House Phiarlan. The fledgeling house also carries the Mark of Shadow. While its members are skilled artisans, they are also said to be deadly assassins and spies, and they are considerably more aggressive than their Phiarlan counterparts.

House Vadalis carries the Mark of Handling, which allows an heir to influence the behavior of animals. Vadalis trains and breeds all manner of creatures, from simple livestock and mounts to hippogriffs and other exotic beasts. For centuries, the heirs of Vadalis have been working to enhance mundane creatures with the power of magic. These magebred creatures are superior to their traditional counterparts in many ways. The heirs of Vadalis are human.

The City of Sharn

Sharn is the largest city in Khorvaire and one of the wonders of the modern age, a symbol of what can be accomplished with magic and skill. Little useable land exists on the edge of the Dagger River, but Sharn stretches up into the sky. The tips of its tallest spires are over a mile in height. Only magic could support the columns of Sharn, and the spells woven into the stone are unique to the city. Sharn is built on a manifest zone, where the wall between physical reality and the mystical domain of Syrania has worn thin. The energy of Syrania lends power to spells of flight and levitation, and it is this that keeps the towers from tumbling. Skycoaches, levitating disks, and flying beasts are all used to support commerce and communication within Sharn. It is truly inspiring to see the hippogriffs circling the glittering spires of Daggerwatch as the last rays of the sun fall over the towers.

Sharn is divided both horizontally and vertically. Along the base of the city, it is split into five regions called *quarters*. The five quarters of Sharn are Dura, Central Plateau, Tavick's Landing, Northedge, and Menthis Plateau.

Vertically, these clusters of towers are broken into three distinct levels or *wards*. Thus a citizen of Sharn may refer to Upper Central, Middle Dura, or Lower Northedge.

Each Ward is subdivided into a cluster of neighborhoods known as *districts*. Each of these districts often caters towards a particular segment of the population or a particular field. The Bazaar of Middle Dura is a mercantile district, while the Daggerwatch district of Upper Dura is a garrison.

In addition to the system of quarters, wards, and districts, Sharn extends farther above and below. The district of Skyway actually floats above Sharn, supported by a vast disk of magical force. Below the streets of the lower wards lie the twisting tunnels of the Cogs and Khyber's Gate, home to the sewers and foundries that maintain the city. Deeper still are the remnants of human and goblin settlements buried by shifting stone and ancient wars.

Sharn has been a center of trade and communication for centuries. When this Last War began, the population of Sharn included people of all of the Five Nations along with Zil gnomes,

Mror dwarves, Talenta halflings, goblins, and others. Many of the nationals fled and returned to their homelands, but others had been established in Sharn for generations. While they still held to the customs of their homelands, they nonetheless had deep roots in the city. Over the course of the war, many of these foreign nationals were relocated into secured districts, such as High Walls. Nonetheless, the population remained. In the wake of the destruction of Cyre, many refugees from that ruined land have traveled to Sharn in search of relatives still living in the City of Towers.

The Outer Planes

Twelve moons circle Eberron, but in addition to these physical satellites, the world has spiritual satellites—mystical shadows that move in and out of phase with physical reality. These planes are ideas made manifest, realms governed by a single concept. Death, darkness, ice, light—all have their place in the outer planes.

There are many fanciful tales of people who have managed to visit one of the outer planes, either through powerful magic or bizarre circumstances. The halfling hero Calazar Tash is said to have dived into the mouth of a fire-breathing dragon only to find himself in Fernia. But travel between Eberron and these spiritual shadows is a rarity. Instead, people typically perceive the planes through the effects their motion has on Eberron itself. Just as moons shape the tides, the strange motion of the planes influences reality. When the plane of Lamannia is remote, crops fail and animals become infertile. When it comes into close alignment with Eberron, all life seems to be more vibrant and fertile. In addition to these shifting influences, there are a few places where the spiritual walls are unusually thin. In these manifest zones, the laws of nature and magic may be twisted. One of the best-known examples of this is the city of Sharn, which is located on a manifest zone tied to Syrania. This connection to the Azure Sky enhances magic of flight and levitation, and this in turn empowers the enchantments that support the massive towers.

To date, mystics have identified thirteen distinct planes of existence.

Daavni, the Perfect Order, is a realm of absolute structure and law.

Dal Quor, the Region of Dreams, is a realm touched by mortal spirits when they sleep. It is a place of nightmares and wonders and is said to be the source of the spirits of the kalashtar.

Dolurrh, the Realm of the Dead, draws in the souls of those who die on Eberron. It is a bleak and dismal place, but in time, all memory fades. Many sages and priests believe that when memory fades away, the spirit passes on to another form of existence. The Church of the Silver Flame says that noble souls join with the Flame, increasing its power and purity. Some followers of the Sovereign Host believe that when souls pass beyond Dolurrh they join the Sovereigns in a higher realm, while others believe that the Sovereigns send souls back to Eberron to be born again. The true answer—if there is one—remains a mystery.

Fernia, the Sea of Fire, is an ocean of lava interspersed with firestorms and plates of compressed ash. Legends speak of vast cities of brass, powerful spirits formed of living flame, and glorious treasures waiting to be plucked from the depths of the fire.

Irian, the Eternal Day, is a realm of pure light. A brilliant white sun bathes a crystalline landscape broken by rivers of liquid glass and mountains of quartz. Healing energies suffuse this realm, and when it is close to Eberron the world is filled with color and life.

Kythri, the Churning Chaos, is a realm in constant flux. All things can be found there but nothing remains stable.

Lamannia, the Twilight Forest, is the plane of primal nature. Elemental spirits, exotic animals, werewolves, and strange creatures inhabit the primordial groves and plains of Lamannia, and when it touches Eberron nature reaches its peak.

Mabar, the Endless Night, is a region of pure darkness. It devours the life and light of anyone unfortunate enough to be drawn in. When it touches Eberron the nights grow long and cold, and the forces of darkness reach the height of their powers.

Risia, the Plain of Ice, is an endless field of ice and snow. Stories speak of giants, dragons, and fantastic treasures buried beneath the ice, frozen and trapped until the end of time.

Shavarath, the Eternal Battlefield, is the embodiment of war. Armies of fiends and celestials engage in endless battles over these barren plains. Whirling storms of blades sweep across the region, deadly manifestations of pure violence. When the realm draws close to Eberron, these blades can spill into areas of great violence. During the Last War, a few battles were ended by the whirling blades of Shavarath.

Syrania, the Azure Sky, is a realm of silver towers floating in an endless sky. It is a place of perfect peace and beauty, as well as being the plane that gives strength to the magic of Sharn.

Thelanis, the Faerie Court, is a sylvan realm filled with all manner of mischievous and elemental spirits. Naiads, dryads, and sylphs watch visitors with curious eyes, while in the great citadels the fey lords engage in eternal revels and cunning games. It is a place of powerful magic, but bargaining with the fey can be dangerous for mortals.

Xoriat, the Realm of Madness, cannot be tied to a single description. Each visitor sees it differently, and it is the rare traveler who looks upon Xoriat and returns with his sanity. It is the home of the Daelkyr, malevolent spirits who destroyed the goblin empire of Khorvaire and sought to shatter the world itself. The Gatekeeper druids stopped these fiends, and those trapped on Eberron were bound in the depths of Khyber. The magic of the Gatekeepers prevents Xoriat from moving into alignment with Eberron, but the Cults of the Dragon Below have long sought to counter the druidic magic and pull this realm back toward reality.

The Religions of Eberron

The primary religions of Eberron draw on a system of shared beliefs. The creation myth of the three dragons forms a common foundation for all of the common religions. Both the Sovereigns and the Silver Flame arose after the world was created, as opposed to shaping the universe through divine power. Likewise, few people question that the souls of the dead go to the plane of

Dolurrh, but spirits only remain in Dolurrh for a few decades, and there is a considerable difference of opinion as to what lies beyond. The Church of the Silver Flame believes that true followers join with the flame beyond Dolurrh, while those who worship the Blood of Vol claim that oblivion is all that waits after the plane of death.

The most influential religions on Khorvaire are the Church of the Silver Flame and the Sovereign Host.

The Sovereign Host and the Dark Six

The worship of the Sovereign Host and the Dark Six is the oldest known religion in Khorvaire. Each of the Sovereigns embodies a particular concept, and slight variations of the Sovereigns can be found among many different races and cultures. Some say that even the dragons worship the Nine, and in some of the oldest images the Sovereigns are depicted as dragons themselves.

Worship of the Sovereigns varies by culture. While there are churches and shrines dedicated to each deity, it is largely a matter of personal devotion. A merchant will call upon Kol Korran to guide him through a trade, offer a prayer to Olladra when he goes to gamble with the proceeds, and beg Dol Dorn to guide his hands when he's mugged later that night.

There are a total of fifteen deities associated with this mythology. The nine Sovereigns embody positive and benevolent ideas and are called upon for guidance and protection. The Dark Six are sinister and malevolent, and their names are not spoken. The followers of the Host rely on the Sovereigns to shield them from the powers of the Six. Different races often have different names for the Sovereigns. The names presented here are those used by the people of Galifar.

Arawai is the Sovereign of Life and Love, and she brings good harvest to the land and fertility to the living. Nature is her domain, and she also holds influence over the weather. Farmers and sailors alike ask for her blessings on their endeavors.

Aureon is the Sovereign of Law and Lore, the source of order and knowledge. He gives guidance to rulers and those who pass judgment, guides the scribe and the student, and is said to have devised the principles wizards use to work their spells.

Balinor is the Sovereign of Horn and Hunt. He is the lord of the wild world and those who venture within. The hunter and the hunted are both his charges. He is seen as a protector of the natural world but gives guidance to the hunter who acts in moderation and takes only what he needs.

Boldrei is the Sovereign of Home and Hearth. She lends her strength to the family and the community, bringing people together in times of need. Boldrei is the patron of marriage and mediation, and her wise words can help her followers set aside their differences and become part of a greater whole.

Dol Arrah is the Sovereign of Sun and Sacrifice. She is a patron of war, but she fights her battles with words and cunning strategy as well as steel. She is a god of light and honor, and her holy paladins seek to bring her sunlight to the darkest places of the world. In addition to soldiers, she is seen as the patron of diplomats, generals, and those who make sacrifices to serve the greater good.

Dol Dorn is the Sovereign of Strength and Steel. He is the lord of war and patron to all who raise their arms in battle. He is the patron of physical arts, and the greatest sporting events of the year are held to mark his holy days. His followers are not held to the same standards of nobility and sacrifice as those of his sister, Dol Arrah, but he still encourages honorable conduct. Those who rely on treachery to win their battles must turn to the Mockery for aid.

Kol Korran is the Sovereign of World and Wealth. Merchants, miners, and any who desire to improve their lot in life trust that Kol Korran will help them achieve their dreams, while the wealthy often sacrifice to the Sovereign in the hopes that he will maintain their fortunes.

Olladra is the Sovereign of Feast and Fortune. She is the bringer of luck and joy, and her priests are skilled entertainers and healers, who can salve the wounds brought by misfortune and spread cheer with song and music. She is the patron of bards, gamblers, and others who live by their wits and their words, though those with only malice in their hearts should look to the Dark Six for a patron.

Onatar is the Sovereign of Fire and Forge. He is the patron of both smith and artificer, lending skill to those who follow the traditions of old and wisdom to those who seek to develop new ideas.

The Dark Six are not named and are known only by their titles.

The Shadow is said to be the literal shadow of Aureon, stripped away and given a life of its own as a price for Aureon's study of magic. It represents the darkness that lies within magic, and its power corrupts both life and soul. Most worshippers of the Shadow are wizards or sorcerers who are willing to make any sacrifice for arcane power, but it also has a following among many of the monstrous races, some of whom see the Shadow as the founder of their species.

The Devourer represents the destructive power of nature. He is strongly tied to the sea and the mystery of the deep waters, but earthquakes, avalanches, and tornadoes are all his children. Once a member of the Sovereign Host, he was cast out after raping his sister Boldrei and thus fathering the Fury.

The Fury is the embodiment of passion and madness. While she can bring love and joy, her touch all too often leads to despair and murderous rage. Nonetheless, some artists seek to draw on the Fury for inspiration, and there are those who are willing to risk madness to bring passion into their lives.

The Keeper is the embodiment of greed and decay, hunger so great that it lets all else fall to rot and ruin. While he amasses gold and jewels, the Keeper covets the souls of the living. He seeks to snatch the spirits of the dead as they pass to Dolurrh, hoarding these souls and gloating over his treasures.

The Mockery is the lord of terror and treachery, patron to thieves, assassins, and tyrants. He is said to be the brother of Dol Dorn and Dol Arrah, but he was flayed and driven from the Host after he betrayed his siblings. The Mockery has one of the largest followings among the Dark Six, as many criminals and warriors seek his blessing on their endeavors.

The Traveler is the most mysterious of the Dark Six and cannot be tied to a single form or gender. It is the embodiment of deception but also of cunning and wit. Both bards and artificers may call upon the Traveler for inspiration. Its followers include changelings and doppelgangers who wander the world in a thousand shapes, carrying out strange and subtle plans that often seem benevolent but bring harm in the end. This has spawned a number of proverbs. When dealing with strangers, one is warned to "beware the gifts of the Traveler." Someone who is argumentative for no reason is often said to be "taking the side of the Traveler."

The Church of the Silver Flame

The Church of the Silver Flame was founded in 299 YK. When an ancient evil rose from Khyber, an army of fiends threatened Galifar itself. This darkness seemed unstoppable, until a woman named Tira Miron challenged the demon king and gave her life to bind him below once more. Tira was guided and empowered by an ancient force of spiritual energy—a silver flame that had been forged to bind the demons. In death, she became a conduit for that force, allowing other noble warriors to touch the Silver Flame and use its power to drive evil from the world.

The Church of the Silver Flame has grown exponentially since that time. It is based in Thrane, where a font of silver fire rises from the point of Tira's sacrifice, but it has spread across all of Khorvaire. Only the Sovereign Host has more worshippers, and the followers of the Flame are typically more fervent in their beliefs.

In principle, the Church of the Silver Flame is a benevolent entity, a powerful force for good. Village priests seek to spread humanitarian values, while the knights of the Flame battle the physical manifestations of evil. However, as the church has grown in size and influence, some of its followers have strayed from the path. Many truly believe in the nobility of their actions but allow their zealotry to justify acts of ruthless brutality. Others—particularly in the Brelish branches of the Church—have allowed the lure of gold and power to draw their eyes from the true path of the Flame. While the ideals of the Silver Flame are noble, all too often its followers fail to live up to them.

Traditionally the militant warriors of the Church are sworn to protect the innocent against supernatural threats—werewolves, demons, ghosts, and other monsters. During the Last War the forces of the Church of the Silver Flame played an integral role in the nation's defense, and ultimately the people of Thrane set aside the monarchy in order to place the rule of the land in the hands of the Church. The Silver Flame has worshippers in many other nations, but Thrane is the seat of its power.

The Blood of Vol

Those who worship the Blood of Vol refuse to bow to the power of death. Drawn from the traditions of an ancient line of elven necromancers, the Blood of Vol seeks to abolish death. They revere vampires and other undead creatures as champions in this struggle. This tradition is especially strong in the nation of Karrnath, and while it is not inherently evil, there are subsects—notably the infamous Order of the Emerald Claw—that have turned the battle against death into a struggle to dominate the living. As a result, throughout most of the Five Nations the common image of a follower of the Blood is that of a crazed necromancer leading an army of zombies as part of some mad scheme. As a result of the actions of extremists, the Church of the Silver Flame takes a particularly hard stand against followers of the Blood, and knights of the Flame may assume the worst when dealing with acolytes of Vol.

The Cults of the Dragon Below

According to ancient legend, the dark wyrm Khyber was bound within Eberron and became the underworld, giving birth to fiends and demons. Later, the fiends known as the Daelkyr were bound in the depths of Khyber, adding to the dark legend of the subterranean realm. Over the millennia, many have come to worship the darkness that lies beneath the world. These cults have little in common, save that they are dangerous and prone to madness. Some believe that a promised land lies beneath the earth, but that pilgrims must earn their passage with the blood of the innocent. Others ally themselves with one of the malevolent forces bound beneath the earth, forming a bond with the rakshasa or servants of the Daelkyr, gaining power in exchange for unholy service. The cults are most often found in the Shadow Marches, where different cults fight one another as often as they battle the forces of light, but they can appear anywhere where there is greed or madness—and in the wake of the Last War, both of these things are easy to find.

The Undying Court

Although the elves of Aerenal live far longer than humans, they were not content with this span, not willing to let their heroes slip away into Dolurrh and the mystery of death. In time, the elves found a way to preserve their ancestors beyond death, anchoring them to the world of the living through devotion and spiritual sacrifice. These deathless elves inhabit Shae Mordai, the vast necropolis in the center of the island of Aerenal, and from this city of the dead they continue to guide their nation. Unlike the vampires of the Blood of Vol, the elves of the Undying Court are not undead in the traditional sense. They are sustained by the devotion of their descendants and have no need of blood or life energy. Followers of the Undying Court despise the Blood of Vol and those undead creatures that prey on the living, seeing these as abominations and perversions of the ways of the Undying Court.

While the members of the Undying Court are not gods, they are ancient, wise, and powerful. Just as a paladin can draw on the pure essence of the Silver Flame to lend strength to his sword,

the members of the Undying Court can lend their power to those
priests who honor their memory.

The Druidic Sects

The druids worship Eberron itself, as the embodiment of the
world and nature. While they share certain common features—
reverence for the creatures of the wild and the natural order—there
are a number of different sects, each with its own unique beliefs.
The **Gatekeepers** seek to defend Eberron from unnatural forces,
such as the Daelkyr and other fiends of Xoriat. The **Wardens of
the Wood** fight to preserve the balance between nature and civilization, protecting each from the other. The **Greensingers** have
a strong bond with the fey of Thelanis and are typically seen as
tricksters. The **Ashbound** believe that arcane magic is a violation
of nature and often use violence to stop its use. The **Children of
Winter** embrace death as a natural part of the cycle of life. They
believe in a coming apocalypse that will cleanse the world, and
many actively seek to bring about this devastation.

The Path of Light

The kalashtar are a mysterious race—humans touched by spirits
from another world, and are an enigma to the people of the Five
Nations. They believe in a celestial force they call il-Yanna, "the
Great Light." The followers of the Light engage in meditation
and strict physical discipline, preparing mind and body for battle
against a force they call the Dreaming Dark. However, the nature
of this conflict is difficult for outsiders to understand. While the
kalashtar occasionally engage in physical combat with their foes,
the true struggle is one based around philosophy and dreams-
something that cannot be seen with the eye.

The Paths of Magic

Magic permeates Eberron. Its energy is all around us. The Seren Tablets say that it is the breath of Siberys, released when that great dragon was slain by Khyber in the battle that formed our world. Skeptics and scholars claim it is a natural force like the lightning and the wind. Regardless of its origin, its presence cannot be questioned. The force is there, and there are many ways it can be shaped and controlled.

The oldest road is that of faith, the adept and the cleric. Those who believe claim that the gods and their celestial servants work miracles on behalf of their chosen, allowing the priest to minister to the wounded, protect those in need, and smite the enemies of his faith. Skeptics say that the cleric works his miracles through will alone, the pure strength of his belief reshaping reality to meet his desires. Whatever the truth, it is a path that requires no knowledge of esoteric laws and formulae. All that is required is faith and will, but in such quantities that few men possess.

However, those who lack faith can make up for it with cunning and skill. Scholars and sages saw the powers of the pious priests and were determined to unlock the secrets of this force that granted miracles. In time, they succeeded, decrypting the codes of the universe itself. This arcane magic still requires willpower above all things, but where the priest calls upon his god to smite his foes, a wizard visualizes a force of fire, speaks an ancient word embodying the flame, and flings a pinch of sulfur into the air. This combination of gesture, incantation, thought, and substance summons the fire from the air, drawing on the invisible energy to make thought reality. The true wizard can master any spell he can find, but these gifted sages are few. The most common spellworker is the magewright, who may only master a single spell or two over the course of his life—the augur, the mender, the blacksmith who shapes his steel with magic. Between these two extremes lie the bard and the sorcerer, both of whom possess more power than the magewright but lack the wizard's talent to master every spell.

In recent centuries a new path has arisen—that of the artificer. She cannot pull fire from the air or heal with a touch. Her talent lies in binding magical energy into objects, creating tools that mimic the powers of wizard and cleric. The artificer excels at creating mystical treasures, wondrous elixirs, amulets, enchanted weapons, and many other fantastic items. Given time and access to rare and exotic materials—notably dragonshards—an artificer can make such items permanent. Otherwise, their powers quickly fade.

Regardless of the path a spellcaster follows, the act of performing magic takes a toll on mind and spirit. Only so much energy can be channeled each day, and once a spellcaster reaches this limit he must rely on his mundane skills until he can rest and restore his spirit. Each path has its own rituals. The cleric prays while the wizard studies musty tomes and prepares the formulas he wishes to use the following day.

Some say that the kalashtar follow a different path to power, drawing on the power of mind and dream to produce effects never seen. But this tradition of so-called "psionics" is still a mystery to the people of Khorvaire, and its powers and limitations remain to be seen.

Appendix 2:
Glossary

Aberrant Dragonmark: There are twelve dragonmarks, as described on page 331, but stories say that when dragonmarked bloodlines mingle, they can produce warped marks. Like the true dragonmarks, these bestow magical powers, but these powers are dark and dangerous and said to take a terrible toll on the mind and body of the bearer. See *dragonmark, House Tarkanan, War of the Mark.*

Adar: A small nation on the continent of Sarlona. Adar is the homeland of the kalashtar, and its mountain terrain serves as a natural defense in the constant battle against the Inspired.

Aerenal: An island nation off the southeastern coast of Khorvaire, Aerenal is known as the homeland of the elves.

Alina Lorridan Lyrris: A gnome wizard with considerable wealth and influence. Whether she is a true criminal or simply amoral, Alina is a dangerous woman who usually works in the shadows. Once she lived in the city of Metrol, where she employed *Daine*. Currently she resides in the Den'iyas district of Sharn.

Arcane Congress: Established by King Galifar I in 15 YK, the Arcane Congress was tasked to study the mysteries of magic and place these powers at the service of the kingdom. The congress has its seat in *Aundair*, and when the kingdom collapsed in 894 YK the congress swore its allegiance to the Aundarian throne.

Arcanix: An institute of arcane studies in the nation of Aundair. Many of the greatest wizards of Galifar learned their craft within the floating towers of Arcanix.

Artificer: A spellworker who channels magical energy through objects, creating temporary or permanent tools and weapons.

Asdren: A young halfling employed by the Jorasco house

in Tavick's Landing. Asdren is studying the healing arts and dreams of one day earning a place in the hierarchy of the house, but for now she is tasked with administrative chores.

Aundair: One of the original Five Nations of Galifar, Aundair is houses the seat of the Arcane Congress and the University of Wyrnarn. Currently under the rule of Queen Aurala ir'Wyrnarn.

Auger: A professional fortune-teller or diviner.

Bal: An influential member of *House Tarkanan*, Bal is a gifted unarmed combatant. His skills are enhanced by his aberrant dragonmark—a chilling touch that drains the life from his victim. Bal is covered with boils and sores, and a superstitious soul might say that Bal's aberrant mark was responsible for his unsightly appearance. See *House Tarkanan*.

Bandit King of the Whistling Woods: The title adopted by Horas Calt during his infamous career. Born in Breland in 845 YK, Calt developed impressive sorcerous powers and soon turned his magical abilities to crime. He earned his place in the songs of bards by being the first man to rob the lightning rail, and ultimately settled in the depths of the Whistling Woods. Many vagabonds and rogues joined his gang, and it is said that he found allies among the fey spirits of the wood. A group of the Sentinel Marshals of House Deneith finally cornered the Bandit King in 872 YK. The battle left a trail of destruction across the woods, and in the end Calt threw himself into a fire to avoid capture. It was a great victory for House Deneith, but some bards maintain that Calt's friends among the fey saved him from the flames and spirited the bandit king away to the plane of Thelanis, where he lives to this day.

Battle of the Three Moons: A vicious conflict that occurred in the conflicted territory between Breland, Darguun, and Cyre. The Battle of the Three Moons began on the evening of Barakas 20th, 990 YK, when a Darguul troop and a Brelish army launched a surprise attack on a Cyran encampment. But the Darguuls had failed to account for the presence of a Valenar warband. While the elves were not allied with the Cyrans, they saw more sport in fighting the larger force. The battle lasted for four days, with the worst of the fighting occurring at night; fortunately, the unusual conjunction of three of Eberron's moons provided enough light for the humans and elves to match their goblinoid foes.

Black Arch: A garrison district in the Lower Tavick's Landing ward of Sharn.

Blade Desert: A harsh region in the southeast of Khorvaire. Once part of Cyre, it is currently claimed by the nation of Valenar.

Blademark: The mercenary's guild of *House Deneith*.

Breland: The largest of the original Five Nations of Galifar, Breland is a center of heavy industry. The current ruler of Breland is King Boranel ir'Wyrnarn.

Bronzewood: An unusual form of lumber that has many of the traits of metal. The elves of Aerenal use bronzewood in the creation of arms and armor.

Byeshk Mountains: A mountain chain on the western coast of Khorvaire, separating Droaam from the Eldeen Reaches.

Cadrian: A soldier who served in the Cyran army under Daine's command. Cadrian was killed in the battle of Keldan Ridge.

Calis, Lailin: An augur living in Sharn, Lailin is an old friend of Lei d'Cannith.

Calazar Tash: A halfling hero of the Talenta Plains, said to have lived in the first days of the Kingdom of Galifar. There are hundreds of tales of Calazar's exploits, and with the aid of his clever clawfoot Shurka he is said to have battled dragons, challenged demons, and even outwitted the Traveler himself.

Callol: A small Cyran village captured by the Darguuls in 995 YK.

Cannith, House: The dragonmarked House of Making.

Cantrip: A minor form of magic. A cantrip might be used to clean the dirt from filthy clothing or to open a door from across a room.

Carnival of Shadows: The traveling circus of *House Phiarlan*, filled with illusion, acrobatics, and exotic creatures and entertainers from across Khorvaire.

Carralag: A gargoyle who immigrated to Sharn from Droaam. Carralag represents the district of Malleon's Gate in the Race of Eight Winds.

Changeling: Members of the changeling race possess a limited ability to change face and form, allowing a changeling to disguise itself as a member of another race or to impersonate an individual. Changelings are said to be the offspring of humans and doppelgangers. They are relatively few in number and have no lands or culture of their own but are scattered across Khorvaire.

Chyrassk: A cult leader who has been gathering followers in the dismal district known as Khyber's Gate. Chyrassk has never been seen by those outside of his cult, and he remains shrouded in mystery.

Cloudsilk: A form of glamerweave, cloudsilk is almost weightless and has the appearance of diaphanous white mist. A popular variation of this is stormsilk, which has the appearance of dark clouds laced with lightning.

Cold Fire: Magical flame that produces no heat and does not burn. Cold fire is used to provide light in most cities of Khorvaire.

Cogs: This network of tunnels stretches deep beneath the towers of Sharn. The foundries and workhouses of Sharn are mostly located in the Cogs, along with sewers and tunnels dating back to the ancient empire of the goblins.

Council of Thronehold: Following the Mourning, princes and ambassadors of the surviving nations gathered at Thronehold, the traditional heart of the kingdom of Galifar. Negotiations lasted for many months, until a treaty was finally signed on the 11th day of Aryth, 996 YK.

Crown: The copper crown is the lowest denomination of coin minted under the rule of Galifar. See page 330.

Cyre: One of the original Five Nations of Galifar, known for its fine arts and crafts. The governor of Cyre was traditionally raised to the throne of Galifar, but in 894 YK, Kaius of Karrnath, Wroann of Breland, and Thalin of Thrane rebelled against Mishann of Cyre. During the war, Cyre lost significant amounts of territory to elf and goblin mercenaries, creating the nations of Valenar and Darguun. In 994 YK, Cyre was devastated by a disaster of unknown origin that transformed the nation into a hostile wasteland populated by deadly monsters. Breland offered sanctuary to the survivors of the Mourning, and most of the Cyran refugees have taken advantage of this amnesty. See *Mourning, Mourners, Mournland*.

d'Cannith, Aaren: Dragonmarked artificer, one-time baron of Metrol, and member of the Cannith Council based in Cyre. The official records of the house credit Aaren with the mystical breakthrough that gave true sentience to the warforged. Aaren was fascinated by the mysterious continent of Xen'drik, and some say his work was based on ancient secrets recovered there. Aaren passed away in 984 YK. He is survived by his son *Merrix d'Cannith*.

d'Cannith, Aleisa: A dragonmarked artificer of House Cannith and mother of *Lei d'Cannith*. Aleisa was involved with the development of the warforged, but all records of her work were lost in the war. She is believed to have died in Cyre on the Day of Mourning.

d'Cannith, Casalon: A legendary artificer of House Cannith, who lived in the third century of the kingdom of Galifar. Dasalon's most noteworthy achievement was the development of cold fire, allowing artificers and magewrights to bring light to the cities of Khorvaire.

d'Cannith, Dasei: A dragonmark heir residing in Sharn. Dasei studied the mystical arts with her cousin *Lei d'Cannith*, but she has accomplished far more as a socialite than as an artificer.

d'Cannith, Dravot: The warden of the Cannith enclave in Sharn, Dravot distinguished himself during his service with the elite Blackwood Watch. During the final decade of the Last War he served as the warden of the Whitehearth armory in Cyre, but he was reassigned before the Day of Mourning.

d'Cannith, Hadran: A dragonmarked heir. Hadran's ancestors were one of the first branches of House Cannith to set roots in Sharn, and he possesses considerable wealth and influence. A widower with no children, Hadran arranged a betrothal with *Lei d'Cannith*.

d'Cannith, Lei: A dragonmarked heir, daughter of *Aleisa d'Cannith*. Lei studied the mystical arts in Sharn and Metrol. Like many young artificers, she chose to serve in the Cannith support corps during the war. She served with the military forces of the Five Nations to maintain the warforged soldiers and other weapons each nation had purchased from Cannith. In 990 YK, Lei was assigned to the Southern Command of Cyre, where she served with *Daine, Pierce,* and *Jode*. In 993 YK, her parents arranged for her betrothal to *Hadran d'Cannith*, but before her term of service came to an end she was caught in the Day of Mourning and nearly killed.

d'Cannith, Merrix: As a baron of House Cannith, Merrix oversees house activities in the vicinity of Sharn. Son of *Aaren d'Cannith*, Merrix is a skilled artificer who has spent a decade working on new warforged designs. In the wake of the Last War he has shown shrewd political instincts and has moved to take advantage of the chaos created by the destruction of the House Council. He is the most influential Cannith baron in Breland, and many believe that he hopes to seize control of the house itself.

d'Deneith, Doran: A general of the Blademark of House Deneith, Doran is known for his brilliant tactics and his utter devotion to the principles of his house. During the Last War he led troops on behalf of Cyre, Breland, and Karrnath, taking pride in his impartial service.

d'Lyrandar, Dantian: A half-elf of House Lyrandar, Dantian is a trade minister of his house. Dantian devotes a great deal of time to the needs of his house, but he is also renowned for his lavish parties and galas.

Daeras: A half-elf woman serving in the Daggerwatch garrison of the Sharn Watch. Daeras has a great love of sports, particularly the aerial races of Sharn.

Daggerhawks: A breed of hawk found in the mountains that run along the shores of the Dagger River. Daggerhawks are also known as dire hawks; they are massive creatures that can support the weight of a human rider while in flight. During the reign of Galifar II, daggerhawks were domesticated and used as aerial mounts. However, they are difficult to manage and today they are generally only seen in the sporting arenas of Sharn.

Dagger River: One of the largest rivers in Khorvaire, the Dagger runs south through Breland into the Thunder Sea.

Daggerwatch: 1) One of Sharn's garrison districts, located in the ward of Upper Dura. 2) A specific garrison building within that district, commanded by Captain *Grazen ir'Tala*.

Dailan: The grandfather of Daine. Dailan was a master swordsman and taught Daine to wield a blade. He passed away in 984 YK, passing his heirloom sword to his grandson.

Daine: A soldier and one-time mercenary, Daine prefers not to speak of his past. Born in Cyre, he is known to have worked for *Alina Lorridan Lyrris* for an extended period of time. In 988 YK he took up service with the Queen's Guard of Cyre, ultimately rising to the rank of captain in the Southern Command.

Dalan's Refuge: A wealthy residential district in the Lower Tavick's Landing ward of Sharn.

Dal Quor: Another plane of existence. Mortal spirits are said to travel to Dal Quor when they dream. See page 337.

Darguun: A nation of goblinoids, founded in 969 YK when a hobgoblin leader named Haruuc formed an alliance among the goblinoid mercenaries and annexed a section of southern

Cyre. Breland recognized this new nation in exchange for a peaceful border and an ally against Cyre. Few people trust the people of Darguun, but their soldiers remain a force to be reckoned with.

Darkhart Arms: The home of *Jura Darkhart*, located in the Ocean-view district of Upper Tavick's Landing.

Darkweave: Minor enchantments woven into this cloth give it the appearance of solid shadow. Garments woven of darkweave allow the wearer to blend into darkness and are favored by thieves and spies.

Darkwood: This rare lumber is named for its pitch-black coloration. It is as hard as oak, but it is remarkably light—almost half the weight of most types of lumber. It is often used in the creation of magical wands and staves.

Dassi: A halfling whose family immigrated to Breland from the Talenta Plains. Dassi owns and maintains the Manticore Inn in the High Walls district of Sharn.

Daughters of Sora Kell: The three hags that rule the nation of Droaam. The Daughters are figures of myth and legend, and possess impressive mystical and oracular abilities.

Dek: A changeling gambler and bookmaker. Dek spends most of his time at the King of Fire in Hareth's Folly.

Demon Wastes: A barren land in the northwest of Khorvaire. The Demon Wastes are said to be filled with savage barbarians, deadly spirits, and ruins that predate human civilization by hundreds of thousands of years.

Deneith, House: A dragonmark house bearing the Mark of Sentinel. See page 332.

Den'iyas: A district in the Upper Menthis ward of Sharn. Den'iyas is a prosperous area primarily inhabited by gnomes. It is sometimes known as "Little Zil.' "

Dolurrh: The plane of the dead. When mortals die, their spirits are said to travel to Dolurrh and then slowly fade away, passing to whatever final fate awaits the dead. See page 337.

Dolurrh's Doorstep: A dangerous and rundown tenement in the High Walls district of Sharn, inhabited by Cyran refugees.

Domo: A warforged servant at the house of *Hadran d'Cannith*.

Donal: A soldier in the Cyran army. Donal served under Daine at the battle in Keldan Ridge. He has not been seen since the Mourning.

Doraashka: A Goblin term translating to "gray eater." A name for the acidic oozes that inhabit the sewers of Sharn. Also known as eaters or gray ooze.

Doras: This half-orc was the reeve of Cytal, a tiny village in the south of Cyre. He managed to escape the effects of the Mourning, but his village was destroyed and he has become twisted and bitter. He currently lives in Dolurrh's Doorstep, a tenement in the High Walls district of Sharn and has built up a number of followers among the refugee community.

Dragon: 1) A reptilian creature possessing great physical and mystical power. 2) A platinum coin bearing an image of a dragon on one face. The platinum dragon is the highest denomination of coin minted under the rule of Galifar.

Dragon Towers: A district in the Middle Central ward of Sharn. Most of the dragonmarked families maintain enclaves in Dragon Towers, and it is the primary place to do business with these houses.

Dragonmark: 1) A mystical mark that appears on the surface of the skin and grants mystical powers to its bearer. See page 331. 2) A slang term for the bearer of a dragonmark.

Dragonmarked Houses: One of the thirteen families whose bloodlines carry the potential to manifest a dragonmark. Many of the dragonmarked houses existed before the kingdom of Galifar, and they have used their mystical powers to gain considerable political and economic influence. The dragonmarked houses are described in detail on page 332. See *dragonmark, War of the Mark*.

Dragonshard: A form of mineral with mystical properties, said to be a shard of one of the great progenitor dragons. There are three different types of shard, each with different properties. A shard has no abilities in and of itself, but an artificer or wizard can use a shard to create an object with useful effects. *Siberys shards* fall from the sky and have the potential to enhance the power of dragonmarks. *Eberron shards* are found in the soil and enhance traditional magic. *Khyber shards* are found deep below the surface of the world and are used as a focus binding mystical energy.

Dreamlily: This powerful opiate comes from the continent of Sarlona. Brelish healers imported elixir of dreamlily for use during the Last War but discontinued use once they determined how addictive it was. It has since found a market as a recreational narcotic in Sharn, and use is spreading across Khorvaire.

Dreamsilk: A form of glamerweave produced on the looms of Zilargo. Minor illusions are woven into the threads, producing stunning visual effect. Clebdecher's Loom in Sharn is renowned for its sunset gowns, dreamsilk dresses that seem to glow with the orange-and-rose light of a Sharn sunset.

Droaam: A nation on the west coast of Khorvaire. Once claimed by Breland, this region was never settled by humans and was known as a wild land filled with all manner of monsters and creatures who had been pushed back by the spreading power of Galifar. In 986 YK there was a movement to organize the creatures of Droaam into a coherent nation. While this has met with some success, the new nation has yet to be recognized by any other country.

Dura: One of the five quarters of Sharn. Dura is the oldest quarter of the city and is home to the most impoverished inhabitants of Sharn.

Eaters: See *doraashka*.

Eberron: 1) The world. 2) A mythical dragon said to have formed the world from her body in primordial times and to have given birth to natural life. Also known as "The Dragon Between." See *Khyber, Siberys*.

Eldeen Reaches: Once this term was used to describe the vast stretches of woodland found on the west coast of Khorvaire, inhabited mostly by nomadic shifter tribes and druidic sects. In 958 YK the people of western Aundair broke ties with the Audairian crown and joined their lands to the Eldeen Reaches, vastly increasing the population of the nation and bringing it into the public eye.

Elymer: An elderly Cyran blacksmith who became a refugee after his village was destroyed by the Mourning. Currently he lives in the High Walls district of Sharn. The hardship has sapped much of his strength, and he is beginning to go blind.

Eternal Fire: See cold fire.

Everbright Lantern: A lantern infused with cold fire, creating a permanent light source. These items are used to provide illumination in most of the cities and larger communities of Khorvaire. An everbright lantern usually has a shutter allowing the light to be sealed off when darkness is desirable.

Excoriate: A person who has been expelled from a dragonmarked house. An excoriate is stripped of the family name and any property held by the house and is not welcome at house enclaves. Members and allies of the house are urged to shun excoriates. Prior to the foundation of Galifar, houses often flayed the victim's dragonmark off of his body. While only temporary, this was a brutal and visible way of displaying the anger of the house. See *dragonmarked houses*.

Eye of Deneith: Most of the dragonmark houses have two heraldic emblems—a magical beast associated with the history of the house and a simpler, iconic symbol. The three-headed chimera is the beast of Deneith, while its icon is a silver eye surrounded by the golden rays of the sun. This symbol is known as the Watchful Eye or the Eye of Deneith.

Felmar Valley: A stretch of land on the border between Breland and Cyre. Towards the end of the Last War, Daine and his fellow soldiers were assigned to hold the Felmar fort against the Brelish.

Fernia: A plane of existence known as the Sea of Fire. See page 337.

Firebinding: A technique taught to artificers. This art includes the creation of cold fire and true flame, allowing an artificer to produce a flaming sword or to slay an armored knight by boiling him in his armor.

Fireblossoms: These rare flowers are found in the gnome lands of Zilargo. Ruby red in color, when properly tended they produce an inner radiance similar in nature to cold fire.

Firepine: An exceedingly rare tree. Firepines can only grow in manifest zones linked to Fernia. The wood of the firepine does not burn; instead, it draws the fire into itself, absorbing the heat while still glowing cherry-red. Between the beauty, rarity, and practical value of the wood, it is one of the most expensive forms of lumber in Khorvaire.

Five Nations: The five provinces of the Kingdom of Galifar— Aundair, Breland, Cyre, Karrnath, and Thrane. See page 327.

Flamewind: A mysterious sphinx from the distant land of Xen'drik. The Carradan Expedition found her in the ruins of a city of giants. Flamewind claimed to have been waiting for the explorers and declared her intention to accompany them back to Khorvaire. Fascinated, the explorers agreed and even provided her with a residence at Morgrave University. Flamewind has the body of a predatory cat, the wings of an eagle, and the head of an elf-maiden. She clearly possesses oracular powers, but her motivations remain an enigma.

Flameworms: These parasites enter through the digestive tract and reside in the stomach, causing internal lesions and fever in the host. While uncomfortable, these symptoms are rarely lethal among adults, but children can easily die from a case of flameworms.

'Forged: A slang term for the warforged.

Foundling: Dragonmarks are bound to the blood of a single family. Anyone who possesses the Mark of Making has some tie to House Cannith. However, the marks have existed for thousands of years, and those families have grown and spread over that time. When someone develops a dragonmark but has no known link to the house that bears that mark, he is known as a foundling. The dragonmarked houses traditionally embrace foundlings in order to maintain control of the mark, but foundlings rarely rise far in the ranks of the house and cannot use the full house name. The child of a foundling and a full heir of the house can take the name of the house. See *dragonmark, dragonmarked houses.*

Galifar: 1) A cunning warrior and skilled diplomat who forged five nations into a single kingdom that came to dominate the continent of Khorvaire. 2) The kingdom of Galifar I, which came to an end in 894 YK with the start of the Last War. 3) A golden coin minted by the kingdom, bearing the image of the first king. The golden galifar is still in use today and is worth ten sovereigns. See page 327.

Galt: A young goblin from Malleon's Gate.

Ghallanda, House: A dragonmarked house bearing the Mark of Hospitality. See page 333.

Ghaal'dar: A Goblin term that can be translated to "mighty people." The goblinoids of Darguun use this word to describe the people of their nation, emphasizing their martial strength.

Ghostfish: A large, freshwater fish similar to a trout, with one key difference: the ghostfish is invisible. This bizarre condition persists even after the fish is killed, and many diners relish ghostfish for the sheer experience of eating an invisible meal.

Glamerweave: A general term used to describe clothing that has been magically altered for cosmetic purposes. A glamerweave outfit may enhance the appearance of the wearer—concealing blemishes, adding color to hair or eyes—or it may simply possess colors or patterns than could never be replicated with mundane fabrics. Cloudsilk and dreamsilk are two examples of glamerweave.

Glass House: A restaurant and inn located in the Hareth's Folly district of Sharn. The Glass House is based on the theme of invisibility; the walls are made from Riedran crystal, the staff wear translucent glamerweave garments, and the kitchen serves unusual dishes, such as Aundairian ghostfish.

Goblinoid: A general term encompassing three humanoid species—the small and cunning goblins, the warlike hobgoblins, and the large and powerful bugbears.

Gold Wings: A mounted unit of the Sharn Watch. The Gold Wings ride trained hippogriffs, and the unit monitors the upper towers and responds to aerial crimes.

Gorlan'tor: A word from the language of the halflings of the Talenta Plains, roughly translating to "stampede."

Half-orc: When humans and orcs interbreed, the offspring typically possess characteristics of both races. These half-orcs are not as bestial in appearance as their orc forbears, but they are larger and strong than most humans and usually possess a few orcish features, such as a gray skin tone or pronounced canine teeth. Half-orcs are most common in the Shadow Marches but can be found across Khorvaire.

Halfstone Street: One of the main streets of the Black Arch district in Sharn. Much of the commerce in the district is located on Halfstone.

Halodan Meal-worms: These grubs are considered to be a delicacy in the Talenta Plains. Halfling traders brought the worms with them as they spread across Khorvaire, and while most humans find them repulsive, many gnomes and shifters enjoy these treats.

Hareth's Folly: A district in the Middle Dura ward of Sharn. Hareth's Folly is an entertainment district, with a focus on gambling and aerial sports.

High Walls: A district in the Lower Tavick's Landing ward of Sharn. During the Last War many foreign nationals living in the city were relocated to High Walls, and the majority of the Cyran refugees living in Sharn reside in this district.

Hila: A humble seamstress, Hila was born in a small village on the southern edge of Cyre. She was widowed during the war and traveled south to Sharn after the Mourning.

Hollow Tower: An arena for aerial sports, located in the district of Hareth's Folly.

Holas: A half-orc serving in the Sharn Watch. Born in Malleon's Gate, he fought his way up from poverty and destitution and earned a place in the watch. Currently he serves as a sergeant in the Daggerwatch Garrison.

Horas: A dwarf serving with the Guardians of the Gate. Horas spends most of his days processing travelers at Wroann's Gate in Tavick's Landing.

Hugal Desal: A young Cyran refugee. Hugal and his identical twin brother *Monan* came to Sharn after the Mourning and found a home in the High Walls district.

Hulda: This dwarf served as a field medic in the army of Cyre. After the destruction of her homeland, she traveled south to Sharn to lend her skills to the refugee community in the city. She maintains a makeshift infirmary in Togran Square in the district of High Walls.

Hu'ur'hnn: A giant owl with the power of speech and a quick wit matching—or exceeding—that of a human. Hu'ur'hnn used to be a racing beast, and he won the Race of Eight Winds in 970 YK. Age has forced him to retire, but he has found great success as a mediator and advisor in the Bazaar of Dura.

Illithid: An abomination from Xoriat, the plane of madness. An illithid is roughly the same size and shape as a human but possesses a squidlike head with tentacles arrayed around a fanged maw. Illithids feed on the brains of sentient creatures and possess the ability to paralyze or manipulate the minds of lesser creatures. Illithids are more commonly known as *mind flayers*.

Iltrayan: A dark, dry wine from Aundair. The Iltrayan vineyards lie within a manifest zone tied to Shavarath, and many soldiers claim that a goblet of Iltrayan readies the blood for battle.

il-Yanna: A word from the Quor tongue, translating to "the Great Light." This mystical force is the focus of the religion of the kalashtar. See page 345 for more details.

ir': When attached to a family name, this prefix indicates one of the aristocratic lines of Galifar. The descendants of King Galifar I belong to the ir'Wyrnarn line.

ir'Dain, Jairan: Proud scion of a noble line, Jairen ir'Dain is the Cyre's ambassador to the city of Sharn—or was, before the Mourning. The Lord Mayor of Sharn has allowed the Cyran embassy to remain open, and Jairen is doing what he can to promote the interests of Cyran refugees.

ir'Dalas, General Bail: The commanding officer of the Cyran forces at the Battle of Three Moons. General ir'Dalas survived that conflict, but fell in battle against a legion of Karrnarthi undead the following year.

ir'Lanter, Alais: A noble from the nation of Aundair. Along with his brother Helais, Alais serves as an ambassador, representing the interests of the Aundairian crown in Sharn.

ir'Ryc, Greykell: Scion of a noble Cyran family, Greykell ir'Ryc served as a captain in the Queen's Guard of Cyre. Known as "the laughing wolf" due to her tenacity and good humor, Greykell was renowned throughout the southern command for her cunning strategies and her ability to inspire her soldiers. The blood of dragons is said to run through her house, and in addition to being a gifted swordswoman, she possesses a minor talent for magic. Following the destruction of Cyre, Greykell traveled to Sharn. She has established herself as the unofficial sheriff of the High Walls district, though she prefers to maintain order through diplomacy as opposed to the use of force.

ir'Soras, Teral: Once a councilor to the court of Cyre, Teral ir'Soras retired from politics to enjoy his middle years. This quiet life came to an end when the Mourning destroyed Cyre. Teral survived the disaster and traveled to Sharn. As one of the few Cyran nobles in the city, Teral feels an obligation to use his skills to preserve the remnants of Cyran civilization and he has devoted himself to organizing the refugees of High Walls.

ir'Talan, Grazen: Born into House Deneith, Grazen served in the Blademark and earned a place in the *Sentinel Marshals*. During an assignment in Sharn, Grazen fell in love with an heir of the Tala line. As the Galifar Accords prevent the heirs of dragonmarked houses from holding royal titles, Grazen chose to leave House Deneith to marry his beloved. Between his own skill and the influence of his new family Grazen obtained a commission in the Sharn Watch. Today he is the captain of the Daggerwatch Garrison in Upper Dura.

ir'Talan, Hareth: An aristocrat and architect who lived in the early days of Sharn. Many believed that Hareth was mad, but the gold and connections of the ir'Talan family gave him the opportunity to design one of the districts fo Sharn. Now known as Hareth's Folly, this district is a bizarre conglomeration of building styles from across Eberron—and at least according to Hareth, from across the planes of existence.

ir'Wyrnarn, Wroann: The daughter of King Jarot ir'Wyrnarn, the last king of Galifar. Prior to her father's death, Wroann served as governor of Breland. When Jarot died in 894 YK, Wroann turned against the tradition of the kingdom and crowned herself Queen of Breland. To the people of Breland, Wroann is a heroine who took a stand against outdated traditions. To many others—especially the people of Thrane and Aundair—Wroann was the worst of the rebels, responsible for a century of war and the destruction of Cyre.

Ivy Towers: A residential district in the Upper Menthis ward of Sharn.

Jani Onyll: A Cyran soldier who served with *Daine* in the Last War.

Jask Roots: Alchemists claim that the jask root is the most nutritious vegetable that can be grown in Khorvaire. The root was first discovered in the Talenta Plains, where it is a staple of the halfling diet. However, most humans—especially human children—are revolted by the taste of jask root. As a result, roots are typically served with thick, sugary glaze.

Jhaakat: A hobgoblin warrior from the land of Darguun, Jhaakat led a bad of Darguuls to Sharn following the war, in hopes of finding mercenary work. Currently he lives in Malleon's Gate. The lack of work has fueled his frustration, and he often picks fights with humans and elves.

Jhola': This is a salutation used by the halflings of the Talenta Plains. It can be translated many different ways, depending on the time, location, and the relationship between the speakers.

Jholeg: A goblin scout who served in the Cyran army under *Daine's* command.

Jode: This halfling has revealed little about his past. He bears the Mark of Healing but has never admitted to having a tie to House Jorasco. While he occasionally speaks of a childhood in the Talenta Plains, Jode moved to the Five Nations at a young age. In 988 YK he took up service in the Queen's Guard of Cyre in the company of his friend *Daine*. He never sought to hold any sort of command and instead served as a healer and occasional scout, using his dragonmark and quick wits to assist his friend.

Jol: An old Cyran refugee. Jol was born in the village of Callol. His family was killed when the Darguuls captured the village, and Jol was tortured. He now lives in High Walls, but is widely considered to be insane.

Jorasco, House: A dragonmarked house bearing the Mark of Healing. See page 333.

Jura Darkhart: Born Jura d'Cannith, this dragonmarked aristocrat was expelled from House Cannith after marrying a dryad. He remained in Sharn even after being condemned as an excoriate. His wife died in 995 YK.

Kadran: A servant of House Lyrandar, Kadran serves as the major domo in the household of Dantian d'Lyrandar.

Kalashtar: The kalashtar are an offshoot of humanity. Stories say that the kalashtar are humans touched by spirits from another plane of existence and that they possess strange mental powers.

Karris: A grim Cyran dwarf. Karris was once a soldier, but following the Mourning he chose to serve Teral ir'Soras as an assistant and bodyguard.

Karrnath: One of the original Five Nations of Galifar. Karrnath is a cold, grim land whose people are renowned for their martial prowess. The current ruler of Karrnath is King Kaius ir'Wynarn III.

Kasslak: An authority figure in the district of Malleon's Gate.

Kazha zar: A Draconic incantation often used to activate arcane spells involving movement or teleportation.

Kela: The hostess at the King of Fire.

Keldan Ridge: A remote region of hills in southern Cyre. While passing along the ridge in 994, Daine's soldiers encountered a heavily armed force of unknown nationality. This enemy scattered the Cyran forces; it was this forced retreat that pushed Daine, Lei, Pierce, and Jode outside the radius of the Mourning.

Khorvaire: One of the continents of Eberron. See page 326 for more details.

Khyber: 1) The underworld. 2) A mythical dragon, also known as "The Dragon Below." After killing Siberys, Khyber was imprisoned by Eberron and transformed into the underworld. Khyber is said to have given birth to a host of demons and other unnatural creatures. See *Eberron, Siberys*.

Khyber's Gate: This name is used to cover a vast stretch of the Cogs of Sharn. It is a lawless area where the Watch will not go, and many criminals, goblinoids, and Droaamites make their home in this dark district.

King of Fire: A tavern and gaming hall located in the district of Hareth's Folly.

Korlan: A half-orc from the Shadow Marches, Korlan developed an aberrant dragonmark when he was ten. He was driven from the Marches, but found a home in Sharn with House Tarkanan.

Korluaat: "Hero's Blood." A highly alcoholic beverage favored by the hobgoblin warriors of Darguun.

Kundarak, House: A dragonmarked house bearing the Mark of Warding. See page 333.

Lakashtai: A kalashtar woman residing in Sharn.

Lamannia: A plane of existence known as the Twilight Forest. See page 337.

Last War, The: This conflict began in 894 YK with the death of King Jarot ir'Wynarn, the last king of Galifar. Following Jarot's death, three of his five children refused to follow the ancient traditions of succession, and the kingdom split. The war lasted over a hundred years, and it took the utter destruction of Cyre to bring the other nations to the negotiating table. No one has admitted defeat, but no one wants to risk being the next victim of the Mourning. The chronicles are calling the conflict "the Last War," hoping that the bloodshed might have finally slaked humanity's thirst for battle. Only time will tell if this hope is in vain.

Lhazaar Principalities: A collection of small nations running along the eastern cost of Khorvaire. The people of this land are renowned seafarers, and there is a strong tradition of piracy in the region.

Lorrak: A Brelish dwarf. Lorrak holds the rank of sergeant in the Sharn Watch.

Lynna: A soldier who served in the Cyran army under Daine's command. Lynna was killed in the battle of Keldan Ridge.

Lyrandar, House: A dragonmarked house bearing the Mark of Storm. See page 333.

Magewright: A general term for any professional who uses magic to enhance the skills of his trade. The typical magewright can only perform one or two spells; examples include the blacksmith who uses magic to improve his craft, the lamplighter who produces everbright lanterns, and the auger who uses magic to divine the future for her clients.

Mal: A soldier who served in the Cyran army under Daine's command. He was killed in the battle of Keldan Ridge.

Malleon's Gate: A district in the Lower Tavick's Landing ward of Sharn. This area is largely inhabited by goblins, Droaamites, and other inhuman creatures.

Manticore: 1) A magical beast with the body of a lion, the wings of a dragon, and the face of a man. 2) An inn located in the High Walls district of Sharn, which uses a Manticore as its trade sign.

Marcher: An inhabitant of the Shadow Marches.

'Mark: A slang term for the bearer of a dragonmark. See *dragonmark*.

Menthis Plateau: One of the five quarters of Sharn. Menthis is noted as a center of education and entertainment. Most of the theaters of Sharn are spread throughout this quarter, and Morgrave University is located on the Upper Ward.

Metrol: The capital of Cyre. Metrol was destroyed by the Mourning.

Minal: A member of the Sharn Watch, serving in the Dagger-watch Garrison.

Mind flayer: See *illithid*.

Mithral: A silvery metal that is just as strong as iron, but far lighter and more flexible.

Monan Desal: A young Cyran refugee. Monan and his identical twin brother *Hugal* came to Sharn after the Mourning and found a home in the High Walls district.

Moresco: A halfling pickpocket who makes his home in the drains of Daggerwatch.

Morgalan: A human with a minor gift for sorcery, Morgalan served in the Brelish army but grew tired of the military life. Morgalan deserted the army and along with a group of his friends, he became a bandit, preying on those traveling along the road to Sharn.

Morgrave University: Located in Sharn, Morgrave University is the largest institute of learning in Breland. Compared to the other great colleges of Khorvaire, it has a shady reputation; many claim that the scholars of Morgrave University are more interested in grave-robbing than actually unlocking the secrets of the past. Regardless of its standing, Morgrave can be a valuable resource to inquisitive inhabitants of Sharn.

Mourner: A slang term for a Cyran refugee.

Mourning, The: A disaster that occurred on Olarune 20, 994 YK. The origin and precise nature of the Mourning are unknown. On Ollarune 20, gray mists spread across Cyre, and anything caught within the mists was transformed or destroyed. See *the Mournland*.

Mournland, The: A common name for the wasteland left behind in the wake of *the Mourning*. A wall of dead-gray mist surrounds the borders of the land that once was Cyre. Behind this mist, the land has been transformed into something dark and twisted. Most creatures that weren't killed were transformed into horrific monsters. Stories speak of storms of blood, corpses that do not decompose, ghostly soldiers fighting endless battles, and far worse things.

Mror Holds, The: A nation of dwarves and gnomes located in the Ironroot Mountains.

Olalia: A Cyran refugee and servant of *Teral ir'Soras*. Olalia has been disfigured, supposedly through magical means.

Olaran: A village in the northeastern edge of Cyre. Olaran was destroyed during a Karrnathi attack in 989 YK.

Old Road: A trade road built on the orders of King Galifar II. Today, the Old Road still links the capitals and great cities of the Five Kingdoms.

Olladra: The Sovereign of Feast and Fortune, goddess of luck and plenty. Those who follow the Sovereign Host will ask Olladra for aid in risky ventures, and the phrase "Olladra smiles" is used when someone has a stroke of good luck. See page 340.

Oranon, Mulg: A dwarf windchaser who races in the aerial events of Sharn. Mulg is best known for riding Daggerhawks.

Orasca: A word from the language of the halflings of the Talenta Plains. It can be translated many ways, but a standard usage is "one who seeks to steal my livelihood."

Phiarlan, House: A dragonmarked house bearing the Mark of Shadow. See page 334.

Philan: A Cyran refugee living in High Walls. A minstrel by trade, Philan survives by telling tales to children in exchange for copper or scraps.

Pierce: A warforged soldier, Pierce was built by House Cannith and sold to the army of Cyre. He was designed to serve as a skirmisher and scout, specializing in ranged combat. His comrades named him based on his skill with his longbow. Following the destruction of Cyre, he has chosen to remain with *Daine*, his last captain.

Precarious: One of the districts of Sharn. Precarious is located on the lowest levels of Dura Plateau. It serves the shipping trade, and is dominated by warehouses and the mystical cranes that haul goods up from the docks of the Dagger.

Pride of the Storm: The personal airship of Lord Dantian d'Lyrandar.

Prospers Street: A street in Deniyas. Most of the upscale merchants and inns of the district can be found on Prospers Street.

Q'barra: A young nation hidden within the jungles of eastern Khorvaire. Q'barra was formed by refugees and rebels who refused to fight in the Last War, along with bandits and other ruffians.

Queen's Guard: One of the titles of the army of Cyre.

Race of Eight Winds: An aerial sporting event that takes place in the Dura quarter of Sharn. In this annual event, riders race different types of flying beasts. Each Dura district is represented by a different beast, and preparations and rivalries between the districts play a major role in daily life.

Rakshasa: Ancient fiends from the dawn of time. Rakshasa are cunning shapeshifters with considerable mystical powers, but the most powerful of these demons were bound in Khyber hundreds of thousands of years ago.

Ralus: A human windchaser. Ralus specializes in handling hippogriffs, and represents Daggerwatch in the Race of Eight Winds.

Rasial Tann: A guardsman with a gift for handling hippogriffs. Rasial had a bright future in the Sharn Watch and the sporting arenas of Dura quarter. He rode the hippogriff to victory in his first time in the Race of Eight Winds, but the second year his mount died in an unexplained accident. Following this disaster, Rasial disappeared into the underworld of Sharn.

Rattlestone: One of the residential districts in the Lower Dura plateau of Sharn. Many of the poorer inhabitants of Dura gather in Rattlestone Square to watch the major aerial races.

Rhazala: A young goblin girl who lives in Malleon's Gate in Sharn.

Riedra: The largest country on the continent of Sarlona. Once a collection of warring states, Riedra overcame its internal conflicts only to break all ties with the rest of Eberron. After a thousand years of silence, Riedra is only beginning to re-establish diplomatic relations with the nations of Khorvaire, and much about the realm remains a mystery.

Round Wind: The ancestral estate of Hadran d'Cannith. Round Wind is located in the district of Dalan's Refuge in Sharn.

Saerath: A wizard who served in the support corps of the Queen's Guard of Cyre. Saereth served under Daine but has not been seen since the Battle of Keldan Ridge.

Sagal Powder: A pungent spice commonly used by the halflings of the Talenta Plains.

Sarlona: One of the continents of Eberron. Humanity arose in Sarlona, and colonists from Sarlona established human civilization on Khorvaire.

Sarris: A young woman from Cyre. Sarris served as a scout in the Cyran army, under the command of Greykell ir'Ryc.

Seawall Mountains: A mountain chain in southern Breland. The Seawall separates Darguun and Zilargo, and many kobolds and goblinoids still lurk in its shadows.

Selas Leaves: First found in the Shadow Marches, the use of these aromatic herbs has spread across the Five Nations over the last three centuries. They have become a staple of Cyran dishes, particularly those involving red meat.

Sennan Rath: A simple keep in southern Cyre, Sennan Keep was heavily fortified after the rise of Darguun. Daine and Pierce spent a year walking the walls of Sennan Rath.

Sentinel Marshals: The dragonmarked House Deneith is the primary source for mercenary soldiers and bodyguards in Khorvaire. The Sentinel Marshals are a specialized form of mercenary—bounty hunters empowered to enforce the laws of Galifar across Khorvaire. This right was granted by the King of Galifar, but when Galifar collapsed the rulers of the Five Nations agreed to let the Sentinel Marshals pursue their prey across all nations, to maintain a neutral lawkeeping force that would be respected throughout Khorvaire. See *House Deneith*.

Seren Tablets: An ancient set of tablets recovered from the Seren Island chain off the coast of Argonnessen. The tablets are a written account of a tale handed down among the dragons for hundreds of thousands of years, describing the war between the first dragons and the creation of the world.

Shaarat: A Goblin word that translates to "sword" or "blade."

Shaarat'kor: A Goblin word that translates to "blood-colored blade." This is the sobriquet of the Lhesh Haruuc Shaarat'kor, the ruler of Darguun. Goblinoids loyal to Haruuc often use this as a warcry.

Shadow Marches, The: A region of desolate swamps on the southwestern coast of Khorvaire.

Shae Mordai: An Elvish name translating to "City of the Dead."

Shae Mordai is the home of the Undying Court of the elves of Aerenal.

Sharn: Also known as the City of Towers, Sharn is the largest city in Khorvaire. See page 335.

Sharn Watch: The force that maintains order in the city of Sharn. The Watch is spread throughout the city, and each quarter of Sharn has its own garrison. In addition to the main force of guards, there are a number of specialized divisions of the Watch. The Gold Wings provide aerial reconnaissance and support. The Blackened Book deals with magical crimes. The Guardians of the Gate monitor the activities of foreigners. And the Redcloak Battalion are an elite military unit that can be deployed against deadly foes —demons, enemy commandoes, or similar threats.

Shifter: A humanoid race said to be descended from humans and lycanthropes. Shifters have a feral, bestial appearance and can briefly call on their lycanthropic heritage to draw animalistic characteristics to the fore. While they are most comfortable in natural environs, shifters can be found in most of the major cities of Khorvaire.

Siberys: 1) The ring of stones that circle the world. 2) A mythical dragon, also called "The Dragon Above." Siberys is said to have been destroyed by Khyber. Some believe that the ring of Siberys is the source of all magic. See *Eberron, Khyber.*

Silver Flame, the: A powerful spiritual force dedicated to cleaning evil influences from the world. Over the last five hundred years, a powerful church has been established around the Silver Flame. See page 342.

Silver Tree: A luxurious inn located on Prospers Street in Deniyas.

Sivis, House: A dragonmarked house bearing the Mark of Scribing. See page 334.

Sivis Tower: The central enclave of House Sivis in Sharn. This structure is located in the district of Dragon Towers.

Skyblade Joust: A sporting event where participants fight while mounted on flying beasts. In a typical joust, the goal is to unseat all opponents and send them tumbling to the ground, but there are many variations of the sport.

Skycoach: A small flying vessel, typically shaped like a rowboat or gondola. The magic that allows a skycoach to fly is tied to the manifest zone around Sharn; as a result, these vehicles will not function far from Sharn, and are only found in the City of Towers.

Sorans: A family of Cyran refugees living in High Walls. Bakers by trade, the Sorans have struggled to acquire enough supplies to continue their trade in Sharn.

Sovereign: 1) A silver coin depicting a current or recent monarch. A sovereign is worth ten crowns. 2) One of the deities of the Sovereign Host. See *Sovereign Host*.

Sovereign Host, the: A pantheistic religion with a strong following across Khorvaire. See page 339.

Star of Cyre: A five-pointed star. The points represent the Five Nations; the top point and the center of the star are gold —representing Cyre—while the remaining points are red, blue, black, and silver. The silhouette of a crown is often placed in the center of the star. As Cyre maintained its claim to the Five Nations throughout the Last War, it continued to use this symbol throughout the war.

Stone Eye, The: A title the goblins of Malleon's Gate often use to refer to Kasslak.

Stormchild: A slang term for an heir of the dragonmark of House Lyrandar.

Sundown: A fast-paced gambling game traditionally played at the end of the workday.

Syllia: A matron of a Cyran farming family, Syllia came south with her surviving sons after the war. The family found a place in Dolurrh's Doorstep, but Syllia turned to dreamlily to wash away the pain and soon became an addict.

Tal: A beverage from the Talenta Plains. Tal was introduced to the Five Nations by the halflings of House Ghallanda. Made by steeping herbs in boiling water, it serves many purposes depending on the herbs that are used. There are dozens of varieties. Milian tal is typically served cold and is said to settle a fever, while blackroot tal is served hot and is a popular mid-day drink.

Talenta Plains: A vast stretch of grassland to the east of Khorvaire, the Talenta Plains are home to a proud halfling culture. The people of the Talenta Plains live a nomadic life-style that has remained more or less unchanged for thousands of years, though over the centuries a number of tribes have left the grasslands to settle in the Five Nations. A wide variety of large reptiles are found in the Talenta Plains, and the half-ling warriors are known for their fearsome clawfoot mounts.

Tanda: This salutation from the Talenta Plains can be translated in many ways depending on the circumstances but is generally friendly. A common usage is, "Greetings, one who is not my brother in blood but yet might become one in friendship."

Targath: A metal found in the land of Argonnessen. A charm fashioned from this metal is said to provide its wearer with good health.

Tarkanan, House: A criminal organization based in Sharn, specializing in theft and assassination. Only people possess-ing aberrant dragonmarks can join House Tarkanan, and the members of the house are taught to hone these skills to aid in their work. The organization is structured as a mockery of the true dragonmarked houses, in remembrance of the aberrant alliance that arose during the War of the Mark. See *aberrant dragonmark, War of the Mark*.

Tavick's Landing: One of the five quarters of Sharn. Travel-ers arriving by foot or by rail must pass through Tavick's Landing, which is a blend of residential, entertainment, and business districts.

Test of Siberys: Members of dragonmarked houses are not born with their marks. Anyone who possesses the blood of a house has a chance to manifest a dragonmark, but typically a mark only appears under stressful conditions, when its power is truly needed. The Test of Siberys is a formal ritual administered by the house. In theory it will force a dormant mark to the surface, though there have been those who failed the test but still developed a mark late in life. The precise nature of the test varies from house to house. In some cases, the test can be quite dangerous. See *dragonmark, dragonmark houses*.

Tharashk, House: A dragonmarked house bearing the Mark of Finding. In Sharn, House Tharashk serves as a clearinghouse for the services of monstrous mercenaries from Droaam, including gargoyle couriers and ogre laborers. See page 334.

Thrane: One of the original Five Nations of Galifar, Thrane is the seat of power for the Church of the Silver Flame. During the Last War, the people of Thrane chose to give the church power above that of the throne. Queen Diani ir'Wynarn serves as a figurehead, but true power rests in the hands of the Church, which is governed by the council of cardinals and Jaela Daeran, the young Keeper of the Flame.

Three Stones: A popular gambling game played with a deck of cards sporting an elemental theme. The three stones of the title represent the three dragons that are said to make up the world.

Tsash: A common greeting in the Goblin tongue.

Traveler, the: Loosely aligned with the Dark Six, this deity is the embodiment of intrigue and artifice. See page 341.

Xoriat: Another plane of existence, known as the Realm of Madness. See page 338.

War of the Mark: Five hundred years before the creation of Galifar, the dragonmarked families joined forces to eliminate those who possessed aberrant marks. Ultimately the aberrants joined forces and formed an army of their own, under the leadership of Lord Halas Tarkanan and his lover, the Lady of the Plague. Despite Tarkanan's skill and personal power, his troops were few in number and poorly organized, and he could not stand against the dragon-marked. In the aftermath of the war, the families formally established the first dragonmarked houses. See *aberrant dragonmarks, dragonmarks, dragonmarked houses, House Tarkanan*.

Warforged: A race of humanoid constructs crafted from wood, leather, metal, and stone, and given life and sentience through magic. The warforged were created by House Cannith, which sought to produce tireless, expendable soldiers capable of adapting to any tactical situation. Cannith developed a wide range of military automatons, but the spark of true sentience eluded them until 965 YK, when *Aaren d'Cannith* perfected the first of the modern warforged. A warforged soldier is roughly the same shape as an adult male human, though typically slightly taller and heavier. There are many different styles of warforged, each crafted for a specific military function—heavily-armored infantry troops, faster scouts and skirmishers, and many more. While warforged are brought into existence with the knowledge required to fulfill their function, they have the capacity to learn, and with the war coming to a close, many are searching their souls—and questioning whether they have souls—and wondering what place they might have in a world at peace.

Windchasing: A popular sport in Sharn. Windchasing is a form of aerial racing, in which riders mounted on flying beasts follow a dangerous course in and around the towers of Sharn.

Windguard: The organizers of the Race of Eight Winds.

YK: Most of the nations of Khorvaire make use of the calendar of Galifar. The current date is reckoned from the birth of the Kingdom of Galifar, in the Year since the founding of the Kingdom, or more simply, YK.

Zae: This halfling is one of the youngest members of House Tarkanan. She seems to be able to mystically communicate with vermin and influence their actions. This is not an aberrant ability that has been seen in recent history, but it is reminiscent of the powers of the legendary Lady of the Plague—if on a far smaller scale.

Zilargo: Located on the southern coast of Khorvaire, Zilargo is the homeland of the gnomes. Known for its vast universities and libraries, Zilargo also possesses considerable mineral wealth in the form of gemstones and Khyber dragonshards. The gnomes themselves are masterful diplomats, shipwrights, and alchemists, renowned for their cunning and inquisitive nature.